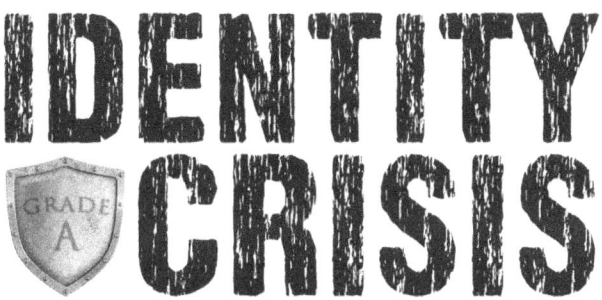

Blood Brothers #4

MANDA MELLETT

Published 2017 by Trish Haill Associates
Copyright © 2017 by Manda Mellett

Edited by Elizabeth Wright

Book and Cover Design by Lia Rees at Free Your Words
(www.freeyourwords.com)

www.mandamellett.com

Disclaimer

This is a work of fiction. Names, characters, businesses, places, events and incidents are either the products of the author's imagination or used in a fictitious manner. Any resemblance to actual persons, living or dead, or actual events is purely coincidental.

Warning

This book is dark in places and contains content of a sexual nature. It is not suitable for persons under the age of 18.

ISBN: 978-0-9954976-7-2

CONTENTS

Two years ago

"Come in, Van. Sit down." As I step into his office, I can almost feel Ben's assessing eyes burning into me, tracking my progress across the room. When I've complied with his instructions I, at last, dare to look across the desk in time to see his sympathetic smile. I manage to respond with a tentative one of my own, as he continues, "How are you doing?"

Looking down to where I'm picking imaginary dirt from under my fingernails, I know I won't be able to deter him with a shallow answer, so offer him the truth, "I've been better, but I'm getting there slowly."

Glancing back up, I find Ben Carter, my boss at Grade A Security, still studying me carefully, seeming in no hurry to get to the point of the conversation. Eventually, he gives a small nod, as though satisfied with what he sees. "You sure you're ready to return to work?"

I've that response prepared, "I'm fed up with wallowing in my misery. At least being here will give me something to occupy my mind." And that's the truth, sitting alone with nothing to do but relive my ordeal, wondering time after time whether I could have done something to prevent it, is doing me absolutely no good at all.

Now his eyes crease as if my situation pains him, and

appears genuinely sorry as he shakes his head, "I'm sorry I couldn't do anything more to help. I tried, Van, I did what I could. At least the smug bastard won't be bothering you again." He leans forward, "I put the fear of God into him and made sure he knows not to come near you in the future. But I couldn't get him to admit to anything."

"I know you did what you could, Ben. And thank you." Ben had visited Simon himself. But Grade A has a reputation to maintain, and while my boss would have probably preferred to have had the conversation with his fists, he'd had to restrict himself to a verbal confrontation to stay on the right side of the law. He is the senior partner of a prestigious security company after all.

Currently used to my emotions making rapid changes from one direction to the polar opposite in just seconds, the tears that come to my eyes are not unexpected. Ben's support when no one else had believed me is something I value. Just about managing to prevent another bout of crying, as that's all I seem to have been doing lately, I blot my face with a tissue. "I'm just grateful that you believed me. No one else did."

"There wasn't any evidence. And it is an incredible story, I admit. But the bastard confessed to you, even if he didn't to anyone else."

I nod in agreement. He certainly hadn't come clean with the police when I'd tried to report him.

Ben's frown deepens, "That he told you was a crime in itself. That knowledge was meant to hurt you." Small spots of red appear on my boss's cheeks, "I wish there was more I could have done. He raped you, Van. Oh, not in the normal sense." He holds up his hand as I go to correct him, "But what he did was entirely without your consent…"

He doesn't have to spell it out. Simon had taken my baby from me. After first walking away when I'd told him I was pregnant, he'd returned a few days later, and proceeded to convince me he hadn't meant the vitriol he'd spat at me in the heat of the moment. That, after thinking it through, he'd come to the belated realisation that he did want a child with me and did everything he could to convince me he really had changed his mind and that he loved me. And it wasn't just words, he proceeded to demonstrate how much he'd had a change of heart, becoming the most attentive and caring man in the world. Even while feeding me the drugs which would cause an abortion. Easy for him to get hold of, his brother's a pharmacist.

I'd have put my miscarriage down to bad luck if he hadn't so proudly told me what he'd done before disappearing out of my life, hopefully for good. I'd have been upset in any event, but I wouldn't have been devastated, violated, and had my trust in men destroyed. *How could I have been so blind not to see through him?* And the reason he'd gone to such lengths was to avoid paying child support for the next eighteen years. Money was more important to him than a life.

I put my face in my hands, and brush away yet another errant tear, then look up at Ben once again, "I didn't think men were capable of such evil. Or that I wouldn't be able to spot such a diabolical example a mile off." And my poor baby was dead because of my bad judgement. Simon was a murderer and had gotten away scot free. When he'd eventually come clean, there was no proof; all the drugs had gone from my system.

"You're still going to therapy?"

"The doctor set that up for six weeks, so yes, I've got another couple of sessions left." The doctor might have put my explanation for my miscarriage down to fantasy, but he'd grasped I needed treatment for my extreme reaction, even if he didn't believe the cause. The psychiatrist, equally doubtful, concentrated on the resulting symptoms rather than the cause. She even had a name for it, post-traumatic stress disorder. But identifying what I was suffering from didn't give me much comfort.

Ben leans forward, his elbows on the table, his chin resting on his clasped hands. "What can I do to help?"

So ashamed of what I'd let happen, I hadn't wanted anyone to know that didn't need to. Especially when, with the exception of my boss, all the people I had told thought I was making it up. But I hadn't been able to keep the reason why I wasn't coming into work from Ben; he saw my sick certificates after all. I'd broken down in tears when I'd given him the full story, expecting him to dismiss it like everyone else. But being used to working with the underworld and the bottom dwellers that feed there, Ben was the first person who didn't question my allegation, taking it upon himself to try to get justice for me. But even his proficient interrogation techniques failed to elicit an admission of guilt. But he did help in other ways, spreading the rumour I'd had my appendix out, hence explaining my absence from work. And now he is offering more support. And I know exactly what I'm going to ask for.

Inhaling a deep breath, I take the plunge, "I need something new to focus on. I need a new challenge." If I'm going to convince him to agree to my request, I've got to appear strong even while I'm wilting inside. So, putting as much strength into my voice as I can, I state my case. "I want to train to be a Close Protection Officer. I want to work in the field as a bodyguard, Ben."

His eyes widen, though it's the only part of him that moves, and he takes a moment before he clears his throat and finally speaks. "All our current CPOs have a military background. And there's a reason for that." It might sound dismissive, but from his thoughtful expression that he's not rejecting the idea out of hand. "I know you, Van, you'll have looked into this already and wouldn't be suggesting it if you weren't serious." At my nod of confirmation, he continues, "We need people at the highest level of fitness." Now one finger of his hand points toward me, "I'm not sure you appreciate what will be required simply to achieve that."

Four weeks languishing on the couch feeling sorry for yourself doesn't help show you're in peak condition, but I'm prepared for this. "I'll work with a personal trainer; work on my strength and endurance training."

A slow bob of his head shows me he appreciates I've thought it through.

"And self-defence, martial arts training. Hand to hand combat," I continue. In fact, when the idea first came to me, it had been this part which attracted me the most. Taking control of my body after the way I'd been debased. And hopefully, it would help improve my mental state too.

"Then there's the training for your licence. You'll need a Level 3 Certificate in Close Protection, and there's a lot involved in that."

To show him I'm taking this seriously and know what's involved, I pick up from where he left off. "I understand, Ben. It will involve courses on evasive driving, firearms, anti-ambush. Then there's all the law and legislation, reconnaissance, journey planning and route selection, threat and risk assessment. Oh, and I'll need to be qualified as a first responder through a first aid course as well."

"You have given a lot of thought to it. There are other things involved, but that's the gist of it." Sounding impressed Ben gives me a smile of encouragement, "You really want to do this, don't you?"

My head bobs up and down eagerly.

"Well," his eyes seem to penetrate into mine, "You've got some of the right skill set; you've proven that in the office. You've shown excellent communication abilities, and you resolve conflict well." He laughs, "I saw you step in when Ryan and Nat were arguing the other day. Fuck knows what that was about, but you soon shut them up," he chuckles softly at the memory. "And you stay calm whatever the crisis and can focus until the job's done. But whether you can apply that outside the office remains to be seen. We haven't tested your ability to adapt and react out in the real world when different things are thrown at you from all directions at the same time."

"I know I'll have to prove myself, Ben. This is something I want, need, to do. I want something to get my teeth into."

Tapping his fingers on his desk, I notice while Ben's not saying no, he's not being too enthusiastic about the idea either. The observation makes me sit up straighter, wondering what else I can say to persuade him.

"Van, let me be honest here. And this is something I'd warn anyone about. While there's nothing to keep a CPO from being married or having a family, it's not a job that lends itself to that. For a man or a woman. It can be hard to have any kind of personal life when you might be sent God knows where at any time. And, let's not forget the risks involved. While your training will endeavour to minimise any personal risk, every bodyguard accepts they might be facing a bullet or a knife as part of their day to day job."

"I realise that. Look, how can I put this? I've just come out of the most damaging relationship it's probably possible to have. I assure you, the very last thing I want to do is jump straight into another one. I'm only twenty-five, I can put a good few years into this job before my biological clock starts running down. If I'm ever prepared to start thinking about a family, it will be a long way into the future, but to be quite honest, after what happened to me, I don't think I'll ever want to go there again."

He sits back and folds his arms, and now's the time for me to keep quiet and let him think about my request. The clock above us ticks off the seconds while he deliberates. Finally, he reaches a decision, and sits forward again, "Okay. You can do the course to get your Security Industry Authority licence under day release. The firm will pay for that. We'll pay for your gym membership, and I'll get you on the martial arts and firearms training that we approve. Likewise, with the first aid requirements. But you'll need to keep up with your day job here. Van, you're one of our best analysts, and we need you to focus on that in the meantime."

"Ben." Again, I have to brush away a tear but, this time it's not one of sadness, "I can't thank you enough…"

As he waves his hand to dismiss my appreciation, he has one final warning for me, "I'm not going to be sending you out until I know you're one hundred percent ready Van, and that will be my decision. You might not ever be sufficiently prepared for me to risk a client to your care. You have a long way to go to get up to speed and reach the point where the others even started. But to help, Jon and I will give you our support and assistance with your training, and we'll be assessing you ourselves."

That's a great offer, both Ben and Jon used to conduct close protection training for the SAS, the elite of the British Armed forces.

"It could take two years or more before we're satisfied with your progress."

"I don't mind that. It gives me something to focus on and work for." I'm so excited, it's hard not to start bouncing in my seat.

Another careful examination, and then his face breaks into a smile as he stands and reaches his hand over the table, "Good luck then, Van. And I look forward to having you on the team."

CHAPTER 1
Sean

"Hi Master Sean, it's good to see you. It's been a while. How the fuck are you doing?" The Master Dom, who's doing his stint as bartender, holds his beefy hand over the bar and vigorously shakes mine. I manage not to grimace, and successfully resist the impulse to rub my bruised fingers as he pulls back and asks, "Your usual?"

Shaking my head, I place my order, "Just water, please, Ralph." As I don my orange Dungeon Monitor vest over my black T-shirt, he nods, recognising that I'll have to keep a clear head for at least the next couple of hours.

After passing me the requested bottle of water, he does what everyone else has been doing over the last few months and enquires after my injuries, "How are the legs coming along? Are you healed up now?"

Patting my leathers, I offer up my standard response, "Left one's completely healed now, that was only a flesh wound. Still getting physio on the right, but it's getting there. At least I've ditched the darn crutches now!" I'd been shot in both legs during my last overseas mission—something I wouldn't recommend and personally hope never to repeat. Although my left leg only required stitches, the injury leaving me with a nasty scar; the bullet that entered my right tibia had smashed the bone to smithereens, and it's only down to the great skill of the surgeons and copious amounts of nuts, bolts, and plates that six months later I'm now able to walk with only a slight limp.

Recuperation hasn't been fun. The amount of metal they used to screw me together is going to make going through airport security interesting in the future. Luckily for him, the bastard who shot me is already dead, though sometimes I'd like to be able to dig him up and kill him all over again. Slowly. St John-Davies had died far too fast for all the havoc he'd wrought.

Ralph's innocent question seems to have triggered a dull ache in my right leg. Leaning with my back against the bar, I realise I might have overdone it today, pushing myself too hard. I'm determined to get full movement back, hence the intensive physio and exercise regimen I'm putting myself through. And there's a reason I'm trying so hard. If I don't get back to full fitness, I won't be able to do my job. As one of the lead CPOs for Grade A security, if I can't run or fight, I won't be able to protect anyone. And, as a black belt in a variety of martial arts, for me, my legs are my secret weapons.

My hand automatically rubs my aching limb to try to erase the throbbing as I turn away from Ralph, leaving him to serve the other patrons. I stand scanning the main room of the club in front of me. Club Tiacapan, named, rather appropriately, after the Aztec Goddess of Love and Passion, is an exclusive BDSM club with strict membership rules, located in South London. Were it not for the fact I worked for Grade A, and hence for two of the club's owners, I wouldn't be able to afford the astronomical joining fees in a lifetime. Luckily Grade A employees get membership rights as a perk of our employment, though only a number of us with certain proclivities take up the offer. It's not exactly in the same league as a subscription to the local gym.

But it suits me and my appetites right down to the ground. I took up the opportunity shortly after I was hired on at Grade A and, having played in similar clubs previously, it wasn't long before I'd earned Master rights and privileges. Along with those come responsibilities. Master Ralph chooses to take his shifts tending the busy bar; I prefer to take my turn at monitoring the dungeon, making sure all play is conducted as per the strict rules of the club. Of course, due to the intense vetting before allowing members to join, the duties are not onerous, and it's rare I have a need to interrupt a scene.

Downing the water, I push off from the bar, ready to take a turn around the club, just to ensure everything's as is should be, when I spot something that causes my experienced eyes to sharpen. One of the stages is being prepped for a very particular type of play. Hoping all the proper precautions are going to be followed and wondering who the Dom or Domme is, I start walking over in that direction, trusting he or she knows exactly what they are doing. Gritting my teeth, I only slightly favour my right leg as I make my way across the dungeon, my eyes intent on my destination.

Drawing closer to the brightly lit stage area, I discover candles are being set out on a shallow tray resting on a small table. Sir Duncan, who in his daily life I know to be CEO of one of the major banks, walks into the area carrying a bucket of water. I sigh to myself, knowing he's a fairly new Dom, which means I'll have to confront him. I approach, clearing my throat to get his attention, interrupting as he sets up his scene.

"Duncan." I greet him, pleasantly enough at this point. I may need to toughen my stance if I need to call a halt to his plans. I know him quite well, having been one of his mentors during his training, but to my knowledge he hasn't performed this particular activity before.

Intent on preparing for his scene, my voice startles him, but glancing my way he notices my bright orange vest and straightens as he understands I'm here in an official capacity. "Master Sean. Is everything alright?"

I nod toward the play area, "Have you got permission for this?" Wax play, if not done correctly, carries a risk of serious injury for a submissive, and obviously, a small, but one that cannot be dismissed, hazard of fire for the club.

His head dips down then up again enthusiastically, "I had a training session with Master Ryan last week."

I nod in return, happy to hear that. But Ryan, who's coincidentally a Grade A colleague of mine, should have been in attendance the first time his protégée, quite literally, plays with fire. The club's rules are very comprehensive. "And where is Master Ryan?"

Duncan looks a bit sheepish. "He was supposed to be here, but he hasn't turned up yet. I thought it would be okay to go ahead, at least with the preparations. The training covered everything. I know what I'm doing."

I can't be annoyed that Ryan hasn't appeared. In our line of work, it's never possible to guarantee where you'll be at any point in time; providing protection and security to a vast range of diverse people with varying requirements means you can't predict when you might be called out of the country on short notice. And it's hardly a nine-to-five job where you can just clock out when your shift is over. If the person you're protecting suddenly needs extra security, or decides on a whim to alter their plans, you've no choice but to drop everything else to provide what's necessary. And you can't excuse yourself to make a phone call when you're neutralising a threat. It's far from unlikely that Ryan could have been held up, or won't be able to make it to the club at all tonight. But I'm here, and wax play is one of my specialities. I don't mind standing in for him.

I tell Duncan so, then add, "Carry on setting up, and I'll be back in a moment. Who's your sub?" He mentions the name of someone I haven't heard of. "I'd like to be in on your negotiation, if that's okay?" Wax play doesn't suit everybody, and the sub has got to appreciate what she, or he, is getting into.

Duncan seems quite relaxed as he gives his confirmation, and shows no awkwardness that he's going to have an audience, making me recall the titbit I'd forgotten, that he's a bit of an exhibitionist. Leaving him to continue getting ready, I stride away, giving a slight gesture with my hand to catch the attention of one of the other dungeon monitors on duty. There are four of us in attendance at any one time, three in the main club while the fourth monitors the hallway leading to the private rooms. I quickly explain the situation, and that I'll need to be focused on the one particular scene for now. He confirms he's happy to cover my allocated area of the dungeon as well as his own. Satisfied I'm not neglecting my duties, I return to find a male sub kneeling at Duncan's feet.

Although Duncan is relatively new to Club Tiacapan, I know from our previous conversations that he's been in the lifestyle for a while, but I've not met his sub before. It's soon clear from their interaction their relationship is well established. Duncan's hand is on the younger man's head, and he's affectionately caressing his hair. I watch, discreetly, as they have a private moment. The successful businessman leans down, lifts the man's chin with his hands, and places his mouth on his, sharing a deep, and surprisingly gentle, kiss. While they are enjoying their intimacy, I take a second to examine the sub. He's certainly not what I expected. A burly man with an unruly crop of curly hair and tattoos down his arms and across his chest. Rings adorn both his nipples and moving my gaze downwards I see he's got a Prince Albert cock piercing. This chap is no stranger to pain, and it is easy to see why this sort of play would appeal to him.

The idea that he likes a bit of discomfort is reinforced when I make my presence known with a purposeful clearing of my throat. Duncan reaches out his hands, takes hold of his sub's nipple rings, and uses them to pull the man to his feet. The hard nubs stretch out from his chest, and the sub gives a loud groaning sigh, a sign he's enjoying the combination of pain mingled with pleasure. *He's a pain slut!* I begin to feel easier about the situation.

Standing aside, I let them negotiate the scene, close enough to hear, but far enough away to give them a semblance of privacy. Then I nod, giving my approval for the scene to proceed, and take a further few steps back, letting them have the stage to themselves.

Duncan first binds his sub to the table, making sure the hand and ankle cuffs are tight enough to keep his body taut, but loose enough so as not to restrict blood supply to his appendages. After stepping back to admire his work, he applies a lotion all over his sub's body, massaging it into the skin. The careful attention causes the man to start to writhe, and for that he receives a sharp slap and terse instruction to be still. A command he obviously struggles to obey as the lotion is applied to his half erect cock, which quickly becomes hard under his master's touch. I smile, whether or not wax will be dropped there, Duncan is certainly making sure his dick and balls are well covered, almost reverent in the care he's giving to that part of his anatomy.

Moving to his table Duncan collects a blindfold, and, after tenderly smoothing his sub's head, insists on a verbal assent he's doing okay and correctly reminds him of his safe word. Then he ties the black cloth around his head. If I had a checklist for a perfect BDSM scene, I'd be ticking every item off right now. As far as I can see, Duncan hasn't put a step wrong. Pulling up a chair, I relax into it, taking the weight off my aching leg. Tonight's duties aren't arduous at all, in fact, I'm transfixed by the tableau in front of me. I've been on both the sub and Dom's side for wax play before, and it's something I personally enjoy. My cock twitches and begins to swell as if in camaraderie with that of the man tied down on the table.

Now we're getting to the main event, I notice, as Duncan lights the candles which I've already checked are made of soy wax—they're the safest, burning at a fractionally lower temperature than other types, and slightly less likely to cause skin irritation. Ryan's obviously taught the Dom well.

Not wanting to keep his sub waiting overly long in anticipation, Duncan pauses for just the right length of time before picking up a red candle, and, after a terse command to 'stay still', begins to dribble wax in a line from just below the sub's throat, following down the sternum, but halting just above his neatly trimmed pubic hair. The sub's body jerks as the hot liquid causes a momentary burn, but his bindings hold him firmly in place. Next Duncan draws a horizontal line, just under the nipples across his chest, this time the man keeps control, and a slight twitch is the only sign he's feeling any discomfort. Then Duncan pulls back, and a large glob of wax is allowed to drop onto a nipple, the heat intensified by the metal of the nipple ring. That causes the sub's whole body to shudder and for the first time, a groan escapes his lips. I can almost feel the sting and burn myself, and I adjust myself in my leathers, engrossed in the smooth performance of what I now realise is a Dom who's taken his lessons to heart, and the palpable enjoyment of the sub.

Another candle, this one blue, and now Duncan pays attention to his sub's legs, drawing on them as if on a canvas. From experience, I know exactly what the young man will be feeling, a burn creeping over his skin, almost unbearable for a split second, and then fading away to a pleasurable, gentle warmth. Theoretically, his body should process the pain and transmute it into arousal, which is evidently the case as his cock is bobbing against his stomach, and even from my position I can see it hardening to almost impossible proportions. Duncan takes his time, painting his picture, weaving the wax close to, but never quite touching that most painful area on a man's body. Captivated, I can't draw my eyes away, my cock's straining almost unbearably against my leathers, mentally I'm sharing every drop of wax with the sub.

Duncan's drawing this out, the sub's excitement is growing; audible sounds of longing and frustration coming from his lips until the Dom builds up to the finale. And there it is! A line of wax along his shaft. A scream rings out, almost too shrill for such a burly man.

Duncan immediately pulls away, blows out the candle and reaches for his sub, taking his dick in both hands. Massaging his balls, heavy strokes up and down and pulling at the piercing until the man suffering his attentions doesn't stand a chance. Within seconds the sub is shouting out in ecstasy, cum is shooting out in long white ribbons up and over his chest. Duncan rubs it into his skin, mixing it with the cooled wax. I can't see from my position, but I suspect the man's eyes have rolled up into his head, and that he'll be floating on the most incredible high. I breathe deeply and concentrate, far too close to coming myself, and needing a moment to bring myself under control.

When suitably composed, I stand, intending to leave them their time to indulge in aftercare, but I wait to check the last stage and am satisfied when Duncan takes a plastic card he left for this purpose on the table beside him and starts to remove the hardened wax gently; a job made easier by the lotion applied earlier. He glances over at me and we exchange nods, mine hopefully conveying the scene was a pleasure to watch, even though it's left me with churning balls. As I watch the competent Dom take care of his sub with such glowing affection, an unexpected wave of envy comes over me.

Making my way through the now heaving club, I retrace my steps to the bar area and, seeing by the clock that I've completed my allotted time, pass my DM vest over to Master Donavan. My lips curl up as I see he's been chatting with a very pregnant Mia, wife of Jon Tharpe, my boss at Grade A and part owner of the Club Tiacapan. It's hard not to remember the first interaction between Mia and Donavan, as it wasn't exactly quiet or reserved. It had to have been a year ago, her first visit to the club and she'd hit him. But if I recall correctly, it was his fault, and his actions that had triggered such an extreme reaction. She'd earned her first punishment from Jon that night, and at that time it wouldn't have seemed possible she and Donavan would have become friends. But it's clear, over time, that's exactly what's happened.

Sweeping the memories from my mind, this time I take the offered whisky from the bartender who's replaced Ralph, having decided I won't be playing tonight, so there's no longer a need to keep my head clear. If truth be told, I haven't scened for a while now. My last mission in Amahad was so frantic I had no time for extra-curricular activities, and of course it was there that I'd been shot. On my return, I had the excuse that my legs needed time to heal, but that justification no longer holds sway. I still get a thrill out of coming to the club, but my heart just hasn't been in playing.

But the reason why completely escapes me.

CHAPTER 2
Sean

When you figure it out, let me know." Although I'm only hearing the words in my head, the sentence seems to echo around me, hovering in the air.

Gazing into the bathroom mirror as I shave, the question Zoe, now the wife of the Emir of Amahad, had asked all those months ago, as well as the answer I had given to her, rattle round my head as though they're haunting me. Just one day was enough for her to sum me up as an enigma, unable to understand who or what I was. I'd asked her to let me know when she'd worked it out. But she never did get back to me with an answer. Even after we'd become close friends, while I was serving as her, as it turned out, rather unsuccessful bodyguard, and we both ended up kidnapped and injured, the mystery remained. Who, and what, am I?

Fuck if I know.

Oh, the basics are easy enough; I'm thirty-six years old; I have a great job working for Grade A, work which takes me all over the world, a role that I enjoy, or did, before I was wounded. But my private life is another matter. Zoe's comment that I was neither one thing nor the other hit down deep. Was it time I made a decision and came out on either one side or the other?

Holding my head still, as I carefully trim my goatee, I look into the blue eyes reflected in the glass, then note what are politely called 'laughter lines' are now undeniably obvious. Although my shoulder length, but nonetheless carefully groomed, dirty blonde hair isn't yet showing signs of graying, I'm unable to hide it; age is creeping up on me. Is it time I started to leave my playboy days behind and settle down? Fuck, I've no idea what a life like that would even look like.

Slowly shaking my head I, yet again, shelve such deep thoughts for another day, unsure whether I'll ever be able to come up with an answer. All I know is a sense of deep dissatisfaction with my life has come over me, and it's as if I'm standing at a crossroad, not knowing which way to turn.

Stepping back, I straighten, but my mind refuses to stop racing. Saturday night at the club, for example, I got my kicks watching a scene but came away restless and unwilling to find a sub to play with or to submit to someone myself. Since my recent injury and extended recovery, I don't seem to have the same appetites I once had, and one night stands don't interest me like they used to. What previously gave me gratification seems jaded now.

Was it that I'd come so close to death? The insight into my mortality? The knowledge that I'm vulnerable, just like anyone else? That I'm getting older? Giving up hope my reflection will be any better than me at providing any answers, I finish my daily ablutions and return to the bedroom, pulling on a tailored shirt and expensive suit. Grade A ensures that its operatives are paid well, very well.

But then we ought to be. In the field, we risk our lives almost on a daily basis. Being a CPO means being prepared to take a bullet for the person you're protecting. And that's part of the problem; that question of my expected longevity that makes me cautious about introducing any stability into my life. I might not be around long to enjoy it. But is that what I crave? Something more meaningful? Fuck, it's probably the fact I've been desk bound for too long while waiting for my leg to fully mend that has engineered this sense of restlessness and discontent. Perhaps when I'm back out in real world, I'll relish my freedoms again.

Glancing at the alarm clock by the side of my bed I see, despite the time taken for introspection, I'll still be in good time to make this morning's briefing. With any luck, Ben will have relented, will have accepted I'm fit enough, and will assign me to a real case. Since I returned to work five months ago, I've just been doing paperwork, and my feet have become itchy staying close to the modern offices situated in the Docklands area of London. Assigning others to do the job I love so much has become wearing. I'd rather be out there, on the front line myself.

I took this flat, which is nothing more exciting than a typical bachelor's pad, as it's centrally situated and not too far from the office. A twenty-minute hop on the tube via the Jubilee Line and then another on the overground Docklands Light Railway will take me there in thirty minutes. Like any other morning, I have no expectations there'll be a vacant seat on either train in the busy rush hour, and now I've ditched the crutches no one will offer me their place. Not that they always did even when my disability was more visible. Unless I sidled up to someone sitting under a 'Please give up your seat to someone who needs it' sign and exaggerated my incapacity.

Reaching the platform, pausing only to grab a copy of the free paper, Metro, I leap on board the first tube to arrive, and stand, leaning against a pole. In a practiced move, I read what's going on in the world swaying gently with the train as it rattles around the curves. The DLR is only slight less crowded, and again I've no option but to stay on my feet, but I'm used to that. Then a short trek from the station and I'm walking through the glass and chrome business district of the Docklands to arrive at the building housing the headquarters of Grade A.

"Hey, Sean! Good Morning!"

I wave at Sandra, the receptionist, as I enter the building without stopping to chat, hopefully giving off the vibe that I'm in a hurry. She's the worst gossip in the world, always good-naturedly trying to extract information to titillate her fellow workers at break time. I've suggested to Ben we should use her in interrogations; a couple of minute's conversation with her and you're spilling the beans about things you never expected to divulge! I've quickly learned it's best to steer clear unless I want my personal life known throughout the organization. Sandra's innocent enquiry of 'did you have a good weekend?' is usually followed by questions which tend to prompt far more than you ever wanted to say. I've often wondered whether she was trained by the intelligence service.

So, I avoid her after acknowledging her pleasant

greeting and, swiping my card through the reader, enter through the security gates. Taking the lift to the third floor, I pause at the coffee machine to grab a drink before heading into the conference room where we hold 'morning prayers', the name given to our regular early Monday morning meeting. This normally takes the line of a general catch up, an update on current assignments, and, hopefully in my case today, the allocation of new ones.

"Good weekend?" A slap on my back has me turning, and I acknowledge Jon Tharpe, one of the partners, with a grin and a jerk of my chin.

"Great and yours?" As I give the practiced and expected, if not quite truthful response, an image of the sub I'd seen subjected to wax play comes into my mind. I shake my head to dismiss it. "I saw Mia at the club on Saturday, Jon, with Donovan." I pause, and we share a grin, each of us remembering their first inauspicious meeting. Then I politely enquire, "Pregnancy going okay? She must be due any day now." It's something of a miracle that she conceived, and I know everyone's behind the couple in making sure it proceeds smoothly this time.

"She's still got three weeks to go. On one hand, I can't wait, on the other, fuck, I think I'm more worried about it than she is."

"She'll be fine," I hasten to reassure him, "She's a strong, brave woman."

Jon laughs in agreement, then adds a comment about how his weekend was spent buying up last minute stuff for their expected addition as we make our way to the meeting just in time to be called to order by Ben, the senior partner. Noticing Ben's staring intently at me as I walk in, I concentrate on hiding my residual limp, knowing his eagle eyes will be assessing the way I'm moving. It makes me hopeful he's considering putting me out in the field soon. I know he gets the medical reports, but hope he'll prefer to rely on the evidence in front of him rather than the, in my view, overly pessimistic predictions of the medics. As a good employer, Ben is sometimes known to be over-cautious with his men, but fuck me, I hope he can see it would be bad for my mental health if he doesn't assign me something soon. I'm going stir crazy stuck in the office.

It's the day after the weekend, and Grade A is an informal place to work. Our roles as Close Protection Officers often require intense concentration, the slightest loss of focus could mean injury or death to the client or the CPO themselves. Back at base we tend to relax, so it takes Ben a while to shut down the individual conversations about what everyone did on their days off, and to get all of our attention. Used to the shenanigans, I pass the time flicking through the documents that have just been downloaded to my tablet in front of me, hoping that I'll see my name somewhere on the agenda. I don't. Fuck.

Curbing my frustration, I look around the table, noting who's here. There's Jon and, of course, Ben. Ryan's seated a little way down the table, and Harry, Nat, and Seth are also present. Vanessa's sitting opposite me, and Nafisa next to her—the pair making up our office support staff—which means almost the full top team is present today. Jason Deville, the other senior partner, is still absent, engaged in work abroad. In fact, he seems to have been missing in action during all my six years with the company. I've never seen him, and sometimes think he's a figment of everyone else's imagination.

A surprise additional attendee is Hunter Wright. Although a paid employee of Grade A, we all know that he's working for the British Government in some capacity or other, even if no mention of that is ever made outside the third-floor offices and this conference room.

Hunter's report is first on the agenda, and I listen carefully as he fills us in on the current situation in Amahad, the country where I was working when I got kidnaped and shot six months ago. Despite the horrific position I'd ended up in, I do have a fondness for the country where I've often been assigned to provide protection for the Emir and his family, as well as security for their oil operation, so I'm interested in Hunter's summary of what's happening in the region. I listen, making notes on my tablet of facts I'll need to remember.

"What's your view on the current risks at the oil field development, Hunter?" Ben asks a direct question. "Is our team big enough on the ground in Amahad?" Having recently found oil under the sands of Amahad and its neighbouring countries, getting the drilling for the wells underway and establishing a pipeline to take the liquid gold to the coast is a risky venture in these troubled times. A target for terrorist attacks.

Hunter's eyes tighten before he gives his considered response, "I think so. Neighbouring Alair is supplying part of their army, and Ezirad seems quiet right now. I'm going out there again next week, so I'll keep you informed if anything changes."

"And anything from Amir al-Farhi?"

Shrugging, Hunter gives only a vague reply. "Most of the world's governments are hunting for him. We can only do our best to stay on guard." They're referring to the number one terrorist, responsible for so many terror attacks across the globe. Only last year al-Farhi had plotted to fabricate reports falsifying the results from the original test wells, making people believe there was no oil to be found in Amahad and, as a result, causing discord amongst the desert tribes. When the truth came out, instead of causing civil war, the tribes had become united in the potential exploitation of the wealth under their lands. But none of us would be stupid enough to believe Amahad had heard the last of the international terrorist.

"Okay, on with the agenda then…" Ben's interrupted by a knock on the door. He tilts his head, his brow furrowed. Team meetings are sacrosanct, confidential, and normally never disturbed. We all turn off our phones when entering, guaranteeing no interruptions from that quarter, unless it's for something critical. He glances around the table, sharing our puzzled looks. Then, as if deciding no one would butt in without good cause calls out, "Enter!"

The door opens cautiously, as if the messenger is frightened to put his head in the lion's den. "I'm sorry to interrupt," starts David, Ben's personal assistant, rather sheepishly. He wavers on the threshold as though uncertain whether his message is significant enough to intrude on us or not. "But there's a bit of a commotion in the lobby. Sean needs to get down there as soon as possible."

Me? A commotion? What the fuck? "What's up, David?" I'm as puzzled as Ben and annoyed at the disruption to the meeting. I wanted to get on with discussing the new assignments.

"Sorry," his hands flutter apologetically, "I don't know the details. But I think it's personal."

Personal? For me? Jon snorts beside me, "You forget to wrap it up, man? Is that your baby mama down there?"

I should have guessed he'd jump to something like that. I thump his arm, "Shut it!"

"Probably an angry husband!"

"Fuck off, Ryan." I scoff at the light-hearted ribbing.

"Or an angry wife!"

Even I smirk at the amusing comment. The ribaldry round the room is not unexpected, but I give an exaggerated sign of resignation and get to my feet. *My reputation precedes me.* If only they knew the truth. I haven't dipped my wick since before the shooting.

Ben nods at me, his head tilted to one side in question, unable to completely suppress a look of annoyance at the disturbance to our meeting, but giving me his permission to go find out what's so important David's felt the need to disturb us. Ignoring the remainder of the snide comments still coming from various quarters and flipping a two-fingered salute over my shoulder as my parting shot, I leave the room with nothing more than mild curiosity, to find out what the fuss is all about down in the lobby. Whatever it is, Sandra will probably be having a field day.

CHAPTER 3

Vanessa

Monday morning team meetings can go one of two ways. They can be as boring as hell or edge of your seat gripping, depending what cases we're currently working. The time we were trying to locate the erotic fiction writer Mia Fable, who's now the wife of one of my bosses, Jon, and who'd been kidnapped by a dangerous stalker, definitely came under the heading of the latter. It had quickly become a matter of life or death, and being part of that team was nail-biting and exhilarating, particularly as we won out in the end. But today's agenda holds nothing like that. Having helped prepare it, I already know it's comparatively boring stuff coming up, and no exciting new assignments of note either. At least none which will be assigned to me.

When will Ben relent, and assign me my own client? I keep asking, but to date have only received non-committal answers, which is frustrating seeing I've worked so hard over the last couple of years. I've completed all my official training, have got my firearms' certificate, have proved proficient in a number of different martial arts and, a few weeks ago, finally received my SIA license, making me a fully qualified Close Protection Officer. But the partners continue keeping me close to the office. True, I'm the only female CPO on the books and don't have a military background like most of the others, but that shouldn't be holding me back. And if my sex was any part of the reason I'm being kept office bound, I could threaten to take them to the employment tribunal.

Not that I would, of course; I enjoy working here too much, even though it's amongst a group consisting predominantly of overly protective males. For now, it seems I must remain content with being the in-house 'go to' expert, together with my colleague, Nafisa. Nafisa and I work with logistics, extracting information from computer systems. Together we map coincidences and join sometimes obscure pieces of information to give the CPOs on the front line the intelligence they need to do their jobs. Most of the time it's damn boring, but oh, so necessary and exciting; particularly when we're doing our part and working against the clock to save a life. But it doesn't stop me craving to be out there, putting my new skills into practice.

Prayers start at nine. As usual, I leave my desk ten minutes early and arrive before anyone else, carefully carrying my near over-flowing cup of coffee. While officially anyone can sit where they want, except for Ben's place as Chair, of course, being creatures of habit we tend to navigate to the same positions. Seating myself opposite the chair Sean normally takes, I bide my time, and then, when he eventually enters the room, greedily soak in his tall, slender frame and roguish good looks. I've waited all weekend for this chance to feast my eyes on the man who haunts my dreams and is the image I see in my mind when

I allow myself time with my battery-operated boyfriend. Oh, the fantasies I have about him. Whoops! Now I have to cast my eyes downwards and pretend to study my screen, in case he glances across at me and correctly interprets the red flush that's come to my cheeks betraying the inappropriate direction of my thoughts. Christ, now that would be embarrassing!

Sean Cooper joined Grade A soon after I started, and for the first four years I admired and lusted after him from afar. Then, when my one attempt at a relationship came to such a disastrous end, even he could no longer tempt me. I'd sworn off men. Or so I thought.

While he's been office bound and we've been working in closer proximity over the last few months, I've found myself regaining that earlier attraction. There's just something about him which draws me in, even while knowing I'll never have a chance to be more. He's so self-assured, well-built and handsome, any woman would want to fall at his feet. And often do, if the conversations I overhear have much truth to them. What chance would I have? If, in all these years, he hasn't looked at me twice, he's hardly going to start doing so now. I sigh, my hand covering my mouth, pretending to hide a yawn. Eye candy, that's all he can ever be. But while others might resent Monday mornings, I look forward to them as they signify five days ahead working with Sean.

As conversation goes on around me, I cast another quick glance at him, soaking in the sight I've been waiting for since Friday evening, and then take a moment to give equal nods and smiles at all my other colleagues who are now in their seats. It's my usual ploy, I work hard on not giving myself away.

As we wait for the various discussions to cease and jokes to be laughed at, I consider the members of the team. Jon, Ben, and the absent Jason Deville are co-partners in Grade A, but Jon and Jason also part-own an exclusive BDSM club in South London. As employees, if we have such an inclination, we can join without having to cough up the very hefty membership fees. Most of the men sitting around the table haven't been able to resist the offer and have become members, and I happen to know Sean is one to have taken up the opportunity.

So far, I've not been able to summon up the courage to join myself, but my fantasies often lead me there. If I was brave, and took the leap, could it be a way of getting him to notice me? For Sean, I understand, that lifestyle is an important part of his life. Since Mia's stalker case a year ago, I've known secrets about him that even Sandra doesn't know. As part of the investigation, when Sean had been tasked with going into the seedier BDSM clubs to expose a wannabe Dom, I'd been called on to research similar clubs and activities, and admit what I learned intrigues me.

My position in the company means I know a lot about the employees and partners of Grade A, more so even than Sandra, the nosy receptionist who could probably get a dead body to give up his secrets. Such as the fact that Sean's unusual, even in the lifestyle he's chosen. Not only is he devastatingly handsome, but he's also a switch; meaning he can be a Dominant or a submissive. And as if that isn't enough, he isn't particularly selective as to which sex he played these roles with. I risk a quick look across at him, recalling the rumours I've heard about how he likes variety. Perhaps he's just looking for the right person to settle down with. And though I doubt I could ever be that special someone, it does nothing to dampen my attraction to him. Damn hormones!

Allowing myself a quick daydream, I know exactly what role I'd like to take with him. *I just need the man to see me as a woman, not a piece of office furniture!* Without thinking, I exhale a long breath, loud enough to get a few looks thrown at me.

"Keeping you up, Van?" Jon jokes from across the table.

"Late night?" Ryan, sitting next to me, nudges me in the arm and winks knowingly.

Shaking my head in response and thinking, *I wish*, I notice the man who's captured my interest hasn't once glanced my way. *Oh well, par for the course.* Sometimes I think I must be invisible.

Ben coughs, and at last gets the meeting started. I force my thoughts back to where they should be, and concentrate on Hunter's briefing about the situation in Amahad. We might joke and laugh our way through, but our work is serious and having up to date information is imperative.

The abnormal interruption of the meeting comes as a surprise to us all, particularly as it's a personal matter concerning Sean. Ben's assistant knows better than to interrupt for anything trivial, so immediately I know it must be serious. Bemused, I look on as Sean gets to his feet and leaves the room, unable to dismiss my feelings of concern as he derides the teasing thrown at him with the contempt, in my view, it deserves. Even after he closes the door, the comments continue.

"A tenner says it's a dissatisfied lover." Jon throws a crisp ten-pound note into the centre of the table.

Dissatisfied? If Sean leaves any lover wanting I'd be very surprised. Not that I would know what satisfied feels like if it jumped up and bit me.

"He's got a woman in trouble." Ryan's opening his wallet and extracting an identical note.

"He's got a speeding fine."

I would have thought Ben would have been above all this, but he puts his money down too.

"Insider knowledge, Ben?" Jon narrows his eyes, then his lips curve as he grins at his partner's response.

"Fuck no! But we all know how he drives!"

As laughter rings around I frown, being worried about the man in question, I can't help myself. "You lot are awful! What if his mum's had an accident or something? Shisk! It might be something dreadful!" It's common knowledge that Sean adores his mother, his only relative. And we all appreciate the delicious cupcakes she bakes and sends in with him occasionally. Even if just a whiff of them makes me gain a few kilos.

One corner of his mouth twists and turns down, and after throwing me a sheepish glance of acknowledgment, Ben bangs his hand on the table. "Van's right. Come on, let's move it along now. Anything that's our concern we'll know soon enough." He eyes the pot on the table. "Van, if it is something serious we'll donate the money to charity, okay?" His eyes question me. At my nod of agreement to the compromise he continues. "It's probably none of our business and we've got important things to discuss here. Next item on the agenda then."

After such an unusual interruption, I have difficulty trying to concentrate during the rest of the meeting. To everyone else, Sean's a well-respected work colleague and friend, but to me, at least in my head, he's something more, and I can't suppress the flicker of worry inside me. I hate myself for even thinking it, but if something awful has happened to Sean, he might need a shoulder to lean on. And I'm certainly willing to make myself available for that. Whatever has happened, if he needs support, I'm determined to be the one to provide it.

CHAPTER 4

Sean

Though I successfully hid it from the rest of the team, my leg is giving me jip today, and as I stand in the lift, pressing the button for the ground floor, it throbs with pain. That I'm not as fit as I hoped I'd by this point makes me hit the side wall with my fist in frustration. Fuck! I think back to that bastard St John-Davies and can almost feel the bullets tearing into my legs once again. I'd been powerless and helpless at the time, handcuffed, with six men all targeting me with their guns. If only I can get rid of this pain, I might also be able to escape the recurrent nightmares about that day.

The aching I'd been trying to conceal momentarily takes my mind off the strange summons to the reception area of our building. But as the lift descends floor by floor I force memories of the past which I can't change out of my mind, and turn my thoughts instead to wonder what on earth I'm going to find at my destination. It must be something important if it was enough to cause David to break into our sacrosanct meeting.

At first, I'm intrigued, but as I get closer to street level, I get the twitchy feeling in my spine that's given me an early warning of danger in the past. *What if something's wrong?* Fuck it, I haven't spoken to my mum in over a week, I hope she's okay. Cursing myself, I realise I should have checked up on her over the weekend. I tend to forget she's getting on, and though she's not exactly old and frail, she's as likely as any one of us to have had an accident. Shit, I hope that's not it. Wracking my brains, I can't think what else it could be. But wouldn't I have received a phone call rather than a summons? Unless the police have turned up to deliver bad news in person. Wiping my hand over my face, I find my forehead's damp, and I'm starting to sweat. *Fuck it, Mum, you haven't done anything stupid, have you?*

The last ping and the announcement we've reached the ground floor comes, then there's the customary torturous interval before the lift doors open. Making a hasty exit, having now convinced myself something must be terribly amiss, I hurry over to the security guard who's currently manning the reception desk. Sandra's not there, she must be on a break.

"What's up, Matt?" My voice is breathy, concerned. But, glancing around, I can't see anyone else here. Certainly, no police officer wearing a sympathetic frown. That's something, I suppose.

Matt nods to the side of the desk, his expression professional and impossible to read, though he's leaning forward as though struggling to remain completely composed, "Someone left something for you."

"What?" It can't be a normal parcel, if it is, someone's going to get a bollocking for the interruption if it was just due to a simple delivery. But then again, working where I do, finding I've been sent a box containing a severed finger might not be off the cards.

Matt just shrugs and points down to the side of his desk. Wondering whether we might need to summon the bomb disposal squad—and if that's the case, he should have bloody called them already—I take a step to one side and follow the direction his finger's indicating.

And there I see, to my astonishment, a pram. On closer examination, there's a sleeping baby, covered in a pink blanket, inside. I glance up at Matt, and then down again, and now notice Sandra kneeling beside it where she'd been out of my immediate line of sight. Sensing my presence, she stops cooing at the baby and glances up, her eyes wide and full of excited curiosity. As I stare on in disbelief and confusion—why call me for a fucking baby? —she holds out an envelope for my inspection. Why I'd got the summons all becomes clear. There's a name clearly marked on the outside. Mine. Sean Cooper.

The first and obvious thought flies through my head, and I immediately dismiss it. *Shit! Jesus fucking Christ! No, there's no fucking way that baby is mine!* Momentarily frozen to the spot, I recover quickly and give an inward chuckle. Whatever reason the baby's been left here, it's certainly not because I'm the daddy. *It's impossible, isn't it? I've never forgotten to use a condom!* Reaching out to take the note, I notice my hand is shaking and I can't seem to stop it. A seed of doubt has planted itself in my mind. *Is this the moment every man dreads?* I think fast, have any of my friends got babies? I've no family other than my single remaining parent, so it can't be a relative's. But the only baby I can think of is the one currently happily residing in Jon's wife's stomach. Why the fuck has an infant been left here for me?

Gingerly holding the note in my hand as if the object itself could harm me, I look at the two members of staff, and force myself to remain calm, treating it as I'd treat any other unexpected package. With intense suspicion. "Who left it here? What did they say?"

Matt and Sandra look at each other, and both start to speak at the same time. Sandra waves at the security guard. "Matt was here, I'd popped to the loo, I was desperate for a wee."

TMI, Sandra, you could have just said you were taking a break! I look to Matt. "Well?"

He shuffles, looking embarrassed. "I didn't really see. Someone came in pushing it, I assumed they were coming over to the reception desk. I looked down at the CCTV screen, next I looked up and the pram had been left, and I caught sight of a person wearing a hooded coat going out of the door again. I went to the door, but they'd disappeared into a waiting black cab."

"Did you catch the number plate?" There are thousands of black cabs in London, operated by all manner of firms and licenced individuals.

He's shaking his head, "Sorry." He purses his lips together, looking sheepish.

Don't we pay him to be attentive? Yes, we fucking do! Someone could have snuck in explosives, and it seems he wouldn't have noticed. But right now that's not my most immediate concern, so I won't get into that at the moment. "Okaaaay," I start, drawing out the word as though I'm speaking to a child. "There are security cameras all over this area and the outside of the building…"

"Mr Cooper, I've already checked those. This is the best I can do." Matt beckons me around to the other side of the desk and shows me what he explains is the clearest image of the person who dropped off the unusual package for me. It's impossible to see whether the person is male or female; they're wearing a long, thigh-length coat and have a hood pulled up over their head. All it's possible to discern is that they are about five foot eight or so, wearing jeans and trainers, moving quickly as they get into the cab. The angle is wrong and there's no way to see the licence number.

"No facial shot?"

He shakes his head and looks apologetic, "No, I've checked. Whoever it is kept their head down. They didn't want to be recognised." Obviously not.

If I were to hazard a guess, I'd say the person was female, but perhaps I'm leaping to the obvious assumption that it was the mother dropping off her offspring. Shrugging, I turn away from the screens with their next to useless information, and only then realise I'm still holding the unopened letter in my hand. I tap it against the reception desk for a second, feeling Matt and Sandra watching me inquisitively. Their curiosity can't rival mine, but I'm far from as keen as they are to find out what's inside the envelope with my name so clearly printed on the front. They've already jumped to their own conclusions. I can see Sandra almost twitching in her impatience to share the news throughout the building. There's a reason we keep her in the dark about some of the more discreet goings on at Grade A.

With a quick glance down to make sure the baby is still

sleeping, and, for the moment, needs no attention, I take myself off to the visitor chairs situated in front of the sheet glass windows to give myself a little privacy while I read the note. I seat myself, automatically unbuttoning my suit jacket as I do so, and lean forward, my elbows on my knees, and my hands cupping my face. I stare across to what looks like a high-end quality pram, lurking like a beast lying in wait, on the other side of the large reception area. Fuck knows what this is all about. And fuck it, I'd rather not know.

I can feel eyes burning into me, and gather Matt and Sandra probably think my proclivities have come back to haunt me. The rumours about me are all true. I don't hide that I like sex. Lots and lots of sex. With whom, how many, it doesn't matter to me. I'm an incorrigible flirt, and if it's offered, I take it. Or at least I did before I was injured. They probably think I'm about to get my just desserts, and a horrible tight feeling in my chest tells me they just might be right.

Well, I can't put it off any longer. When my dread of what I might find turns into curiosity to discover what's going on, my hands tremble as I tear the envelope open and slide out the contents. There are two pieces of paper inside, and I take the first, unfolding it carefully. It's a handwritten note—the writing's legible and neat but I don't recognise it. The content is short and sweet, to the point. I read and re-read it.

Sean

I hate to do this to you, but I have no other option. Please look after my daughter, I leave her in your hands as I am unable to look after her. Please believe me, I wouldn't do this unless I was desperate, but it's not safe for her to be with me now. I can't keep her out of danger. I can't even save myself. Please protect her with your life. I trust you.

Please tell her I will always love her.

Dannie

She's leaving her daughter with me? *Do I even know her?* I wrack my brain to see if I remember a 'Dannie', but nothing immediately springs to mind. I notice there's no emotion toward me, the letter starts and ends abruptly with no salutation, no crosses denoting kisses. It's cold as if I don't even know her, and perhaps I don't. The frantic beating of my heart slows. *The baby's not mine!* But fuck if I know why she's entrusted her to me. Nodding, I throw a relieved grin in the direction of the reception desk. From Sandra's disappointed expression I see it's been correctly interpreted. Feeling relief, amused that I could ever have thought I'd sired a child I had no knowledge about, I extract the other paper that accompanied the letter. It's a birth certificate.

I must have stared at it for a couple of minutes before letting it drop from my hands onto the floor. As the blood drains from my face, I wipe unsteady hands over my eyes as though to erase the words I've just seen, but they're written in indelible ink, etched on my brain, and now I know I'll never be able to unsee them.

The child's name is Mollie Jane Smith, the mother's name—still unhelpful as I don't recollect it at all—is Danielle Smith. And the father's name? Well, that's clearly printed so there can be no misreading it. It's mine.

FUCK!

CHAPTER 5

Vanessa

Sean's been gone an awfully long time. I can't stop fidgeting in my seat, and again flick my eyes to the clock on the wall behind Ben, noticing it's actually only been twenty minutes. But I'm consumed with curiosity tinged with concern, longing to know what's going on in the life of the man who's captured my interest, selfishly yearning to know what's going on in his life, and hoping that it will be something I can help him with.

"Van! The latest on the Archer situation?" Ben's voice snaps, and I jump as I hear him bark my name.

"Sorry." I quickly look down at my tablet, feeling my face going red yet again. Being damned with red hair and the complexion that goes along with it, my pallor always betrays my emotions. And this time my guilt is plain to see. I flick through the tablet screens trying to reach the right one. I miss it and go back hearing Ben impatiently tapping his pen on the table. "Right, Archer…"

"We're all concerned about Sean, Van. But if it's anything we need to be involved with, we'll know soon enough. Otherwise," he breaks off and gives a pointed glance to the money pooled in the middle of the table, "Otherwise it's none of our business until Sean makes it ours." Shit, how did he even know what had distracted me?

Wow! I've just had my wrist slapped. I decide that putting my professional hat on and giving my update without comment is the best way to proceed. "We've identified where the threat against Archer came from." Ben's nodding, he'll have read my report already, this update is just info for the others. "It was a disgruntled ex-employee. He's been arrested, the police are now dealing with the case and the protection for Archer has ceased." Ben starts to speak but I stop him by raising my hand, asking him silently to give me a second to finish. I'm pleased to be able to tell him something he doesn't already know. "Archer was so delighted with Grade A's discreet services, he's put in a recommendation for the Government to send more work our way." Archer is a member of Parliament, so in a good position to promote us. I can see Ben is pleased with the news.

"Well, that's great!" Ben glances around the team, a proud look on his face, and exchanges satisfied looks with Jon. Together with the Jason Deville, the three of them built the business from scratch. "Should help us keep our bellies filled if we get more government contracts and…" He breaks off as the door opens.

As people sit up straighter around the table, it appears I wasn't the only person intrigued to discover what had called Sean away. And I'm certainly not his only colleague to find their mouth dropping open when our normally sedate meeting is suddenly interrupted by a very angry cry.

"Oh shit! Fuck! What the fuck do I do now?" Sean's pushes his way through the door, his arms full. "And what the fuck do I do with *this*?" His normally tidy hair flops down over his face, his usual calm expression now one of outright panic.

He enters the room carrying a baby in a car seat, one that sits on top of a pram and a bag slung over his shoulder! *A baby!* I can't stop the loud gasp that comes from my mouth, too late my hand goes up to cover it but luckily everyone else is in a similar state of disbelief, and no one notices. He's got a bloody baby? *Is it his?* No!

Whosever it is, the baby's not happy; it's screaming at the top of its voice, and despite everything, I can't help but admire the set of lungs it must possess to summon up that level of volume. Sean's face is white and his eyes flick around us all in a silent plea for help. He hasn't a clue what to do. I'm sitting motionless, all I can think of is if that's Sean's baby, where's the mother, and who is she to him? *Fucking selfish.* Looking around the room, I see Ryan grinning, and pulling the pile of money toward him. Jon's smirking, Ben's eyes are open wide in astonishment, Nafisa's looking shocked, and Harry is laughing out loud.

"For fuck's sake!" Ben suddenly pushes his chair out from the table and gets to his feet, shaking his head. "Sean needs help!"

"Whose is the baby, Sean?" Jon finds his voice.

"Ask questions later," Ben says sharply. "Let's sort it out first. Get the noise level down at least."

I can't move, can't do anything but keep that hand covered up over my mouth. Well, what do I know about babies? My face is no longer flushed as I feel the blood draining away.

"It's a her. Not an it." Sean speaks with a vehemence

that surprises me. It seems Ben's movement has sparked him into action. Very gently, he places the baby seat on the table and unfolds the blankets. I watch his face. An intense expression I've never seen before crosses it as he gazes at the tiny creature below him. Running his hands through his hair, completely mucking up any remaining styling, he's completely at a loss what to do. Suspecting, from his wariness, he's probably never even held a baby before, I'm frozen to the spot as Sean's large hands come out, and oh so carefully, he picks up the small thrashing body and holds it close, rocking back and forth as he dredges up some innate instinct. The baby's cries diminish to an acceptable volume, but I suspect it's only a brief interlude. Don't they need feeding or changing or something?

It appears someone knows what they're doing when Harry steps forward. "Whose the fuck is it, Sean?" When Sean doesn't immediately offer an answer, he focuses on the most important thing, getting the baby to stop crying. "Oh hell, never mind about that for a moment. Have you got a bottle or nappies?"

After looking at him as if he's speaking a foreign language, Sean seems to remember what else he brought in, "I don't know—there might be something in there." Sean rocks his body to indicate the bag on the table.

Harry, father of two, albeit his children are now both teenagers, draws the bag over and opens it. Sure enough, he finds what he wants in there as he pulls out some bottles and a few nappies and places them to one side.

"Nafisa—can you go put this in some boiling water to

heat up a bit, doesn't need long, just until it's lukewarm?" Harry waves a bottle in her direction. Spurred into action everyone stands at once, and Nafisa nods and leaves the room. I'm just thankful that he hasn't asked me, I'm not even sure I could get to my feet at the moment. "Can I?" He nods at the baby.

"Yeah, here." Sean lets go of his precious bundle.

Harry holds her up and then touches her tiny bottom. He nods toward the bag, "Sean, unfold that, it's the type that doubles as a changing mat."

I watch wide-eyed and transfixed as Sean finally figures out what to do, and Harry lays the baby down on the padded plastic. Expertly he takes a clean nappy, undoes the press studs on the all in one the baby's wearing, and has the old nappy off. He doesn't falter at all when he cleans the private bits that we all can now see belong to a baby girl.

The look on Sean's face is priceless. "Cover her up! Quick, man! Everyone's looking at her."

"She's fucking baby, for Christ's sake, Sean."

"Yeah, well I don't want you all ogling her bits." His growling protest brings a welcome burst of laughter around the room which releases some of the tension. Harry puts on the clean nappy and extracts a dry Babygro from the bag and to Sean's obvious relief, has her dressed again within seconds.

Almost simultaneously Nafisa returns. Harry tests the temperature of the milk by dripping a few drops on the inside of his wrist, and then passes the now dry baby and bottle back to Sean who sits, and somehow as if he's always been doing it, cradles the baby in one arm, holding the teat of the bottle to her mouth. She begins to suck noisily, and thus, to an extent, peace and calm are restored to the room.

As one, we all let a collective out a sigh of relief. Ben indicates everyone should take their seats again. The sight of Sean, the renowned playboy, carefully feeding a baby would be extraordinary even if it wasn't taking place in the conference room at Grade A. My gut clenches at the paternal sight, I try to take deep breaths, concentrating until I've staved off the threatening panic attack. *Would my baby have looked like that?*

Tearing my eyes away from Sean and the bundle in his arms, I notice Ben looking straight at me. Oh shit, he must have noticed my clenched hands. Taking them off the table I put them in my lap, and bravely throw a nod of reassurance toward my boss. That man can read me like a bloody book!

But for some reason, my gaze is then drawn to Sean again. *I* want to know if he's the baby's father, and if so, what kind of relationship does he have with her mother? Just the fact he has a baby that he's never admitted to is as effective as a bucket of cold water being thrown over me. My attraction I had felt for the man disappears in one fell swoop.

CHAPTER 6

Sean

I've never heard such a racket in my life. It's hard to believe so much sound could come from such a small body. Now that awful heart-wrenching crying has stopped, my relief is immense. Mollie seems content, lying in my arms, sucking at her bottle, making little gurgles of appreciation. Her eyes are gazing up into mine. It's impossible to ignore they're the same brilliant blue colour as my own. *Fuck, could it be true?*

The rest of the team is silent now, all watching me, eyeing up the now settled baby in my arms, their expressions all questioning—except for Van who seems to be looking at me, almost with contempt. All seem to be enjoying the welcome silence and holding back their comments for now, but it's time I come clean. I nod toward the baby seat, "There's a letter there, Ryan. Could you pass it across to Ben?"

The envelope is handed down the table. Ben inclines his head as though asking for permission, and at my nod, opens it. He extracts the two sheets of paper.

Impatient as always, Jon recognises the birth certificate and snatches it away. He lets out a slow whistle and turns to me. "This suggests she's yours. You've never mentioned a baby or pregnant girlfriend. Can I assume you knew nothing of this?" As I shake my head, he looks back down again. "If you didn't know about the birth and weren't there to register her, I'm not sure it's official."

"I didn't know of any pregnancy, let alone a birth, I can assure you of that." I'd immediately known that I couldn't handle this alone as soon as I'd read and digested the paperwork down in the lobby. It's why I brought the baby up to the conference room. And if I'm going to need the team to help me sort out this mess, I'm going to have to tell them everything. It's going to be messy and I'm not going to come out of it well. I throw a glance at Van, noticing she's watching me intently. For some reason, I know it's her I'm going to disappoint the most, but what I don't understand is why that thought upsets me. Realising they're waiting for me to tell them what I do know, I close my eyes briefly, and then let it out. "I've no fucking idea if she's my baby or not."

Ben looks searchingly at me, "You can't say for definite that it isn't?"

"She," I correct again, automatically, "And no." Before they can start reproaching me, I add pointedly, indicating the men around the table, "Nor could any of us."

It's that moment when I can see most of my male colleagues shift awkwardly, as they acknowledge there's truth in my words.

"So, what do you know about this," Ben pulls the certificate away from Jon and lays it out in front of him, "Danielle Smith?" His eyes question me.

Shaking my head I sigh, "I don't recognise the name." As much as I could once Mollie started screaming, I'd been wracking my brains to remember.

After letting out a short breath he continues, "She's four months old. That would make it around thirteen months or so ago that you did the deed with Ms Smith, if, indeed, you did so." Again, he consults the form. "She's listed her occupation as 'self-employed'. That doesn't help much. But do you remember anything? Remember forgetting something?" He raises an eyebrow that somehow appears at once to be both quizzical and censoring.

He means going without a condom. Something that would never happen at Club Tiacapan. None of its members, including myself, would ever go in un-gloved. I look around the table, giving them the assurance they expect. "I have never, ever, forgotten to use a condom." I pause for a moment, seeing their nods. It's fucking unusual, but accidents can happen, even if you take all the precautions you can. Everyone knows that condoms are only ninety-eight percent effective, and any of us can only hope that we'll never end up in the unlucky two percent.

"Had one break on me once," Jon admits.

"Bloody persistent fuckers." Ryan's comment breaks the tension in the room, and everyone laughs, especially as he adds, "Knowing Sean, one probably karate chopped its way through the latex." He's referring to my martial arts expertise. Or what was my expertise before I was shot.

Glancing down at Mollie, I see the bottle has slipped out of her mouth. As she catches my eye, she smiles up at me. *She fucking smiles at me!* I feel a tightness in my chest which I can't describe and certainly don't understand. Pushing the feeling down, I get back to the business in hand. "I can't remember fucking anyone called Dannie or Danielle," I admit to the room then continue, knowing I'm going to have to be completely honest, "But I couldn't tell you that I didn't." I can feel Vanessa's eyes burning into me. I don't even have to look in her direction.

And she's the one who speaks, "You can't remember the names of the women you've made love to?" She sounds incredulous.

"Fucked, darling, fucked. I don't make love." I give it to her directly. It's the truth, and it's also true I'm probably about as much of a bastard as she considers I am at this very moment. But total disclosure is required if my colleagues are going to be able to help me. I make it worse. "I don't need to know their names."

Van's hand goes over her mouth, and she glances around the room at the others to see if they think as little of my admission as she does. But except for Harry and Nafisa, we're all Doms, we all play in clubs. What does she think happens? Half the time people use pseudonyms in any event, so what's the point in asking? The others shift uncomfortably under her gaze, but it's Ben who takes the lead, ignoring my confession, and thankfully simply concentrating on the main issue.

"First, Sean, you'll do a DNA test, check whether she's yours or not. Nafisa, can you sort that out?" Nafisa nods in agreement. DNA tests are something we've arranged before, though not exactly under these circumstances. Grade A has connections with a lab who is willing to fast track the results for us. "If Sean does the tests now we should get the results back first thing tomorrow."

"Should we involve child services?" Harry butts in, his brow creased in concern. "Who's going to look after the baby?"

"I am!" I snap, indignantly, making the decision on the spur of the moment. "I'm named as the father."

Ben's isn't the only mouth that falls open, but he's the one that voices what they're all thinking, "Are you sure, Sean? You don't even know how to change a fucking nappy."

Looking into Mollie's lovely face, now relaxed in sleep once more, I know if there is any chance that she's mine I won't be letting anyone else take responsibility for her. And I definitely don't want to hand her over to the authorities and end up with a possible fight on my hands to get her back if the test comes back as a match. "How hard can it be?" I ask, half to myself.

"Huh!" Harry's been there, done that and so will know from experience. But surely it can't be that difficult?

Ben's drumming his fingers on the table,; he's frowning, "How do you read this letter, Sean?"

His question causes me to review what I'd read in the reception area, "Probably the same way as you do. Whoever the mother is, she's in some sort of trouble. Whether Mollie's mine or not, I can't ignore it, Ben. It's a plea for help. And a pretty desperate one at that if she's left her child with a stranger." Shifting the baby in my arms so I'm holding her more comfortably, I continue. "I may need to take a leave of absence. The baby's been left with me, so I've got to find this Danielle. No one abandons their child without good reason, even if it turns out to be the case she's left her with the man who fathered her." I feel bad asking for more time off when it's only been a few months since I returned from sick leave.

"*We* need to find her," my boss announces softly, "She brought us into it when she left the baby at our building, and you're one of ours." He effectively lets me know I'll have the full resources of Grade A at my back. I start, I hadn't expected that. I'd hoped to be able to call on some of the available expertise, but not that he would pledge such support. Lost for words at the generous gesture, I jerk my chin toward him, simply nodding my thanks as I let him know how much I appreciate his offer. It's a comforting suggestion and one which takes a weight off my mind.

"Thirteen months ago, you were in Amahad." Van has, at least momentarily, put aside her condemnations of my sex life, and is looking up last year's work schedule. Yes, that was the time before last that I went to that Arab country. The last time being six months ago, when I'd received bullets for my pains. "You were there with Harry in place of Jon." I do notice her voice sounds a little unsteady as she speaks.

I think back. Ah, yes, that's right. At that point in time Jon wanted as little to do as possible with the old Emir and his sons. It was when the world still thought the younger son, Sheikh Nijad, guilty of a terrible crime, and seeing it as a betrayal of his previous close friendship with the man, Jon had steered as clear of Amahad as he could.

"You were there for just over three weeks. It's the right time frame," Van continues.

"Unless the baby was premature or late," I say. Nothing is ever simple. I learned long ago it's best to never assume anything. "But thanks for reminding me, Van. That seems the place to start." I try to bring to mind exactly what I did there.

Harry's thinking along the same lines, "Our duties were fairly light, Sean. We had most of the evenings free when the Palace security took over. You were out a lot at the clubs, and at the casino. Do you remember meeting anyone in particular?"

A different girl each time. And no, I couldn't remember any of their names. A simple shake of my head lets me escape without having to spell out my indiscretions with words.

As my colleagues digest my admission, I think about the country I'd been working in. Amahad, a small Arabic state, is a country of two halves. The north, being the coastal area and home to the capital Al Qur'ah, is being developed as a tourist destination with all the associated attractions. The south of the country is mostly deserted, inhabited by the nomadic tribes who seem to live in a different era. Being situated in the modern northern half, Harry's right, I'd made good use of the tourist facilities while I'd been there.

Ben's pen taps rhythmically on the table and his brow creases. After a few seconds, he turns to his partner. "Well, let's see what we can do to trace her from here first. We have a name and address on the birth certificate. Sean's going to have his hands full," he pauses to give a grin and his glance at Mollie leaves none of us in any doubt as to what he's alluding to, "So Jon, can you get someone to head out to…" he checks the certificate, "Watford and check it out?" There's a round of smirks at the thought of me trying to cope with the baby, but Jon dips his head as he agrees to help.

"Do you think it's going to be that simple?" I frown, having doubts about that. It didn't sound like she wanted to be found, so why leave the birth certificate with an address in plain view? "I don't even know if it was her who dropped the baby off this morning. It could have been a friend, relative. Heck, she could have paid a stranger to do it."

"Let's take the obvious steps first, Sean. Get the DNA test done, and we'll meet again in the morning and see what we've got so far. Despite what it says on this piece of paper, the baby might not be yours. And although we're reading it as though she's in danger, it could be we're overreacting. There might be a simple answer. This Danielle might be running from an ex, for example. She could be right under our noses."

Or more likely, in my opinion, she might not.

CHAPTER 7
Vanessa

While Ben is announcing we'll reconvene again the next day, I start getting my stuff together ready to leave the conference room. My mind races with everything I've just heard, and what I've learned about Sean today leaves me very confused. My attraction to Sean had lurked in the background since the day I'd first met him but now has taken a nose dive with the realisation that if he ever looked at me, it would probably only result in a one night stand. The fact that he can't remember—or even bothered to find out in the first place—the names of the multitudes of women he's slept with has shaken me. And particularly that he could well have fathered a child he knew nothing about. His casual approach to sex is very far from my own.

What approach to sex? My traitorous mind asks me. I haven't seen any action in the last two years! Shit! I pause, my hand hovering halfway to picking up my tablet. In all honesty, am I so unlike him? I've never had much more than one night stands in any event. Okay, so the difference was that these were preceded by the dating ritual, a dance between partners trying to assess compatibility over dinner or a drink in the pub, before taking the decision to jump into bed. But whether it had been days or weeks before taking that final step to slide under the sheets together, nothing earth shattering had come of any of the rather limited number of liaisons that I'd had. Something had been missing, that spark, that excitement, that experience I've only read about, two heaving, sweaty bodies coming together, shouting and screaming a release of such intense satisfaction to both partners that they were left sated, unable to do anything but sleep. Until round two.

Hmm, I can honestly say that my half dozen attempts had been little more than awkward fumbling between friends, going through expected motions with predictable, but ultimately disappointing results for both parties. *It will get better in time. We have to get to know each other first.* How often have I heard that, or words to that effect? But I think half a dozen times was the most I gave it with anyone before giving up and, for the most part, making the mutual decision to continue with a friendship and the admission to an incompatibility in bed. I've got a lot of male friends.

Except for my one try at a proper relationship with that bastard, Simon. Usually I try not to remember the one time I did go back for seconds and a whole lot more. It was the idea of the companionship and everything else I'd believed was on offer that was the attraction. And even though no bells pealed in heaven when we were in bed together, the engagement ring on my finger had made me overlook any deficiencies in that area. And look how badly that had ended. Total fucking disaster. I shake my head as if I can physically force thoughts of *him* right out of it, but it's hard. The baby held in the arms of the man sitting opposite me is bringing it all back.

I'd always imagined that Sean would be different. Just

one look at his confident face suggests he's a man who'd pride himself on satisfying his lover in any way they could want to be gratified. And how often have I yearned to put my suspicions to the test, especially after learning about his lifestyle? No man I've ever been with has had a clue what I wanted them to do in bed or has picked up on my subtle hints. It seemed impolite to instruct them to touch me in a certain way or was too embarrassing to express my darkest desires. The knowledge I've gained from reading about the life style has made me wonder, what if I could direct and control a man in bed?

Until today, the man holding the baby in front of me, the man who openly admits he's happy to either top or bottom, had played a starring role in my fantasies. But now my dreams are shattered. Because of the very thing he's holding in his arms. A baby.

"Vanessa, are you with us?"

Embarrassed I discover I've been lost in my thoughts and have missed that my boss hasn't quite concluded the meeting.

"Sorry, Ben?" Again, I feel my face flushing. Shit! Not only am I ignoring what's going on around me, but I'm also thinking of sex in a business meeting. Dragging my mind out of the gutter I give him my attention.

The slight smirk on his face suggests Ben suspects I'm consumed by the revelations about Sean's sex life. *Could he possibly know I had had a crush on the man?* Christ! I hope not!

"Vanessa, if needs be, I'm going to want you to work on this case with Sean. I appreciate it's the first time for you out in the field, but your investigatory skills might come in handy, as he seems to have lost track of a woman. I take it you'll be okay with that? Nafisa can take up the rest of your workload, and we've a new chap coming in next week to help as well. That should free all your time."

I think my heart might have stopped momentarily. My God! I hadn't expected that today. An opportunity to work outside the office? But the smile that started at my lips doesn't complete its journey to my eyes as reality hits. He wants me to work with Sean? Well, finding a woman doesn't seem to be a very risky mission, so perhaps he sees this as a gentle way to ease me in. But to see Sean daily, now that I've heard his secrets and his attitude to women? To be in close contact now that I know he's not looking for 'the one', but lots of ones? *To help him sift through all the women he's slept with to find the baby's mother?* Shit! I've just been handed the proverbial poisoned chalice. And on top of all that, he could well be a father!

It would be foolish to pretend I've recovered from what happened two years ago. Just the sight of an infant being pushed in a pram in the street causes me to have palpitations as all the bad memories come rushing back. If the baby *is* his, will he keep her around? *I won't be able to cope.*

Wondering if I can protest, when everyone is waiting for me to jump with excitement as they all know I've worked hard for this for two years, I force myself to think rationally. With any luck my first assignment as an operative might not even get off the ground. Danielle might very well be found by our paperwork search today. So, before my lack of response can be misinterpreted, or quite possibly, correctly construed, I hurry to speak, "What if it doesn't come to anything and we find Ms Smith quickly?"

"Then you'll get the next assignment that comes up. As a CPO."

It takes a moment for his words to sink in, but as they do, a full smile comes to my face when I understand that, in front of everyone, I've just been promoted. That working with Sean isn't going to be a one-off, he's suggesting a proper operative role! As the others rush to congratulate me, Ben waves away my thanks and a bolt of excitement hits me. This is what I've aimed for, and what I've been working so hard toward. At last, Ben's agreed I'm going to be sent out in the field.

As the others stand and leave the room, I sink back down into the chair and put my head in my hands. The first woman CPO at Grade A. Wow!

A baby's wail from out in the corridor brings me back to my senses. Shit, before I get sent out on a proper assignment I'm going to have to help Sean find the mother of his child; to work alongside a very real reminder of the worst thing that ever happened to me.

What the hell do I do? Torture myself by being placed in an impossible situation? I wait a few moments, thoughts racing round my head. Babies and I do not mix. After a few minutes, I leave the room, make my way further up the corridor, and rap on an office door.

"Enter." I do so, and find Ben relaxing back on his large manager's chair, his hands laced behind his neck. "Ah, Van, have you had some thoughts on Sean's *little* problem?" He smirks at his own joke.

Not too sure how to put my concerns, I pull out the seat on the other side of the desk and I sit down, my posture stiff. "Not exactly, Ben. I came to say I don't think I should be the one to work with Sean."

Slowly he slides his hands down from his neck, his arms extending until his elbows are resting on the table. His eyes probe mine. "Strange," he tuts, "I thought you'd enjoy it."

I look down and worry at a snag on one of my nails. How can I explain? "I just don't think I'm right for this case."

His fingers move in a gimme gesture; I haven't explained enough. "You know my background, Ben. I don't want to be around a baby."

His brow furrows, "I understand your worries, Van, but I asked you to work with Sean. I didn't pick you for any maternal skills you may or may not have. I don't expect you to act as a babysitter, so get that out of your head if that's what you're thinking. I didn't select you because you're a woman." He sighs, "Look, Van, I know you think I've been holding you back, but I need to know you're properly prepared and can put your training to use out on a mission. I realise you're desperate to get out working a protection role, but like any of my team, you need to prove yourself before you can take the lead on a case. Sean's one of our best men, and you could learn a lot from him. Plus, there'll be some puzzles to solve, and that's your strong point. I put the two of you together because I thought it would work."

"But Ben…"

"No, listen to me, Van. How would it be if everyone

wanted to pick and choose the jobs they were assigned to? It would be chaos, and you know that. I know two years ago, you trusted me with what happened to you, and I supported you then. I let you undertake training that I know you wanted to do, partly to help put what happened behind you. And now I need you to prove yourself. Are you asking me to vet all cases I assign you to? What if a mother with a child needs a CPO? Are you telling me that I wouldn't be able to use you on that? If you can't take on whatever I give you, maybe this kind of work isn't for you after all."

"Ben, you know how hard I've worked." I've done all the requisite training, spent hours at the shooting range getting top scores, and suffered more than enough bruises honing my hand to hand combat skills. I don't have to tell him that, he'll have got all the reports. "It's just this particular case…"

"It's this case, or nothing, Van. I need people I can rely on. If you've a problem, tell me."

I stare down at my hands and mumble, "I don't think I can work with Sean."

"Now, unless you can give me a professional reason as to why you can't work with him, then you'll either suck it up or revert to your office role." He sits back again, folding his arms, "And let me tell you now, having a dislike for the way he conducts himself in his private life is not sufficient reason not to want to be his partner. I'm not asking you to jump into bed with the man. Christ, that's the last thing I want. Operatives getting involved?" He shakes his head to emphasis the point.

I go to speak, but he hasn't finished.

"In fact, Van, I'm reassured to find you don't like him very much. It means that's one worry off my mind. But I expect you to have his back, just the same as if I'd sent one of the men with him."

I've been pushed into a corner; any argument would come back to the fact I'm female. None of the men would use an objection to his sexuality as an excuse not to team up with him. If I want this new role, I'll just have to suck it up. "Of course, I'll have Sean's back, Ben. You can rely on me."

Now he looks smug, "I know I can. And hopefully wrapping this up won't take long, and we can see what else there is to offer you."

He's left me no choice. Either I work with Sean and help him find his baby mamma, or I give up a chance to work as a CPO.

CHAPTER 8

Sean

I've never even considered the possibility of having children. Well, for a start I always believed you'd need to settle down for that, and I'm about as far from a settling down type you can get! *So how the fuck did I get into this position?*

Walking into my flat carrying a gurgling baby in my arms, I stare down at her, unable to comprehend where she's come from. If she's actually mine, why didn't this Dannie or Danielle person tell me she was pregnant? Didn't I deserve to know, even if it was a mistake? Did she just assume I wouldn't want to be involved? But if that was the case, ruefully, I accept that she could have had a point. Nothing about me screams paternal instinct.

Or could it be that Dannie just hazarded a guess as to who the father was? Surely that's more likely? Not wanting to become involved in a relationship, I only play with like-minded women who know the score, so anyone I slept with is likely to have morals as loose as my own. Shit, what a debacle. If she's in trouble she might have picked me as I work for Grade A. But how would she have known who I was or my job? If I didn't know her name, I doubt I'd have given her mine.

A shuffling in my arms warns me Mollie's awake now,

but she seems happy enough. Well, she should be given the amount of attention she was getting on the tube. No one, fucking no one, on the underground system in London ever looks another person in the eye. Never. That is, unless you happen to be carrying a baby who's kicking off the blankets just for the entertainment of seeing her adult carer pick them up time and time again. An activity which caused everyone around me to smile and even laugh, including the person who kindly gave up their seat for me. Someone giving up their seat? Un-fucking-heard of.

"Jeez, Moll," I suppose I might as well be talking to myself as to a baby, but as she swings those blue eyes, already seeming to shine with intelligence, round to meet mine, I'm certain she can understand the sentiment, if not the words. "What the fuck am I going to do with you?" She stares at me intently, then, slowly, her face starts to pucker and grow red, and she begins to grow rigid in my arms. Shit, is she having some kind of fit? Her smile has gone, her cheeks are clenched. Suddenly there's a loud farting sound—too loud to come from such a small creature—and a stench fills the air. Oh, shit! Literally. What the fuck do I do now? And then she giggles as if she's done the funniest thing in the world. Yeah, right. *Perhaps she is mine after all!*

When I'd left Grade A today, it had taken me a while to get out of the office. Everyone wanted to coo at the sweet baby that had arrived in such an unusual way, and I'd had lots of offers of help. Thankfully, one of the girls at the office, who had a young baby of her own, had run out to get the stuff she expected I'd need to see me through tonight. In fact, another had even offered to take Mollie for me, but already something I can't describe makes me reluctant to let her out of my sight. But at least I'm prepared with everything I need, even if I know fuck all about how to use it.

Is she mine? Shaking my head, I dismiss the question. As soon as I saw my eyes mirrored in hers, I knew I didn't have to wait for the DNA test results; I already know I sired her. And no one else is going to be fucking looking after her.

Carrying her through to the bathroom, still not quite believing I, Sean Cooper, a Grade A CPO and a Master Dom, am now removing a cute little baby's all-in-one Babygro, and attempting to take off a dirty nappy. Christ, how could one tiny baby shit so much? *Is it normal?* It's gone everywhere! I look round, fuck, what the hell do I do? I can't use these flimsy wipes; there's far too much crap for that. Trying to balance a shitty baby on my arm I reach over to switch on the bath taps, before realising that she's probably too young to use the big tub. Fucking hell, though, she needs a bath. Reaching the only conclusion I can, I decide there's nothing for it, but to get in with her.

So, that's how it comes about that I'm lying naked with the youngest girl I've ever had in my arms in a bath half full of water, far cooler than I'd usually have it. And I'm loving every second. Her giggling, as I splash water over her little body, is infectious. She seems to find it one big joke as I hold her awkwardly and try to wash her, and at the same time, clean myself up. Fuck, how did I get crap in my hair?

Finally, and admittedly clumsily, I manage it. Both of us clean, I get her out, dry her, lay her on a towel and have her into a new nappy and clothes, before I even notice the cooling drops of water causing goosebumps on my own skin. Huh! That's the Dom instinct for you, putting someone else's needs before my own.

****

It's a bit like déjà vu when I arrive at the office the next morning. Sandra might have added a probing look as I entered the lobby, but her cheery 'Good Morning' is exactly the same as it was yesterday and every day before that. It's almost as if nothing had happened, and it would have been the same old same old had I not driven here from my mother's house instead of taking public transport from my own home. And, of course, if I hadn't still been reeling from a rather stern parental tongue lashing the night before.

After my triumph with the bath yesterday evening I quickly discovered babies need more attention than I knew how to provide. Soon, I was regretting my rather rash decision to take Mollie home with me and finally admitted that I needed help. And there was one point of call for that. Mum.

I might have long been out of nappies myself, but I'd wilted as my mother had left me in no doubt how disappointed she was with the whole situation. The problem wasn't that I was presenting her with a possible grandchild, but the admittedly rather unsavoury fact that I hadn't introduced a serious girlfriend to her first and, not the least, that I had no fucking idea who the mother was. Oh yes, my one surviving parent didn't pull her punches on that one. But that didn't stop her getting down to business and sorting out what was to be done with the little one. I'd left her this morning surfing the net researching modern child care methods. She is, after all, thirty-six years out of date. I'm not abdicating my responsibility for Mollie, just admitting I'm going to require some support if I'm going to look after her.

Last night I'd slept in mum's guestroom with a baby curled up by my side; cushions and pillows plumped around to keep her safe and to prevent me rolling on her. And although now I might be bleary eyed and having to suppress a yawn, there's a sense of pride that I managed the night feeds and changes without asking for help. And waking up to that smiling face and being greeted with baby gurgles, which I like to interpret as a 'Hi Dad'? Well, that made the lack of sleep worthwhile.

Now I'm back at Grade A, Mollie safely left in the already doting care of her new grandmother. Exiting the lift on the third floor, a couple of people glance at my empty hands as if they'd expected me to bring the baby in with me, and a couple throw me quizzical looks, as though wondering what I've done with her. I'd already had to ignore Sandra's pointed looks and now want to evade the rest of the inquisition. I make my way to the same conference room where we assembled only yesterday. It might only be twenty-four hours ago, but it seems a lifetime away when I was a single man with no responsibilities. Pausing before entering, I think about the devastating change to my life that's happened in such a short time. Yesterday morning I was a carefree bachelor, now I find I'm a father. Talk about a shock to the bloody system.

It's a few minutes before nine, and already half the team is assembled when I push open the door and join them. Glancing around before entering, I see rest of my colleagues either exiting the lift behind me or, having arrived earlier, coming out of their office doors carrying cups of their preferred brew.

It's soon evident that lack of sleep has shortened my temper and it doesn't take long before I start to get fed up of explaining where Mollie is, and start giving people the short version consisting of just one word. "Mum's." I need to explain no further, my mother has a sort of notoriety around Grade A—her cupcakes are famous, and she often makes batches to bring in for someone's birthday. Being her only son, I'm still somewhat spoilt even at my advanced age. And then, of course, her chosen career is always a topic of interest. Being a scriptwriter, people are often trying to pry and try to find out what's going to happen on one of the popular soaps. But to no avail, mum never lets on, even to me.

Ben's the last to enter, and he gives me a querying look before taking his seat. Suspecting I know what his silent question is, I respond with a quick shake of my head, confirming I've had no news as yet. But as I'm giving him the negative signal my phone buzzes with a text coming through, an out of place sound to interrupt our meeting. But today I've kept my phone switched on lying on the table in front of me, now vibrating and threatening to jump onto the floor.

We're meeting for just one reason today, and there's no point starting until I read the gist of the message and let the others know what it says. My hand hovers in the air, knowing the confirmation I want to read, dreading it in case I'm wrong. I hope my colleagues can't see me crossing the fingers of my other hand under the table.

Taking the plunge, I pick up the phone then nod to show that it was indeed the text I'd been waiting for. As I read the results I let out a breath I hadn't known I was holding. Briefly, I roll my head back on my neck, letting the words sink in, trying to analyse my feelings, a mixture of fear and elation, but no disappointment. *I knew it from the moment I saw her. There was never any doubt.*

Ben's cough makes me look up. They're all looking at me, trying to interpret my reaction, so I quickly put them out of my misery. "She's mine. Mollie is mine!" I repeat, trying to keep the triumph out of my voice.

"Good news?" Jon glances over at me. He would take it that way, Mia, his wife, is eight months pregnant and after her miscarriage would count any baby as precious.

However unprepared I feel to be a father, however much I never expected to be in this position, I feel I've won the lottery with the news. I smile tentatively, as I reply, "Yes."

My reaction is clearly unexpected, but apart from varying degrees of amusement and incredulity being exchanged, no one says anything. I glance down and re-read the text, astounded by the feeling of elation that I *am* that beautiful baby girl's father. But just as quickly reality sets in. How the fuck can I raise a daughter? I'm simply not that kind of man; my lifestyle has no room for a child. That Mollie's mine is amazing. That I could ever look after her by myself is impossible. Dragging my hand across my eyes, I grasp what's now most important. "We have to find her mother." And return the baby to her proper place. I can't understand why that thought causes my stomach to drop.

Ben, like the others, is watching me, giving me time to process the life-changing news I've just received, and I'm grateful when he simply says, "That's what we're here for. We've got this, brother."

Brother. Yes, this team is family. We work together, have each other's backs in dangerous situations, and often, well, some of us at least, we play together. They might rib me, but they'll support and help me too.

I nod in thanks, then pose that all-important question, "So where the fuck is she, and why did she drop Mollie off?" Leaning forward, I rest my elbows on the table and cup my chin. "Mollie's been well-looked after. She's a well fed, happy child. So, what made her mother leave her with me?"

"Postnatal depression? Could be any one of a number of reasons." Harry's obviously been thinking about it. "That can be a nasty thing. If she's suffering from anxiety, she might not think the baby is safe with her. She might be worried she'd hurt her, or not be able to look after her."

With a dip of my head, I acknowledge the possibility. But, "I don't like the wording of the note." I'm thinking out loud. "The way it was written, phrased, it's like she was panicking and had no other option. You might be right, Harry, it might something of that ilk, but I have to find out."

Obviously, Ben agrees, as indicated by his next words. "Van, Nafisa. You've done some digging already. What have you managed to come up with?"

Van had had a curious expression on her face as I'd disclosed the results, one I couldn't read. Now I examine her carefully, seeing a flush on her face as she shakes her head, and after only a moment's hesitation begins to speak, "Not a lot. We tried the obvious route first. The address on the birth certificate was a false one. Well, the house and street exist, but a Danielle Smith never lived there. The house has been owned and occupied for fifty years by a couple now in their eighties. They have no children and no knowledge of a recently pregnant woman. Just in case they were hiding anything we queried enough of the neighbours to know it's a dead end." As she finishes her spiel, she glances across at me, catches me watching her, and looks back down at her tablet with a frown. Her blush deepens.

I see everyone around the table sitting up a little straighter. When nothing's simple, it often means there's one heck of a lot of complicated underneath. "Does Danielle Smith even exist?"

A snort of laughter comes from Ryan. "I've heard of immaculate conception, but not immaculate birth. I think we can safely say somewhere, out there, is the mother of your child."

73

"For fuck's sake Ryan, you know what I mean." My hand rubs my chin in frustration, not only at his asinine comment but also that there are no obvious leads. "I know the bloody woman exists, but is Dannie, or Danielle Smith, even her real name?"

"But why put a false name on a birth certificate? And why put yours on, and then not tell you about it? Why register the birth at all if you're going to do that?" Jon's face tightens, he's deep in thought. "It's been proven you are the father, so presumably she's the mother."

I give it some consideration, "Could she have put my name on so Mollie would come to me if she got into trouble? Could she have known even then that she might be in danger?"

"So why not warn you?" Jon's shaking his head, "Why not at least pick up the phone and tell you to expect her? Why the subterfuge?"

"The name's all we've got to go on. Working on the principle it's her real one, can we track her movements via her passport?" Ben tosses his question at the girls.

Again, Van glances at her tablet before saying anything. "With only a name, no age or legitimate address, I can't track Danielle Smith at all. The surname's too common. There was no maiden name listed, so presumably she hasn't been married before, and the place of birth was given as Dover, Kent. There's not enough to go on."

"She must have a passport. It had to have happened in Amahad. Or Paris. I went straight from Amahad to France. Can't we track her arriving in Amahad? Or leaving?" I'm grasping at straws here.

"Sean, I don't have access to every bloody system in the world. If you could remember the girls you fucked it might make things simpler," Van snaps.

Vanessa's vehemence startles me, and quickly I look her way, surprised at her outburst and the censure in her words, but make a rapid decision to ignore it. She's got a point, I suppose, I'm hardly in the position to contest it. Rubbing my hand over my short beard, I think rapidly. "Chasing down a name is one thing, but if I'm going to find the actual woman, Amahad is the place to start." Plus, Cara's there and might be able to help. Having to stay the right side of the law as a Grade A employee, Van might be limited as to what systems she can legitimately get into, but Sheikh Nijad's wife accepts no such boundaries.

Ben's nodding thoughtfully. After a moment, he agrees, "That's the place to start, Sean. Go back to the scene of the 'crime' so to speak." Pausing, he chuckles at his small joke, "Something might well trigger some memories for you. It's all you've got to go on after all. You'll need to make a list of the women you were involved with at the time and seek them out. Get yourself out there as soon as you can, and take Van with you. Nafisa, can you continue digging and tracking down that name? My gut feeling is there is something very wrong. A woman doesn't just drop off a baby and disappear off the face of the earth."

My heart misses a beat at the thought I'm going to have to leave my child when I've only just found her, but whichever way I look at it, I can't see I've got any other option. If I want to find Danielle, that is. Then I frown, realising what else Ben's said. He'd mentioned Van helping me yesterday, but with my mind taken up with Mollie, I'd assumed he meant helping me search in England. But he's suggesting she comes to Amahad as my partner? What's the fuck's he thinking? She's never worked out of the office before. "With all due respect, Ben, I'd prefer Ryan to have my back." The looks Van's been throwing my way suggest she hates me and would happily stick a knife in me herself.

Ben draws himself up, leaving me in no doubt he's Grade A's senior partner. "We're doing this as a favour to you, Sean. With you gone that's one less man on the team, I can't afford to lose two. Vanessa's got to start somewhere. This will be good training for her. Ease her into working in the field."

The woman under discussion seems to have been expecting this outcome as she's making no protest, but she's looking down, her hair falling over her face so I can't read her expression. I wouldn't be surprised if she was gloating. She's been so eager to get out of the office her bags are probably already packed and ready. But that doesn't make me feel any happier about her being the one by my side. I've always been dubious about her ability to be a CPO. Oh, I know she's had all the appropriate training, she was proudly waving her licence around in the office a few weeks ago, but so far, her knowledge is only theoretical.

Ben must be confident she's gained sufficient skills to be out in the big bad world, but she's got no practical experience. And I've got my doubts about this slender framed redhead who looks like a strong breeze would blow her over. Still, perhaps Ben figures this is a low-risk case to get her started. I'm going to track down a woman, not go into a firefight. Just how dangerous can that be?

Interrupting my assessment of the woman who'll be accompanying me on my search for Mollie's elusive mother, Ben raps his fingers on the table, "I'll get in touch with Kadar, as a courtesy. I'll let him know you're coming, and he might be able to smooth your way. Cara may be able to help too."

That Ben's on the same page about Cara doesn't surprise me. And I'm grateful he's offered to make first contact. Kadar is the Emir of Amahad, the highest authority in that country. I hadn't expected to be returning so soon, and my leg chooses this moment to give a twinge, bringing into mind the last time I was in there and the injuries I sustained doing my job protecting the woman who is now Kadar's wife.

In truth, I could do without going back, but no other alternative presents itself.

With everything decided, Ben wraps up the meeting, wishing my new partner and me good luck in our search. With one last glance at a frowning Van, I gather my stuff together and leave the room. Now I've got to persuade my mother to look after *my* baby for an indefinite amount of time. But the revelation she truly is her grandchild might prove to be just the sweetener I need. And, of course, I'm lucky she has a career that allows her to work from home.

CHAPTER 9
Vanessa

Sometimes the jobs that come to Grade A are planned months in advance. Other times, we have to react fast to provide a response to an immediate threat. It's not unusual for an operative to be sent out with minimal notice, as is the case now. As soon as the decisions were made, our journey was arranged and the very next morning, Sean and I found ourselves landing in Amahad.

That Sean doesn't want me here is obvious. He'd given it away when his face had fallen in the meeting yesterday, his jaw dropping when Ben made clear I was going to be the one to partner him. His mood had also been quite distant during the flights from England. While I'm fully cognisant of my reasons for not wanting to be here with him, I don't understand his objection to me. That he has any at all perversely annoys me. Is it just due to my inexperience? Or is it the fact I'm a woman and he doesn't think I can do the job as well as a man?

We've danced around the subject, being as polite as colleagues should be, but neither of us spell out our reasons why I shouldn't have been the operative accompanying him to this Arab country. And in my case, I really want to avoid having to explain that I'd been given no option; that this is my sole opportunity to prove myself to Ben.

Underlying it all, despite recent revelations and the knowledge I could never mean anything to Sean, hidden just beneath the surface is a continued simmering attraction to the man however hard I try to suppress it. Damn it! The long hours of the flight when we were forced to sit together in cramped proximity, the warmth of his leg inevitably touching mine due to lack of space, ramped up my hormones all over again. Just what is it about the sound of his deep voice that makes my pulse beat faster? What is it about those innocent and accidental touches which start my insides quivering?

Determined to do the best I can in my assigned role, I've got to keep buried and well-hidden the slightest indication that he has any effect on me. I know it was wrong for me to come with him, he's got me twisted into knots, and for the life of me I don't understand why. After Simon, I didn't want to get close to any man again and even if I did, Sean is unattainable and just completely wrong for me. But my traitorous body seems to have other ideas when it comes to him. Why didn't I protest more about this assignment? *Ben gave me no choice.*

Now in the accommodation that's been assigned to us, I force myself to concentrate on the positives, and admittedly, there are a number of them. Leaving aside my intense relief at finding Sean's left Mollie behind and I'm not going to have to contend with a baby on top of everything, this is my first mission and I'm staying in an honest to God real frigging palace! Well, perhaps not in the ancient building itself, but in a house in the royal compound. It all happened so fast I've hardly had time to catch my breath. *This is what the life of a CPO is all about!*

I'm in a foreign country working on behalf of Grade A! Yeah! Pausing my unpacking, I flop down on the bed and look back on the last twenty-four hours.

Once Ben had contacted the Emir of Amahad, his old buddy Kadar, things started to happen quickly. Or, as Ben told us, they had once Kadar had managed to stop laughing. Apparently, he knows Sean well, and the image of him being landed with a baby caused so much amusement he'd had a coughing fit. Until he calmed down, and understood the seriousness of the situation. Then he couldn't have been more helpful, offering us accommodation in one of the houses they keep vacant and available for foreign guests.

And he'd gone one step further. As soon we arrived, obviously no stranger to the perks of this particular abode, Sean had opened up a gun safe hidden at the back of the wardrobe in the main bedroom, and extracted weapons that had been provided for us to use. He'd passed me a shoulder holster and taken one for himself. I'd chosen a Glock and, as I'd balanced the gun in my hand, it was then that it dawned on me this is real and though I'd been trained, I hoped I'd never have to use the weapon in earnest. Shooting a paper target at a range is one thing, pointing it at a person quite another. *But this is what I've trained for.*

Flinging my arm up over my eyes, I realise being assigned to a case as an active member of the team, rather than working behind the scenes in an office, AND being assigned to work with Sean Cooper AND, at least for a few days, staying in the same house as him would have been, until only recently, all my dreams come true at once. But the reasons why we're here, and the revelations about the man himself, have shaken me to the core. All my preconceptions of my handsome co-worker, who I've lusted over for aeons, have flown out of the window, and I've had to re-examine every carnal thought I've ever had about him having now discovered he's a complete manwhore. I shouldn't be attracted to him. Damn my libido.

Who fucks, to use his word, women without knowing their names or even bothering to find out who they are? Not just once, but quite possibly hundreds of times? All my hopes and fantasies have been smashed into dust. I'm certainly about as far from his type as you can get. Realistically I know I'm not a woman who'd be content with being just another one night stand, another notch on his bedpost. And in the unlikely scenario where I did get him to notice me, that's all I could ever expect to be.

But it could be different with you!

Shit! My optimistic mind doesn't want to give up. Not just yet.

I could change him…

Oh yes, and just how many women have thought that since the beginning of time? He's beyond redemption, and I'd do well to remember that, and suppress the little glow inside every time I see him. Why can't I control myself around him?

Hearing a voice downstairs I pull myself up, swinging

my legs over the side of the bed and carefully composing my features to avoid giving any indication of the direction of my recent thoughts. Whatever my disgust at Sean's behaviour, which, contradictorily seems to do nothing to dampen his desirability, I need to act as I've been trained to do. I'm here to do a job, nothing more, nothing less. He's my partner, so personal feelings—whether positive or negative— must be locked away. As Ben had impressed on me, my views on my partner's sexual proclivities should have no bearing on working with the man. Pulling back my shoulders, I leave my room to go down to the living area where I spot the man in question with a phone to his ear. He throws a nod of acknowledgement at me but continues his call.

"Sorry, Mum…" He waits, then grimaces, holding the phone away from his ear for a moment, then sends me a self-deprecating glance which makes him look endearing and boyish. Ignoring the traitorous flip-flopping feeling down low in my stomach and giving him some privacy, I go to the small kitchen and start checking the fridge and cupboards, pleased to find they've been well stocked with food, and that a lot of it is the British brands I recognise.

Sean's deep, velvety voice drifts over to me. "I don't know how long I'll be away. I've got to do this, Mum. I'm sorry to leave you literally holding the baby." And then in a quieter, almost loving tone I hear him say, "Give her a kiss from me." God, that gets me. A man getting gooey over a baby only fuels my perfidious body's reactions, so far removed from my experience before. I steady myself against the worktop as I reel when a memory hits me, *You did it on purpose. So, I sorted it for you.* Shaking my head, I try to rid myself of the hateful words thrown at me two years ago and instead concentrate on those I've just overheard.

Give her a kiss from me. There's a hundred and eighty-degree difference between Sean and the man who hurt me so badly. Sean's accepted his responsibilities. But as a warm feeling begins to fill me, it's doused just as fast as I remember that baby has got a mother, and finding her is the reason we're here. *That* woman has more claim to him than I could ever have.

A knock at the front door draws me out of my reverie. Having finished his call, Sean moves faster than I, going into professional mode as he checks out the security system finding out who it is before undoing the lock. *Shit. I would have forgotten that!* Giving myself another mental reminder that we're on a job, not here on holiday, and I could do worse than mimic him as I to learn how to slip automatically into the role that I've been trained for. There's so much for me to get my head round. *What if we'd been on a real case with a threat lurking around every corner and I'd just thrown open the door?*

At Sean's cheery greeting I swing around, and am shocked when I see who enters. The last person I expect to pay a visit is Emira Zoe, Emir Kadar's very obviously pregnant wife. What have we done to deserve a greeting from such an eminent person? Then, as I watch, I'm surprised at the level of familiarity with which she greets my partner, throwing her arms around him and giving him a loud smacker of a kiss on his cheek.

I recognise her, of course, from photos we used when Grade A was helping to rescue both her and Sean from their kidnappers. But wow, she's changed so much since then. Her very bearing is regal now, her clothes the height of fashion. And here I am, standing to one side, feeling dowdy, annoyed that I've not been introduced and forced to listen to their exchanges of, *How have you been?* and *It's so good to see you.* My body tenses at the easy relationship there is between them.

Then, when I hear Sean ask, "When you going to leave that husband of yours for me, Zoe?" however joking the tone, I hate the woman on sight. *I'm jealous!* Once again, my colouring betrays me as my pale cheeks flush red and my freckles blaze, and then I want the earth to open up and swallow me, when I notice the second woman who'd entered behind the Sheikha and recognise the smirk on her face. My cheeks burn redder. *She knows!*

After far too long, my co-worker releases the emira and lets her step back from the circle of his arms, eyeing her from head to toe at arm's length. "You're looking great, Zoe!"

Zoe's looking around her examining the room, eyes gleaming with mischief. "This brings back memories, doesn't it?" Suspicious, I want to know what she's referring to, and just how close she'd been with Sean. *Has she been one of his one night stands?*

Sean gives a laugh as his answer to her question, and then, at last, he greets the other woman and, finally remembering I'm here, turns to make the introductions. "Vanessa, this is Sheikha Cara Kassis, who's married to

Sheikh Nijad." As he indicates the second woman first, I step forward and shake her hand. I've worked with her before, but only in the virtual world and have never met the renowned hacker face to face.

"And," Sean continues, "I also have the pleasure of introducing you to Emira Zoe Kassis, Kadar's wife." Well, it might be his pleasure, but it certainly isn't mine! Especially when he continues to gaze at the woman in question with a fondness in his eyes, "We shared this house when Zoe first came here."

Just as I was wondering what else they'd shared, Cara steps forward, speaking enthusiastically, "You ought to see the harem now, Sean. Zoe's done absolute wonders with it!" Her words help me recall the details, Zoe originally came to renovate the harem, and ended up marrying the emir.

"How are the plans going, Cara?" Sean shows his interest.

"Well! We're taking our first bookings at this very moment, and have a magazine shoot coming up. We're hoping the publicity will put Amahad on the map and attract more tourists." Cara turns to me, at least she's noticed I'm being left out of the conversation and that I haven't a clue as to what they are talking about. "We've kitted the harem out as a venue for hen parties." I'm grateful to her for the clarification and, as she continues, for her invitation. "You'll have to come and see what we've done while you're here! I'd like to know what you think." She looks me up and down, before adding, "You're the demographic we're aiming for."

Stifling a laugh, I refrain from telling her that the chances of me getting married, let alone having a hen party in an exotic location, are extremely remote.

Cara obviously doesn't expect me to answer, as her attention has already turned back to Sean. "I hear you've got a small problem, Sean," she holds her hands about a foot apart and is unable to keep the grin off her face.

The other woman steps back, and throws a disappointed look at him, while indicating her growing belly. "You've beaten me by a few months, Sean. Way to steal my limelight, fella."

Sean glances from them to me and flushes, his body language showing he's embarrassed. He runs his hand through his blond hair, leaving it spiky and dishevelled. *I wonder if that's what he looks like when he gets up in the morning?* The thought makes me momentarily lose concentration. Dragging my mind back to the matter in hand, I realise he's speaking, explaining the situation he's in, and why we're here.

I hadn't noticed the laptop bag at her feet, but now I do, as Cara bends and opens it. Indicating the dining table, she asks, "Shall we?"

Without words, we agree by congregating around as she takes a seat and logs in. "Ben sent me the information that you've got, Sean, which isn't a lot, is it? We're looking at the time before last that you came to Amahad, aren't we? About thirteen months back?" At his nod, she waves her hand toward the screen, "I've already looked into all the databases we have; passport control and employee records at the casinos and hotel complexes, but I can't find anyone with the name Danielle Smith anywhere." Cara's ability to hack into computer systems is legendary, not that she's permitted to use those skills much nowadays. But her position in the country means she has legitimate access to some of the information she's providing. And it's legend that she doesn't stop there. If anyone can make a computer jump through hoops, she can. I pride myself on being good, but Cara's in a different league altogether.

She waits for us to digest what she's given us so far, but before any of us can express our disappointment, she continues. "I've pulled out a list of female employees who were around at the time in question. Sean, is there any way that we can narrow it down, further? Can you remember anything that might help?"

He shrugs as he thinks, and then comes up with, "The baby is obviously Caucasian."

"Okay." Cara's fingers flit across the keyboard. "What else? Can you recall anything about the women you were with during that period? Anyone or anything, in particular, stand out?"

Another shrug and a dismissive shake of his head. "Well, I obviously gave my name to her."

"And you don't do that to everyone?" I can see Cara biting her tongue as if stopping herself from saying something. Zoe, on the other hand, seems to be finding this amusing and doesn't try to hold back her peal of laughter. Having drawn herself back from a sarcastic comment, Cara probes for more. "What about age group?"

"I'm not fussy," Sean responds with a smirk, "Obviously, they have to be legal, but I don't turn much away." He makes an effort to be serious; his brow creases as he thinks, "Okay, she's got to be of childbearing age, clearly, and I'd have gone for someone attractive. Very attractive."

"Christ, Sean!" Even Zoe exclaims at this. I have to turn my face away, and that affords me a glimpse of myself in a mirror hung on the side wall. I wish I hadn't, I'd gone without makeup today and my hair's still awry from all the travelling. Right now, I very much doubt I could class myself as a member of the category he's described. Or even if I'd ever match up to his exacting standards.

Biting her lip, intent on her task and not showing any outward reaction to his revelations, Cara's fingers tap the keyboard again. She's all business as she glances up, "Ok, I've narrowed it down to people in the age group twenty-one to forty. I can increase the age range if needs be, but this will do for a start."

"What about tourists? Could just be someone passing through?" I add my contribution.

"Yup, looking into that. We'll have taken copies of their passports at the hotels as obviously, like anywhere else, we're under the constant threat of terrorism. I'll get Sean a list of every female I can identify as being in Amahad during the period he was here." The look she gives me is a bit condescending; clearly, she's already got all avenues covered. Then she continues, "I'll pull up their photos from the employee and passport records and leave you a file to go through. Anyone you recognise, we can then look into further and see whether they've been pregnant while in our employ. It won't be quite so easy, but I'll try and track the visitors' medical records too."

"Wouldn't medical records be confidential? How can you match those up?" I can't see how she can get all that data. I wouldn't be able to.

But all I get are looks of disdain from the other three. Oh, yeah. Cara can hack into anything. Feeling a bit of an idiot I change the subject, "Anyone want anything to drink? I'm going to make a coffee."

"No thanks, we've got to be going," Zoe tells me with a bright smile. If anything, the expression makes her look even prettier. Yup. Still hate her.

"Yes, Zee and I have an official function later. With some foreign diplomats or something," Cara explains offhandedly, still concentrating on the screen in front of her. "It takes hours to get ready." She glances up with a grin. "And before you say sarcastically what hard work being primped and preened is, let me tell you it's right down on the bottom of my list of favourite things to do!" She lets out a long sigh. "But, it's part of the job."

"I hate it too," Zoe adds.

Sean reaches over the table, and his hand strokes her cheek. "You're already beautiful, Zoe. I can't believe anyone can improve on that."

As she glows under his praise I turn away, my hands tightly fisted by my side. *Bitch!*

"I'll take a coffee, Nessa if you're making one. I'll just see the girls out."

Nessa? With a violent shake of my head, I tell myself now is not the time to make a fuss about his unique shortening of my name, but instead, I nod and say a brief 'Goodbye' and the polite, but not entirely genuine, or at least, in one case, 'Nice to meet you,' and disappear into the kitchen.

"What's up?" Having seen the women out, Sean's silently come up behind, and his amused voice interrupts me as I place two mugs noisily on the worktop, coffee slopping over the sides.

I reach for a cloth and clean up the mess then, keeping my back to him and placing my two hands on the surface in front of me, I try to keep my voice neutral. "Nothing."

His hand rests gently on my shoulder. "Nothing? Are you certain about that?"

Ignoring the inappropriate effect his touch has on me, I huff. "Hearing what a whore you are? About you having every woman in sight? And that you can't remember anything about them? They weren't very bloody remarkable, were they, Sean? No names, no distinguishing features…"

"It wasn't their facial features I was looking at!"

Swinging round I throw a punch at him, hitting him in the chest. "How dare you say that! How dare you use women like that. Like, like…. Sexual objects. That's all women are to you!"

"They used me too, Nessa. None of them was unwilling, in fact, completely the opposite." The wide grin on his face undoes me.

Suddenly all my rage and frustration bursts out of me, focusing on just one thing. "For fuck's sake, don't call me that!"

"What?" He's taken aback at the words I've screamed. "Nessa?"

"Shut it! And make your own damn coffee!" Pushing past him roughly, I take myself off to my room. I'm stupid to let him get to me, but how can he be like this? So cold about the women he's made love to, even the woman he got pregnant? They mean nothing to him. And what is really making me angry isn't Sean or his attitude at all, but the fact even knowing what I do, he can still turn me on and make me want to be one of those foolish women. His only redeeming feature is he's stepping up and taking responsibility for his mess. And, of course, he's sex on legs.

I take up my position on the bed again, my head in my hands. The bloody man can't even see what he's done wrong. There won't be any changing him; it's not possible and he doesn't even want to try. My mind might know there isn't a chance. But a wicked frustrated feeling lower in my body tells me I'd still want to take a shot if the opportunity presented itself.

CHAPTER 10
Sean

F ucking hell! What was all that about? Women! *Ben, what the hell were you thinking sending her with me?* She's already driving me crazy! It was impossible to miss the cold vibes coming off her while I was greeting my old and very good friend, Zoe. Fuck, we'd been kidnapped together, almost died together. And yes, I had wanted her, but I'm happy she's ended up with Kadar. He's very much the better man for her, and they are madly in love. But after what we'd been through? That forges a bond that can never be broken, and I'll hug and kiss Zoe as much as I'm able to get away with, just not in front of the emir of course.

Briefly, my mind turns to their state wedding I'd attended five months ago. Being on crutches at the time I was unable to take part in any of the more vigorous activities, but what an occasion it was, a fitting celebration of two people so obviously in love being officially joined together. There had been celebrities and politicians from all over the world rubbing shoulders with the fierce desert sheikhs together with their tribespeople and, of all things, members of an outlaw bikers' club from America, proudly wearing their Satan's Devils' cuts. Yeah, it had been one hell of a party that would surely go down in the record books. I smile as I recall one of the bikers beating the Arabs at horse racing, much to the consternation of the sheikhs.

Grinning at the memory, I toss away the half-filled cups of coffee and make a fresh one for myself, debating whether to make another for Nessa, but as I have the distinct feeling I'll probably end up wearing it, decide against it. And why did she object to my nickname so strongly? Vanessa's a mouthful, Nessa or Ness suits her. Far better than the shortened 'Van' used in the office. Smiling an evil smile, I decide I'll keep using it. She's quite attractive when riled; her pale complexion turns almost as bright a red as her flaming hair, and her freckles become more pronounced. She's unable to hide her emotions to save her life. I can only hope she doesn't play poker. Or, if she does, that it's only with me. And she can be assured the bets won't involve money.

Fuck? What am I thinking? I give a short laugh. This is a first for me, I've never thought about getting a work colleague naked before, but then, I usually work with Ryan or Harry, and though I've seen their junk when we've been at a club, I could have happily lived my whole life without the sight. But Nessa? Her tight jeans and tank she wore today revealed a far more shapely figure than the dreary suits she usually wears in the office, and had definitely sparked my interest. Yeah, I wouldn't say no to seeing what's hiding underneath. Huh, but not on the office time, I remind myself, Ben would shoot me and probably aim for my balls. Down boy!

Taking my coffee into the lounge area, I seat myself at the table and get out my laptop, preparing to start work.

Clicking on an email, I see there's a file attached. Great! Cara's worked fast and has already emailed me a selection of photos I'll have to wade through. Quickly I flick through the file. Fuck, there must be a hundred here. *Even I couldn't have gone through that many!* There must be some I can rule out, some I didn't fuck. Jeez, that would be a record, even for me.

The thought makes me bring up my hands, lacing my fingers behind my neck, leaning my head back as I think. Perhaps there's some valid basis for Nessa's disgust. But I like women, and they like me. All women know what they are getting into when I take them to bed or any available horizontal surface. Or up against a wall for that matter. Christ, if I don't ask their name, I'm hardly going to ask for their number. They all go into it with eyes open, and all want the same thing as me, a no strings attached way to satisfy a physical need.

A muscle spasms and I reach down to rub my leg. As I try to ease the ache I remember. The truth is, my cock hasn't actually seen any action since before the last time I came to Amahad when I was Zoe's bodyguard and ended up being shot. Did the bullet in my left leg take more than a chunk of bone with it? Did it affect my brain? Rob me of my libido? Fuck if I can understand it. Pain eased, I lift my hand and rub it over my chin. Ner, I just need more time, that's all. Time to heal fully and get back to my old self.

Closing my eyes briefly, I spare a thought for Mollie's mother. Whoever she is, she got a lot more than she bargained for from our one night stand. While wondering what made her carry the child, I know I'll be forever thankful that she didn't abort her. I imagine a woman on her own, alone in a strange country knowing she was pregnant with a stranger's child. It couldn't have been an easy decision to make. So why didn't she come to me, if she knew I was the father?

I might have doubted her claims, but I'd have helped her out. Even though I would have told her it couldn't have been me, I'd have thought it impossible. I might be indiscriminate, but I'd never forget to glove up. What the fuck could have gone wrong? As it hits me just how many women I've used along the way to satisfy my itch, I feel a shiver down my spine. *I fucking well hope there aren't other children of mine out there.* The air's warm, but I grow cold. Condoms, as I now know first-hand, aren't one hundred percent reliable. Next woman I go with, I'll check she's on the pill as well. And pull out.

Forcing that rather unpleasant thought down, I drag myself back to the task at hand and get ready to look at the portrait photos contained in the file Cara has sent, while musing it might be easier to recognise them if there were other body parts on display rather than just faces. Which again makes me concede Nessa's view.

I click the mouse on the first image. No, I'd remember her, her short hair cut in one of those bobs where one side is longer than the other. And the streak of purple? Not my type at all. I click onto the next one. After ten negatives, I feel some relief at the confirmation I didn't manage to fuck my way through all the female employees and tourists.

The task is mind numbing, so my mind drifts. What Nessa doesn't understand is that sex, for me, is a bodily function, just like any other. I don't go with hundreds of women for variety's sake; it's because I've simply not found many I'd like a repeat performance with, and even fewer, scratch that, any, with whom I want a relationship outside of the bedroom. Or outside of the dungeon. Most of my sexual activity either takes part in clubs or, if actual intercourse is prohibited there, as it is in some, at the woman's home after an extended play session as the ultimate culmination to the evening's entertainment. But if I were to find that one special woman, the one who satisfies me so much that I want her, and only her, then I'd probably change. But the problem is, I doubt such a woman exists.

Mollie comes into my head. Could I commit to one woman for the sake of my daughter—fuck, how strange it is even to think that word—to enable her to have a stable female influence in her life? If I find her mother, could I make a go of it with her for our child's sake? Sadly, I recognise the answer almost certainly no. A family man is not what I'm wired to be, any compromises I make could only end in misery. Although I'll have to think about it at some point, for now, I shelve the question of Mollie's care if I don't find Danielle. What place would someone like me have as the main figure in an innocent child's life?

My finger swipes the screen, and another picture appears. Bugger it! I remember her, her photo triggering memories. She'd come on to me, and how was I to refuse? Christ, I hope it wasn't her. Her shrill voice had grated on my nerves until I used her mouth for another purpose. That hadn't been bad. My cock twitches at the memory, and I rearrange myself to find a more comfortable position. Then I make a note of the .jpeg number and move on to the next. And then the next. I'm now about three-quarters of the way through the photos, finding eight definites and two probables. Well, I had stayed in Amahad for three weeks.

Click, a quick scan with my eyes, then on to the next. Click, scan, move on. Click, scan. Hang on a moment. The next picture is someone I recall. Gently I trace the image in front of me, dredging up the memories. I remember her tinkling laughter, her sheer enjoyment of life. She'd been adventurous in bed, just my type of woman. There'd been no pretence between us, both looking for a good time, ships passing in the night. Could she be Mollie's mother? I try to recall the baby's features and realise I need a photo of her to compare, and wonder why I hadn't thought of that before.

Captivated by the face on the screen, I sit gazing at the image, trying to dredge up more details. What was her fucking name? Danielle? She doesn't look like a Danielle, or a Dannie, but then, what the fuck is a woman of that name supposed to look like? Taking my hand from the screen, I rub my fingers across my chin, feeling the goatee there, idly noting it needs a trim.

A hand lands on my shoulder, I notice it's shaking slightly, and I feel someone leaning over me.

"Is that her?" Nessa's voice is uncertain; I hear a catch in it.

"Fuck if I know," I reply, wondering why her voice sounds unsteady.

"Did you sleep with her?"

"Well, she wouldn't be on the shortlist if I hadn't." Not really paying attention I take my phone out of my back pocket and send a quick text, then look back to the picture on my screen. It's one of those official photos where you're not allowed to smile, but this woman's got a disdain for authority showing in her eyes, and a suggestion of a grin in the quirk of her lips.

Nessa squeezes my shoulder. "How many so far?"

"She," I point at the picture still displayed, "Makes it eleven."

"*Eleven?*" she repeats, incredulously. "You're a complete slut!" I take it from the words and the tone of her voice she doesn't find the tally impressive.

The vibration of my phone means I don't have to comment. I'm not surprised mum's answered so fast; she's always got her iPhone to hand. Swiping the screen, a photo comes into view. Mollie's awake for once, her big eyes staring at the screen as if she's looking straight at me. I glance from baby to woman in front of me, but can't find any resemblance.

"She looks like you." Nessa's hand comes around my side and takes the phone. I notice she's trembling and she's almost forcing herself to look at the picture. "She's got your eyes, your nose. Even your mouth. And the shape of her chin is yours too."

"Poor thing." I retort, I take my phone back, and look at Mollie again, having to admit Nessa's right. Mollie, heaven help her, is all me. No fucking help at all with identifying who gave birth to her.

Pointing at the laptop, Nessa asks, her voice hesitant. "Would you like it to be her?"

I put my head on one side, "I remember her better than the others. I'd lost my wallet earlier that evening. I was looking for it around the casino when she came up with it and returned it to me. I bought her a drink to thank her, and things progressed from there. Fifty quid was missing."

"Did she take the money?"

Shaking my head, I consider the question, "I didn't think so at the time, and I don't think so now. She didn't look like she needed the money. I assume I'd dropped it, she'd found it, checked the ID inside and saw my picture, so she knew who to return it to." *She would know my name.*

"Do you want another coffee while you go through the rest?" It's a conciliatory gesture, and one I welcome. I accept her offer then continue wading through the rest of the employee and visitor photographs while she busies herself in the kitchen. I end up with a dozen that, hopefully, Cara will be able to get more information on.

My neck's stiff from leaning over the computer all afternoon, I roll my head back, turning it to one side and then the other hoping to ease the ache. A yawn escapes from my mouth. We'd suffered through night flights on the plane, and it certainly wasn't conducive to sleep. Having arrived at the palace mid-morning, I'd since been working almost constantly and as a result am dead beat, but also hungry, and aware that my companion must be feeling the same. Realising this is the first time Nessa's been to Amahad, I decide to make a suggestion.

"Hey, Nessa?" I call out; she's gone back upstairs, leaving me to my task. As she hears my voice, she comes down the stairs, dressed, as she had been all day, in tight fitting blue jeans but her tank top's now covered by a flowery blouse and again I notice the figure I hadn't taken any notice of before. She's always successfully hidden that delightfully rounded arse and long slim legs from my sight.

"Sean?"

My eyes glow in appreciation as I take in her lithe body. I take a second too long to answer.

As if she notices my appraisal, she fidgets, and then prompts, "Sean! What do you want?"

Hmm, now there's a question. Recovering my wits fast, I remember why I called her down. "Do you want to go out into the city, Ness? Take in the sights, have a meal? There's not a lot more we can do tonight. I'll send the shortlist to Cara and let her work on it."

She looks surprised that I asked her. I don't understand why. Had Ryan or any of the others been with me we'd have done the same thing. Mind you; we'd also probably have parted company later on, or not as the case might be, and certainly not returned to our own beds tonight. Or at least, not alone. I sigh, I can't leave Ness alone in a strange town, a foreign country. And I certainly can't see her hooking up with someone and going off to have a good time. Fuck, there are major obstacles when partnered with a member of the opposite sex. Try as I may, it's impossible to suppress my innate urge to protect her while, technically, as colleagues we should be equals.

But given my lack of appetite over the past six months,

even if I had a different companion, would I want to seek out female company tonight? Probably not. *And haven't I learned my lesson?* Fuck knows. But I'd certainly check any condom I intend to use extremely carefully from now on.

"That sounds fun, Sean." For a second there I'd forgotten what I'd asked, so turn to look her way. Her face lights up and then dulls as she waves a hand down at herself, inadvertently causing me to look at her all over again. Fuck, she's got great tits too. How did I miss those? "Should I change? What should I wear?"

Now my question comes back to me, "What? Oh. No, you're fine as you are, Nessa. Al Qar'ah is very cosmopolitan, everything goes here. We're not going anywhere special."

"Ok. I'll just go freshen up then. Five minutes?"

I nod, suppressing a grin. If a woman can get ready in just a few minutes, I'll eat my hat. But she surprises me. I'm just checking my gun when she's clumping down the stairs again, looking at me in amazement.

"You're armed?" She frowns, "Should I be?"

For goodness sake woman! I narrow my eyes at her. "You're on assignment in a foreign country, Nessa. What do you think?"

"Oh." Again, her face grows red as she makes an abrupt about turn and rushes back to her bedroom.

Shaking my head in disbelief, I check my weapon then slip it back into my shoulder holster, feeling like I'm wearing an old friend. Like the rest of my team, I feel naked when in England where we're unable to go armed. And Amahad is not the safest of countries to be in, particularly when I don't know what I'm dealing with. It's impossible to forget, last time I was in this small Arab state I was kidnapped.

With high temperatures reigning when the sun is blazing in the sky, like most countries with a similar climate, Amahad comes alive during the cooler night time hours and Al Qu'rah, the capital city, is no exception. Leaving via the main gates of the palace compound, I lead her off the main boulevard, and into the narrow winding streets that characterise the ancient town. Spice and other pleasant aromas surround us, and all around a loud chatter of voices calling to each other. Being a fluent Arab speaker, their conversations hold no mystery for me, but Nessa isn't a linguist so won't understand, which will be adding to the mystique.

She draws closer to me, and automatically my arm goes around her. Well, it's one way to make sure I don't lose her in the hustle and bustle around us, though I certainly wouldn't be holding onto Ryan in a similar fashion. She doesn't pull away from me, presumably for the same reason. I'm over six foot tall, and at about five foot seven, she settles quite nicely beside me, her stride just able to keep up with mine.

I take her to the main souk, and her eyes dance with delight at the stalls with their colourful displays of clothing, leather goods, vegetables, meats, bread and, of course, spices. Some are set up to sell cooked food of all different types. A squawking draws us to a stall selling live chickens, but she blanches at their tightly cramped cages, and we move on quickly. She pauses at a place selling jewellery just a little too long, and I pull her away when the excited stall keeper thinks he has a sale. I notice he hasn't missed my arm around her, and his eyes flitted toward his display of rings. No fucking way, mate. Quickly I move her on.

I have a destination in mind, an authentic restaurant on the edge of the souk, close to the beach, but not so close as to be an easy find for tourists. I've eaten here many times in the past, but am still pleased to find I'm recognised as I walk in through the door. A conversation in fluent Arabic establishes that both myself, and the restaurant owner are well and living happy lives, and then we're shown to a low table. A little more awkwardly than I used to, I fold my long limbs under me, seating myself on the cushions provided. With just a raised, curious eyebrow, Nessa follows my lead.

"How's your leg?" As she expresses her concern, I'm annoyed she's noticed.

"More of a nuisance than real pain," I answer, trying to dismiss it.

"You'll get there." She gives me the reassurance I'm grateful for, getting directly to the heart of the matter and I narrow my eyes at her perceptiveness. Does she know how much I worry I'll never be one hundred percent back to full fitness? Ninety percent won't cut it for the work I do.

After admitting she doesn't have a clue what most of the dishes are, she leaves me to deal with the food, then we sit back and take in the ambience. I'm pleased she seems enchanted with my choice of eatery.

After I've ordered a starter of mezze, and a lamb kebab

dish to follow, Nessa picks up her can of coke and takes a drink. Alcohol is not available outside of the tourist resorts, but the universal soft drink seems to be found everywhere. I watch, transfixed, as a drop of moisture remains on her upper lip, and her tongue sweeps out to gather it in. My damn cock jumps. *Fuck off! This is Vanessa! Shit, man, draw the line somewhere.* Trying to imagine it's Ryan seated opposite, I switch my brain into work mode. *Ryan doesn't have a rack like that!*

"Didn't anyone tell you it's rude to stare?" Nessa asks, dipping a piece of bread into a delicious garlic and oil concoction.

Caught out, I drop my eyes down to the table, and tear off a piece of the doughy mix for myself. Work seems to be a safer subject, "Hopefully Cara will come back with something useful tomorrow. If we're lucky, it will be someone who's easily traceable, and we can get back home."

She pauses, with her hand halfway between the table and her mouth and tilts her head to one side, "How do you feel about it, honestly, Sean? Having a baby dumped on you out of the blue?"

I shrug, "It's about the worst thing a man like me can imagine. I've never thought about having a family." I take a mouthful, chew, then swallow. "If a woman came and told me she was pregnant I, well, I don't think my initial reaction would be very positive. But having Mollie dropped off like that? A fait accompli? There's no way on this earth I could wish her not to have been born. Not for one fucking moment. She's a bloody miracle."

Nessa quickly looks down at her food, making me wonder what I've said wrong, but when she looks up again, she appears to be composed, "So, if Danielle had told you she was pregnant, you'd have wanted her to have an abortion?"

But when I glance at her, her relaxed state appears to be at odds with the tension in her eyes. "Fuck no!" I tell her, adamantly. Then, knowing she deserves an honest answer, give it more thought. "I might have questioned whether it was right to bring a baby into the world under the circumstances, but if she wanted it, then I'd have done all I could to support her."

She looks at her hands; I notice the whiteness in her knuckles and I get the feeling it's a difficult subject for her. For my part, I'd be quite happy for her to get onto something else.

But she's not leaving it yet. "Is Mollie going to stay with you?"

I sigh, "Not saying that, honey. I'd love to say yes, but hell, I can barely look after myself, let alone a baby. Half the time I'm travelling around the world, you know that as well as I do. And I can't ask Mum to have her full time. No, the best thing I can do, the *only* thing I can do, is to find this Dannie person, make sure she's ok, and reunite her with her daughter. I'll help her and would like visiting rights, but I couldn't be the main carer."

"What if Dannie is someone you could settle down with?"

The look I shoot her obviously warns her not to go there. She fidgets, makes a show of looking around the restaurant, then gets back to her food. For a while we eat in silence, finishing our starter, and tackling the main course.

"How can you do it, Sean? How can you go with so many different women?"

As her face creases into a frown of such censure, it almost makes me lose my appetite. Almost. "It's not how you're thinking, Nessa. Not really." God, I wish Ryan was here. Then we'd be having a totally different sort of conversation.

"Well, what's it like then? Explain it to me. And *don't* call me Nessa!"

Toying with my kebab, I wonder how I can explain. In the end, I decide to try to elucidate my lifestyle. "I play at BDSM clubs, *Nessa*. Do you know what that means?" I grin, saying the name I've coined for her deliberately. Somehow I like calling her something nobody else does and enjoy the resultant flush it brings to her cheeks.

Narrowing her eyes, she shakes her head. "Apart from what I learned working Mia's case, I don't know very much. I've read about Doms and subs, but don't really understand the dynamic." As she throws me a hopeful look, I can see she's now more intrigued with getting me talking than fighting the losing battle over her new moniker.

Wiping my hands on the napkin provided, I try to explain. "You know Jon's a part owner of Club Tiacapan, don't you? And one of our employee perks is reduced membership?" At her nod, I continue, "Most of the time I play there, or at other clubs like it. People go there to scene. Yes, there are lots Dom/sub pairings who are either couples, or who play regularly together, but there are also people who go just to team up with someone for the night."

"It's just sex then."

"Not just sex, sometimes, often, not even sex."

She's shaking her head, not understanding, and definitely not believing.

I'll have to give her more. "Okay, here we go. BDSM clubs cater to a variety of kinks, but the relationships I'm talking about involve a Dominant and a submissive, and the power exchange between them. In the vanilla world, relationships tend to just happen. A couple will meet, and go to bed. They'll tear each other's clothes off, have a quick fumble, do the deed, and hopefully both, or sometimes just one will get off. Sometimes one or the other will even fake an orgasm. Both parties will be left unsatisfied, but 'it's just sex', and so they might even go on to get married, hoping it will get better over time." I can see Nessa shifting uncomfortably, her eyes looking anywhere but at me and I wonder if I've struck a chord. Regarding her intently, watching her reactions, I continue. "Dominance and submission is focussed on communication, exactly what's lacking in a vanilla relationship. If you, for example, need something in particular to get you off, your nipples pinched or bitten, a finger probing your arsehole or a slap to your bum; you can't expect a partner to know what you need unless you ask for it."

"Sean!" her harsh whisper and her hand moving swiftly to her mouth make me smile. "You can't talk about things like that!"

"Why not?" I challenge her.

She's gone that lovely shade of red again, and looks around the restaurant, making sure no one is listening to our conversation. Then she hisses, "But all you're talking about is sex!"

"If you'll let me finish?" I raise my brow; she drops her eyes to the table under my intense look. *Hmm, interesting.* Noting her reaction, I pick up where I left off. "A Dom/sub relationship involves what's known as a Total Power Exchange. Some people live the life twenty-four seven, others just during sex, and others only when they are playing in the dungeon. For whatever period is agreed, the submissive will give all their power over to the Dominant who will then make all the decisions and be in control. Though, of course, ultimately the sub retains all the power." *Or they should do.* I suppress a small shudder at an unwelcome memory.

"But you've contradicted yourself there. You said the Dom was in control," her brow creases, perplexed.

I breathe in deeply as I try to drag up the right words, "Go back to my original scenario about the vanilla world. Two people, trying to please each other, with the possible result that neither comes away fully satisfied. In the D/s scenario, the Dom will control the scene and will give the sub what she, or he, needs. The sub has the power to say they don't like something or if they want it to stop. They don't have to worry about being put in any situation they don't like, or being forced to do something they don't want to. Once the roles are agreed, the Dom will take control. The sub doesn't have to worry about whether they should initiate or reciprocate oral sex, for example, whether they should undress themselves or let their partner to it. They will be given commands and directions to follow, and the Dom will take the lead."

"But you said it's not always about sex?"

"No, sometimes it's just experiencing the freedom of giving up responsibility, for a period of time having to make no decisions whatsoever, putting yourself into someone else's hands."

"That must involve one hell of a lot of trust." She's starting to understand it more, now.

"Absolutely. Which is why it's always best to play in a club such as Tiacapan which has people monitoring the scenes at all times. Any walk of life attracts people for the wrong reasons, and yes, there are people who use BDSM to abuse the trust of their subs. In a true D/s relationship, the sub can take back control at any time. It's the Dom's job to avoid pushing his or her sub so far they have to safeword out." *Well, that's the way it should be.* I know, to my cost, that it doesn't always work out like that. And I have the scars to prove it.

We've just been served small cups of strong, dark coffee which I've developed a taste for, having been in Amahad so often before, but I can see by the grimace on her face that Nessa isn't keen.

She tries a second sip, before asking me, "But you've gone far away from the original subject, Sean, how does this explain how you could have sex with so many different women?"

Sighing, once again I try to make her understand, "Some people are Dominant, they live to fulfil the needs of another. Some people are inherently submissive; they want to have their needs fulfilled, to be directed and commanded, not to have to think what they are doing. Many submissives love to serve their Doms. In their everyday lives, such people are forced to suppress their natural inclinations. Many subs work in powerful jobs where they have to make decisions all the time and want to switch off by playing a submissive role in their free time. When I go to a club as a Dominant there'll usually be a sub who wants to give up their control for just one night. Like me, they are not looking for anything permanent, just an outlet to give them mental and physical release from their otherwise demanding daily grind."

She's given up with the coffee and is now tapping her fingers against her lips, as though in thought. "You're a switch, aren't you? That's why you were sent in on Mia's case. Doesn't that mean you're submissive as well?"

I chuckle, "Sometimes, babe, yes. Sometimes I'm as happy as the next sub to give all my control over to someone. It's incredibly freeing." *Or I was.*

A strange glint comes into her eyes, "So, as a sub, you have to make your Dom happy?"

Now I laugh, ""Look, there's a symbiotic relationship between the Dom and his sub. Doms have an innate desire to make their *subs* happy. And will take their pleasure from that."

Her brow furrows, forming a delightful little V over the bridge of her nose. I can see she still doesn't really understand.

"So, what you're saying... In these clubs, there is no expectation on either side of anything permanent?"

"Oh, people exchange real names and telephone numbers if they want to take it further, just like in any other walk of life. But many subs and Doms use fake names for anonymity, so don't have a clue who each other are outside of the clubs." Feeling all talked out and that I've tried to explain it as best I can, I decide to call it a night. "Come on; I'll get the bill, and we'll go back to the compound. I don't know about you, but I'm knackered."

As I'm getting to my feet, my right leg protesting as I've been semi-lying on it for so long, she puts a hand on my arm. "But there aren't any BDSM clubs here, are there, Sean? So how did you get through a dozen girls in three weeks last time you were here?"

Cupping my hands around her face, I smirk, and give her the honest answer, "I'm just a jerk, babe."

CHAPTER 11

Vanessa

J erk! I'll say he's a bloody jerk. I glare at him as he pays for our meal, and then follow him out into the dusty street which consists of hard packed sand under our feet, rather than tarmac. When he takes my arm, I permit it, but only because I'm worried about getting lost in this foreign city. As we walk back through the souk, still teeming with life, I try to get my head around who the man by my side is. I can perhaps understand him having sex with anonymous women he meets in kink clubs—despite his strange assertion that it isn't always about sex—but I have difficulty with the fact he seems to jump in and out of bed with anyone who takes his fancy without even bothering to learn their names.

Surely this man is someone I'd want nothing to do with outside of the work environment? That's the sensible part of me talking, but my perfidious body is at odds with my brain, betraying me as I acknowledge my state of arousal. All this talk of BDSM has intrigued and excited me. *What would it be like to play in a club, with Sean?* Even if it was just for one night. If my suspicions are right, it would be a night I wouldn't forget for a very long time.

"You've got noisy thoughts, babe. Want to share what's made you go so quiet?" His face creases into a delicious grin as he opens the door to our abode and ushers me inside.

The last thing I want to do is let him get a whiff of what I'm currently thinking about. "I'm tired, is all. I think I'll go straight to bed." It would be far too dangerous to have any more deep discussions tonight. I know my face is flushing, I can feel my skin burning. All this talk of sex has turned me on. And that's something I definitely can't afford for him to know.

Cupping his hand around my chin, he looks into my eyes, and sniggers, as if even without me telling him, he knows perfectly well what the conversation over dinner has done to me. That my reddened cheeks have betrayed me is clear when he says with a smirk, "Okay if that's the way you want to play it. Sweet, *very* sweet dreams, darling." Releasing me, he points me at the stairs and has the nerve to pat my bum as I move toward them. To my shame, I don't react, I don't protest, just wanting to get far away from this man's touch, from his silky voice, as quickly as possible.

As I go through the normal preparations for bed, including adjusting the air con, so I won't be sleeping in the Arctic, then slip under the sheets, I know a restless night is on the cards. Our exchange in the restaurant keeps going around my mind, as I try to get straight some of the things that had resonated with me. What was it he said? *Once the roles are agreed, the Dom will take control. The sub will be given commands and directions to follow, and the Dom will take the lead. Doms want to make their subs happy.*

Am I remembering that right? Surely I've got it the wrong way round? Sean must be muddled, despite his experience. If the Dom is the one giving the instructions, how's he to know what gives a sub pleasure? I can't understand it at all. In my fantasy, it had been me giving very precise instructions to a man as to how to please *me*, something a man has never done before because they hadn't a clue what to do. Which make me the dominant partner, doesn't it?

The sub doesn't have to worry about whether they should initiate or reciprocate oral sex, for example, whether they should undress themselves or let their partner do it.

I close my eyes, imagining having a man under my command. Being able to initiate the proceedings and undress him, slowly unbuckling his belt and drawing it through the loops, pushing his trousers and pants to the floor. Telling him to keep still as I take out his cock, hearing his gasp of appreciation as I run my hands over it, his masculine scent making me want to reach forward and sip that drop of pre-cum into my mouth, discovering whether it tastes as good as its promise.

My hand moves down under the covers, gradually reaching my clit and circling round. *I'll tell him to keep his hands at his sides, and take him into my mouth, using my hands to fondle his heavy sac, then smoothing them around his thick, hard, and oh so long shaft, too much length to take it all inside my mouth. My cheeks would burn as I stretch them wide to accommodate him.* My fingers work harder, finding my natural lubrication, and using it to slide my fingers around and over my clit, pressing harder with each rotation. *Then I'll step away, make him watch as I take my clothes off, watching his eyes flare as I remove my bra, letting my breasts hang free, playing with my own nipples until they peak. Then slowly, oh so slowly to tease him, I'll hook my thumbs into the elastic of my underwear and take my time in sliding them down my legs, revealing my strawberry coloured and neatly trimmed pubes for his view. But I wouldn't allow him to touch. Not yet.*

As his eyes dilate with approval, I'll go to the bed, and lie down on my back, drawing my knees up, and directing him to come to me. Then tell him to kneel, to put his mouth on me, to suck my clit, to probe his tongue inside me, while instructing him to touch and pinch my nipples, increasing the pressure each time until I come with a primal scream.

Only then will I let him inside me. I'll feel him feed his large cock into me, inch by torturous inch until he's fully seated, still completely under my instruction. He'll pull out, and press in, each time hitting that perfect spot. Does that actually exist? Outside romance novels? Oh, well, he'll have to do his best. *Then I'll control the speed, telling him to thrust hard, to take me, to use me, to hammer inside me with all his might until I'm screaming …*

One hand thrumming my clit, the other stuffed into my mouth as I try to suppress my cries as I come, harder than usual, my body trembling with the force of my release, lungs heaving and the face of my fantasy still hovering in my mind. Sean. I bloody well fantasised about Sean. Again! Fuck!

Rolling over I bury my head in my pillow in shame, and try to talk sense into myself. It wasn't Sean that had me so aroused; no, it was the idea of taking control. God, but that felt so bloody good, even if it was all in my imagination. Directing someone to see to my pleasure. *Perhaps I'm a Domme?* Hmm. Sean's a switch.

The possibilities that could come out of that are the last thoughts that flit around my head as the long day and my self-induced state of relaxation catch up with me, and I drift off to sleep.

"Coffee?" Sean's voice disturbs me, and I wake with a start. Daylight shines in through the drapes, and the object of my dream is standing over me with a cup in his hand and a very sexy grin on his face. "Christ, woman. You sleep like the dead. I've been knocking for hours, then thought I'd better come in and make sure you hadn't shuffled off your mortal coil."

Reaching for the dose of caffeine, which hopefully will revive me, I scowl, "Shakespeare? At dawn? It's far too early to quote the bard. Why are you waking me at the crack of dawn anyway?"

Sean's grin widens, "Dawn? It's gone nine." Then, as he assesses me, he adds, "Back home it's only five o'clock, so I expect you're a bit out of kilter. You're not used to swapping time zones." Goddammit! He's laughing at me.

Nine o'clock? I've overslept. Very professional. The realisation I've cocked up by not setting the alarm, and his subtle reminder of how much of a novice I am, make me snarky. "Well if you'll get out of here and leave me alone I'll get up," I know I'm scowling, but I don't feel particularly friendly when I'm not fully awake. My body clock is decidedly out of whack, and I just wish I could roll over and go back to sleep. Shit, he would already be up bright and breezy, wouldn't he? And what the fuck is he wearing, or not wearing more like? The top button of his jeans is undone, and he's gone without a shirt, allowing me to see the smooth skin of his chest and an impressive six pack. I supress the urge to lick my lips.

There's amusement in his eyes as he remains by the side of my bed, as if he knows the effect he's having on me. But his words are all business, "You might want to get a move on. Cara's already been over, and she's got more information on the er, likely candidates."

This helps clear the final vestiges of sleep as well as the beginnings of arousal. Sitting up, pulling the sheet with me even though I wore a perfectly adequate t-shirt to bed, I ask quickly, "What's she found out?"

"You're just going to have to get your lazy arse out of bed and come down to find out." He smirks. And then leaves.

Bastard!

CHAPTER 12
Sean

Laughing to myself, I make my way back downstairs. Nessa is clearly not a morning person, and I'm probably lucky to escape alive, and might well not have done so, had I not taken that coffee up to her. Still smiling, I make my way to the kitchen, refresh my cup, and then rake through the cupboards seeing what I can pull together for breakfast pausing only to pull on the tee I'd brought down with me.

I just love that woman's skin, the way it betrays her emotions. And that gorgeous hair, untamed, spread out over the pillows—what would it look like spread out around my cock? That thought has the obvious reaction, so with difficulty, I force myself to get back to the task at hand. Greeting her with a morning hard on would probably only reinforce the impression she had of me last night. *And how the hell did I end up explaining Dominance and submission to her?* Hoping that's not going to turn out to be a mistake that turns around and bites me in the arse, I resolve to keep all conversation strictly to business today.

The kitchen's stocked with a range of Western and Eastern delights, so I've got the bacon cooking, filling the house with its enticing aroma, when there's a knock on the front door. Automatically going through the security checks, I grin when I see who it is.

"Déjà vu!" Zoe laughs as she comes through the door. "I remember you making breakfast before, Sean!" Her expression becomes mischievous, "At least you've got your clothes on this time!"

An ill-suppressed snort makes me turn to see Nessa descending the stairs, the look on her face is priceless. Oh, for fuck's sake! I couldn't have planned that better if I wanted to worsen her already poor impression of me. But that doesn't stop me exchanging an amused glance with Zoe who's blushing, instantly realising how her comment could be misconstrued. I might not care, but she does.

With a glare toward me, seeing as I'm not going to help, she turns to face Nessa with a welcoming smile, "Morning, Vanessa. The smell of bacon just reminded me of when Sean was my bodyguard. He used to cook breakfast for me…"

"I'm sure he did." Nessa doesn't wait for the emir's wife to finish her sentence and pushes past to go into the kitchen. "Is there more coffee, Sean?"

I wink at Zoe, still trying to hold back a laugh. "Yes, and I'm just about to ask *the emira* whether she'd like a cup."

Nessa's back stiffens as my words let her know the faux pas she's just committed with her rudeness. To her credit, she tries to recover the situation, "Er, Emira, would you like some coffee?"

Throwing me another sharp look, Zoe, responds, "No, that's ok, Vanessa. I just popped in to invite you both to join Kadar, Nijad, Cara, and myself for dinner tonight."

"I'm fine with that. What about you, Nessa?" I hope she

understands what an honour this is, the emir is a very busy man. It's akin to being invited to dinner with the queen in our country.

She returns to the hallway to join us, her freckles glowing on her face. Christ, she really can't hide a thing. "I, er,", then she asks a feminine question, "Will it be formal? I haven't got anything fancy to wear."

Zoe laughs softly and rushes to put her at her ease, "No, just the six of us. Very casual, I assure you. We have enough of getting dressed up here." She smiles as she looks between the two of us, and I have a flashback to the frightened woman I'd once been protecting, awed at how much she's changed in the six months since she'd first come to Amahad. Pregnancy suits her as well; she's glowing.

"Well, that's settled then. We'll see you around eight-ish?"

"Thanks, Zoe." She might be the wife of the emir, but I still brush her cheek with my lips before allowing her to depart. As she steps out of the door, two bodyguards take up their positions to escort her to the palace.

"Hmm." I turn to see Nessa behind me, her hands on her hips, a scowl on her face.

"You want to ask me something?" I don't mind leading her on for a laugh, but we're having dinner with Zoe's husband tonight, and it wouldn't look good for Grade A if there was any awkwardness.

"No, I'll just…"

As she starts to back down, I give it to her straight. "I wouldn't have kicked her out of bed, Nessa, I'll be honest about that, but it never happened. Ok? I. Did. Not. Sleep.

With. Zoe. Are we quite clear now?"

She lowers her gaze to the floor, then mumbles, "But you wanted to."

I sigh. "Of course, I fucking wanted to. But I take what's offered, Nessa. And if it's not offered, it's of no consequence. Now can we have some fucking breakfast and get back to what we're supposed to be doing? Working!" I start to turn away, and then swing back, wanting to get this straight, "What I do, will do, or have done, in my private life is no concern to you except where it affects the case in hand. You're my co-worker, Nessa, nothing more, nothing less. If you don't like me or how I live my life, then sod it. You're going to have to put up with it. I'm not fucking apologising to you. Ok?" Yes, there it is, the red flush on her face showing her embarrassment. I know I stepped over the line in our discussions last night, revealing more of myself and my lifestyle than perhaps I should have done. But showing jealousy? What does she think we're in, a fucking relationship?

In the end, we skip breakfast. Neither of us seems to be hungry. Stinging from our confrontation Nessa barely looks at me as we start to look at the information Cara's sent. She's emailed it to both of us, so we have our laptops open; Nessa's sitting on the couch, I'm at the table. Out of the corner of my eye, I can see her fidgeting, she's unsettled, unable to concentrate on her work. It doesn't surprise me in the slightest when she suddenly closes her laptop.

"Sean, I need some fresh air. I'm going to take a walk." Her voice isn't at all steady. Thinking that perhaps it will do us both good to have some distance for a while, I agree and acknowledge her statement with a chin lift, before turning my eyes back down to my screen.

I didn't expect her to get up and almost run out of the door. My mouth falls open at the speed with which she wants to get away from me, and when I spy her handbag lying on the table, my gut clenches in disbelief. Jumping to my feet I open it and check what she's left behind, it's just as I thought and proves me right to be worried that she's gone out unprepared. I hurry after her, but she's already disappeared by the time I get to the front door. Lifting my eyes to the heavens and back down again in despair, I shake my head, sadly. I'm going to have to prepare a report for Ben, assessing her suitability for working in the field. And right at this particular moment, I don't have much that's positive to say.

Sighing deeply, knowing she'll probably be safe enough if she sticks to the palace grounds, and that at least one of us should keep working, I return to the table, clicking open the file Cara has sent.

Christ, she must have worked all night to amass this amount of information. She's drawn up profiles on the each of the women I'd identified with as much background as she could dig up, including whether there were any extraordinary circumstances over the last year that would suggest a pregnancy and birth. It doesn't take long before I open the last file, and begin to read through. There's one hell of a lot more information here, and what I read makes me drop my head into my hands.

Oh, Mollie! What the fuck has your mother got into? And, by way of association, got me into, too?

CHAPTER 13

Vanessa

I'm well aware it was very unprofessional of me, running out of the house the way I did, but I just had to get away. Why the hell had I been so rude to the emir's wife? If word gets back to Ben, I could be sacked! Grade A has a very close working relationship with Amahad, and I've just snubbed their first lady. *What the hell made me do that?*

Making my way through the compound with no destination in mind, I only vaguely notice I'm passing the modern houses built to accommodate the palace servants and visitors such as ourselves, and come to a gate in the wall, beyond which I can see the sea. Breathing in the ocean air might calm my troubled mind, so I wait until the guard nods me through, and then go out beyond the palace walls.

It's not a long walk to the beach, well, if you define beach as sand, I'm there already. Low sand dunes, covered in sparse grass, lead down toward the brilliant blue sea, sparkling in the harsh sunlight. As I make my way across the sand, lizards scuttle out of my way, and I cast a wary look around for snakes, not yet familiar with the wildlife in these parts. *Perhaps I should have found out any possible venomous ones to look out for, before venturing out alone?* Hmm, that probably would have been a good idea, but my one thought had been to escape, to put some distance between myself and the man who seems to have got me tied up in knots. *Where has this jealousy come from?* As he put it so bluntly, the way he wants to live his life has absolutely nothing to do with me.

I walk on, having the urge to reach the water without really knowing why. Maybe the vast blue openness will help clear my mind. But I quickly realise I came on impulse and am not equipped for an outing; being so fair I'll quickly burn under the blazing hot morning sun, already I can feel the heat attacking my skin. Oh, bugger it, I'm still determined to reach my goal.

A five-minute trudge through the shifting sand and I'm there, the shimmering water just in front of me, a cool breeze blowing across the water taking some of the harshness out of the sun's rays. Kneeling on the baking ground, grateful for the denim of my jeans protecting my knees, I put my head in my hands. Fuck, I'm so mixed up.

I'd been so excited to be sent on my first assignment, even though it wasn't the normal sort of case Grade A takes on, but still one sanctioned by my employers, and one for which I was getting paid. I wouldn't be surprised if Ben expected a report of some sort from Sean, assessing my ability to work in the field, and what the fuck could he tell him? Lifting my head I gaze ahead, entranced by the waves approaching and receding, the only sound I hear coming from the murmur of water moving over the sand. Looking right, then left, I appreciate how lonely this place is. Then I remember.

Oh shit! I've left my gun and phone in my handbag

back at the house, and it dawns on me like a plank of wood hitting me round the head just how stupid I am. This isn't Margate; this is Amahad, the country where Sean was kidnapped and shot only a few short months ago. How the hell could he report I'd make a good agent? I can't look after myself, so how on earth could I be expected to protect anyone else?

It's his fault that I'm in such a tizz. Why couldn't I have been sent as support for Ryan, Harry, or one of the other men? I'm sure I'd have my head screwed on better if I was working with somebody else. Sean's been affecting me one way or another for God knows how long, and the recent revelations about him have my head in such a muddle I don't know whether I'm coming or going. And that fantasy that made me come so hard last night? *What the fuck was that all about?* And then his outburst this morning. Of course, he's right. It's not my place to criticise him; we're work partners, nothing else. I'm not in a relationship with him, and I never will be. And, unless I pull my socks up, I won't have a job after this either.

The sun's beating down on my head, I need to get back. But before I can pull myself to my feet a shadow falls over me. *I didn't hear anyone approach.* Rolling to my right to give myself space, I curl my body around and leap up, my hands held in a defensive stance, ready to fight, and then relax when I recognise the person who's crept up on me.

"Sean? How did you know where I was?"

He opens, then hands me, a large beach umbrella and a bottle of water. "The Palace Guards don't miss much, Nessa. They told me where you'd gone." Nodding toward the sunshade, he adds, "Sit yourself under that, you're going to burn if you stay out here much longer." Then he points out, as he examines my face, "You've already caught the sun."

Shit! That's really going to improve my complexion. "Shall we head back now?" I try to keep my voice even.

"No, I need to talk to you." Putting his long legs under him with an almost inaudible groan, he sits beside me in the shade. Of necessity, so the umbrella can shade both of us, closer than I would like. *Or perhaps, not close enough.*

Feeling I need to get my side in first, I'm the first to speak, "Sean, I'm sorry…"

His finger comes over my lips. "No need to apologise, Nessa." Taking his hand away but not before I get the scent of the sandalwood soap he must have used, he looks away from me, out over the blue sea. "This is so fucked up, babe. Look, it's obvious you think you've got feelings for me. That you think you fancy me." As I gasp and go to protest, he touches his hand to my mouth again, "No, let me finish." At my nod, he moves his hand and turns his head again. "I'm not the man for you, sweetheart, and deep down you know that."

At my indignant squawk of rebuttal, he again stops me from remonstrating and denying any attraction to him, this time by putting his hand in the air. "Be honest, Nessa. You were jealous this morning. While that's flattering, this isn't the right place or time, and I'm not the right person." His hands do that characteristic swipe through his hair. "And this situation? I've no idea how it's going to end. Nessa, you're a beautiful woman, but what you are looking for

126

isn't what I'm able to give. You need a nice guy who'll do the relationship thing."

Remembering my thoughts of last night, he doesn't have a clue what I'm after. "Sean, I don't…"

"Please, Nessa, be honest." He points his hand toward me, and then back at himself, "Us— working together is a bad idea. I thought that when Ben suggested it, but he seemed to see some merit in the notion."

I draw in a sharp breath, and suddenly I'm worried, for my future. He's put it so plainly. *Have I cocked up that much?* "Are you going to send me back?" My words come out as a whisper.

"What? No! What the fuck gave you that idea?" He's surprised I even considered it. "We've just got to keep things professional, sweetheart. No more discussions about BDSM for a start. Look, I won't deny if you offered me something, babe, I'd take it, you're a lovely girl, and you could easily tempt me. But I wouldn't be giving you anything back; I just can't. I don't do relationships, and you wouldn't want a quick fling."

I might, just to be with you, even if it was only the once. Mentally, I slap myself. However attractive he is, however much he appeals to me, and however much I'd like to be subjected to the expertise that must come from his experience, he's right. A one night stand isn't who I am or what I'm after. If I ever wanted to go there again, I'd like the pretence something might turn into a relationship even if it didn't work out.

He doesn't say anything more, and I don't trust myself to open my mouth. For a while we sit in silence, staring at the waves approaching and receding until I recognise it's time to pull myself together and put my professional hat back on.

"So, what's next?" I say, brightly, as if we hadn't just been skirting around the subject of having sex, "We plough through the files?"

"Already done that," his voice trails off, and when I glance at him, his eyes have tightened as though he's in pain. He stares out at the sea, before turning back to me. "I know who Mollie's mother is, Nessa."

Something about his reaction tells me exactly who it is. "It's her, isn't it? The one who returned your wallet." I'd put money on it being the one I'd have given anything for it not to be. The picture that had him so entranced.

"Yes." After his simple confirmation, for the moment, he doesn't offer any more.

I sit quietly, realising the implications, already having read the signs. This woman means more to him than any of the others. This one he remembered. *He liked her.* So, what will happen when he finds her? And if he's so close to locating her, does this mean our time here is nearly over? Even if we can't have anything together, it means something to me that I've had this opportunity to be partnered with him. I doubt he'd volunteer to work with me again.

"She's trouble, Nessa." His voice, coming out of the blue, startles me. "She was kicked out of Amahad when she was caught cheating at the casino."

My mouth drops open; that wasn't what I'd expected. "Oh shit, Sean. What did she do?"

"Hand mucking." At my quizzical look, he continues, "Hiding the better cards to replace them for poorer cards later in the game. She's an expert at it, apparently."

A *card shark?* "Was she prosecuted?"

Sean gives a quick shake of his head, "No. Apparently, they didn't want the bother or the fuss, so she was deported from the country."

"Do you know where she went? Or where she is now?" Perhaps it's not going to be so easy to find her. After having accepted our time together was nearing an end, my mind does an abrupt about turn at the thought I might have longer with Sean. *Will I survive it?* Right at this moment, I don't know if I wouldn't prefer to have this case wrapped up and concluded so I can go back to admiring him from afar.

Idly running his hand through the sand, he gives me more details, "Not yet. Cara's trying to track her down. She wasn't using her real name, she acts under a number of aliases, and Cara's already come across several. The police want to question her under several different false names in several countries across Europe. For fraud and robbery."

Fuck. That doesn't sound good. "Are you certain it's her?"

Sean turns his attention to the sea again, and says, softly, "Four months ago, she booked into a private clinic where she delivered a baby. It's her, Nessa; it's her. And she's a wanted criminal."

"Is Interpol looking for her?"

"According to Cara, not yet. Cara's joined the dots, but the authorities haven't; they're still looking for different women."

I'm amazed that Cara's got so far so fast and, again, I find myself in awe of her skills. "How does Cara do it?"

"She's a bit like you in that respect. She researches patterns which others miss. Of course, she's not one hundred percent sure, but it's highly likely that as Mollie's mother is a felon, she could very well have crossed some people that perhaps she shouldn't have crossed. And that's why she's in trouble and left her daughter with me."

I put my arm round him, and pat him on the back in an imitation of the man hug I've seen my male colleagues give to each other. Just a gesture of support. Then I get to my feet, "Come on then, I suppose the next step is finding her."

As he stands I notice him favouring his right leg, and I grimace, suddenly full of remorse that my hasty exit has caused him to walk over the loose sand; obviously not beneficial considering his injury. One more thing for me to feel guilty about. But it would make it worse if I mentioned it, intuitively knowing he doesn't want people to draw attention to his weakness. I stay quiet as I watch him put on his aviator sunglasses, my eyes greedily soaking in his model handsome features. My gaze lingers a little too long, and he wraps his arm around me, hugging me close. A brotherly hug.

"I'm sorry I can't give you what you're looking for, Nessa," he says, softly.

I shrug, taking one last glance out over the gleaming water, thoughts of yesterday evening's conversation going through my head, as well as my late night fantasy. I might have to give up my dreams of being the one to make Sean settle down, but when one door closes, why not open another? My voice decisive, I ask, "When we're home, will you take me to Club Tiacapan?"

By the tensing of his muscles, I know my request has surprised him. He turns me around to face him, and his hand gently caresses my face. It takes all my willpower not to lean into his touch. "I can't be your Dom, Nessa. I can't be the one to introduce you to the lifestyle. I've already told you I can't offer you what you want."

Giving a short laugh I respond, "I'm not in the market for a Dom, Sean. I'll be looking for a sub."

CHAPTER 14

Sean

She'll be looking for a sub? Fuck, I didn't see that coming. It takes everything I've got not to laugh out loud. A few seconds ago, I wouldn't have believed anything could distract me from the issue of finding the missing mother of my child, but that statement stopped all other thoughts dead in their tracks. *She thinks she's a Domme?*

Unbidden an image comes into my mind of her slim, lithe figure strapped into a leather corset, her red hair falling down her back, thigh length black boots wrapping her slender legs, and wielding a whip. Her cheeks reddening with effort, freckles standing out as she lashes an unknown sub. Well, fuck me if that image doesn't turn me on.

I might have refrained from chuckling aloud, but I can't stop a wide grin spreading across my face as I watch her striding ahead. I'm struggling to keep up, the loose sand playing havoc with my bad leg, weak muscles unable to compensate on the uneven ground. But my mind is racing ahead. If she's a Domme, I'll be very, very surprised. What the fuck could have given her that idea? I think back to our conversation the night before, re-running it in my head, but for the life of me, I can't think what I might have said that could have left her with that impression.

We're still not quite back to the compound when I admit defeat and give it up. But heck, if she wants to give it a try, who am I to argue? Nessa a Domme. Now I do bark a laugh as we enter the palace gates, making her turn and toss me a strange look. But I shake my head to discourage any questions and wave my hand in the direction of the quarters which the palace has assigned to us.

Having given up on breakfast, by the time we get back to the house I'm more than ready for something to eat, so as Nessa goes into the living area to catch up with the information we currently have about Danielle Smith, I go into the kitchen and throw together a quick snack. Taking a plate, I place it down beside her on the couch with strict instructions she's to clear her plate. I wait, unmoving until she starts eating. She needs to eat.

I smile to myself as she cleans it up, chewing and swallowing almost automatically as she continues to read, her face frowning every now and again as she clicks back and forth through the information Cara's provided as though double checking the thought processes the Sheikha had followed. It's about half an hour later when her face lights with excitement, and a little exclamation catches my attention. "What's got you so animated?"

She's bouncing with excitement, "I've got an idea. Cara's not the only one who can work with behaviour patterns," she breaks off, looking down, obviously having something to ask. "Do you think it would be possible for me to pick her brain?"

"Ha!" I laugh, "Is that a euphemism for getting her to hack into systems that you can't?" I adore the way her cheeks redden all the bloody time. We'll never be able to send her undercover.

"Busted," she laughs self-consciously, "But I could be onto something."

"Want to share?"

She hesitates, "I'd rather I check it out first."

Now this is the Nessa I know, back home she'd always want to be one hundred percent sure of her facts before sending any operative on what could be a wild goose chase. This is what she should be doing, solving a puzzle, not toting a gun in her handbag. She should play to her strengths and someone ought to explain that to her. Wondering once again why Ben indulged her desire to be out in the field, I extract my phone from my pocket and dial a number; it gets me straight through to Cara's office, and as luck would have it, she has some free time this afternoon. Having arranged the appointment, I ensure Nessa is provided with a guard-come-guide, and I'm left alone.

Taking the opportunity to check in with Mum, I place the call to hear Mollie screaming in the background. The sound pulls at something inside me, and I wish I wasn't three thousand miles away. But at the reassurance it's perfectly normal and probably the beginnings of teething, my mind's put at rest. And Mum tells me she's stocked up with Calpol—a child-friendly painkiller, apparently—and a soothing gel, I know she couldn't be in better hands. Especially when she adds that I'm not to worry when I apologise for taking advantage of her caring nature. Apparently, my situation has provided her with some ideas for a future plot. I just hope she gives it a happy ending.

Hmm. Wondering whether I'll see something about how Mollie came to me featured in one of the soaps at some point and not too sure how I feel about that, I end the call with a smile on my face. Then I try to analyse why I'm wishing I was there to comfort my daughter, when only days before the sound of a crying child would have me running for the hills. It must be the knowledge that she's mine. Mine to care for, mine to comfort, and mine to keep safe. Well fuck me, I would never have expected to feel this way.

But at least I know she's in good hands, and being well looked after by her caring and efficient grandmother. It gets me thinking about Danielle, and what she must have got herself into to make her so desperate as to give up her child. That's, of course, presuming she wanted her in the first place. But then why put herself through nine months of pregnancy if she was only going to give her up? And, if that was always her intention, why wait until the baby was four months old before doing so? No, there had to be something which forced her into this position. Nothing else makes sense. And thief, liar, cheater, or not. I've got to find her.

It's late afternoon before Nessa returns, and from the satisfied look on her face as she enters the house, I know that her hunch must have paid off. But though I ask her, she refuses to give me any details, offering only the explanation that Cara is still following through on something and hopefully we'll get an update later. Knowing Cara as I do, she's probably working on her algorithms to hack into yet another system. I'll have to apologise and thank Nijad and Kadar when I see them; I know they try to restrict her more nefarious activities which, at one time, was all but an addiction for her. I do know, however, Cara herself, will be delighted with this opportunity to flex her mental muscles again.

Although dinner was described as casual, I don a smart suit in readiness, and when Nessa descends the stairs I see she's also dressed up, and for a moment my breath is quite literally taken away. She's wearing a knee length flowing dress in a shade of olive green which compliments her skin tone, and the way it's nipped in at the waist emphasises her curvy figure. Her wavy, shoulder length hair has been pulled back in a sparkling clip, and glittering drop earrings complete the picture, combining to emphasise her rounded face. She's used some makeup to cover her freckles, a shame in my opinion. As she walks past, I get a waft of a musky perfume.

She looks utterly gorgeous, and once I'm able to breathe normally again and have my semi-erection under control, I'm proud to take her arm and lead her across to the palace. As we pass one of the full-length mirror panels in the foyer, I can't fail to notice what a striking couple we make.

I've spent a lot of time in and around the Palace of Amahad over the past few years, so have become somewhat immune to the almost decadent surroundings. For Nessa, however, it's a new experience. Her little sighs of appreciation as we pass through the formal areas don't escape me and, while I've become used to seeing the odd

Rembrandt and Constable lining the walls—originals of course—she has to pause to look at each one. Until I remind her we need to get a move on, as we shouldn't be late. Wide eyed she walks alongside me, her mouth dropping open as she takes in the sights. Grinning I explain to her everything here that appears to be gold, *is* gold. Door handles, taps, decorations. The Amahadian country is extremely wealthy and isn't ashamed to advertise the fact.

The palace guards, stationed at intervals, are intimidating to the newcomer. Armed traditionally with functional scimitars in their belts, they now also sport shoulder holsters and guns, many carrying automatic rifles. Although Kadar has largely overcome the initial objections to his succession to the throne, there's always a constant threat both within the country and externally and, of course, the ever-present risk of terrorist activity. Unfortunately, nowadays the latter is an issue wherever you happen to be in the world. Hence the necessity for the well-trained and highly vigilant palace guard.

Eventually, we arrive at the emir's private quarters, and once the guards announce us, our escorts leave us to enter alone.

It's not quite a year since the previous emir, Sheikh Rushdi, died unexpectedly. As he was only in his early sixties, his heir, Sheikh Kadar, came to the throne many years earlier than he had foreseen. At the beginning, he'd tried to emulate his father who'd held a tight rein over the country. But gradually, and with the help of Zoe, his English wife, he's developed his particular style of leadership, commencing with a plan to implement a form of government which would have the ability to temper the dictates of the ruling sheikh. Kadar is on the journey to become his own person, no longer attempting to be a clone of his revered parent. But the burden of being in control of a country that's only just hanging on to stability remains a heavy one. There is no doubt that Zoe grounds him, but he remains an austere and aloof man to most. When we enter the room, I'm not surprised to be greeted with formality, and as I feel Nessa falter by my side, I know she's left in no doubt that Emir Kadar is equivalent to a king.

However, knowing the man beneath the robes, I ignore his distant façade and move forward grasping his hand firmly in mine. Kadar had led the team comprising his army as well as Grade A associates when Zoe and I had been rescued six months earlier, and his quick actions to summon medevac had saved our lives. Had he been any later I'd have bled out on the sands.

Zoe smiles at us from beside her husband, and, in the presence of her partner, I greet her politely, but can't resist bending over and kissing her cheek, while casting a sideways glance at Kadar. His jaw tightens, but he says nothing. He won her, after all.

A touch on my sleeve brings my attention back to my companion, and I take it upon myself to make the introductions, "Nessa, can I introduce you to Emir Kadar, and of course, Emira Zoe, who you met earlier. And," I give a chin lift to the man across the room. "Sheik Nijad. You, of course, already know his wife, Cara."

Nessa squeaks a 'pleased to meet you', and I see she's overwhelmed by the elevated status of the four people greeting us. Making a mental note that she's not exactly exuding the confidence that an operative of Grade A should, I place my hand on the small of her back and encourage her across the room to the dining table set for six. It's a pleasant room, part of Kadar's personal suite, rather than one of the formal public areas of the palace, but still with rich furnishings that could leave no one in any doubt they were in the presence of royalty.

Nijad throws off his headdress, the Arab gesture of informality, and Kadar follows suit, suggesting they are planning a relaxed evening, a meal amongst friends. Then the former, noticing what she's doing, glares at his wife and growls, "Cara, habiti. Can't you put that laptop down for one moment?"

Completely unabashed, she smiles coyly, "I'm waiting on some info for Sean, Ni."

After trying to stare her down, he throws up his hands as if knowing he's beaten, then leans over and places a kiss on the top of her head, a sweet, loving gesture. I can't hold back a grin. Despite the understated, but to the initiated, plainly a collar of ownership around her neck, Nijad is obviously only a Dom in the bedroom and dungeon, Cara has him wrapped around her little finger the rest of the time.

Kadar tuts at the tender exchange, and then addresses me for the first time, smirking, "You seem to have got yourself a small problem," he begins, unable to help himself chuckling as he holds his hands about eighteen inches apart, reminiscent of Cara's gesture when she first asked me about Mollie. "About this size, I understand?" Now a louder laugh, "Sean Cooper, a father? Never would have believed it."

Nijad's joined in the laughter; the women don't seem to find it so funny. But then, being surprised with a baby is the pinnacle of misfortune for most men. It's not the first time, and won't be the last, that I'm the butt of this particular joke. Shrugging it off, I grin along with them.

As if a switch was thrown, Kadar's face grows serious as he addresses the reason why we're here. "I hope we can help you find the mother, although I understand she might have got herself in trouble of a different sort."

Now he turns to his brother, but his eyes are fixed on Cara, "Nijad, please ensure Cara understands that she's to leave no trace of what she's been doing. *I* don't want to know the details."

Cara grins, and waves her hand in the air, "I'm here, you know."

Nijad places his hand on her head as though to still her, "Cara knows this is her 'fix', and will have to last her at least another year."

Now it's my turn to laugh, knowing he's referring to what they call Cara's 'hacking habit'. Her amazing ability to get into almost any computer system is a compulsion for her, and she'll jump at any opportunity to use her noteworthy skills. But her position in Amahad now means such addiction could be risky, and if she was discovered, could bring disrepute to the country. Her over-confidence had, in fact, already gotten her into trouble, but she's learned from it by tightening up and now leaves no footprint that can be traced. Or so I hope, feeling a little guilty that this time she's doing it on my behalf.

"Have you been to Club Tiacapan, recently?" Kadar asks conversationally, as we take our places around the ornately carved table.

"I used to go regularly, although my leg put paid to that for a while. But I went last weekend." I pick up the linen napkin, unfold it, and place it on my lap.

"It's been some months since I was there, but Jasim tells me it's doing well." His, and Nijad's brother, Jasim, part owns the club along with Jon and Jason Deville.

"It's the safest club in London, so there's a waiting list for membership." As I assure him the club is indeed a success, servants appear, silently bringing in plates of delicacies, placing them on the table.

"I'd love to go," Cara joins in. "I've never been, but I've heard so much about it. Nijad is going to take me next time we're in the UK. Now Zorah is a little older, we can travel." Zorah is their beautiful daughter. Quickly doing a calculation in my head, I realise she's probably only a couple of months older than Mollie. I glance toward her as she continues, "Jasim was telling us about some of the new equipment he's had installed, and I can't wait to try it out. Tell, me, is the suspension rig as good as he makes out?" She turns to Vanessa, and asks, "Have you tried it, Vanessa?"

CHAPTER 15

Vanessa

I hadn't known what I could expect would be considered polite dinner conversation with the eminent emir, his younger brother, and their wives, but the one topic I didn't foresee was a frank discussion about BDSM. I suppose as their brother owns Club Tiacapan, it's not surprising that Nijad and Kadar would also be Doms, but to openly discuss those appetites with their dinner guests? And now Cara is directing a question to me, as if it's perfectly natural to assume I partake in the same activities. When my face glows and goes blank, she rephrases it, obviously out of kindness, making sure I don't feel excluded from the exchange.

"I understand the rig takes up one whole wall, what do you think of it?"

I know I sound several octaves higher than normal when I have either to respond or look stupid, so simply offer, "I don't go to Club Tiacapan."

"Oh?" Kadar throws Sean a look, and then I'm the victim of his intense gaze. "Where do you play, then?"

"Nowhere!" I wish my voice would return to normal. I turn to Sean, wanting his support, but he's openly grinning. "I'm er, not interested at all in BDSM." *Liar!*

The emir seems perplexed, "Sorry, my dear, I was

certain you were Sean's sub." Again, his gaze turns to Sean, and he raises his eyebrows.

Forcing my tone back to something closer to my normal range, I toss a glare in my partner's direction, and calmly tell Kadar, "I'm Sean's work colleague. I'm here as his backup."

At that comment, Sean chokes on his mouthful of wine, and I feel like running from the room and bursting into tears. *What the heck?* So what if I've forgotten to set the security system when leaving or entering the house, and does it really matter I've gone unarmed through the streets of this foreign city? A stunned silence greets my pronouncement, and just as I'm going to open my mouth and blurt out something stupid just to fill the void in conversation, a gentle hand rests on my arm.

"You're a Grade A Close Protection Officer?" Zoe regards me with something akin to admiration, and while I retain some suspicions about her relationship with Sean, at this moment I'm extremely grateful to her.

"Yes, I'm fully qualified, but only recently. This is my first field assignment. I've been working behind the scenes for Grade A for about six years."

"And she's very good at it!" Cara breaks in, throwing me a winning smile. "We've put out heads together this afternoon and have come up with some leads. Vanessa's ideas were extremely helpful." She waves at her laptop, seemingly always by her side, "The result of which is what I'm waiting on now."

Her interjection seems to have brought the conversation back round to safer topics. Safer for me, that is.

For a while, we all concentrate on eating the delicious food that's been placed in front of us, and thankfully no more mention is made of BDSM. When Kadar speaks again, the focus is, at last, removed from me.

"So, how do you feel about being a father, Sean?" Kadar throws out the question, but his gaze falls lovingly on the stomach of his very pregnant wife.

Shifting awkwardly in his seat, Sean takes in a deep breath. But before he has time to formulate a reply to the difficult question, Cara's laptop pings. Dropping her fork to the table, she opens it, receiving a glare from her husband who's apparently also her Dom. Ignoring him, she eagerly opens the email that's just popped into her inbox, and her eyes light up with excitement. Interpreting her expression, I see she's received something interesting.

Flicking her eyes at me, she gives a slight nod. I raise my wine glass at her in a triumphant toast. The others look on curiously, waiting until she's finished reading. Then, at last, she enlightens us all.

"Found her!" She announces with a flourish, her hand forming a fist and pumping the air. "She's had the audacity to turn up at our Casino in Paris!" I know the ruling Kassis family own several casinos around the world, as well as the one in the home country. "And, for once, she's using an approximation of her real name, Danielle Martin."

"She's got a nerve!" Nijad barks incredulously, as he flicks his long, dark hair back over his shoulder.

"She wants to be found," Sean comments softly. "Martin is akin to Smith in England; it's the most common surname in France."

I realise something, "Only by you. She's been using aliases across the other countries, and she used a different name here as well."

Cara's nodding, "Yes, here she used the name Maggie Saltwell, it's no wonder you didn't recognise it, Sean."

Kadar's all business, his brow furrowed as he asks, "Is she playing her tricks in Paris?" I get the impression he's wondering how much she's costing his casino.

But Cara gives an adamant shake of her head, "She's staying relatively clean, she's card counting, but that's not illegal. Unlike card mucking."

The emir growls, and puts down his cutlery on his now clean plate in a rush, "But it's still cheating."

"How long has she been in Paris?" Sean's fingers tap quickly on the table, obviously anxious for details about the woman he needs to find, rather than what's she's up to.

"She arrived yesterday. She's staying in the casino hotel."

"How the hell did you find her?" Nijad is the one who's interested now.

With a glowing smile at her husband, Cara responds before I have a chance to speak. "Facial recognition software." She points at me, "It was Nessa's idea to start searching in the obvious places."

Sean's ruminating on something; his head is bowed, resting on his hands. Idly I wonder whether his mother had ever told him it was rude to put his elbows on the table, if so, it hadn't sunk in. Just then he looks up, "She didn't want to be found when she dropped Mollie off, so why make it obvious now? Why turn up in a Kassis Casino with a fake name it wouldn't have taken long to discover, even if we didn't have geniuses like Cara and Nessa on our side?"

Suppressing a glow at the implied compliment, I shrug, "Perhaps she doesn't intend to stay long. She was either going to have gone to ground or hide in plain sight. Nijad's right, she might simply be toying with us, thinking we're not clever enough to find her. But my feeling is she's bringing herself to our attention. There's something she needs from Sean. That's why I thought we should search in places she'd be visible." I've often found following my gut feel brought results. Sometimes it wasn't all about thinking logically.

"It's a funny way to go about it." Kadar pronounces, "If she wants help, why not pick up the phone and call?"

Nijad's brow creases, "Maybe she wanted to meet on neutral ground, force you to go to her. Whatever she wants, she's playing games, Sean. And don't forget she's a wanted criminal."

"But it's only Cara who's put all the pieces together and knows she's behind the crimes the police in different countries are looking at as individual cases." Sean frowns, "Nonetheless, I agree with you, Nijad. Nessa and I will be out of here tomorrow morning; we need to get to Paris before she disappears again."

My life has gone from predictable and dull, to jet-setting around the Middle East and Europe in just a few days. But I'm not going to complain, and while I'm not too fussed about seeing Sean meet the mother of his baby, if I'm honest, there's part of me that's intrigued to meet the mysterious Danielle. Hopefully, we'll catch up with her, and I can see for myself what sort of woman abandons her own daughter. And discover what particular trouble she's in. Apart from being wanted by several police forces, that is.

"I'll get the casino manager to keep an eye on her, Sean. We can make sure she stays put by force if necessary." Nijad offers helpfully.

"If she's cheating I want her out of there as soon as possible!" Kadar keeps to the subject closest to his business mind.

"I don't think we should scare her off, brother," Nijad tries to calm his brother, "Play it low-key until Sean gets his chance to have a heart to heart."

Zoe hasn't spoken for a while, but now she places her hand on her husband's arm, Kadar visibly relaxes and turns to her with a smile. "We owe Sean a lot, Kadar." Her softly spoken words remind all of us Sean received his injuries trying to protect her. And as the emir turns his full focus of attention onto his wife, his love for her beaming from his eyes, I know what I'm missing and just how much I want a man to look at me in exactly the same way.

CHAPTER 16
Sean

As Zoe asks Kadar to give me more time I throw her a grateful look, knowing she's exaggerating my part in her rescue. Sure, I had tried to protect her, but the odds had been too great, and all I got for my pains were bullets in each leg to take me out of the action. The emir's wife is one of the strongest women I know, and I don't believe she owes me anything. It was only the good timing of the arrival of Kadar's men and Grade A that means she's here today. Still, if calling in a favour from Kadar means I get to catch up with the mother of my child, I'll resist protesting her generosity and refrain from correcting her.

I wait impatiently to hear what Kadar decides, my good leg bouncing under the table. He's a businessman as well as a politician after all, and I understand how he won't want any one of his corporate enterprises to lose money. By card counting, rather than the outright cheating Danielle used in other casinos, including the one in Amahad, she's staying just the right side of the law as far as gambling is concerned, if not with anything else. She'll probably be on a roll with winnings which have been won dishonestly, but she's not doing anything she could be prosecuted for.

Most casinos are content with banning such sharks from swimming in their waters. Kadar would be quite within his rights to tell the manager to evict her immediately from both the tables and the hotel. I sit, holding my breath, hoping that he'll let her stay. If only until I can catch up with her. I can't offer to make good any losses; the type of money Danielle could be amassing would be way beyond my pay grade.

Kadar's hands are steepled in front of him, his familiar gesture showing he is giving the matter careful consideration. We're silent as we finish our meal, waiting for him to announce his verdict. Then, at last, with an exaggerated sigh, he gives his pronouncement. "I'll let it go, for now, Sean, but I do want her stopped before she breaks the bank. Let's get you there fast. The Kassis jet will made be available to fly you to Dubai in the morning, and you'll be able to get a connection to Paris from there."

I breathe again. Yes! I feel like doing a fist pump myself, but manage to control myself. The fact that Kadar wants it sorted quickly fits in well with my desires. By this time tomorrow I could be meeting the mother of my daughter, and finding out what the fuck is going on. I thank him profusely, but he waves away my grateful comments with a dismissive wave of his hand.

The next hour passes quickly, the conversation animated and interesting, a welcome distraction from my problems. Everyone carefully avoids the two topics which would cause discomfort for myself and Nessa, namely, there's no further talk of dungeons and BDSM and no more unanswerable questions about how I ended up holding the baby. Eventually, a servant enters to tell Cara that Zorah is restless, and needs her mother's touch. Both

Cara and Nijad leave the room to go to their daughter. Zoe pleads tiredness as her excuse to make an exit, and Kadar almost knocks over his chair as he speedily leaps to his feet to help his seven-month pregnant wife out of her chair.

After polite 'goodbyes' Nessa and I make our way back to our temporary home in the compound, and spend the rest of the evening repacking the few possessions we brought with us. Well, Nessa does, I'm too used to this life and never bother to unpack. While she's busy, I treat myself to one last glass of whisky as I try to get everything straight in my mind. Finding Danielle had been far easier than I'd expected, and the question I ask myself is, why? Does she need help, or have her problems now been sorted and she wants Mollie back?

Another sip of the amber nectar, and I rest my head back on the sofa. Kadar was right, all she had to do was to pick up the phone. Why the subterfuge? And what the fuck is going on? And now I know what she is, if she wants to reclaim her daughter, I'm reconsidering that she's the best person to bring her up.

Finishing my drink, I go upstairs to bed. The myriad of unanswerable questions rolling around my brain lead predictably to a restless night. Not being one to function well on lack of sleep, I'm not at my best when the following morning we leave the never-ending blue skies of the desert country behind, and eventually land to rain and dark, cloudy skies in Paris. I know I've not been good company, but Nessa seemed to accept I've got a lot on my mind and kept herself to herself, reading for most of the time.

The French capital can be a glorious sight, but not so

much when you're trying to hold an umbrella in gale force winds, and the swift climate change doesn't do much to lift my mood. But on landing and receiving a welcome text, I appreciate how much I owe the emir. As well as giving us the use of his private jet for the first leg of this journey, I find Kadar has also arranged our accommodation in the extensive hotel complex attached to the Kassis casino, L'Oiseau Bleu.

From Charles de Gaulle airport we take the Metro, the Parisian equivalent to London's underground, to the station close by the hotel. It wasn't worth taking a taxi from there as it was only a short distance. But the atrocious weather means we're both disheveled with water dripping off us by the time we arrive at the entrance to the casino beneath the huge neon sign which, unlike others in the area doesn't flash. Instead, it shows its ostentatiousness by the number of bulbs and fine detail in the gorgeous blue bird that gives away the identity of the place even for people who don't speak the native language. Pushing through the revolving doors, we step inside.

The building hums as we enter. Immediately the dismal day is left behind, and it becomes impossible to say whether what time it is, let alone whether or not the sun is shining outside. To reach the hotel's reception we make our way past the temptations of gaudy slot machines looking deceptively eager to pay out, and tables with croupiers calling for bets to be placed. It's nothing new to me, but an eye-opener for my companion. Her steps falter as she looks around, and I place my hand on the small of her back to encourage her along.

Once we get to the desk to register, I'm amused that

Kadar has arranged a suite for us, but then, emirs probably don't think in terms of basic digs. Personally, I'd have been happy staying in any of the rooms here. Like most casinos around the world, they are all about encouraging people to stay in their opulent surroundings and lose more money than they can afford to at the gaming tables. Everything anyone could need is on site, a variety of restaurants suiting all pockets and tastes, as well as shops selling whatever you could wish for, from clothing to suit every mood to condoms. Despite only being a stone's throw from the attractions of the centre of Paris, I doubt many staying here often emerge into the light of day, seduced into eating, drinking and, of course, gambling their money away, in the building specifically designed to provide everything they might want. All in all, there are worse places to stay.

Receiving the golden keycard, I suspect we've been given one of the suites reserved for high rollers, and for which it's not unusual for the hotel not to receive payment. Keeping punters happy and returning is part of the casino business, and the Kassis family know their industry well. Taking the lift to the penthouse floor, we, at last, arrive at our room.

Nessa's entranced by the opulence of the suite. Moving quickly forward, she stands in the middle, twirling around as she takes everything in. "Wow!" she pronounces, before turning to me with a look of rapture on her face, "Good to have friends in high places, isn't it?"

"This is the norm for Kadar," I chuckle, "Doubt he'd have even thought about it. It's probably where he stays when he's in Paris. Looks like there's two bedrooms—take whichever you like."

She picks up her bag and takes it across to one of the open doors and peers inside. It seems sufficient and meets her requirements as she doesn't bother to check the other, so I guess that one's mine. After dumping my small case, I then return to the sitting room. I stand, undecided. Do I wait for Danielle to come to me? Or take the initiative myself and try to track her down?

Crossing to the desk, my hand hovers over the phone. I know Danielle's suite number, should I call? Or should I go to her room and confront her in person? I'm so close to getting answers but know there's a need to play this right. I don't want her to slip through my fingers again. And it's still up in the air as to whether her being here using such an obvious name was an invitation, or whether she's just become overconfident. The last thing I want to do is to scare her into running before I've had my chance to demand answers from her.

As I stand, wondering what might be my best move, a rap sounds on the door of the suite. Going to answer, I find a bellboy with an envelope in his hand. When I go to take it, he holds it a second longer than he should before releasing it to me. Inwardly grinning, I reach into my pocket and pull out a handful of Euros.

"*Merci, Monsieur,*" he nods, pocketing the notes and making them vanish like a magician's conjuring trick, before disappearing down the hallway.

Closing the door, I lean forward and rest my head on it for a second. Is this it? *Is this what I've been waiting for?* Then, putting it off no longer, I straighten, tear open the letter that I've been given, and extract the piece of paper inside.

There's no greeting or salutation, and the message is clear. "Meet me in the bar at four o'clock." I don't have to ponder who the note is from. And it's confirmation I'd been half expecting that Danielle has been in control of our merry dance, and probably, our every movement. She'd wanted me to trace her here.

Heaving a sigh of exasperation, realising I'm being played every step of the way, I get out my phone and check the time. It's just gone three now, so we haven't got long. Wrapping my fingers around the paper I'm still holding in my hand, I wonder how I'm going to take back control, hating feeling like a puppet with someone else pulling the strings.

"Nessa!" I call out, then hearing no response, go to the open door of the room she chose. Oblivious to my shout for her, she's neatly putting her clothes away, folding them and selecting which drawers to put them in. Tunnelling my fingers through my hair in frustration, I pause to watch. Knowing how quickly things can change on this job I just live out of my suitcase, a quick getaway being always on the cards.

So intent on her task, I have to clear my throat loudly to get her attention. At last, she looks around and I tell her about the message I've just received.

Her eyebrows rise, "So soon? I thought we'd have a problem finding her."

Slowly, I nod, "So did I. But it seems like the mountain is coming to Mohammed for once." And thank fuck for that. Soon, perhaps, I'll be able to get the answers I'm looking for. And will be able to get back to Mollie.

CHAPTER 17

Vanessa

I thought I'd have more time to mentally prepare before meeting the mother of Sean's child. But no, before I'd even got halfway unpacked, Sean told me to get a move on as we were about to meet her. And now I'm dreading what we might discover. Despite her dubious profession, if you could go so far as to call it that, and the bizarre fact the police want to speak to her in several countries, will Sean overlook her shortcomings and want to be with her for the sake of his baby?

Sitting at a table, a glass of orange juice in front of me, I glance across at my companion. His styled but longish hair flops down, framing his face, the muted light complimenting his features. He's such a handsome man, only just the right side of being too pretty to be a member of the male sex but his shortly trimmed beard and light moustache corroborate his masculinity. What would it be like to have all his attention focussed on me? To have him under my command, to be able to tell him what I want him to do to me? I feel myself becoming wet, and my nipples start to peak as I imagine it, and I try to resist squirming in my chair. And then try to knock some sense into myself. With Danielle in the picture, who he'd obviously thought attractive enough thirteen months ago, I would never get a chance. He's told me in no uncertain terms that he's got no interest in me.

I shiver at the thought he might decide to make a go of it with this unknown woman, and he chooses that moment to catch sight of me.

"Cold?" He sounds solicitous, and looking up, frowns at the air con unit that's right above our heads. "Want to move?"

"A bit." I lie, and a flush of betrayal comes to my face. "But I'm alright sitting here."

His eyes are watching me too intently, and he smirks. Bloody man, how could he know what I'm thinking? I turn my head away, and it's at that point I see her. It's easy to recognise her from the photo I'd seen.

Danielle's beautiful, just as her picture had suggested she'd be. But it hadn't shown me she was also tall, statuesque, with colouring like a Nordic blonde, blue eyes matching Sean's own. She's gliding toward us, her dress flowing around her as though it's been programmed to show her off in the best possible light, clinging in all the right places, showing off her cleavage, but just the correct amount. Her makeup is flawless, her skin unblemished. Confidence radiates from her, and I feel myself sinking into my seat as she approaches, knowing there's no way I could compete with someone like her. Sean gets to his feet, his hand outstretched, a cautious half-smile on his face, just one corner of his mouth turned up as though he's unsure how to greet her. She's got no such reservations, she pulls him to her and hugs him. For far too long, in my opinion.

In the end, it's Sean who pulls away, holding her at arm's length and examining her closely. Well, he is meeting the mother of his child, for the second time, of course. Or perhaps the first when they'll get into any conversation. They clasp hands; something goes between them; a recognition of sorts, and I wonder whether she'll end up warming his bed tonight. Oh shit, God, why didn't I let him come to this meeting alone? She's so glamorous she makes me feel like a clumsy frump in comparison. Giving myself something to do, to avoid looking at the suave, well-matched pair, I reach for my drink and take a gulp of my orange juice. But it's too big a mouthful, and I choke, noisily.

It breaks the spell, Sean thumps me on the back, and gives me a curious look, then with a gesture, he invites Danielle- I can't think of her as Dannie—she's far too sophisticated for such a shortening of her name—to sit with us. She puts her hand around his back one last time before taking a seat, and then I watch Sean watching her as a waiter appears out of nowhere to take her order. She unashamedly demands a glass of champagne; why am I not surprised? As she issues her order, Sean's drinking her in with his eyes, the flare I see showing me whatever attracted him the first time is still there. And why wouldn't it be? She's perfect.

"So," As soon as the waiter leaves us, Sean leans forward and cups one elbow and rests his chin on the fingers of his other hand. "Danielle, I think you have some explaining to do." He wastes no time getting to the heart of the matter.

She laughs, a tinkling sound, "No pleasantries? No 'how

are you' after all this time?" Her voice is husky, seductive.

Shaking his head Sean tells her, "We didn't know each other long enough for that. As I recall, *you* left me in the middle of the night. I didn't even know your name."

Shrugging, she laughs again. "You got used by a user, Sean." She scans the room, as though looking for someone. The waiter comes and puts her drink on the table. Looking up she tells him, "Put it on my tab, please. Suite 105."

"I'd have bought that."

"I've taken too much from you already." After throwing her strange comment, she puts her perfect lips to the tall glass and takes a mouthful of the fizzy liquid. I note the bubbles don't tickle her nose, and neither does she choke.

"I'd have phrased it more that you've given me something." Sean's eyes narrow, "Can we talk about that? This isn't a social meeting, Danielle."

It surprises me that he sounds harsh; he can't possibly be immune to her charms.

"Call me Dannie, please." She smiles seductively, and it's at this point I realise she's not once looked at me, it's as though I'm invisible, insignificant.

It spurs me on to make my presence known. I join in the conversation. "That's your real name?"

Looking almost surprised to hear someone else speak, she at last deigns to acknowledge my presence, "Yes, actually, it is. I use others, of course, but Dannie, Danielle Smith, is who I am."

"Thirteen months ago, I was in Amahad, Dan.. Dannie. We had… a one night fling. Obviously, there was a problem, I know we used contraception, I've never gone without, but…" Sean's hesitant as he describes the little he knows about their encounter.

"But you left me pregnant. And you think the story starts there, don't you?"

"It doesn't?" Sean asks, his eyes opening wider.

Dannie shakes her head, her smile teasing. "You got played, I'm afraid."

Now his eyes narrow once more, and his mouth compresses into a thin line. He leans back in his seat, his hands clasped behind his head. "Well, why don't you tell me about it, then?" It's probably only noticeable to me, but there's a tinge of impatience in his tone.

After another scan of the room, she nods and puts down her drink. Her hands cross one over the other in her lap, the movement drawing attention to her perfectly manicured nails. "I'm a thief. I don't need to be," self-depreciatingly she indicates her designer clothes, "Despite the common surname I was born into riches, Mother left when I was small, Daddy dear died a few years ago, and left me his fortune. But I found I had the knack for taking things, so I do."

Why would this rich, gorgeous woman want to steal anything when she doesn't need to?

It's what I'm thinking, but it's Sean who voices the question. "Why?"

Another dismissive shrug, it's a gesture that looks far too common for her. "It's who I am, how I'm wired. I can, so I do. I chase thrills. Life's so boring without some excitement."

"You stole my wallet," Sean states.

"Yes, but I gave your *wallet* back." She doesn't look at all concerned that he'd recognised she'd been the guilty party.

"Minus fifty pounds which, presumably, you didn't need." His voice is censoring, but there's no shame on her face.

Instead, there's another grin, "No, but the homeless man hovering around outside did. I gave the money to him." She doesn't stop and wait for us to comment, but continues, "I also stole the condoms you had in there."

Sean looks baffled. He runs his hands through his hair, and then gives her a sharp look as a memory comes back to him, "We used your condoms." It was almost an accusation.

Her mouth widens in a broad smile, almost as if he'd said something clever. "That's right, my carefully prepared condoms full of little holes. I was hoping some of your swimming buggers would get through."

Sean turns his head away; his nostrils flare as he takes in a deep breath. I watch his body tense, as he understands how he'd been set up. He's furious. "Why the fuck did you do that? And why the fuck did you choose me? It was me you targeted, wasn't it? You came on pretty strong." His voice isn't quite a shout, but loud enough to draw attention. Reaching out my hand, I rest it on his arm, willing him to calm himself. I can understand how angry he is. Mollie was no accident. Dannie had done it on purpose. Placing his hand over mine, he gives it a squeeze and continues to hold it, as though welcoming my comfort.

"I told you, I'm a thief." Nothing about her suggests she's contrite in any way. "It was going to be someone that night, it *had* to be that night, everything told me I was ready. I was thirty-five, my biological clock was ticking, and I wanted a baby. But I didn't need or want a man in my life."

"So you stole it from me." Sean's voice has lowered, "Why me?"

Taking another sip of champagne, "I'd been watching you. It was obvious you're a Dom," she says, nonchalantly.

"Are you a sub?" I butt in, she certainly doesn't look like one, but then Sean had told me powerful, strong women can be subs too.

She glances at me as though she'd forgotten I was there. "No of course not, I don't go in for all that silly business at all. I have absolutely no desire to be controlled by, or control anyone." Before I can query the mystery further, she carries on, "Doms, though, my dear, make the best lovers. Even in a vanilla sense. They care, you see, about the pleasure of the person they are with." She puts down her now empty glass and waves her hand toward Sean. "And you, my love, did not disappoint in any respect. It was a fantastic night, a great way to conceive my child."

"*Our* child!" Sean growls. "And you were never going to tell me about her."

"No," she confirms drily, "I didn't think you'd ever need to know."

As Sean growls before going quiet, I know he's grappling with the notion that this woman had cheated him, had made him the unknowing father of a child he might never have discovered existed. "So why put my name on the birth certificate?"

"A forgery, my dear. So you knew who she was to you, when I arranged to have her delivered to you."

She's a cold-hearted bitch, and with great difficulty, I resist the urge to slap her.

"But what do you care?" she continues, "You're not the type to want children. What you didn't know wouldn't hurt you." She sips her champagne and speaks as though she's discussing the weather.

"You know nothing about me, Danielle," Sean leans forward and hisses, "You have no right to make that assumption. And if you think I'm so far from a family man, why the fuck did you leave Mollie with me like that? How could you know that I'd care for her properly?"

"You're a Dom; you're wired to care. She's a baby!" Dannie airily waves her hands as though making a point. "Anyone can look after a baby. I thought you'd find a nanny or something."

"Bloody hell!" Sean almost chokes the words out.

"And I hadn't any choice." She shrugs her shoulders, "She's half you. There wasn't anyone else I could trust with her. Even if you didn't look after her yourself, and I wasn't expecting you to, I knew you'd do the best for her once you'd checked you were the biological father. And you did check, didn't you?" She pauses then scoffs, "Mind you, one look should have told you. The one chance I get to have a mini-me, and she looks just like her bloody father! Just my damn luck."

I think both Sean and I have identical incredulous looks

on our faces, but it's Sean who asks her, "Do you give a flying fuck about her at all?"

Now she gets angry, showing the most emotion she has so far. "Of course I do. I love her. She's my daughter." Leaning forward, she puts her head in her hands and just for a second I see her mask slipping. "I can't have her taken from me. I can't have her used against me. She needs to be protected, removed from danger. I sent her to the one person who I thought would keep her safe." Unbelievably, a tear drops from her eye. "It doesn't matter what happens to me, so long as my beautiful baby girl is safe."

Sean leans forward, legs open, his hands clasped between his knees. His eyes are fixed firmly on the beautiful, but frosty woman in front of us. When he speaks, his voice seems to have dropped an octave lower. "Why would she be taken from you? Why wouldn't she be safe with you?"

As though mesmerised, Danielle stills, her face fixed on his. "I'm a thief," she starts, and from her tone, I'm certain this is the point when we'll start to get the truth. "I stole something that I shouldn't have done." She breaks off, and for a brief moment, again inspects her perfectly manicured nails, picking at some invisible dirt. Then she looks up, her look sharp and certain. "I didn't know I had it at first, it was in a wallet I'd appropriated from another man. An innocent looking thumb drive."

As though he's one step ahead Sean frowns. "You looked at what was on it?"

"It wasn't difficult," she shrugs. "It was encrypted, but

the idiot had written the password on a piece of paper tucked behind some bank notes."

"And…?"

Now she slants her body toward him, her voice lowered, and I crane forward to hear. "I hit the jackpot, Sean. It's the hierarchy within Amir al-Farhi's organisation."

"Jesus H Christ!" Sean runs his hands through his hair, and I sit up and pay attention. Amir al-Farhi is *the* number one terrorist wanted all over the world and responsible for horrendous attacks from the USA, Australia and the UK, to his native Arabia. "What have you done with it? Where is the information now?" Sean quick-fires questions.

"I was going to sell it to the highest bidder, of course."

"You're fucking what?" Sean almost jumps out of his seat. It's the first time I've seen him this angry.

Another shrug. "Well, a girl's got to make a living."

It's at that point I realise the charismatic exterior hides something rotten inside. If she's telling the truth, the information she found could save lives if it was put into the proper hands.

Rubbing his hands over his face, Sean cups his chin and throws her a look of utter disbelief. "Who are you dealing with?"

"The UK's SIS or MI6 as it used to be called and the CIA. The DGSC here in Paris, of course. They have a particular interest. There are a few other agencies fishing around."

"They're not going to buy it from you." Sean's shaking his head at her naivety.

"Well, I know that now!" Danielle smiles a strange, sad

smile. "Once I understood the true value of what had come into my possession I decided to give it away for free. Don't worry, I've made sure I've got it to the right people. I'm a thief, but not a bad person."

With a sigh of relief that she'd done the right thing, even though it might not have been her first decision, I see Sean relax a little. Then he asks, in his very serious voice. "Who did you give the information to? And who, exactly, are you in danger from?"

As if she can't believe how stupid she's been she inhales in a deep breath and shakes her head. "You'll find out who I gave the details to in good time. And it's Amir al-Farhi or someone in his organisation who knows I took the thumbnail drive. I must have been caught on CCTV or something." She lets out her breath on a sigh, "The body of the man I'd taken the wallet from turned up on the bonnet of my car. It was obviously a message, and I've been running ever since."

"Why haven't you gone to your Embassy for protection?"

She shakes her head and gives a small laugh, "I've not exactly got a clean record in the States. If I go back, I'm likely to be arrested."

"Surely that's preferable to being dead?" I butt in, speaking bluntly.

Sean's considering her carefully, and I wonder what he's thinking. She's the mother of his child, but that pedigree is nothing to shout home about. We're all quiet for a couple of minutes, then he starts the interrogation again. "When you sent Mollie to me, you did so completely anonymously. You regularly change the way you look, your identity, and you're clever. If you hadn't wanted me to find you, I probably wouldn't have done. Or not so fast, anyway. So why, Danielle? Why bring me to Paris to meet you?"

"I didn't care who you were that night, you could have been anyone. But I'd kept your business card with the details, just in case they ever came in useful. When I needed someone to keep Mollie safe, I discovered more about the organisation you work for. Grade A. If I'm to stay alive I need the very best and Grade A's reputation is second to none. Don't worry, I can pay for your services." Brazenly, she summons the waiter and requests another glass of champagne. I can't understand it; this woman is on the run from one of the most frightening and dangerous men in all the world with an organisation so large it's impossible to say who might be a member of it, and she's sitting here in the open, flaunting herself.

"With your track record, I doubt Grade A would want to offer you protection," Sean speaks calmly, and a sense of relief floods over me that he doesn't feel any personal responsibility for her, otherwise I think he'd be handling this differently. "The partners might want to hand you over to the authorities."

"The information I've found will save lives, Sean," she justifies herself succinctly, "That will count for something."

Again, he stares at her, his eyes darkening as he contemplates. Then he gets to his feet. "I'm going to ring Ben Carter, my boss, Danielle, and see what he thinks of this fuck up of a situation." He frowns, "I can't promise anything." He nods at me while he speaks to her, "Wait here until I come back."

"I just need somewhere to be safe until this all dies down, that's not too much to ask. Surely there's a safe house somewhere and a bodyguard you could assign to me?" And I wonder whether she'd expected Sean would offer himself and that they'd end up playing happy families. *But that could still be on the cards if Ben suggests it!*

Shaking his head, Sean walks away from the table, leaving us alone.

I've sat here listening to the conversation in disbelief, but not contributing much. She stole sperm from Sean which resulted in Mollie and never intended to tell him he had a daughter. How could she do that to a man? Then, on discovering vital information on a terrorist organisation, she decided to try to profit from it. In my view, she deserves everything she's brought on herself.

"You don't like me, do you?"

Realising she's addressing me directly, it takes me no time at all to respond with the truth, "To be brutally honest, no."

Again she summons the waiter, and orders more champagne, then, palming her hand over the top of the glass which has just been placed in front of her she passes it across to me. "Here, drink this. You look like you need it."

I'm not one to turn down a glass of the very expensive elite sparkling wine, I mean, it's not every day a girl like me gets to partake, so I take the offered drink, throwing a quick nod of thanks.

"You like him, don't you?" Again, it's a straightforward question.

I don't want to get into this with her, whether I do or not is none of her business. Ignoring the enquiry, and raising the glass to my lips I take a long sip.

"Does he know you want him?" she asks, curiously.

Bloody hell, the bubbles in the champagne are making the alcohol go straight to my head. I try to open my mouth to refute her assumption that there's anything between the father of her child and myself, but my tongue seems stuck to the roof of my mouth. She's saying something else, but my hearing's gone fuzzy, and when I try to concentrate, her face is shimmering in the light, colours radiating out like a kaleidoscope. I comprehend too late what's happening. *She's bloody gone and drugged me!*

CHAPTER 18

Sean

At last, she starts to stir, and her hand goes to her forehead. I'd had to carry her up to our suite, ignoring the curious looks thrown at me as I'd taken her out of the bar. I leave her alone for a few minutes, and this is what happens. Christ!

Shaking my head in exasperation, I cross over to the bed and gently put my hand on her shoulder. She jumps at my touch then rolls her head as though in pain, but I find it hard to summon sympathy. When she opens her eyes, I haven't the patience to wait any longer.

"What the fuck happened, Nessa? I come back from making a five-minute call to find you looking like you drank yourself under the table."

Her pupils are dilated, and her eyes are unfocused as she blinks rapidly. Then, sitting up too fast, she groans, pressing her fingers to her temples. Her face is a bit green, not a good shade with her colouring.

"Are you going to puke?"

She takes a moment to consider it then, very slowly and carefully, moves her head from side to side, and at last she finds her voice, it's hoarse as though her mouth is dry. "She drugged me. It must have been in the glass of champagne she gave me."

And she thinks she's going to make a field agent? Shit! "How the fuck did she manage to do that?" Tunnelling my hands through my hair in disbelief, I throw her an incredulous look.

"I don't know!" she huffs out. "If I'd seen her doing it, then I wouldn't have drunk the bloody drink, would I?" She's recovered sufficiently to manage a glare. "But why on earth did she do it?"

"So she could disappear." I respond, drily. "Again." I'd returned to find Nessa slumped on the table and no sign of Danielle. Fuck, I thought Nessa had picked up I wanted her to make sure she stayed put. Ryan would have done.

"But you were trying to see if Grade A could help her. Why wouldn't she wait to hear the outcome of your chat with Ben?"

I'll allow that she's still somewhat out of it and incapable of putting it together right now, so I give her the answer, "In case we weren't going to help. And I returned with a gendarme or two in tow."

As she swings her feet off the edge of the bed, she whimpers. "My head hurts."

Suspecting this would be the case I've already got a couple of paracetamol ready and I hand them over with a glass of water. She rewards me with the beginnings of a smile.

"Thank you." Downing the tablets, she exhales, "I've cocked up again, haven't I?"

It's so obvious, there's no need for me to comment on her observation. Pleased to see her colour is starting to return to normal, I decide to bring her up to date. "Ben's sending Hunter."

She takes a second to digest that information. "Hunter Wright works for the government; he's SIS." She knows as well as I do that that's only supposition. Ben would know, but we underlings aren't privy to the same level of detail as our employers. But we've got our suspicions, and it's interesting that when raised, the suggestion has been met with a laugh, but never actually confirmed or denied. But if he is working undercover at Grade A, it makes him the perfect man for the job.

"She's a criminal." As she says the words, she glances at me as if seeing how I'm taking it.

I just lift my chin. "That's most certainly the case, but all she's admitted to is petty theft." I walk across to the window and look out at the view of Paris spread before me. "Ben agrees with me that there's more to it than she's saying. I can understand her not appearing on Amir al-Farhi's Christmas card list, but if what she's said is true, and she's presumably put the information in the hands of the right authorities, why would he put effort into coming after just one woman? He got his revenge on his incompetent soldier."

"But who did she give the thumb drive to? She didn't tell us that."

My brow creases, I've been giving some thought to that too.

"She doesn't act like a frightened woman, Sean."

"No, I noticed that." Danielle had been remarkably calm for someone whose life was in danger.

"She's something more than an over-privileged bored heiress."

I look at her sharply, pleased her mind was working the same way as mine. I'd come to that conclusion, too. Danielle needs to enlist the help of Grade A, but exactly in what capacity I don't yet know. I suspect it's not just to provide her with protection. And now she's disappeared. Again.

Of course, I've already checked her room at the hotel while waiting for Nessa to come around. She's skipped without paying her bill, and all her luggage has gone, and, despite Kadar's assurances hotel security would make sure she didn't run, she seems to have got out from under their noses. But we hadn't finished our conversation, and something in my gut tells me we'll be hearing from her again very soon.

"How's your head?"

Nessa looks up ruefully at my change of subject. "Throbbing."

A knock at the suite door interrupts our discussion. Leaving her bedroom, I cross the living area and check through the security peephole to see who could have come calling. For the second time today I see a man in the hotel livery standing outside. My hand goes to the gun that I've slipped into the back of my waistband as I cautiously turn the lock and pull the door open. He hands me a large bouquet of flowers. I exchange them for another handful of euros, and he disappears after throwing me a nod.

Taking the flowers inside I carelessly place them on the side table, knowing it will be whatever has accompanied them that's going to be more important. Opening the envelope, I extract a card, and then cannot suppress a laugh. Danielle's got a sense of humour. I read it again, and then throw an amused look over to the woman who's just stepping out of her bedroom, wondering how she's going to take the invitation, or whether it might be better for me to go on my own.

"What is it?" Nessa's staring at the flowers. Even I have to admit they are a rather remarkable display. "Who sent the bouquet?"

Waving my hand in the direction of the stunning blooms I hold up the card. "Danielle hasn't wasted any time. She's arranged a new meet with us."

Nessa's eyes narrow as she homes in on the invitation in my hand. "Where? When?"

I snort. "Somewhere with excellent security and where the police would stick out like a sore thumb." I pause, and can hardly suppress a chuckle as I ask her, "How do you fancy going to a BDSM club tonight?"

You can read a lot in someone's expression, often things they don't want you to see. Interested to see her reaction I'm studying her carefully. I'm not sure what I was expecting, but the flash of excitement takes me by surprise. Oh, fuck. She was jealous of Zoe, and I hadn't missed her reaction to Danielle earlier. Perhaps going to an intimate club with a woman who can't hide that she's got the hots for me is not the best idea in the world. I wait for her answer, hoping that she'll find some excuse not to go. The Parisian BDSM club we've received invitations to is not for the faint-hearted.

She brushes her hand across her forehead as though trying to wipe a residual headache away. Whether she's succeeded or not, I don't know, but she surprises me when she looks up with a determined expression and asks just one question, her voice husky and full of anticipation. "Where can I buy fetwear?"

Oh! Shit!

My mouth drops open, and immediately my cock jerks at the thought of seeing this woman dressed in the minimalistic clothing of my lifestyle. Wanting to object in order to keep my sanity, instead I find myself pointing her in the direction of the concierge to get the information she needs. Half of me is hoping she'll have second thoughts and decide not to accompany me—having issued the invitation I can't very well retract it—and the other half hopes she doesn't. Going to a BDSM club with a woman who, though she doesn't know it, with just one look can command my dick to stand to attention is not the best idea I've ever had. I certainly wouldn't be harbouring such thoughts about Ryan or another work colleague. If I play this wrong, I could end up giving her totally the wrong impression. And Ben would certainly fire me if he knew what was going through my mind. Fuck Ben, why did you put me in this situation?

It's a couple of hours before she returns to the suite—heaven knows what she's been up to. Returning in the middle of the evening, she slides into her room carrying some bags, unable to meet my questioning eyes, and doesn't emerge until shortly before it's time to leave. And then she's wearing a trench coat which leaves everything to the imagination. Despite my misgivings, I'm curious about what she's chosen to wear. If I was her Dom

I'd make sure I approved before we set off, but I'm not, and she will never be wearing my collar. Even enjoying her obvious assets for just one night would be a mistake of the greatest magnitude.

Deliberately damping down my growing attraction, I decide my best course of action is to help her. If she's determined to play, perhaps I'll try and find her someone suitable to initiate a novice sub and help her negotiate a scene. And I'll certainly be matching her up with a Dom. Nessa's a sub, through and through, whatever she thinks. A blind man would be able to see that. But taking advantage of the dungeon we'll be visiting, will have to wait on the back burner until after we've had our meet with Danielle. Tonight is all about business. And business always comes before pleasure.

She doesn't open her coat or give me the slightest hint of what she's wearing underneath until we've entered the club, and she checks in her outer clothing. And that's when I discover what she's been hiding under the black gabardine.

It stuns me. Even under her dowdy clothes, I'd already noticed she had a decent figure, but the shiny black leather corset, cinched tight, narrows her waist and enhances the size of her breasts so they almost spill out of the top. Too shy to wear a thong, black leather boy shorts cover her well-formed arse, and dark fishnet stockings attached to the red suspenders show off her slender legs and thighs. To complete her outfit, she's wearing shiny black boots which come to just above her knees, the high heels making her legs go on forever. Her striking auburn hair left loose and long flows around her shoulders, complimenting the sombre colour of her outfit. She might be dressed as a Domme, but her attitude is that of a nervous newbie sub.

Taking her hand, I lead her into the club proper, feeling her pulse quicken and seeing her mouth drop open in apprehension as the scenes taking place around us immediately signify this is not a fancy dress party. Her eyes settle on me, widening slightly, a silent plea for help.

Suppressing a sigh, I realise this was inevitable; I'll have to take her under my wing, take responsibility for her while we're here. She's too innocent to be left alone. Telling myself I'm regretting not being here with Ryan, while acknowledging a certain part of me is intrigued by the woman at my side, I eye up my surroundings. There's a discreet table in the corner of the bar area, away from the main activities going on, but visible enough so Danielle will see us, and which will afford me with a good view of the dungeon. I guide her across to it with my hand on the small of her back, the slight contact enabling me to feel her jump as she hears screams of pain and pleasure echoing around the dungeon.

Glancing round, I see my target is nowhere in sight. We're early, so I've got some time to address the matter at hand. "I need to talk to you," I tell Nessa, pulling her chair out so she can sit. I take the opposite side of the table, my back to the wall.

"It's not what I thought," she whispers, her voice breathy as though she's having difficulty getting air into her lungs. It's clear she's out of her depth, and also apparent she's forgotten the reason why we're here. She's sparing no thought, not even looking around for the woman we're supposed to be meeting.

I attract the attention of a waitress and order some non-alcoholic drinks. Then I stare intently at my companion, and sigh, "Nessa, what do you think you're going to do, here? Apart from meeting Danielle, of course." As I add the last, she looks at me in consternation. I was right. In her excitement at coming to a BDSM club, she has forgotten why we're here. "You've dressed the part." I wave at her costume, "And you wear it well." I give her the slight compliment while thinking she looks like a sheep in wolf's clothing. "Are you planning on playing tonight? You certainly look ready for it."

The way her shoulders lift and fall tell me she hasn't thought this through at all.

"Okay." I pay the waitress, and then turn back to Nessa, knowing I'm going to have to educate her about a few things as she's never been to a club like this before. "You see that area over there?" I point to a circle of couches, just to the left of the bar area. When she looks in the right direction, I continue, "That's where the unattached subs wait to catch the eye of a Dom or Domme who interested in playing with them."

She shrinks a little in her seat, as though trying to hide, then asks, "Would you sit there? If you wanted to play with a Domme? If we weren't waiting for the meet, of course."

I laugh loudly, appreciating the way she's tried to bring it back to business, and then answer her loaded question which was aimed to see if I'm going to be playing as a sub tonight. "No." My answer is emphatic.

"Why not?" Is that disappointment I discern in her tone?

Keeping my eyes scanning the dungeon on the lookout for Danielle, I understand I'm going to have to set her straight. I know she's aware of the rumours about me, that anything goes, but in truth, I'm not quite as liberal as gossip would make out. Especially after what happened to me last time I played a submissive role.

"It's true I will occasionally bottom, but only in limited circumstances, and not with just any Top." As I say the words it occurs to me she might have had expectations of playing with me. My cock twitches at the thought, and as I shift myself in my chair, it's harder to remain immune to her than I hoped.

If anything, her hazel eyes are opening wider. I hadn't appreciated how beautiful they were before. Lost in their depths, I'm only just aware she's asked another question. I have to ask her to repeat it.

"If we have time, will you be playing as a Dom tonight then?"

As I give my eyes a break from checking the room, I spare another glance for my companion, taking in her lily white breasts trying to spill from the restraints of the corset, her wide, eager looking greenish brown eyes, the freckles on her face that refuse to be entirely hidden by make-up and I suddenly know that there's only one person that I'd like to play with tonight. And the role I want to take is certainly not that of a bottom. Picking up my drink I lean back in my chair, my long legs stretching under the table, crossed at the ankles, squashing any expectations in that direction right away.

"I'm a Dom, Nessa. We call it play, but I don't play at being what I essentially am. Through and through, that's what you get with me, love. I can't turn it off and on at will."

"But you're a switch!"

It's such a brash statement; it makes me laugh. I watch her flinch as a loud crack of a whip lands close by, and briefly, I wonder what her back would look like with light welts across it, making a bet with myself that her fair skin would redden easily. Cupping my hands around my face, I run them down my skin, smoothing across my short beard. "During my training to be a Master Dom I acted as a sub and found I didn't dislike it. There's something intensely satisfying giving up control over your pleasure to someone else. With the right Domme, and in the right situation, I still bottom occasionally." In truth, there's only really one Domme I play with, Mistress Beatrix. There's nothing sexual between us, but she can launch me into subspace like a rocket.

"But you subbed for a Dom when Jon Tharpe's wife was kidnapped." She's starting to look uncertain, making me think she'd thought she had me pegged and is now finding out she's been reading me wrong.

"I'm happy to top men, as well as women, or to play a third in either role. I'm versatile, and I don't have many boundaries. If you recall, that case meant weeding out Mia's stalker, who we suspected was a wannabe Dom. I volunteered to try to find him." I know she'd typed up the transcript of the verbal report I'd given after the event. But what she doesn't know is the trouble I've had coming to terms with the aftereffects of that occasion.

She obviously remembers all the details, "You had oral sex with him."

She's got to get a bit freer with the language, if she's serious about getting into the lifestyle, so I correct her. "I sucked his cock."

"But how could you do that?" She's frowning, and her eyebrows pull down into a delightful V that my hands itch to smooth away.

Her question makes me glower as I remember. It hadn't been a particularly pleasant occasion, but I had done what I had to do and made the most of it. It had turned into one of the worst situations in my life when the wannabe Dom had ignored my safeword, and I still carry the scars, both mental and physical. But Nessa doesn't need to know about that. So, I restrict myself to just one part of it, and tell her with a chuckle, "I used one of my condoms, love. It was strawberry flavoured. Just like sucking a lollipop."

Now her mouth falls open, she doesn't know whether to be disgusted or laugh. Then a smile starts to spread over her face, and a giggle escapes her. "You're awful, Sean!"

"Don't knock the goods until you've tried them," I send back, raising an eyebrow in question. Quickly her head snaps away, and she's taking in her surroundings again, though, at this point, I think if Danielle walked in ringing a bell she wouldn't notice. I examine her again. She's dressed as a Domme, with absolutely no fucking idea of how to handle the fire she could end up playing with.

Suppressing my overwhelming desire to take charge and rid her of that corset that's pushing her ample breasts up toward her neck, I decide to talk to her about where we are, and get my mind off what I want to do.

"This is what's known as a 'vanilla gateway' club, Nessa." I begin, and wait to check I've got her attention. "Anyone can come in off the street and have a go at playing here."

I've caught her interest. "You say that like it's a bad thing."

"Not necessarily," I give a quick shake my head in rebuttal, "It's somewhat freeing how people can play out their kink, can have an experience that they might not otherwise feel able to explore."

"I don't understand what you're saying." As she comments, she looks around her. I follow the direction of her eyes with mine so I can see what she's looking at. Several spanking benches are in use, a couple of St Andrews crosses, naked men and women of all sizes and ages are being led around in collars. An overweight, middle-aged man is crawling behind his mistress, barking and pretending to cock his leg. As he does so, he receives a belt from a crop on his backside. He's led on a few more steps then stops to do it again. It's a bit much for Nessa, and I sense she's not into puppy play as she turns her eyes back to me.

I double check that my target's still not made an appearance, and then expand, as much as to fill in the time as anything. "People come to clubs like this to explore, to feel free to do whatever they want." I wave my hand toward the alert looking monitors either propping up the walls in readiness or walking around inspecting the scenes. "Club Tiacapan caters to the more serious BDSMers, people who are sincere about the lifestyle, rather than just wanting to get their kicks on a Saturday night."

Her eyes narrow in thought. "What do you mean?" She thinks. "You said you were trained to be a Dom, Sean," breaking off she waves her hands around, indicating the variety of people around us. "Has everyone here been trained?"

"At Tiacapan all the Doms will have been. Here? Some perhaps, but most at this club are just dipping their toes in the water to see whether they like it. If they do, they may go on to get trained, or just continue to play in places like this."

"So why bother to be trained?"

Exhaling a frustrated breath, I know I'm not explaining this properly, and it occurs to me how little knowledge she has. If she's serious about exploring the lifestyle further, she needs to understand. "BDSM should be all about safe, sane, and consensual. While this place isn't particularly fussy, and allows people who maybe want to experiment for just one night, a true Dom or Domme will have undergone training, or at least mentoring, before attracting a play partner."

This makes her sit forward. "Why?"

"You're aware of safewords?"

She nods, and looks scornful. "Of course."

I grimace, nearly everyone in the world is now if they've

read *that* book or watched the film. Some think that's the be all and end all of the knowledge required. "Along with safewords, a Dom wielding a whip, or a cane or flogger should understand the human body, so they know which parts to avoid otherwise they might cause permanent damage or scarring. A Dom has to understand anatomy, what areas to avoid during a whipping and what toy can go where or not. He should also know rudimentary psychology and should be able to recognise triggers that might initiate a psychotic episode. A good Dom or Domme can read their sub—it's the only way to make the experience good for them, and the sub's pleasure is the ultimate goal.

"Look at the people around you, really look at them." Discreetly, I point to the spanking bench in the furthest corner of the room. Even from here I can see the sub is tense, not relaxing into the flogging she's receiving. The 'Dom', on the other hand, is clearly getting excited by the red marks he's leaving across her body, his erection obvious even from here. "Does that sub look like she's enjoying herself to you?"

She follows the direction I'm indicating and gives her head a quick shake, her face wrinkling in disgust. "Why's she doing it, then?"

I shrug, "Who knows? Could be her boyfriend wants to try something new, to put a spark into their love life? It could be the way many vanilla women regard sex—get the act over and done with to get on with the cuddling and aftercare that follows. My guess is she wants to make him happy. I just don't believe his focus is on her pleasure."

"He might think it is." She defends the unknown man.

"If he'd been properly mentored, he'd know," I retort.

As her brow creases in confusion, I think, at last, she understands she's not ready for this, and that the lifestyle is far more complicated than she had expected. I find myself longing to go around the table, take her in my arms and show her how a Master Dom treats his sub, as it dawns on me it would be absolutely no hardship at all to divest her of her clothes and sink my cock into her soft depths. Her breasts call out for me to fondle them, to find out what colour her nipples are, to take them into my mouth and suck them. Would she like the bite of pain as I sink my teeth into them, or twist them? Nipple clamps decorated with rubies would surely complement her complexion, or perhaps emeralds to match her eyes and a chain running in between so I could tug it to keep her attention on me. Her arse would colour up well beneath my hand, I'm certain. And would her freckles become even more prominent as she comes beneath my hand, my mouth, my cock? Shifting awkwardly in the chair, I finally admit to myself that despite my best intentions, if she keeps on like this, I'm not going to be able to keep this relationship purely professional for very much longer.

But how to get over the biggest obstacle of all? She's interested, *intrigued* by BDSM, but something is preventing her wanting to give up control. That's why she's presenting herself as a Domme. How do I get her to see what she is? Submissive right down to her very bones.

A man approaches our table, I glance up, my quick appraisal showing I've never seen him before. He's looking at me, and my companion, as though checking he's got the right people. Nessa stands out with her long red locks, so I'm not surprised when he greets me with a question, "Master Sean?"

I nod, keeping my face neutral.

He holds out an envelope. "This was left at reception earlier this evening, with strict instructions to give it to you at this particular time." His face splits into a grin. At this type of place anything goes, and as far as he knows, the contents could be instructions for a scene.

Taking it, I thank him, knowing he'll be just the messenger and there'll be no point questioning him. Closing my eyes for a second, I realise in all probability the contents will explain Danielle is not going to be putting in an appearance tonight. Nessa's looking at me curiously as I slit the envelope open and slide out the single card, idly noting it's the same stationery that came with the flowers. The message is simple, just six short words. *Check your wallet. Enjoy your sub.*

My wallet. Has Danielle been up to her tricks again? Reaching into my back pocket, I'm at least relieved to find it's still there. Pulling it out, I check the contents. My euros are safe inside, my bank cards and driving licence, and a handful of condoms that weren't there before. That's curious enough. Condoms? Well, if they're from Danielle I certainly won't be using those. Nothing's been taken.

Nessa's watching me closely, fidgeting as she tries to curb her curiosity. There must be more to it. Surely she hadn't stolen my wallet just to give me her special brand of condoms? To check it more thoroughly, I empty the contents onto the table and then feel inside the wallet. At first, my fingers trace the lining, and then I find it isn't quite empty. A tiny USB drive has got wedged at the bottom. My fingers trace it for a second.

I've got it to the right people.

As Danielle's words come back to me, I close my eyes in horror knowing exactly what I've been given. Looking around I see no one looking at me, no one seeming to take any interest in a Dom and his sub sitting at the table.

Putting everything back into my wallet, I cast my eyes at Nessa, keeping all expression from my face. *She hasn't noticed I've found something's been added to the contents.* Quickly, I run through my options. Hunter's arriving tomorrow. I can't do much about it now except accept I've been made an unwitting target. There's no point worrying the woman sitting beside me, and from what I've seen, if she knew the danger we could be in, one look at her face would give everything away. The worry would be visible to anyone who cared to notice.

"What is it?" Now she's leaning forward, her fingers gesturing, asking to see the paper in my hands.

I read it again, my gaze focusing on the last three words.

I've been set up. Fuck knows what conversation the girls had had after I'd left them alone, or perhaps she hadn't even needed to speak. Nessa had made her attraction to me obvious, and now Danielle's pushing her into my arms. The note and condoms make that clear. Not that I hadn't already made the decision to get her there. Crafty, crazy bitch. I can help but bark a laugh.

"What is it?" Nessa repeats, leaning over the table, her

inquisitiveness making her forget the precarious nature of her costume, and that it's almost possible for me to see the half-moon of the tops of her areolae. *So that's their colour!* I can't wait to see more. I just say, "She's not coming."

Her mouth opens in feigned disappointment; she can't hide her pleasure that our evening won't be interrupted. I suppress a scowl, the whole reason for us being here has decided not to turn up, and my colleague should be disappointed. Perhaps I need to shoulder some of the blame. Once again, she's got me onto topics that should have been avoided like the plague if we're going to continue to be professional toward each other. And right now, keeping our relationship to work matters is the last thing on my mind.

It's time for us to leave, initiating her into BDSM in this environment would be like throwing her into the deep end of a pool without armbands. She hasn't understood anything I've been telling her. A smile slowly spreads across my face as the answer comes to me. A demonstration is worth more than any words. Finishing my hardly touched drink in one long swallow, I stand and hold out my hand across the table. "Let's go back to the hotel, Nessa." The depth of my voice makes it only just this side of a command and my slight breathlessness carries a promise. I wait, arm outstretched, as I wonder what she will do.

CHAPTER 19
Vanessa

I don't know what I expected when we came to the club tonight, but I didn't anticipate anything like what I'd walked into. Hell, of course I know BDSM is about whips, collars, and spankings but somehow, I thought it would be more polite, not people walking around semi-naked, or even completely bare. And some having full-on sex in plain sight. It's overwhelming, and I don't know which way to look.

Having pestered Sean to bring me, having spent time choosing the right outfit to wear, and having got up the guts to enter the door behind him, now I don't know what to do. To be honest, I've seen so much more than I ever imagined, not that I had known what to envision. Men and women, all shapes and sizes doing heaven knows what; and the sounds! Christ, I can't stop myself flinching as I hear a whip fall. Instead of being turned on, I find I'm getting less and less aroused and unable to picture myself in the role I thought I'd relish. *Is it possible to be dominant but not want to whip or spank someone, or want to lead them around on a leash?* Surely there must be some other way of taking the Domme role? *Maybe I'm just in the wrong club.*

While Sean's been talking to me, something odd has happened; he seems to have become a different person.

The sights and sounds of the dungeon do nothing to move me, but my companion's deep voice, full of authority, seems to have a link straight down to my girly parts. It's been difficult to keep my mind on the reason why we're here, and impossible to be disappointed when at last Sean receives a note and it becomes clear we'll be conducting no business here tonight. Which means I won't have to see *her* again. *Or worse, see him play with her.* Yes, that had been my deepest fear.

Then, when he stretches his hand across the table to me, somehow with a gesture not expected from a work colleague. His eyes are slightly dilated and his breathing has quickened, the signs letting me know I'm not misreading the situation. He's not just suggesting we go back to the hotel; he's issuing me an invitation into his bed.

I hesitate before giving into the temptation, my womb clenching, my palms feeling sweaty. I should turn him down. *But this is what I've been dreaming of since the first day he joined Grade A, and I was introduced to him.* Ok, he might be the most fantastic experience I've ever had in bed, and let's face it, it wouldn't be hard to beat my previous partners, but knowing his track record, it will only be for a very limited time. *And how will I be able to work with him afterwards?* No, this would feature among one of the biggest mistakes in my life if I go through with it. *But it's Sean. How can I turn him down?*

Swallowing rapidly, I try to get my mouth to work, to make a comment letting him know I'm ready to leave the club, but will not be joining him in his room. To dismiss him succinctly so he doesn't offer again. I can't jeopardise my career for a one night stand.

But as I find my voice to put him in his place, the words that come out are at odds with my decision, and as I tell him in an embarrassing squeak, "Okay," my hand reaches out across the table to take his. It's so much bigger than mine, his fingers encase my palm with room to spare. Glancing down to where we're joined I focus on the size of his thumb, if what I've read is true he's not going to disappoint me tonight. *Fuck! What the hell am I thinking?*

I try to get back on track, "Danielle?"

Pulling me from my seat, he simply shrugs and says dismissively, "*She's* not here tonight." The stress he gives to the words makes it clear he means neither in the physical or mental sense. She's not who he's thinking of right at this moment. He means his focus is all on me. *Me!* I don't know whether I should be honoured or terrified.

Hand in hand we leave the club. He summons a taxi; it pulls up immediately. As if he doesn't want to give me a chance to have second thoughts, he refrains from talking during the short journey back to where we're staying, but doesn't break the physical contact. I'm glad he's not asking me for conversation, with thoughts whirling through my mind as fast as they are, who knows what the fuck would come out if I had to speak? Something highly embarrassing, I'm sure. At least the silence has given me time to think, and by the time we reach our destination, I have it all clear in my head. I know what I want from him. *I know exactly how I'm going to play this.*

He hovers between the doors to our rooms, giving me a

choice. Swallowing rapidly, knowing I've got to start taking control, I find my key card and once the door's open, step toward the room I'd taken as mine. Striding inside, I cross over to the chair and unceremoniously dump my bag and coat there then turn, seeing he's followed me into the room and has shut the door exactly as I had expected. Without hesitation or giving him time to speak, I take charge. As a Domme should.

"Strip!" I snap out my one word instruction whilst placing a hand on my hip as I wait for him to obey, stamping down the rogue question, *what the hell would I do if he didn't?*

"I suspected that might be the way you want to play it." His voice is soft, slightly amused, but not offended.

Slowly, decadently, he puts both hands over his head, grasping his t-shirt at the neck, and pulling it up and off, exposing his lean, muscular chest as he does so. Sean's not got the muscles of a body builder, but his well-toned pecs still show his strength. His jeans hang low on his hips, and there's a delicious V and trickle of darker blond hair that clearly points the way downwards to where I so want to explore. In fact, I have an overwhelming desire to drop to my feet in front of him, to pull out his cock and taste him. Rapidly, I straighten my body. What the heck? I've never performed oral sex before, so why the hell would I want to now? Thinking of that, I've never received it before, either. Perhaps Sean could… Fuck, Van. Putting my mouth *there?* It's dirty! Yuck. Sure, I've acted out both ways round in my fantasies, but in real life? Just no.

He throws a look of challenge at me as his hand rests on

the top button of his jeans. I jerk my head, indicating he should continue. With his eyes fixed on mine, he flicks the first button through the hole, and then the next. There are four in all, and my breathing shallows with each one he opens. Finally, his jeans are undone, and I can hardly catch any breath at all. He's commando, he's fully erect, and the size of his thumbs hadn't lied. Jesus! What am I expected to do with *that?*

My tongue skims around my mouth, all but getting stuck on my very dry teeth as I try to get sufficient moisture to speak. Knowing I'd be able to manage little more than a squeak, I resort gesturing, letting him know he should remove the rest.

Falling to one knee with a grace unexpected from a man, he removes one shoe and sock, and then the other. Then, slightly more awkwardly, favouring his recovering leg, he stands and slides off his jeans. I never understood watching a man undress could be so sexy before and, embarrassed, I feel a rush of arousal making the boy shorts I'm wearing decidedly damp.

I've not many people to compare him to, but he tops everything in my limited experience. Even the still angry looking scars on his legs don't detract from his masculine beauty. Sean wouldn't look out of place as a nude model. I can't believe such a specimen of manhood is standing in my hotel room. Mine. I can feel my traitorous skin flushing red just looking at him. He makes the men I've been with before seem like boys. As I moisten my lips in anticipation, worry suddenly chills me. *What's he going to think of my very average body?*

Perhaps I don't need to get naked? But what next? I've got a perfect specimen of a man standing unclothed in front of me. *What the bloody hell do I do with him now?* The slight smirk on his face tells me I better make up my mind fast or I suspect he'll try to swap roles. *No bloody chance, mate!* But I take a moment to drink him in. His cock is springing up, pre-cum glistening on the tip showing he's ready for some action and, because I'm the only female in the room, it must be me that's making him ready to play. The thought makes me feel decidedly feminine. And his state of readiness shows I've probably only got seconds before he takes over the show.

The notion helps me find my voice. "Lie on the bed," I instruct, trying, unsuccessfully, to control the quiver as I speak. *I must find my Domme voice.* But the tone I've used seems to be enough as, without a pause, he complies, lying down, full length stretched out, his hands linked behind his head, his legs immodestly spread open allowing me to see his heavy sac lying beneath that enormous thick, long, prick. I try to keep my cool as I decide where to start my feast, unable to believe this man is laid out before me, mine to do with whatever I want. He's given his control completely to me. Then I remember what he'd told me in the club, the sub gives over their control, but the Domme receives their satisfaction by pleasuring their playmate. It suddenly occurs to me what an immense responsibility that is.

How should I pleasure him? *And* receive my own gratification? Hesitantly, I take a step toward him. He's looking at me curiously, expectation in his eyes. Aiming to please, I avoid the obvious appendage, not too sure what to do with that in any event, and crawl up the bed, hovering over him. Leaning down, I take a nipple into my mouth, circle it with my tongue, and suck it gently. I watch him carefully and notice his look of challenge seconds before he starts removing his hands from behind his neck.

"Keep your hands there, don't move." I can't keep my voice level, but he relaxes his arms again, doing as I asked, and there's a flicker of excitement inside me as I recognise this man truly is under my control.

Giving him as stern a stare as possible, I move to his other nipple, caressing it as I had the first. He pushes up into my mouth, but I don't know what to do. Does he want me to bite him? Won't that hurt? Uncertain, I cease my caress of his chest and instead inch up his body again, and for the first time, I brush my lips over his mouth. Oh, the times I've dreamed of kissing Sean, of our tongues dancing together. I want to taste him, but his lips are closed tight. What do I do? I try sliding my tongue against the seam of his mouth, pressing, seeking entrance until at last, he opens for me. Now I push inside his mouth and he responds, oh so gently. It's an enjoyable, but not particularly earth-shattering kiss. He's following where I'm taking him, but I don't know how to lead.

Feeling a moment's frustration, I pull myself up so I'm straddling his body and run my hands over his chest, daring to tweak his nipples gently. His eyes are twinkling, but… with amusement, arousal? I can't tell; I can't read him. Hoping it's the latter, I reach down behind me, finding his cock with my hand. Still watching his face, I close my fingers around as much of his length as I can and pulse my fist up and down. His head goes back, and he murmurs a sound which I can't translate, but I'm hoping it's one of pleasure. I pump once again and then release him.

I'm wet, and he's hard. Time to move it along and get to the main event, but he's unashamedly naked and I'm still wearing clothes. *Shit, now I've got to get undressed with him staring at me.* I haven't thought this through. What if he finds my breasts ugly? I'm not model thin, the corset is holding in a bit of excess luggage. Even though my body is more toned nowadays, due to the gruelling exercise and fitness regime I've been following, I just can't seem to get completely rid of my tummy bulge. What if he finds that disgusting? Gazing at his body, I see there's not an inch of fat on him. God, I hope I won't be a disappointment. What if his cock deflates at the sight of me? Talk about embarrassing. But even more disconcerting is the fact I'm playing the Domme, and we're not going to get much further unless I remove at least some of my clothes. Could I get away with just removing my knickers?

Oh, for goodness sake, Nessa. Stop overthinking it. There's nothing else for it! In for a penny, in for a pound. Bowing my head, not wanting to see him watching me, I move my fingers to my corset and gradually start to unlace it. Freed from their confines my C cup breasts spill out, flopping down as I remove their support. Looking down I watch them bounce, wishing they were perky, not heavy and full. I continue undoing the laces until soon my not-so-flat stomach comes plainly into view. I hear an indrawn breath, and bravely raise my head, but instead of disappointment, his eyes are dilated in appreciation, and there's a small smile on his lips. Muscles twitch in his arms, showing he's having difficulty remaining still, tethered only by my instruction and will. Confidence returns to me.

Briefly sliding off the bed, I bend over and pull off my boots, then undo the suspenders attached to my corset and push down my stockings. I suppose I could have made more of a striptease about it, but I just want to get this part done. At last, I wriggle out of my boy shorts. Not wanting to give him a chance to stare at my unshaven nether-parts I jump quickly back onto the bed, my knees falling either side of his thighs, shuffling a little awkwardly until I've positioned myself just right.

"Condom."

I feel my face burn as he has to remind me. Christ, I hope he didn't think I'd forgotten on purpose. Especially after he'd been tricked by Danielle.

"In my jeans. Not my wallet." I'm not sure why he's telling me not to use the ones he'd dropped out onto the table in the club, but it doesn't make much odds. Awkwardly clambering off the bed, I fumble in his discarded clothing until I find the item I need. Then, returning to him, I hesitantly slide it on him, fumbling, as I've never put one on a man before. He half lifts his head, then lowers it once he's checked that I've seated it right.

No more delay. Time to find out what Sean can offer me. Lifting my body a little, I take him in my hand again, and place the tip of his cock at my entrance. He's big, bigger even than I expected, and I have difficulty working the head inside. To my mortification, I realise I'm not as wet as I'd thought I was, and, while not impossible, this probably isn't going to be that comfortable for either of us.

I need him to stimulate me. But I didn't ask him. And now I'm not sure I can. I thought I could direct this, I thought I could ask for what I wanted. Unbidden a tear comes to my eye as I feel like a person at a banquet who's not allowed to sample the delicacies on offer. I'm feeling like a bloody fool.

Again, he's giving me that intense look, and all amusement has vanished from his expression. His voice deepens to an almost impossible level as he growls, "Shall we try it my way, now?"

My eyes flick to his. He didn't ask snidely, he's not laughing at me. Nor is there sympathy in his face. He looks like a man on the edge, anticipating taking control. But he's waiting for my permission. The tear rolls down my cheek as I give a slow nod, agreeing to him taking over.

He moves fast. His upper body bows upwards, betraying the strength of his abdominal muscles. One hand reaches out, taking hold of my hair at the back of my head and grasping it firmly, pulling me to him. His mouth crashes onto mine, his tongue doesn't probe politely, but pushes inside, demanding, invading, taking. *And I love it.*

Our teeth mash together as he controls the mating of our mouths. Our tongues duel together and a gnawing ache begins to grow between my legs. Just his kiss ramps up my longing. He's controlling me completely.

He ends the kiss by easing back, gently taking his lips from mine then pulls me away with a slightly painful tug on my hair, sending arrows of arousal shooting through me. I don't stop to analyse the feeling as he draws back, staring me straight in the eyes.

"What's your safeword?" His voice is deep, commanding.

Startled, it takes a second for me to understand what he's asking. "Red," I gasp out.

"Yellow for slow down, Green for good to go." He waits, but at my nod of confirmation tells me, "I need words."

"Yes."

His expression is serious as he continues, "I don't know your limits, so we'll go easy for now. But have you any weaknesses, any pain, any areas to avoid?"

Christ! What the hell is he going to do to me? I feel a gush of wetness which discomforts me. I'm naked so he must feel it too. Remembering he wants me to talk to him, I start, "No, but Sean…"

Another little tug on my hair. "I'm in charge now, and you call me Sir." He waits.

"Yes, Sir." I manage to breathe out.

Without giving me a chance to object, he flips me onto my back, reversing our positions. Now he leans over, taking hold of the stockings I'd thrown on the floor he pulls my hands together, wrapping one stocking around them. Before I can process what he's doing, he's taken the other and, linking it between my bound hands, ties it to the bedstead behind my head, testing with his fingers that the bindings aren't too tight. I tug on my restraints, but there's little give. He's got me at his mercy. The feeling both scares and excites me; my clit starts throbbing, my breath is coming in sharp pants.

He sits back on his haunches, watching me cautiously, studying my reactions and at the same time, being careful to keep his weight off me. Satisfied with what he sees, he nods once, then reverently starts using his hands as well as his eyes to explore my body.

"You really are beautiful," he says, before I have the chance to be embarrassed. He seems able to ignore the excess pounds I'm carrying, "I never guessed you were hiding such a perfect body, pet, not in those clothes you wear in the office."

It's a statement, not a question, and I'm not even sure I could have formed an answer if it was, as he inclines his body, hesitating before taking my nipple into his mouth, and breathing out, "Dusky pink. Delicious." Then his head descends, his tongue swirls, he sucks, and his teeth close hard over my peak, sending me shooting upwards as a shriek comes from my lips. He chuckles, I can feel it against my skin, and he waits, obviously able to interpret that the bite of pain has already changed into a burning warmth that causes my stomach muscles to clench. He does the same thing to my other nipple, but this time I'm prepared and grit my teeth until the pain morphs into pleasure. Heck, I'm already more turned on than ever in my life before.

Sitting back, he stares at my breasts almost worshipfully, and fondles them, his hands pushing and squeezing them together, then, with a grin, "I can't wait to get my cock in between your tits, pet. A bit of lube and it will be fucking heaven."

No one, absolutely no one, has ever spoken so dirty to

me during sex before. Thinking about it, I don't think anyone's ever said much of anything at all while we've been doing it. And Sean's not stopping there.

"I can't wait to taste you, pet. You're dripping for me, aren't you?" I'm thinking to retort that he's already had his tongue in my mouth and tasted me and protest I'm not dribbling, when he sits up and moves down, getting onto his stomach and hanging his legs off the end of the bed.

"Oh!" I exclaim, suddenly aware just what he's about to do. In vain I try to move my legs together, but he easily holds them apart. As I continue to wriggle, he slaps me lightly directly on that bundle of nerves which have only ever had gentle treatment before. He's actually slapped me. "Ow!"

"Keep still. I want to look at your cunt."

He's said *that* word! But somehow, it doesn't seem derogative from him. And he wants to look at it? Again, I try to close my legs to hide myself from view, but his strong hands prevent me.

He continues, ignoring my efforts to evade him, "It's juicy and gushing, just for me. And I like this."

I don't have long to wonder what he's talking about now as he gently pulls my ginger pubic hair, which I keep neatly trimmed, but would never consider removing altogether.

"Love that the rug matches the curtains, babe. I like things smooth, but on you, I think we'll keep it."

We'll keep it? Like he's got a say in the matter.

I'm trying hard not to fidget. He's giving me more of a visual examination that my doctor does when I go for a smear test. I start to feel very uncomfortable, then, all at once, thoughts of humiliation fly away as he blows gently across my engorged nub; that simple breath of air almost causing me to come. Automatically I try to reach my out my hands for him, and the fact that I can't heightens my level of arousal. I'm helpless. All I can do is to let him do whatever he wants.

He chuckles softly at my efforts to encourage him, his hands on my hips, stopping my frantic movements, "Be still."

I want his fingers to touch me, so I obey. But it's not his fingers; it's his mouth sucking as his tongue caresses me at just the exact right spot. Jeez, but it feels good. Then he's replacing his tongue with his finger as he moves the former down, sweeping inside my tight channel. Now I know I'm wet, and that's just dirty. *His tongue's in my most private place!*

"No, you can't…" I start to protest.

For an answer, he proves he can, and he will. I have no option but to sink back on the pillows and experience this new sensation. Then his tongue is sweeping inside me, lapping at me. *He can't be doing that!* But he is, and it feels so good I lose any inclination to stop him.

He lifts his head only enough to rasp out the words, "Fuck, you taste good. I could lap this cream all day." His words, telling me things I never expected to hear, cause a tingling sensation in my spine. Then his fingers enter my channel again, strumming and finding a special spot I'd always been convinced was simply a myth. My leg muscles go taut, scrap that, *every* muscle in my body goes rigid, I'm so, so close. And then he closes his teeth over my nub, and I go flying, soaring, shot to the bloody moon like a rocket as the most intense orgasm I've ever experienced floods over me, wave after wave, contraction after contraction. He keeps licking, his fingers still giving an internal massage, extending my pleasure but pulling back just at that point when gratification transposes into pain, proving he knows my body as well as I do myself.

Without giving me time to catch my breath, his strong arms turn me so I'm lying on my stomach, then pull me toward him and lift so he's placed me on my knees. Gently he pushes on my shoulders. My forehead goes to the pillow, and I turn my face to one side as his hands circle on my back, soothing me as I drag much-needed oxygen into my starved lungs. As my breathing returns to normal, his palms move lower until he's caressing my arse.

Without warning, he pulls his hands away. The loud slap is the first thing I register. *He's spanked me! How dare he?* But before I can chastise him, the pain quickly followed by warmth, spreading through my body causes me to squirm and feel a new rush of wetness between my thighs. Another smack on the opposite flank. I should protest, but the feeling takes me by surprise. *I never wanted anyone to spank me!* I tug on my bindings, but I can't move. All I can do is take what he gives me, but arousal sparks anew, shocking me. *Surely I shouldn't like this?* He spanks me again, harder, both sides in quick succession, then his fingers slide across my vulva, discovering for himself the effect his actions have had.

"You're fucking dripping, pet. You like that, you dirty

girl, don't you?" I know he's smiling by the amusement in his voice.

And I can't even deny it. I know as well as him the effect he's having on me. I'm so turned on despite my satisfaction only moments ago. I feel empty, so empty I'm not beyond begging, "I need you, Sean."

"Who am I?" He's hardly trying to hide his mirth. Another spank as he continues to torture me.

"Sir! I need you, Sir!"

"You need what? You have to tell me."

"You, you inside me!" I'm almost crying with frustration.

A chuckle, although it sounds strained. "You need what, inside you? Be specific, pet."

"Your cock! I need your cock, Sir!"

Without wasting any more time, he takes his hands away from me, and I feel him adjust himself. In seconds, I feel his condom clad dick start to push into me. This time there's hardly any resistance, my copious lubrication easing the way. But I'd forgotten how big he is, and his width burns me as my insides accommodate his size but the pain is delicious, and I welcome it, pushing back into him, asking for more. He claims his way, inching in slowly until, at last, he's resting against my womb. I send up a quick prayer that there's no more of him to take.

He pauses, "You're fucking beautiful, pet. I knew you'd feel good, but you feel fucking fantastic. Your muscles are holding me as if they don't want to let me go." I can't respond, but doubt he's expecting a conversation right at this moment.

Putting one arm under my stomach he lifts me to him, and wraps his other hand tight around my hair, using it to bring my head up and back. Then, at last, he starts to move. Slowly, at first, then gaining pace until soon he's hammering in and out, exciting nerve endings I hadn't known were there. His rigid cock is banging into me, hitting my cervix with every thrust in, dragging across that special spot that so far only he has discovered on each pass. His hand on my stomach inches downwards, circling and pinching on the nerve bundle below. One more pinch and again I fly over the peak, my muscles spasm, clamping down on his cock. With a roar, he starts thrusting erratically then pumps with shorter strokes into me, filling the condom with his cum. At last, he stills, leaning over me, one arm pressed to the bed to keep his weight off my back as we both struggle to regain our breath. Gently, he releases my hair from his hold, and my head drops down.

A moment later he pulls out of me, and he undoes my hands leaving me free once more, rubbing my arms to get my circulation going. After taking a brief detour to the bathroom, he comes back and pulls me into his side, and murmurs softly into my hair, "I think I prefer my way."

I can't argue with that.

CHAPTER 20

Sean

Now I'm in trouble. I've fucked a colleague. More than that, I've dominated her. Our working relationship will never be the same again. Shit! But even while I think that, my lips curl up as I remember how explosive we were together. Eventually, that is. I huff a quiet laugh. Nessa, a Domme? I think we've successfully dispensed with that idea.

She fits well in my arms, and I don't have an immediate inclination to move as I hear her breathing gently beside me, warm exhalations against my skin. She's asleep, her head resting against my chest. I'm just lying here, one arm over my eyes, wondering how I got into this fucked up situation, and more importantly, how do I get out?

Will she be able to understand we were just playing? Like any uninvolved Dom and sub? Bloody hell, I can just imagine her reaction to that; she's no trained submissive, she's barely dipped her little toe into the lifestyle. If I walk away from her now, she'll see it as another of my famed one-night stands, and that I've taken advantage of the attraction she's had to me for some time.

But the sex was good! No, strike that. It was fucking amazing. My cock twitches to tell me it wouldn't mind round two, but I'm not waking her up. I can't take advantage of her again. Not if I want to avoid getting into this any deeper than I already am. Easing my arm out from underneath, I gently roll her to one side. Good. She's a deep sleeper and hasn't stirred. Stealthily, I slide out from under the covers and ease out of bed. I need space to think.

Returning to my room, I pull on a pair of jeans. At least the mini bar in the suite is well stocked, so I pour myself a shot of whisky before sinking onto a couch, leaning my head back and breathing out a deep sigh. Some day this has been. A day that's rocked my life in more ways than one.

Danielle has fucked me over good and proper. First with the revelations about Mollie's conception, then making me the unwilling possessor of dynamite information, and finally planting that idea of Nessa as my sub in my mind. Of course, the idea of getting inside Nessa had been creeping up on me during the time we've been thrown together, but undeniably it was the suggestion on that piece of card that had shot it up the agenda, the realisation that an outsider saw us as a Dom/sub couple, just as Kadar had assumed, that had sent me over the top. And when Nessa had submitted, had given herself into my trust in bed, well, there are no words to describe how that made me feel. Proud to be her Dom. If only for one night.

What the fuck do I do now? She's not someone I met in a club and took home with me with no expectation other than a satisfying fuck and a no strings goodbye. This is Nessa, my colleague and yes, my friend. I should have known better than to shit on my own doorstep, and now it's a mess I'll have to clear up. And as gently as I can. I don't want to hurt her, but right now I'm not sure how to rescue the situation. *What will she expect from me in the morning?*

I top up the whisky and put my mind back to my other problem. Danielle. There's something, quite a lot of somethings, that don't add up. She was so desperate to have a baby that she stole one from me. There's no other way to describe it. I know some women are so anxious to have a child with a partner, particularly as a way to keep them, that they'll go to any lengths to trick them, but a complete stranger? Should I be flattered that she chose me? She was bloody lucky that her plan worked, the odds must surely have been against it. Just bad luck for me that my swimmers took the offered escape route and she must have been fertile at the time.

But if she wanted a baby so much, and her daughter means so much to her, why wasn't a question about her welfare the first thing she asked when we met? And why was there no discussion about Mollie going back to her? So many things which only end up as more questions.

An unfamiliar emptiness assaults me as I imagine a life without Mollie. How the fuck could I have become attached to her in such a short time? But the whys and hows of it don't matter, the fact is, I have. And the one thing I can't run from is my responsibility toward my child.

How the hell could I look after a baby? Me. Dom and womaniser. My life would have to change beyond all recognition. Could I settle down, have a wife, a house with a garden for the kids to play in? That man isn't me, surely? *Nessa would probably be great with the baby.*

Shit! No Cooper, you really did not just think that, did

you? Hmm, well, she's fuck all use as a field operative, to add to all her other faults, she let herself be drugged. I wipe my hand over my face as if it will remove all thoughts of domesticity, as well as inappropriate thoughts of the woman currently asleep in bed in the next room. I know pregnancy hormones do funny things to a woman, could there be paternity hormones that act in a similar way? I give a rapid shake of my head. Settling down is not on my horizon, hell, my job doesn't lend itself to that. The job I'll be returning to just as soon as my leg is fully healed.

Mollie might go back to her mother. But apart from expressing a debatable undying love for her, does Danielle even want her back? And knowing what I do now about the woman, would I be comfortable entrusting her with my child?

The woman appears and disappears like a ghost. And what kind of person carries a sedative around in her handbag? And passes over classified information using her pickpocketing skills?

Putting down my glass, I stand and start pacing across the room and back as I think. She's a master of disguise; she speaks Arabic and French fluently and with an almost native accent as I've personally witnessed, so it's not beyond the bounds of possibility she speaks others too. I think she's American, but she could be putting on that accent for me. Could she be from Canada? Or even Australia? What the fuck do I know about her except for the fact she's carried my baby and she's wanted by the most dangerous terrorist organisation in the world? As well as several police forces. I mustn't forget about that.

And now she's put Nessa and me in danger too. I can only hope that no one knows she's passed the USB flash drive onto me. Fuck! I barely want to touch the thing knowing the information it holds. I have to get it to the right people, but right now, I don't know exactly who that would be. I'll ask Hunter's advice when he arrives.

Glancing at my watch I see it's already five in the morning, and to be honest, I could do with a couple of hours' sleep. Going to my bed, I start to pull down the covers when a sound reaches me, a stifled sobbing.

Fuck! Running my hands through my hair, I suspect I know what it means and don't have a clue how to respond. Usually, a play partner will have got up and left by now, or I'll have left them. All the people I've previously played with have known the score, but that's not true in this situation. The sobs intensify making me realise Nessa has woken up and found me gone, and is clearly upset. Do I leave her to cry alone? Or do I do the decent thing for once, and go back to her?

Oh shit, I've cocked this up. But it's too late to wish I'd kept it in my pants. She was just too tempting, the way she dressed last night, taunting me with her suggestion she was a Domme, piling on my desire to prove her wrong. And being in the dungeon with the scents and sounds of arousal surrounding us, it had been impossible to keep lewd thoughts out of my head.

And now we're both going to have to pay for our indiscretion. Mine really, I was the one who made the approach. Well, what's done is done, and all I can do is man up and deal with it.

Not knowing how or even if I can make this right, I've no option but to go to see her. Returning to the room I so recently left, I cross to the bed and switch on the lamp on the bedside table, and my eyes fall on Nessa sobbing, her fist pushed into her mouth as though to stifle her cries.

"Oh, Nessa. What have I done?" I reach down and sliding my arms under her, pull her to me. I've slipped on my jeans, but my chest is bare, and I can feel the wetness of her tears against my skin. Her bountiful breasts press into me, and my cock, with a mind all of its own, starts swelling. I shift so it's not too obvious.

Holding her to me I rock her gently, and gradually those heartrending sobs start to slow. I pass her a tissue, and she wipes the tears from her eyes.

"I'm so sorry, babe." I don't know what to say to her.

I give her some time, just letting her feel the warmth of my arms surrounding her. After a few minutes, she presses against me. "It's not on you," her voice comes out jerky as she talks through her remaining sniffles, "I could have said no."

Yeah, but I'm the more experienced one. In every way. I've never held a woman before, except to give aftercare, never wanted to cuddle. But strangely, she seems right in my arms. Manoeuvring her with me I move up until my back is against the headboard, and she's lying beside me, her head resting on my shoulder. I'm in no hurry to leave, however awkward the situation.

"You were right." Her voice sounds calmer now, "Letting go, letting you take charge. That was the most intense experience of my life." She hiccups, then bravely gives a soft chuckle, her breath tickling my skin, "I suppose I ought to look for a Dom now."

I stiffen at the thought of her looking for someone else and then tamp that thought down. Although my cock would be very willing for a repeat performance, once was a big enough mistake and one I mustn't make again. But the thought of her submitting to another man makes my hands clench. Another man feasting his eyes on that glorious body that she keeps hidden? Well, that's like a bucket of cold water being thrown over me. The idea I could walk into Club Tiacapan and see her on a spanking bench, another man turning her bum cheeks red with his hand touching that glorious skin—I'd been right, it had coloured up beautifully under my palm. I've never felt possessive of a sub before, have shared subs often enough. So why are these alien thoughts coming to me now?

Resting my chin on her head, I try to think of the right thing to say, what I should do. Is it because she's become a friend? Am I just feeling protective of her as she so obviously can't look after herself? Though I try to compose the words, I'm unable to offer to help her find a suitable man to dominate her. And what's even weirder, I'm finding it hard to walk away and return to my own room. I want to stay here, with her she fits so easily up against me. To my surprise, I search for an excuse so I can remain longer, and try to dredge up something to say.

But she gets in there first, "Sean, Do you wish you'd been involved? In Danielle's pregnancy?" she probes.

That's a difficult question. I take a moment before responding, "Yes, and no. To see a woman's belly swelling with my child, to be there at the birth? Fuck, yeah, that would be good. But Danielle? She was fun, Nessa, and we clicked for the night in bed, but that's all it was. There's something off about her, something wrong. I don't particularly like the woman now I've had a glimpse into who she is. If I were to choose the mother of my child, I wouldn't have chosen her."

She's quiet for a moment, but I can feel her head dipping up and down as she agrees with what I've told her. "Do you hate her for what she did?"

Another difficult question. I hate that she took my choice away, but… I speak my thoughts aloud, "Hate her? How could I? She gave me Mollie. Dislike the person she is? Certainly."

I feel her grow tense as I mention my child's name, something I've noticed before. "What is it, Nessa? Why don't you like me talking about her?"

Dampness on my chest is the only sign she's crying again. Placing my hand under her chin, I lift her head to face me, not surprised to see tears glistening in her eyes. She pulls away, hiding against my pectorals once again.

"Please, Sean, I'm alright now. I've just got bad taste in men; that's all." As she feels me pulling back from her, she adds, quickly, "No, I don't mean I don't like you, I do. I value our friendship, and I want to go on working with you. But as a bed partner, well, I've been there, done that, and enjoyed it. I won't be making the mistake of thinking there's anything more to it than that."

"I enjoyed it too," I tell her, softly, and it's the truth. And something cuts me inside as she takes the initiative and denies wanting a repeat performance.

She huffs a laugh; it comes out as a snuffle, "Sean, don't worry, I know what happened between us is what it is, a one night stand. You don't need to have any concern on that score. I know that's all I can expect."

All at once I feel angry. Angry with her that she thinks that's who I am, and fury at myself that she's right. And all I want to do is to lie her back down and show her that she's wrong. And that would be the biggest mistake of all.

"I want to go to sleep now, Sean. On my own." She tries to dismiss me.

I'd thought she was asleep when I left her earlier. If I'd know she was going to wake, I'd have stayed with her. The way we came together, the way she submitted to my domination, like any sub she should have had the aftercare that I should have provided. Realistically, I muse, that's the reason for her tears, she'd come down hard after an intense experience. That's all it is. And now I've comforted her; she's back to her old self again. If there can be any going back after this.

Smoothing my hand over her face, I look her in the eye. She returns my gaze steadily, as though trying to impress on me that she wants to be left alone. I'm out of my comfort zone, wanting to be her friend, if not something more. I can truthfully say I've never fucked a colleague before. She seems composed, so placing a gentle but platonic kiss to her forehead I disentangle myself from her arms and get off the bed. At the door, I turn, she gives me a nod and a little smile, and a dismissive wave of her hand so I leave.

Back in my room, I get under the covers I turned back another lifetime ago, and slip under the sheets. But it's a very long time before I fall asleep.

I wake to sounds of movement in the suite. Quickly dispensing with the morning's ablutions, I dress and go out to find Nessa unloading a trolley that's just been delivered. Anxiously, I look into her face, but apart from the betraying redness around her eyes, she's pulled herself together. And better than I. Fuck, seeing her hair, not yet tamed, framing her pretty face I have the urge to take her in my arms and kiss her senseless but clamp my hands to my sides to avoid doing anything so stupid. It would only suggest I want a relationship with her. And even if that was my desire, her dismissive words last night suggested I'd be the last man she'd look to for that.

"Hey, Sean," she glances up when she notices me, "I didn't know what you'd want, so I ordered a bit of everything." It's a typical continental breakfast with croissants and rolls, jams and fruit. Not a man's breakfast, in my opinion, give me bacon and eggs any day. But there's coffee there, and I reach for a cup and fill it.

"Thanks, Nessa." I'm about to say more when my phone pings. Looking down, I read the incoming text to find I'm saved by the bell. "Hunter's on his way. He's in the hotel now."

She's nodding, it seems her mind is as last back on the job. Moving on from last night seems to have been easier for her than I'm finding it myself.

While we're waiting for him to arrive I go into my room and discreetly place a quick call to Mum, checking up on

Mollie. I'm relieved to find she's fine, the Calpol having helped with her sore gums and she slept through the night. As I hear her gurgling in the background, I'm suddenly eager to get back to London and see her again. In such a short time, she's become the most important female in my life.

The knock on the suite door brings an end to my call, and returning to the sitting room I'm pleased to see Hunter has arrived. But not so pleased to see him giving Nessa a full-on hug, and at that moment understand why Nijad is so wary of Cara's friend. A low growl rises in my throat, but I swallow quickly to suppress it. Forcing my features into an approximation of a welcoming smile, I step forward.

"Hunter, man. Good to see you." My words make him break away from Nessa at last, and we shake hands.

"Sean, how you holding up? Heard you found this Smith woman?" He slaps me on the back in a friendly manner.

"Found her, but she got away again," I tell him, despairingly, but don't miss the look of concern Nessa throws me, so I give a little shake of my head to reassure her I'm not going to be explaining how. "She left something with me." As Nessa looks puzzled, I extract the USB drive from my wallet and hand it to him.

He turns it over in his hand examining it then his eyes flick to me, "What's this?"

Raking my hands through my hair, I explain succinctly, "Highly explosive, I imagine."

"She left it with you?" Nessa's glaring at me, "Why didn't you say something." At first, her hands go to her hips, then her fingers rise to cover her mouth as the penny drops. "Bloody hell, Sean, we could be in danger if anyone knows we've got this!"

"Look, fill me in, will you? What's on that stick?" Hunter's looking from one to the other of us, a frown settling on his face.

"Information about Amir al-Fahri's organisation, if Danielle is to be believed." As Hunter's eyes widen, and his hand opens as he stares at the tiny device in his hand as though it's going to bite him, I continue, "I wanted your input before I did anything with it, Hunter. Who the fuck do we give this to?"

"I'll need to know what's on it first," he says. He indicates the coffee, and at my nod, pours himself some then waves at the dining table, and we cross over to it. Nessa gathers some plates and pastries and puts them in the middle. Grabbing an inadequate croissant, I dip my head toward him.

He's still staring at the device he's holding as though it's a dangerous snake. "Have you looked at it, yet?"

When I shake my head, he shoots a pointed look toward Nessa. "Fancy doing what you do best, Van?"

Honestly, I swear her eyes light up in excitement and her gaze settles on the stick that he is now holding out. "Gimme." Opening and closing her fingers in the way a child might ask for a sweet, Nessa shows her eagerness to get on with the type of work she's famed for, sorting out puzzles and cracking codes.

Extracting his laptop from his briefcase, Hunter opens it and inserts the USB drive. It clicks and whirrs, and then a screen opens asking for a password. Nessa looks at me, "Danielle said she had the password."

I hadn't remembered that, and I swore under my breath. Out loud I admit, "She didn't give that to me."

With an expression that suggests she's only mildly dissatisfied at that information, without saying another word, Nessa picks up the laptop and disappears into her room.

Hunter grins as she walks away. "Don't know why she wants to work in the field," his eyes fall on the now closed bedroom door, "She's a fucking genius with brainteasers. Don't get me wrong; Nafisa is good, but nothing like Van. We're going to miss her if she permanently leaves the office to take an active role."

He's telling me nothing I don't already know, and from what I've seen so far, she's not going to hack working on the practical side, either. But I say nothing. Just give a jerk of my chin to show I agree.

Knowing there's nothing we can do for the moment, Hunter helps himself to more coffee, and a pastry. "So, Smith. What did you make of your baby mama?"

I tell him the truth, "Huh! Not a lot to be honest. She's a spoilt, privileged bitch playing games with everyone."

He's staring at me, his eyes narrowed, "You going to be happy giving your baby back to someone like that?"

As part of my sleepless night had been spent thinking about that very thing. I sigh deeply, then fill him in on my conversation with her, finishing up by saying, "She says she loves Mollie and I suppose she might in her way, but fuck, Hunter, wouldn't you have expected the woman to come out and ask how her baby is as soon as she saw me? For all she knew, I'd handed her over to Social Services."

Another intense stare from my companion, "You want to keep her?"

I breathe in deeply, and wipe my hand over my face, "If I don't, as far as I see it there's a good chance Danielle will end up in prison or dead if she keeps on the way she's doing. How could I subject a baby to that? Will need some fucking changes to my lifestyle, but yeah, I think I want to find some way to make it work. Fuck knows how. Hunter, it's only been a couple of days, and I miss the little mite already."

"Never thought I'd hear you of all people say something like that." Hunter laughs openly now. I can understand how he's surprised, fuck, the admission of the direction of my thoughts astounds me too.

Getting off the more personal side of the case, we start to discuss what we already know, and the myriad of things we don't. Over an hour passes, and then Nessa appears. We both look up at her in expectation.

"Right, I used the Grade A software to crack the password, so we're in." Ness gets straight down to it. We're still at the dining table, so she comes over and plonks the laptop down. Hunter and I draw up our chairs so we can all see it. "Sean, you read Arabic, don't you?"

"Not as well as I speak it." I glance across at Hunter who doesn't disappoint.

"I do."

She throws a little nod toward him and pushes the screen in his direction. His lips move as he starts to translate the script in front of him. As he reads, his brow furrows. He flicks a glance at me, and I see his eyes have opened wide. Then he brushes his hand down his face. We're both waiting for him to speak, and it's not long before he does.

"Fuck."

Dipping my chin, I tilt my head, "Can you expand on that, Hunter?"

His eyes flick from one to the other of us. But it's Nessa who takes on the role of enlightening me. "The first page is the list of contacts within Amir al-Fahri's organisation." She points to it. "It was a fairly easy password to guess, and possibly, all that Danielle had found and thought was on there. The rest of the info," she points to the document Hunter's now rapidly scanning, "That was securely encrypted. Took me a while longer to get into it."

The list, at least, was as I expected, even though it was possible that Danielle had been lying, and there was nothing of value on the USB at all. The thought that it was all a con had crossed my mind. But it seems she'd been telling the truth. "The list was all she told us about."

Nessa lifts her face up, "I doubt she found what else was there. It was hidden beneath some layers."

Hunter's finished reading through, and he looks stunned, "This is gold dust…" He breaks off, then comes to a decision, "There's no time to waste. Get Emir Kadar on the phone. A secure line."

"That bad?" At his nod, I don't delay ringing Kadar's office and explaining. A quarter of an hour later, my burner phone rings. Putting it on speaker, I put it in the centre of the table.

"Kadar." The emir confirms his identity with just one word. "Cara's assured me this line is clean. And for your peace of mind, the Wi-Fi is securely encrypted in your suite at the hotel; we use it sometimes when we need to discuss business in private."

"Good to know Kadar, thanks. I've got Hunter Wright and Nessa here with me. Hunter's got some info that he thinks you need to hear."

"Speak." The emir's never one to waste words.

Hunter leans forward, "We've had some intel come our way. It's bad, Your Excellency. And it involves Amahad."

"I expected that when I got Sean's call. Bad news doesn't get better for the waiting, so you better give it to me now." Kadar's also a man who likes things told to him straight.

"Amir al-Farhi has got Amahad in his sights again."

There's a brief sigh; then Kadar speaks pragmatically, "Hasn't he always? But I suspect the fact we're having this conversation means you're talking about a specific threat."

Hunter takes a second and then briefly explains how we got possession of the USB drive, "He's going to make some hits on your tourist spots. And soon. Some of his people are heading your way if they're not already in the country."

"Any specific targets?"

"The casino is one. And the main souk is also mentioned."

"Fuck! *Alllaena!*" After his impassioned exclamation in both English and Arabic, the emir is quiet. I sit shaking my head. Kadar's worked hard to make Amahad a tourist destination, attracting visitors from all over the world. It's the last thing he'd want to put his country on the map as one of the places *not* to visit.

"What about the oilfield, Hunter? Any threat to that or the pipeline?"

"Not mentioned, Your Excellency. But it wouldn't hurt to beef up security there as well."

"Hunter, you've had your hands on my sister-in-law, I think we can drop the formalities between us."

Hunter grins, "Thanks, …Kadar."

"So, what's the timescale?"

"They're talking about the week after next. I think we can assume Amir al-Fahri will be putting his plans into action now."

"We'll start looking at who's arrived recently, and upping the checks at the air and seaports."

I step in, "Kadar, we've got a list of people high up in al-Farhi's organisation, I'll forward it to you so you can look out for them. I'll also liaise with Ben, see if we can get Grade A to help with that." I've been making notes of what we'll need to do. "If Ben agrees, Nessa and I will return to Amahad and help in the meantime."

"Where's this Smith woman you were chasing?"

"She's in the wind again, Kadar." As long as she stays away from Mollie right at this moment, protecting Amahad is more important than finding a woman who doesn't want to be found.

There's quiet at the other end of the line, "Amir al-Fahri know she's given you that drive? That you've got this information? He could give up on his plans if he does."

Hunter looks thoughtful, he runs his hands through his

hair and links his fingers behind his neck; he glances at me. "Would she drop you in it, Sean? If she was caught?"

I start to speak, then stop, and clear my throat instead and I realise I know bugger all about the woman who slipped the drive into my wallet. Other than the fact she's my daughter's mother. Rather than the denial that I'd forced back down, I shrug, "She's a thief and a fraudster. And her life is in danger. Who knows what the fuck she'll do if al-Fahri catches up with her?"

Hunter nods toward the phone, "He might think the info was well encrypted, took a genius to break the code." He tosses a smile at Nessa who grins back, "He knows Smith distributed the main info, which at least has probably got all al-Fahri's main men running for cover and must have caused some trouble in his organisation. Or he could think she's hanging onto that drive. In any event, he may believe his coded plans are still safe and will carry on with them."

"Al-Fahri might decide to go ahead in any event. He's an arrogant bugger." Kadar butts in, "He might be confident we won't be able to stop him or will escalate the timetable. I suppose there wasn't a helpful mention of dates and places?"

As the senior operative here, I take charge, there's probably nothing more productive we can do at the moment. After throwing a questioning look toward Hunter and receiving a shake of his head in response, I fill the emir in, "Unfortunately not, Kadar, but you're right, it's sadly lacking on detail. Presumably there are more comprehensive plans, out there somewhere. And there is a risk he'll bring the attacks forward. I'll run things through with Ben, but I expect the three of us, at least, will be coming to Amahad shortly. In the meantime, if you increase the security at points of entry, and start briefing your employees to keep their eyes open, that's about all we can do until we get there."

"Agreed, Sean."

Without wasting much time on goodbyes, we end the phone call at that point.

Hunter tilts his head to one side, and gives Nessa a probing look, "How did you crack the code?"

She grins, and puffs herself up, "The key was his second cousin's birthday."

His head jerks back, "How the fuck did you come up with that?"

Seeming to grow in stature, she replies, "I've been studying his habits, it's a little-known fact that he's particularly fond of that member of his family."

"Fuck, Van, you're wasted in the field."

I agree with him wholeheartedly and hope she takes his message to heart. *And then I won't have to worry about her being safe.*

CHAPTER 21
Vanessa

Instead of offering Sean breakfast this morning I'd have preferred to throw it at him. When I awoke, the first thought in my head was, how mad I was with him and, at the same time, utterly furious with myself. How could I have let that happen? Why the hell did I sleep with him? Not that there was any sleeping involved. No, he just used me for sex; fantastic, mind-blowing sex. *Or did I use him?* Whichever way round it was, I suspect he's completely spoilt me for other men, or anyone I attempt to have a vanilla relationship with, that is. He's shown me how amazing it can be if I give up control. How the hell will I find another man like Sean? Am I destined to spend my life reliving one passionate night?

When I'd come to my senses and found myself alone, I'd cried because of the intensity of the unbelievably powerful experience I'd just been through. And when he'd come to me and comforted me, I'd lied to him when I'd pushed him away. And Christ, told the biggest falsehood I'd ever uttered in my life. *One night would never be enough.*

But I already knew, however incredible our joining had been for me, there's no point wishing for a repeat performance, Sean doesn't do those. And if I suggested it, his rejection would cut me to the quick.

Being with him has opened Pandora's box, and there'll be no closing it again. What if sex with any other man won't match up? Now I know how amazing the act can be, will I find everyone else wanting? It's my fault. I let him show me the wonders that sex can hold. I'm so angry with myself. Why did I give in?

Then, during those few minutes, I'd had alone before Sean emerged from his room I started to put it all into perspective. It wasn't just on Sean, oh, he'd taken what I'd so blatantly offered, but my ridiculous claim to be a Domme had been akin to waving a red rag at a bull. And how wrong he'd proven my assertion to be.

So, while I order the food and then accept the delivery into the room, my anger begins to fade. That we'd ended up in bed together was on both of us, there was no point blaming him. At least half the fault lies with me. Pulling my shoulders back and giving myself a silent lecture, I resolve to act as normally as possible, to pretend last night never happened. I have to; we're partners working on a case after all.

But it's hard, and I'm wishing I could be anywhere else but in that suite when at last he wakes up and emerges from his room. Pulling myself together, I put on the best act of my life and treat him exactly as I should have been treating him all along. As a work colleague determined to avoid any conversation that starts to veer off in any other direction. The message that I'm right to do so is reinforced when I notice he comes out fully clothed for once, Well, he's been there, done that now, and knowing what kind of man he is, I'm no longer a challenge for him. He'll have moved on.

When Hunter arrives, I'm relieved. Knowing nothing about our relationship, or lack of, he's oblivious to the enormous mistake I made the night before. Sean and I are successful in hiding any awkwardness between us despite there being an undercurrent of embarrassment on both our parts.

So, on the surface, it's easy to pretend nothing happened and to carry on as normal. And those couple of hours when I was able to get down to do what I do best—problem solving—helps focus my mind on work rather than the man who was in my bed in the early hours of the morning.

After the phone call with Kadar, Sean and Hunter decide it's best to speak to Ben in person and get the vital information on the thumbnail drive out of our possession and into safe hands. The next item on the agenda has me arranging to the first available flights out of Paris. I busy myself making the arrangements and soon find myself travelling back in first class which had the only free seats, and returning to England.

On the plane we're not able sit together, which, means I'm not forced to sit in close proximity with the man I came to know so intimately in the small hours of the morning, but gives me nothing to distract my traitorous mind from churning over the events of the night before. From remembering Sean's touch, recalling the incredible experience of his lovemaking and the responses he evoked from me. *Oh, for goodness sake, think of something different.*

But it's difficult; he's awoken something within me, a desire to learn more. However much I tell myself there's no point wanting him again, some part of me hangs onto the hope that the door's not shut forever. I wish my head came equipped with an erase button so I could forget everything that happened last night. I'd told him once had been enough for me. *I'd lied.*

He'd been so right when he'd explained the relationship between a sub and her Dom. Having a Dom intent on giving me pleasure, completely focused on my reactions had been mind-blowing. Perhaps it's not Sean I should be focusing on; perhaps I just need to look for someone like him. We're returning to London. What if I get up the nerve to ask for membership to Club Tiacapan? Maybe, when this assignment is over, I can ask Sean to take me there and help me find a Dom? Admitting I could submit to a man *and enjoy it* is something I never thought I'd want to do. If being a sub is in my nature that must have been why sex with manwhore Sean was so exceptional. It couldn't have been just the man himself. *Could it?*

I'm quiet during the flight as I try to analyse my feelings, trying to doze as we didn't get much sleep last night. As I end the journey, if I'm honest I have to admit all my common sense talking to myself, all the good reasons why I should move on, hasn't diminished my attraction to Sean one bit, and I can't see a way any man, even another Dom could come anywhere near a close second. But just like a once in a lifetime holiday in a place you'd love to revisit but know you could never afford to, my one night with Sean has to exist only as a pleasant thing to reminisce on.

Trying to put that memory into a box, locking it and throwing away the key, I force myself think about work again, and more specifically, the information that the thumbnail drive contained.

When we finally reach the Grade A building, it's early evening, and most of the staff have long gone home. But all the senior operatives that are not currently out on other jobs, are ready and waiting for us in the conference room and I'm delighted to see, a welcome buffet of sandwiches laid out on a side table. Breakfast was a long time away, and even the first-class food on the plane wasn't really enough to be adequate. The sandwiches and other bites will keep me going for a while. I fill my plate and then take my normal seat at the table as Ben pops his head round the door.

"Sean, can I speak to you for a moment?"

Frowning, I watch as the two men disappear, presumably to Ben's office. *What does he want to speak to him about?* Hopefully, it's not to give an assessment of how well I've done recently, and I'll be given more time to prove myself. I haven't exactly shown myself in glowing colours so far, my performance has been far from stellar. *Except for my performance last night. Sean didn't seem to have any complaints about that.* I grin to myself at my private joke.

"Hey, Van?" Ryan's waving his hand in front of me, and I realise I'd been miles away. Seeing he's got my attention, he continues, "How do you like working outside the office? We all miss you like crazy here."

That's good to know, because if my suspicions are right,

Ben might be reassigning me to my old job right at this very minute. Ryan's waiting for an answer, I put my hand on his arm, "Nice knowing I've been missed. And it's been a whirlwind few days, but I'm enjoying it." I blush as I remember why I've enjoyed it so much.

Sean chooses that moment to walk back in and take his customary seat opposite mine. I look at him, wondering if his expression betrays anything of the outcome of his discussion with the senior partner of Grade A, but for some reason he begins to glare as soon as his sits down, his gaze fixed on my hand and the man I'm still touching. *Is he jealous? No way, surely?* Then when I pull back and sit with my hands folded across my chest, I see him relax. *Hmm.*

I have no more time to ponder his curious reaction, and whether I can read anything into or not as Ben's taken the chair and the meeting starts in earnest.

Hunter begins by bringing Ben up to speed, and my boss congratulates me on cracking the password and code. Feeling my cheeks redden again, I nod my thanks. Though I try, I can't read anything in my boss's face to give me a hint of what's in my future. *Perhaps Sean wasn't giving a report about me?*

The agenda for the meeting is quite simple as we're focused on only one item; the threats to Amahad. Once we flesh them out, Ben and Jon have a private discussion, jotting some notes on their tablets and obviously discussing options. The rest of us wait to hear their decision. They don't keep us hanging about for long.

"Right," Ben glances around the table, making sure

we're all paying attention, "Hunter. You, Nat and Ryan, will be our men on the ground in Amahad." He waits until they nod their agreement. "Jon will liaise with Kadar as to what other support he might need and, if necessary, he'll round up the additional resources." Grade A can call in extra personnel when necessary, taking staff from our offices in other countries and a number of ex-service men who have affiliation with the company.

Ben hasn't made any mention of Sean or me. Are we being taken off the case?

Flicking my eyes across to my partner his expression confuses me. His brows are drawn down, and he's pinching the bridge of his nose.

"What about Sean and me, Ben?" I prompt, impatient to hear my fate, even if it means I'll end up disappointed. I grow angry that Sean hasn't given me much of a chance to get my feet under the table in my new role. Surely all beginners make mistakes at first?

Ben throws me a curious look, "You're with Sean, of course. I assigned you as his partner, didn't I?" He nods at the man sitting opposite me then leans forward, his elbows on the table, his fists bunched under his chin, "You want to fill her in?"

"Nessa," Sean starts and I sit up straighter as now it seems he's going to let me in on what he'd been discussing with Ben. Seeing the tense look on his face, I'm prepared for something serious. "My mother thinks there might have been someone following her. Her and Mollie that is."

"What?" My irritation recedes fast. "What's happened?"

"Nothing's actually happened, as far as Ben knows, but,

and thanks for this, Ben," he jerks his chin toward our boss, "Ben sent Seth and Harry to keep eyes on her as soon as she contacted him. So far, they've not seen anything out of the ordinary. But mum's pretty certain of what she saw."

Despite having an overactive imagination—which she needs to have, to invent the plots she does—Sean's mother is as sharp as a tack. If she says she was being followed, she probably was. "When was this?" My face creases into a frown.

"Yesterday, when she took the baby out to the shops with her." Ben's nodding, confirming Sean's got the story right.

Sean drops his head down; I can't see his face, but I presume he's taking a moment to think, "It is something to worry about. It could it be Danielle wanting to take Mollie back, or even simply checking up she's okay. We haven't the slightest idea where the fuck she is. Or what she intends to do."

"Was it a woman, or a man?" Had Danielle been there herself?

"Mum was a bit vague; she thought it was one, possibly two men. Darker skinned, which makes me think Arab. She didn't notice a woman."

Sitting back again, Ben shrugs, "Whatever, I don't think we should take this lightly. As it's Sean's family, I want to give him the chance to take the lead on this." Sean's family. Those words are like needles pricking into my skin. *I'm not part of that. I'm just his work partner.*

"I'm with you there, man. Fuck." Sean's eyes narrow, "I don't want Danielle to have the chance of taking Mollie away. I think anyone would agree, if she's telling the truth both she and Mollie could be in danger. It could even be someone wanting to use the baby as leverage. On either myself or her. But how the fuck would anyone know where she is? Unless they've already got hold of Danielle, that is." His face is drawn, and his lips are pursed, "Ben, I don't want to leave Mollie. I can't take that risk."

Jon's looking equally serious, "I'd prefer you out there on the ground, Sean. You and Hunter have both got a better handle on what's going on in Amahad than Ryan and Nat."

Ben scowls at his partner, "While I agree with Jon, Sean, it's up to you to make that call. We can assign men to watch over your family."

"But that leaves you short on the ground." Sean sighs, "I hate the thought of quitting something unfinished, but I can't risk leaving Mollie and my mother unprotected. Guys, I wouldn't be able to concentrate knowing she's in possible danger. And mum doesn't deserve to be right in the middle of something she's nothing to do with."

"Take Mollie with you."

Sean's head comes up quickly at Jon's unexpected suggestion. "What, take a baby into a country where there are active terrorist threats? Come off it. That's a crazy suggestion!"

Ignoring the second sharp look, Ben throws at him in as many minutes, Jon shrugs and continues, "There's been no threat to the palace, and Kadar's got that place sewn up tight."

Sean has his head half turned to one side, "Can't see it

working, Jon. I barely know how to look after her myself, and how I can work when I've got a baby with me?"

"Perhaps Van can help?"

I can feel the blood draining out of my face. No. Just no. My palms start to sweat. No, I don't want to be involved in looking after a baby, As I see all eyes on me, I recognise they're expecting me to offer my assistance. To gain some time, I say the first thing that comes into my head.

"That's a pretty sexist comment, Jon. I've no more frigging idea about looking after a baby than Sean does."

"Thought women were born with a maternal instinct?" Ryan jokes.

"Not this one," I spit out at him in reply.

Hunter's looking thoughtful, "What about Cara? Zorah's what, six months old now? She's not far off your baby's age, Sean, she might be able to help. She's got a nanny to assist her."

I can see the wheels turning in Sean's head; it still seems to be a crazy idea to take Mollie to Amahad, but I can understand his dilemma. It would be difficult for him to focus on work if he's so far away, knowing both his mother and Mollie could be at risk. On the other hand, I know how much he wants to get back to working in the field. And if Sean's not here, as an overly protective boss, Ben will have to assign men from other assignments just in case anyone's going to try to take Mollie. Men he can't afford to have tied up at this time. With the terrorist threats, Grade A are being spread fairly thin as it is.

"If Smith is behind the men trailing your mother and

her intent is to get her child back, she'd follow the baby thereby removing any danger to your mother. She might be lured to Amahad where you'll be able to deal with her, Sean."

Sean nods slowly, "There is that." He raps his hand on the table as though he's come to a decision. "I'll speak to Kadar and Cara, see if it's possible to have Mollie looked after in the palace while I'm working. I must admit I'd like to have her close by, and I don't want to leave Mum exposed to any menace."

Oh shit. Just what I didn't want. Suddenly I go icy cold. *He's proposing to bring the baby with us?*

As Sean goes off to make his call, I stare at the remaining sandwich on my plate, half eaten and now curling up at the corners as my appetite has fled. Returning to Amahad with Sean is bad enough, but add in the baby, and I don't know if I can stand it. I find myself hoping someone will come to their senses and say it's a terrible proposal.

Ben's looking at me, his searching eyes seeing more than I would have hoped, "You're Sean's partner on this case, Van. If Sean returns to Amahad, I expect you to go too. And if he stays here, I'll expect you to provide the necessary protection detail. I take it that's alright with you? If there are any problems, if you've decided working outside the office isn't for you, you can speak to me after the meeting."

That makes me start; the words tumble out of my mouth, "Ben, no, I'm completely fine with working on this case. I'd like to return to Amahad and see it through." I give a sharp nod to emphasise how on board I am. His quizzical gaze looks like he doesn't quite believe me, but thankfully, he leaves the subject and has a brief discussion with Jon about a different matter.

Soon Sean returns to report the Kassis family say it will be no problem for him to take Mollie back with him, and that Kadar's confirmed Jon's assertion that a gnat wouldn't be able to get into the palace itself. Security is already watertight due to the threats against the emir, albeit much lessened now he's married and is putting his idea of an elected government in place. The move toward democracy has been given a cautious welcome and, as I know from keeping up with the news from the Arab country, that the desert sheikhs are giving him their support. In all, apart from the external threats, Amahad is gaining a reputation as a stable country now. But Kadar remains hyper-vigilant, particularly as his own child will shortly be born meaning Mollie's safety can be all but guaranteed.

The meeting concludes after Sean's update on his conversation with the emir. I make a meal of logging out of my laptop and gathering my things together and am the last one to leave hoping everyone else will have gone home. But exiting the room, I find the very man I'd hoped to have a few hours away from, waiting for me in the corridor.

Sean stalks toward me, getting far too close. My back is against the wall as he looms over me, putting one hand on the wall next to my head, "Nessa, I'm sorry. I saw your reaction in there, but this is the only way I can go back to Amahad. If I take Mollie with me."

I understand him but also know myself. "I'm not comfortable with this, Sean. I'm sorry, but I don't do babies." I know he won't be able to comprehend that the sight or sound of a child evokes such feelings inside me. My hands are shaking as I bring them up to cover my face. *How can I do this?* And I also realise, by telling him I don't want to be around a baby, *his* baby, means if there was the remotest chance of us getting together, I've have killed it stone dead. I think quickly, contradicting my earlier response in the meeting, "What if I stay here? Tell Ben I don't like working as an operative after all?"

"And throw away everything you've worked for? If you give up now, Nessa, you might not get another chance."

He leans even closer, his hands come up and pull mine away, "Shit, Nessa, I know for some reason this is painful for you. You might have been able to hide it from everyone else, but in there?" He points to the conference room we've just exited, "It written all over your face. I can't pretend to fathom how you're thinking. Surely you must see kids sometimes, interact with them?" His fingers wrap around mine, squeezing them gently, "Don't you ever see yourself wanting a baby of your own?"

My eyes close, trying to keep back the tears which threaten to fall, hoping to God he doesn't see them. "No."

He pulls me close, his strong arms wrapping around me, "It's okay, Nessa. I suppose some women just aren't wired that way."

If only he knew.

His hands soothe up and down my back, and as he holds me, I feel his erection pressing into my stomach. He feels it too and backs slightly away. "Sorry, babe," he says wryly. "Inappropriate at best."

Yes, the evidence of his physical feeling for me is, but there's still a flicker inside me that makes me pleased I can affect him this way. Equally unfitting at this time.

"What if we changed the accommodation arrangements? If Ryan stayed with me, and you stayed with Nat? Kadar's making another of the houses in the compound available to us."

And not be close to Sean? I might have wanted a little space to sort my head out, but to give up the chance of being with him? Even though I know there'll never be a repeat of last night, I've come to depend on him, to enjoy his company. I'm torn, so torn. My eyes open wide as I gaze up at him. *I don't know what to do.*

He recognises my silent plea. But the solution he comes up with takes me by surprise. "It's alright, Nessa. I've got an idea. Come with me." He takes hold of my hand.

"What? Where, Sean?" My eyes narrow suspiciously.

"Come and meet Mollie." He starts walking down the corridor taking me along with him.

Tugging him back, I force him to stop. My heart rate speeds up, and my pulse is fluttering wildly, "I don't think this is a good idea, Sean."

He turns to face me, "Mollie is my child. Mine, Nessa. She's not some unknown baby that you'd pass in the street. She's her own personality. Come and meet her, give her, us, a chance. If you decide you can't cope having her around, then that's the time to make any decisions."

Shit! This is a bad idea. He doesn't know what it's like

for me. All the feelings that I have to keep buried. But it would be unreasonable for me not to go with him without giving an explanation, and I'm not going to let him into my darkest secrets. Why did I have to become attracted to him? Not only is he the very last man with whom I should be considering a relationship, he now comes with strings attached. Very tight strings.

He collects the keys to one of Grade A's anonymous black SUVs. I follow him down to the underground car park, and we drive in silence. He puts on the radio to a local station, and we catch up with the news that we've missed while being out of the country. Sure, we've kept up with national events, but now we listen to stories of lesser importance, but still critical to the people involved.

I rest my head back, and my hands twist in my lap. The very last thing I want to do is to get to Sean's mother's house and meet his daughter. But maybe my reaction when I see her will convince him that I was right all along. Idly watching the scenery going past, I wonder what Sean intends to do when this is all over. Is he going to look after Mollie himself? Continue to let his mother look after her? Or, marry someone who'll become her mother. In which case, there's no need for me to worry at all.

At last, we come to a pleasant looking housing estate, with each building set back from the road. The house we're arriving at isn't huge, but the front garden and exterior looks tidy and well maintained. Sean pulls the SUV onto the drive behind an older model Volvo and switches off the engine. He glances across at me and gives me a gentle squeeze on my arm.

Then he gets out. There's no point in delaying, so I do the same. Sean glances across the road and throws a nod at Harry who's watching the house.

Before we can reach it, a woman's already opening the door. Although I know she's in her late fifties, now I'm meeting her in the flesh she looks a lot less, her figure alone would be envied by many a decade or so younger. She's got the same impudent grin that I've often seen on Sean's face, and her hands are held out in welcome.

As Sean approaches, she steps forward and pulls him in for a hug. Then she steps back and her face scrunches, "You find Mollie's mother yet?"

"It's a long story, Mum. The short version is yes; I've seen her briefly."

Her eyes narrow, "She coming back for her baby?" I take it she's not overly fond of the idea.

Sean puts his arm around her, "Let's take this inside. I'll fill you in with the details."

He's right, explaining how Mollie came into being, virtually stolen from him, isn't something that should be discussed on the doorstep.

I've moved up behind him, and he reaches for my hand giving me no option but to follow him in. As we cross the threshold, he explains who I am.

"Mum, this is Nessa. She's working with me."

Appearing only now to notice he's brought someone else along, his mother turns and gives me an appraising look. I fidget under her blatant evaluation, but can't have been found too wanting as her lips turn up into a welcoming smile. Stretching out my hand, I mumble,

"Mrs Cooper, it's good to meet you at last. I've heard a lot about you, and of course, enjoyed the cupcakes you make."

Grinning she takes my hand, holding it a little too long, "You don't look like you eat that many. And call me Anna, please."

I nod and smile, taking her comment about the cupcakes as the compliment she's obviously meant.

"Where's Mollie, Mum?" Sean's anxious to see his daughter, and a pang goes through me at his obvious paternal concern, even though he's only known he was a father for a few days.

"In the spare bedroom. She's asleep, but I expect she'll be stirring soon."

As Anna speaks, I notice she's got a baby monitor clipped to the waistband of her jeans.

"We'll go see her, then I'll come back down for that conversation."

She frowns, clearly having to curb her curiosity, then gives a reluctant nod and steps aside. Sean puts his arm around my shoulders, cutting off any chance of escape, and leads me to the stairs. We ascend and come to an open door. There's a cot inside.

Putting his finger to his lips, he murmurs, "We'll try not to wake her," he gives a rueful grin, "But I can't wait to see her again."

I nod, hoping he'll let me go so I can stay out of sight. But no, he leads me inside. And there she is, a perfect baby lying sleeping. There's a dummy by the side of her mouth, obviously having dropped out when she dozed off. Her blankets have been kicked off, and she's dressed in a pretty pink Babygro with grey elephants on it.

Sean reaches out his hand but doesn't touch her. It hovers inches from her chubby face. But it's as if Mollie can sense his presence. She twitches, and he pulls back.

"Isn't she beautiful?" he whispers, his voice full of wonder.

She is. As I look at her, again I can only see him. She doesn't resemble her mother in any way. Her features are all his. Her hair too, already blonde.

And then she lets out a little fart.

"Yup, she's all yours Sean," I laugh as I tell him.

But I've spoken too loudly. Suddenly eyes the same shade as Sean's flick open and I swear she looks at him with recognition as she smiles his smile. Her chubby arms reach out, and he can't resist, bending over and picking her up.

"Hi, sweetie." His voice, soft and so full of an emotion I haven't heard before, does something to me. I'm about to step away when he does the worst thing he can. He turns, and before I have time to protest, thrusts her toward me, "Go say hello to Auntie Nessa."

Automatically my arms go out to hold her. And then a wave of nausea hits me. I can't breathe; my lungs heave for oxygen, but nothing goes in. I stagger. Throwing me a sharp look Sean grabs hold of Mollie, taking her back before I drop her and that's all I know before the world goes black.

I wake to sounds of a baby gurgling downstairs, but I'm lying on a bed, an anxious Sean sitting by my side. He's gently stroking my head, his touch soft over my clammy skin. Enjoying the sensation, I wait a few seconds before showing I'm awake.

"Babe, are you back with us? You fainted. Are you okay? Do you need to see a doctor? I can take you to casualty?"

Violently I shake my head, and then regret it as another wave of dizziness goes through me. As I close my eyes waiting for my equilibrium to restore, he waits patiently.

Then, when I open them again, he prompts me, "What is it, Nessa? What can I do?"

I've got to tell him something. I just fainted for Christ's sake. In his child's bedroom. "Panic attack," I explain succinctly while thinking it's the worst I've ever had.

He regards me searchingly, his hand still smoothing across my forehead as he asks sympathetically, "Do you know what brought it on?"

What the hell do I do? Admit the truth? I gaze at him and then, embarrassed turn my head away. With a gentle touch he turns my face back toward him.

"I'm your partner, Nessa. We work together. If this is a panic attack, then it was an extreme one. You're going to have to tell me your triggers." With his free hand, he pushes back his hair, "I need to know. I can't afford to have you blacking out on me." He's watching me intently, "Nessa, you fainted. And if you're aware of the reason, you're going to have to tell me. People don't faint without cause. You must have been cleared medically for Ben to send you out on assignment. But is there anything else in your medical history that Grade A needs to know?"

I don't want to tell him, don't want to have to explain.

But if he reports this to Ben, if my boss believes I can faint without warning then there's no way he'll let me continue to work as an operative. Now my anxiety is for a different reason. If I want to keep my job, I have to drag up that dirty secret I've kept hidden for so long, my rattling skeleton in the cupboard.

"I'll have to tell Ben, Nessa. Would you prefer to talk to him?" He sits up straight and wipes his hands over his face, pausing on the designer stubble that can only just be called a beard. "It's not lack of food, you've eaten today, possibly not a lot, but sufficient. You don't have a temperature, so I don't believe you're ill. And from that look on your face, you know exactly what happened. You didn't just faint, Nessa. There's a reason for it, isn't there? Something that made you panic so much that all the blood rushed from your head. Are you getting your period or something?"

The blood returns to my face at his forthright suggestion, but I shake my head to deny it, "No, it's not that."

Still he's regarding me with those all-seeing blue eyes. His hands pause, cupping his cheeks, "It was the moment you held Mollie."

CHAPTER 22

Sean

S he doesn't speak. Fuck, I'm going to have to call Ben and tell him, there's no way she can come to Amahad if she has fainting fits for no reason. When I've given up on an answer, and instead start wondering again about her medical history, she surprises me, at last deigning to speak and saying softly, "Yes, it was holding Mollie. That was the trigger."

I frown, it was the likely conclusion, but for the life of me, I can't understand why having a baby in her arms caused such an extreme reaction. I know Nessa doesn't particularly like children or want one herself, but for Mollie to cause her to have a panic attack? There must be more to it.

When I go to prompt her, she stammers out the words I didn't expect to hear. "I, I was pregnant once. Two years ago." It's impossible to miss the tears that come to her eyes.

Fuck me! I breathe in sharply. That was the last thing I expected her to say. Obviously, it ended badly, a miscarriage or stillbirth? Something cruel enough for her never to want to go through again? She's turned her head away, clearly not wanting to expound. But I wasn't lying when I explained the effect it could have on our working relationship, if someone's holding a gun to my head I want a partner who can respond, not one who's passed out on the floor. I need her to let me know what happened. Sympathy isn't going to work, not right now.

In my Dom voice, I ask, "What happened?"

She turns eyes full of hurt toward me, but the authority in my tone encourages her to continue speaking, just as I'd hoped.

The words are spoken in a monotone, "I was tired of being alone, Sean, but I wasn't meeting the right men. I decided to have a go at internet dating, well, everyone does nowadays, don't they? I was careful, never giving personal details away. It took a while, and then I found him, Simon. We clicked. He'd just got out of a long-term relationship and didn't want to be on his own anymore. I didn't take that into account at the time, just was pleased to find someone with the same interests as me. We spoke for weeks on the 'net, and then I decided to take the plunge and meet him. You know me, I looked into his background and knew he was who he said he was, the right age and everything. I took care to make sure I wasn't being conned."

I nod, I'm not going to censure her, I know she'd have used the research tools she has at hand to make sure she'd be safe.

"The trouble, as it turned out, was that in all my investigations I never found out the most important thing I should have taken into account. That he wasn't over his ex."

She swallows a couple of times, and I pass her the glass of water that Mum had brought up earlier, helping Nessa into a sitting position to drink it.

"We seemed to click. We'd only been dating a couple of months when he asked me to marry him. Brought me a ring and everything. I was over the moon. What I hadn't understood was that he was trying to replace her with me and, in the end, I turned out not to be a good enough fit."

The skin around my eyes creases as I think back. Yes, I do remember her flashing a ring in the office. Then, she hadn't been wearing it anymore. But I hadn't heard any story behind it. Although that's not surprising, I tend to steer clear of female gossip, and anyway, most of the time I'm working away.

"So, I had his ring on my finger, but he wouldn't set a date. We looked at houses to buy, but he'd never settle on one." I pull her toward me, her arms hold me tight, as if she's afraid I'll leave before she finishes her story. "I started to think that he was having second thoughts, and I hate to admit how that made me look. I'd told people about the engagement, didn't want to appear a fool. And I'd invested all my emotions in him. I *loved* him. Or I thought I did. I thought he was offering me everything I ever wanted. I didn't look close enough at what lay underneath." I rub my hands up and down her back as she continues, "I got a stomach bug and was sick for a few days. Never thought about the implications or that it might affect the effectiveness of the pill. Well, to cut a long story short, I got pregnant."

I get a bad feeling about how this is going to turn out. "And?" She needs my prompt to encourage her to continue.

"He told me I'd done it on purpose to trap him."

"Babe, you were already engaged to him."

"Yeah," she pauses, "Early on we'd discussed having children, it seemed to be something he wanted. Of course, I knew it was too early, too soon, and when I saw the results of the test I was scared myself and worried. But also, happy. I believed I loved him, you see, and to have something growing inside me that was part of that relationship... Well, the relationship I believed we had, anyway."

I squeeze her gently, "Go on."

"I'd found out early. I'm as regular as clockwork. When I was late by a few days, I took the test. I was stunned but elated. I wasn't sure how it was going to work, but I jumped at my chance to start a family." She sobs again but holds it together. "When I told him, suddenly it was as though I was speaking to a stranger. He threw his accusations at me then turned and walked out." Another muffled sob, "But he came back after a couple of days, all smiles and happy again and I thought everything would be okay. But then he gave me an ultimatum. He said it wasn't the right time to have a baby. If I had an abortion, he'd stay with me."

What a bastard. I don't need a crystal ball to see how this is going to end. To save her having to say the words, I spoke them myself, "So you had an abortion, and he left you anyway."

"No, yes." It's a strange answer, and there's obviously more to come.

She tenses in my arms, "I said no. And chucked him out."

I chuckle softly, "Good girl."

"I wasn't that sensible, Sean. I tried to carry on, I made an appointment to see my doctor so I could start doing the right things for the baby, but had to wait a couple of weeks to see the GP I wanted. I didn't think it was that urgent. In the meantime—and by then I must have been six weeks pregnant—he came back. He walked in carrying flowers and said he'd come to his senses and wanted this to work. That he'd been thinking about it, that he loved me and while it wasn't the best time, he wanted the baby.

"I was so happy, I forgot the man he'd turned into when I'd first told him of the pregnancy, just thought of him as the man I'd agreed to marry. I was so stupid."

I give her an encouraging squeeze, knowing there are many ways this story could end. Had he hurt her? Had she miscarried naturally? "Go on," I urge quietly.

She shudders in my arms. What's coming next isn't going to be pleasant, already I can sense that. "He became so solicitous, couldn't do enough for me. Brought me breakfast in bed, and was googling articles about pregnancy all the time. One evening he made me a special drink that he said had vitamins and nutrients in it. It tasted foul, but he'd taken such an effort with it I drank it all. The next night he made it again. I remember thinking I hadn't the heart to tell him I didn't like it."

Now it's obvious. "What did he give you?"

"I didn't suspect anything at first. Then I started getting terrible cramps, and I was bleeding. It was in the morning, and he'd slept over. When I came out of the bathroom with tears running down my face, he stood there and laughed, an evil, terrible sound and I knew then he'd done something. And that's when he told me he'd taken care of it. That he hadn't wanted to be lumbered with having to pay child support for the next eighteen years, and that this now really was the end. He picked up his coat, collected any of his stuff he had lying around, and left."

"What had he given you, do you know?" My teeth clench so tightly my jaw aches.

"I went to my doctor's appointment and told her what had happened. She wasn't sure whether to believe me until I told her his brother was a pharmacist. She was still dubious but suggested he would have to have given me mifepristone, followed by misoprostol. The timing was right; they need to be taken twenty-four to forty-eight hours apart."

"Fuck! Did you report him?"

She shakes her head, "I tried, but the police said there was nothing to prove anything. Although I was still bleeding, and the doctor said my hormone levels might be raised but that wasn't evidence I'd been pregnant or if I had, that I hadn't miscarried naturally. I bled for nearly a month."

Two years ago. I think back, but am unable to remember Nessa being off sick for any period of time. She's one of the office fixtures, always there. "You didn't take time off work?"

"I took a month off, told everyone I'd had my appendix out. I didn't want anyone to know how stupid I'd been. I'd taken him back after he revealed his true colours to me, I should have kept my distance then I wouldn't have lost my baby. After four weeks, I knew moping around wasn't doing me any good, so I returned to work hoping getting back to normal would help me come to terms with what happened. I think you were out of the country at the time, Sean."

And that's why I don't remember. If I had been around, maybe I'd have been able to help her, to do something about it. *To kill the bastard.* But then again, we didn't have a close relationship at that time. She was just part of the team, no one special.

She sniffs, and then wails into my chest, "My stupidity killed my baby, Sean. *I* killed it by believing him. And I've regretted it every minute since. You might think it's crazy, but if I'd not been so weak as to take him back, I'd have a child in my life right now. Every time I see a baby, it brings it all back, and I feel so empty inside and, as you saw, I can have an extreme reaction."

I just hold her, thoughts going through my head. Her story is difficult to believe, but I don't doubt it's true, and feel honoured she's trusted me with it. I'd like to get my hands on that motherfucker, but something tells me that's not what she'd want. It wouldn't bring her child back, or make her feel better around children. Two years, it's not a long time, not long enough to get over something so evil. To have your control taken away completely, for someone else to decide what to do with your body. It's the ultimate fear of any submissive, and in the circumstance she's described, she didn't have a chance of saying a safeword or taking responsibility for what was to happen.

The man killed his child, and for the life of me, I can't

understand how he could have done that. If Danielle had told me she was pregnant, I would have supported her, even while I'd have been shit scared of the outcome.

She's quiet, now. Whatever I say will seem pointless and meaningless, but I have to try. "Nessa, you were forced into that position, you weren't given a choice. It was forced on you. You had absolutely no control over the situation."

"Yes I did, I was so weak." I hear her inhale sharply, "By then I knew what kind of man he was but I still jumped at the chance of a relationship. I was the one who let him back into my life, who let him woo me with his false platitudes."

Now pull her up, turning her toward me and plant my palms either side of her face, forcing her to meet my eyes, "Nessa, listen to me. You are not weak. You're one of the strongest women I've ever met. It's a fuck of a thing that happened and would be hard for anyone to cope with. Babe, have you had counselling?"

She dips her head, "Although I held it together at work, underneath I was a mess. My doctor sent me to someone. The person I saw, well, they were great. They heard my story and knew I believed it to be the truth, even if they might have had doubts that's what actually happened. So she treated me that way. She told me as I'd been coerced into something I didn't want to do I was suffering a form of post-traumatic stress disorder. I have nightmares still, Sean, and seeing a baby triggers the symptoms." She's quiet, then, "She would have been about fifteen months old now. I think about her all the time. Oh, of course I don't know the baby was female, it was far too early to tell. But I just had this feeling, and always picture myself with a little girl."

Again, I pull her close, resting my chin on her head, noting the perfume of the shampoo she must use, a tang of coconut oil reaches my nostrils. I know how devastating PTSD can be, I've seen my ex-army colleagues go through it, hell, I've suffered it myself and seem to have managed to come out the other side. But it takes time for those memories to fade, and simple things can make you relive it all over again. Like holding a baby girl. Like holding Mollie.

"I get panic attacks around children, so I avoid them."

She's shaking, a vibration I can feel through her whole body. And, for once, I don't know what the fuck to do.

I'm saved by the bell or rather a polite tapping on the door. Mum pokes her head around, gesturing toward the woman in my arms, "Is she okay?"

'She' is currently hiding her head against my shoulder. I nod to answer. Well, she's far from okay, but physically she seems to have recovered.

"I've got some dinner ready if you want to come down?"

"Thanks, Mum. We'll be there shortly."

Closing the door on her way out, she leaves us alone. I move Nessa so I can see her face when I talk to her. "What do you want to do? You're welcome to stay here and eat with us, or if you want, I'll call a taxi to take you home."

Nessa's goes still, and then seems to pull herself up straighter. Her hand comes up and gently touches my cheek, "Hardly anyone knows what happened, Sean. Ben knows, he got my sickness certificates after all. When I explained, he was great. In his view, it was essentially rape.

He was so angry on my behalf. He went to see Simon and made sure he'd never contact me again. And that's when he agreed to me doing the CPO training. And having that to focus on definitely helped. But no one else, other than the bastard himself and my doctors know."

I give silent thanks to Ben for taking care of the problem as best he could at the time, but he probably has no idea how it's still affecting her. Otherwise, why would he push my baby and me on to her? I open my mouth to speak, but she stops me, "Thank you, for listening. And for not being disapproving. It means a lot, you know?"

"Babe, you didn't do anything wrong, there's nothing to disapprove of. I have more trouble understanding what motivated that bastard. He didn't want to support you and a child? Fuck, he's not a man at all." My face twists into a scowl, "If you tell me his name I'll gladly make sure the bastard can never father another child."

Nessa offers tremulous smile, "It's a nice thought, but what would that do to help me? And Ben's already spoken to him." The levity is fleeting, and her mouth turns down again, "That's why I thought I wanted to be a Domme. So that I would have the control."

In my world, the sub always has control; she still doesn't understand that. Yet.

As I gaze into her face, made blotchy by her tears, the thought hits me I'd like to see her belly swelling with my child, to be there through every step of the way while she was pregnant, to see the first scan, to be there at the birth. Everything I missed with Mollie. *And why the fuck would I be thinking of something like that?*

Sensing my thoughts are zooming off in very dangerous directions, I carefully extract myself and get off the bed. Standing I hold out my hand, "Come eat with us, Nessa."

But she shakes her head, "I'd rather you called me a taxi, Sean. I'm sorry. And apologise to your mother for me."

"Nessa, I don't like the thought of you being alone tonight. You've just relived what has to be the worst experience of your life…"

Her fingers touch my lips, "I'm pleased I told you, Sean. We're partners, right? And as you said, you deserve to know if I'm likely to have problems doing the job. I don't think I will. Tonight, holding Mollie was just too much for me. Now I know I'll have to stay away from her." She gives a jerk of her chin and starts to look more positive, "It's been a long time since I've spoken about this to anyone, and I'm glad I got it out. In some ways, I think it's been cathartic. I want to go home; I'm tired. Worn out. But I'll be fine. I'm used to being on my own."

If she stayed with me, she wouldn't have to be alone. But a relationship with me would probably end up being just as disastrous as her last attempt. Not in the same way, but I'd cock up sooner or later. I can't see myself ever committing to just one woman; it's just not my psyche.

I call a taxi and watch it drive away with a broken woman inside, unsure whether I've done the right thing.

After seeing Nessa out of the house, at Mum's unspoken enquiry I brush off her abrupt departure from our home and her fainting fit as being a result of tiredness. A story I'm not entirely sure my mother bought.

But she's easily distracted by her concern about her grandchild going to Amahad, not at all convinced that it is a good idea to take Mollie half way across the world. But as we thrash it out, it becomes clear she was far more rattled than Ben had let on about the person she thought had been following her. And after I dragged everything out of her there is no way I'll be leaving without my daughter, or leaving my one surviving parent at risk.

My mum knows me well, as a mother should, and but her doubts that her playboy son can take on the responsibility of looking after a child seem to dissipate as she watches me hold Mollie and eat my dinner one-handed, and not baulk at changing a dirty nappy. Reluctantly she finally agrees, taking Mollie to Amahad, is the safest bet.

After she'd taken me through all the dos and don'ts of looking after a young baby, she watches me bathe Mollie without drowning her and put her to bed. Then I'm subjected to what I still term a mummy hug, and she looks up and grins, "You'll be okay, you know that, son? I reckon you'll look after her just fine."

"I'll have help, Mum. Cara's got a nanny. You don't need to worry."

"I know I don't. You just keep in touch, okay? I want photos and updates."

"Yes, Grandma."

She flicks me around the head, and I duck in mock surrender. "You could have given me some warning, you know. Just to get used to the idea. You know, the usual kind of stuff? Bringing a girl home, putting a ring on her finger?"

I wish I'd had some warning myself.

And that she hadn't bought my explanation about Nessa's abrupt departure becomes clear when she says, "Now why don't you get out of here and go do what you have to do?"

My lips curl, she knows me so well, "But Mollie…" I start. It doesn't seem fair to leave her when I've only just got here.

"She'll be fine. She's asleep now and if we're lucky might go through the night. Go see your girl."

She's not my girl. I open my mouth to protest, but the look in Mum's eyes says I don't want to go there right now. She's right; I do want to go after Nessa, to check she's okay. Even though it might give her some ideas that she's about to get a daughter-in-law. Fuck, she's a million miles away from the truth there. Even if Nessa and I were romantically inclined, I now come with baggage she wants no part of. But that gleam, that calculating look. It's the kind a mother wears when she wants her son to settle down.

There'll be time enough to correct her assumptions later, so, for now, I just give in. Kissing her cheek, I grab my jacket and go out into the night.

CHAPTER 23

Vanessa

What a fool I am! I knew I suffered from PTSD and panic attacks, but I can't believe I actually fainted when I held Mollie. But it wasn't exactly a conscious choice, there was no warning, nothing I could do to stop it. I haven't been so close to a baby since before *it* happened. Luckily, I've no friends who have just given birth, and if a member of staff brought their newborn into the office to proudly show them off, I would simply make myself scarce or pretend to admire them from afar. I didn't expect actually to lose conciousness. I only hope Sean understood my story and believes that I'm not prone to passing out for no reason at all. And I hope he doesn't rat on me to Ben.

My hand rubs my empty stomach. Why did I let that bastard, Simon, back into my life? Why didn't I see that he had something planned? I suppose I was lucky he took the medical way out and didn't push me down some stairs. Why hadn't I seen much he didn't want the baby? Am I so flawed that I can judge someone so wrongly? Tears prick at the corners of my eyes as my mind goes back to that fateful day.

"You did it on purpose."

"What? No? What are you talking about, Simon? There's no way! And we're engaged… I just forgot my stomach upset would affect me like that."

He'd stomped around the room, his hands pushing back his hair, he seemed to be keeping about as far away from me as he could when all I wanted was a cuddle, a hug.

"Look, it's not the right time. Maybe in the future, but not right now."

I gasp, "What are you saying?"

Now he comes over to me. Although he takes my hands in his, his palms feel cold, "Vanessa, I can't cope with a child right now. We need to get a house, get married first. It just isn't the right time." He waves his hand toward me, and it's the twisted look of disgust on his face that gets to me. "It's early; you can get it sorted. Then in the future, we can try again." He moves away again and half mumbles to himself, "She *wouldn't* have pulled a trick like this."

He's choosing this time to compare me to his ex? Then I freeze, realising just what he's suggesting I do. "You want me to have an abortion?"

His eyes stare into mine, and what I see there, chills me, "I can't do this with you right now, Vanessa. If you keep the baby, you're on your own."

"I'm not having an abortion, Simon. And that's final."

"Well, I tell you something else that's final. I'm out of here. And don't expect me to cough up child support!"

And then he'd gone. And I missed him or missed the man I'd thought he was. When he came back to me, I was over the moon.

"Look, I've had some time to think about this. The timing's wrong, but we said we'd have children one day."

My mouth drops open, "Simon, after everything you said?"

He has the grace to look sheepish, "Well, yeah, but it was the shock. Now I've had time to think I've come around to the idea." He grins, "Let's do this, Vanessa!"

"Do you mean it?" Hope starts building inside me.

"Yes, I mean it! Now come here and give me a hug. I'm going to make sure you're properly looked after."

Yeah, he'd looked after me well.

I put my hand to my mouth, stifling a sob. I've cried enough tears, felt too many pangs of conscience. And now, because of my, over the top, reaction, I've probably offended Sean by bawling my eyes out into his shirt. That bastard doesn't deserve any more of my time wasted thinking of him and what he did to me. Somehow, getting it out in the open, Sean listening without censure, has been cleansing. And, as I remember my colleague's offer and can picture in my head his strong legs delivering one of his famed karate kicks just where it would hurt Simon the most, I manage a small grin.

I could give him his address. No, Van, that's wicked. Still, in some ways, it's a nice thought, that Sean cared enough to volunteer.

Wine. I need wine. Shaking my head as though I could physically dispel the lingering memories, I make the way to my small kitchen and open the fridge. There's a bottle open from before I went away. Lifting it out I think of everything that's happened in the past few days, and how simple it all had seemed before I left for Amahad. Getting up, going to work, coming home again. Then everything got turned on its head. I was given the job I'd been hankering after and spent a night with the man I'd been lusting for. Can I start putting everything else behind me now? Emerge as a new confident woman?

Pouring a glass of the leftover wine, I sniff at it suspiciously. It smells okay, so emboldened, I take a sip. Tastes fine too. No point opening another bottle until I have to, so I might as well finish this one first. A wine connoisseur might object to it having been standing for a few days, but it doesn't bother me.

Taking my drink through to my equally small lounge, I sit back on the couch. Well, if I'd been harbouring any desire to have another night with Sean I've made it pretty clear where I stand now. He knows my aversion to babies is real. But oh, the way he'd taken charge that night, the things he'd made me feel. At least he'd dispelled any notion I'd had of being frigid. I just needed the right man to take control in the bedroom. I need a Dom.

And where was I to find one? Lifting my glass I take a fortifying sip as I find I might just have the answer for that!

Leaning over the couch I take my laptop out of my bag and plonk it on my lap. Not having used it for a while, it meanders through its boot up programs. Eventually I'm able to get into my email, then have to wait until it downloads three days' worth of spam and rubbish. I click on new email, and compose the message carefully, then without allowing myself second thoughts, click send.

Not expecting an answer this evening, I finish my wine and return to the kitchen for a refill. The ping alerting me to new mail doesn't make me hurry back; it's probably just more junk that I'll have to delete.

But when I'm back in my seat I glance at my laptop

screen. Bloody hell! Jon's responded, *and* with the documents I'd asked for. I read his short note; both attachments have to be completed, signed and returned before my request can be agreed. Picking up my wine I take another long sip to bolster my nerves and then replace it on the coffee table. Unable to curb my curiosity, I open up the files and start to read. My God! I didn't realise there was so much to it. In my naivety, I assumed applying for membership at Club Tiacapan would be as simple as joining a local gym.

As my eyes go down the pages of the second document I'd received, I feel them start to bulge from their sockets. Jesus! Some of the things on the paper entitled 'Limits List' I've never even heard of, let alone know if I want to try. Fisting? Anal and/or Vaginal? I'm going to have to start googling fast. Hmm. I glance down at the laptop; perhaps it's best not to use the work computer for this!

Just as I'm wondering whether it's worth going upstairs to switch on an ancient PC that's set up in my spare bedroom, there's a ring at my doorbell. Glancing at the screen in front of me I see it's gone ten o'clock. Who would be coming around at this hour? Then I glance down at myself. I'm hardly dressed for company, wearing my comfort clothes of a tee and shorts, but at least I'm respectable.

Getting up I go to my bag. Damn! The first flipping time I remember to get out my gun, it's not there. Of course, it isn't, before we left France we'd had to turn in all our weaponry to the Parisian based Grade A operative who'd met us there for that very purpose. Not even trained bodyguards are permitted to carry arms in the UK unless they're members of the SAS or the armed police force.

So, taking what precautions I'm able to, I look out of the peephole in the door before removing the chain and opening it. Before doing so, I stand for a second with my back to the door, my mouth dropping open. *What the hell is he doing here?*

If it's about work I can't send him away, so with shaking hands I turn the latch and let him inside.

The door opens directly into my lounge. As I stand back in politeness to let him come in, my small house immediately seems to shrink even more. It's not just that he's tall, it's his presence. Everything about him seems to suggest he's too much for me. He's walked in like a Dom, not like my colleague and partner.

As I close the door behind him, Sean turns and places his hands on my arms and squeezes slightly. His eyes examine mine. A flush comes to my cheeks as I think about the activity he's interrupted. Of course, he doesn't miss it.

"Are you okay, Nessa?" His brow furrows with concern, "Are you still upset about what happened earlier?"

At his reminder, my face blazes redder. I start to speak, but he puts a finger to my lips, "You've nothing to apologise for, Nessa. You couldn't have predicted how you'd react, and I shouldn't have pushed you. Not like that. I wasn't thinking. I'm sorry."

I move his finger away, and he lets me answer him, "It's not your fault, Sean. I'm just so sorry."

"You told me you didn't do babies; I didn't understand that you meant it."

"I should have explained before. You weren't to know. Hell, I didn't know how bad I'd become." I give a short laugh, "Guess I do now, though."

He waves toward the sofa. "Can I sit down?"

Shrugging, I invite him to the seat with a gesture, and then go and sit at the opposite end. Ruefully I eye my glass of wine, wanting another sip, but knowing if I pick up my drink I'll have to offer him one too. And I'm not sure I want him in my house for that long.

"You working?" He indicates the laptop on the table. Another damn blush and I can't meet his eyes. Then I have a horrible thought.

"Why are you here, Sean?" Jon Tharpe couldn't have told him I'd asked for the membership papers for the club, could he?

Settling back into the seat he links his hands behind his head, "I wanted to check you were alright."

Unable to copy his relaxed posture, I sit forward, my arms resting on my thighs and my hands clasping and unclasping between my knees, "I'm fine, really. You can see that for yourself. I was going to go up to bed in a moment." I hope the last will get rid of him.

But the bastard's smirking. He inches nearer, closing the gap between us and with his hand under my chin, turns me to face him. Another of his probing looks. "Are you trying to get rid of me, Nessa?" He gently moves my head one way then the other, carefully examining my expression, "Hmm, what am I interrupting? What have you been up to?" Turning me to face him again, he adds, "What aren't you telling me?"

There's no point in hiding it; he'll know soon enough. The next time he turns up at the club, I'll be there. Taking a deep breath, I admit, "I'm just looking at the forms for Club Tiacapan. I'm applying for membership."

His eyes open wide, then he laughs out loud, the sound coming straight from his belly, "I wondered what was getting you all hot and bothered."

"I'm not…"

The chuckling stops, but a wide grin covers his face, "You're blushing," he touches my face, then he moves his fingers down to my neck, "And I can feel your pulse racing. And I bet if I touched your pussy you'd be soaking wet."

I don't think it's possible for my face to burn any more than it already is, but that's what it feels like. I go to deny that I'm in any way turned on, and then fear he'll know I'm not telling the truth. Deciding it's best to address it face on, I open up my laptop. "I've been going through this." I point to the limits list on the screen, trying to be as matter of fact as I can.

He pulls the laptop closer so he can view it too. "You haven't got very far," he observes. He's peering at what I have filled in.

Pulling my shoulders up to my ears and then letting them drop again I admit, "I don't know what half of these things are."

"That's interesting," he points to an item near the top of the first page, "Anal isn't a hard limit. Something you want to try, sweetheart?"

I smack his hand away, "None of your business."

264

"Oh babe, it most definitely is. I'll have to see your limits list if I'm going to be your Dom."

My eyes widen, and I turn to him, "Sean, you've been there, done that. You'll want to move on."

Something flares in his eyes, "Don't brush me off like that, Nessa. I just haven't found someone I wanted to play with more than once before." He breaks off, and then says more softly, "Until now."

I look at him in surprise, is he saying what I think he is? "Me?" My voice comes out so high pitched I try to lower it, "You want to play with me?"

He indicates the laptop again, "That right there. That shows there's endless possibilities, things for us to try, things for me to teach you." His hand cups my chin again, "We certainly wouldn't be able to get through all that in one night."

I stand up, walk to the window even though the curtains are drawn, and I can't see outside. "Sean, you don't do relationships, and I'm not looking for one. And there's Mollie to consider. I don't *do* babies."

He's come to stand behind me without me being aware that he'd moved. Warm hands reach around me and take hold of mine. "We could keep it to the club. You could be my mine exclusively, my sub."

But how long would it take before he got bored of me? And would I be happy to be with him only for sex? A shiver runs through me as I understand that could be an answer. I get mind-blowing sex without the trappings of a man and a baby. *I'd get Sean.*

"Exclusive? You'd just be playing with me?" If I could

even consider agreeing to this, I wouldn't want him having sex with all and sundry while we were together.

His hands run up and down my arms making me tremble, "Exclusive," he whispers in my ear, his warm breath sending tingles down my spine, "For as long as we both want."

It has to be to do with the forms I was completing before he arrived, but suddenly that option sounds very attractive. With him, in Club Tiacapan I could act out all my dreams and desires, and even those I don't know I have yet. *What is fisting anyway?*

"Okay." My voice isn't quite steady as he turns me to face him. With no warning his lips come down on mine, his tongue teasing, taunting until I open for him. This is no tender approach, this is a demonstration of ownership and oh, how I want to be owned by him. I respond in kind, our tongues twist together, fighting for dominance. Neither of us has closed our eyes. Though his are half-lidded, his smouldering gaze still manages to burn into mine. We mate with our mouths until finally, we have to part, each panting to get air into our starving lungs.

Stepping back from me, he brushes one hand over his hair, his mouth tight, his muscles taut as I watch him fighting to bring himself under control. Slightly bemused my hands flutter, I thought he'd be taking me straight to bed or ripping my clothes off.

He rolls his head back on his shoulders, then looks down at me with a smile, "Hell, Nessa, you steal my breath away."

I have to laugh; he has the same effect on me.

Reaching out his hand, he takes hold of mine and gently brushes his fingertips over my knuckles, "If you're going to play in the club, you need to get that limit list completed. We'll go through it together. Come." His fingers curl round, and with a little tug, he gets me moving back to the sofa. This time he allows no distance between us.

Picking up my laptop he takes charge. "Right," he points to the first item I haven't completed, "How do you feel about this?"

Surprisingly, his casual approach helps keep my embarrassment away as we work through some of my deepest desires. He clicks the boxes as I tell him what I do or don't want to do, or what I might like to try. And then we come to the item I'd got stuck on earlier.

"I don't know what that is."

"Fisting? Well…"

As he goes on to explain, I take a cushion and use it to cover my face then peer out at him over the top, "Is that even possible? Especially… there?"

Giving a snort of laughter, he assures me it is, but adds, "Not that I've done it myself." He shows me his hands, like everything about him, they are on the large side, "Think I might be a bit over equipped for that."

Moving on and completing the list, I'm pleased to find that we're fairly compatible. There's not a lot of things that I get the sense he'd like me to try that I have major objections to, and, being new to all this and fairly conservative, nothing I'd like to try that he dismisses. As we go through and check things off, he takes the time to explain what each activity entails, with the dual results I come to appreciate just how experienced he is and how lucky I am to have landed myself a Master Dom and just how much this conversation is turning me on!

At last, we've finished, and I've added my electronic signature to the documents and have returned them to Jon. Sean explains when I first visit the club I'll be asked to sign hard copies, but at least this way they'll already have them on file. As an employee of Grade A I have regular health check-ups, and so won't need to get tested again to prove I'm clean.

"There's one more thing we should cover while we're here."

I thought we'd done everything. "What?"

His fingers reach out for my laptop. "Can I borrow that for a sec?"

"Sure." I let him take over, watching as he calls up Dropbox and logs into his account. A moment later he's downloaded another document. Peering over his shoulder I see it's a blank contract. A Dom/sub contract. Realising he means to formulate our verbal agreement sends a tremor of anticipation through me. *I'm actually going to do this. I'm going to agree to give my body to this man.*

He types in our names. "I'll put it for an initial month, after that we'll see how we get on, okay?" As he speaks he's looking intently at the screen, "I'll refer to the limits list we've just completed." I notice his lips are pursed, and there's no sign of levity in his expression. "I don't normally bother with contracts, but if we're going to be playing together and as this is all new to you, you need to understand what you're getting into." I notice he's making some alterations, taking out clauses and adding others in. "Right, take a look at this. We can discuss anything you don't understand."

Now the laptop's facing toward me, and I start to read. He's made it an uncomplicated as possible. All our play will be restricted to the club, and only outside with our mutual agreement. Our arrangement is to be exclusive. He will look out for my safety and abide by my safeword. The next section is about communication, setting out that I have a responsibility to tell him my thoughts and feelings at any time during play, to be honest, and open and not to be hesitant or embarrassed. Although I'm not certain how it will pan out in practice, for now, I don't see anything to object to.

Oh, hang on a minute. What's this? I point to the offending clause on the screen, "Sean?"

I expected him to show some sign of amusement, but as his mouth turns down, it's clear that for him this is serious. "The punishment clause. Yes, I thought you might question that." He rubs his hands over his forehead as he starts to explain, "How can I put this? The Dom has a responsibility to keep the sub safe. At any time, if the sub puts herself at risk, for example, she doesn't use her safeword when she should; then a punishment will follow. The point of any reprimand is to enforce the agreement between us and ensure the behaviour is not repeated."

I'm not sure I like that. "I don't understand. What sort of punishment?"

He closes his eyes, and then opens them again, "It can

take many forms depending on the nature of the transgression. Sometimes it's just the withholding of affection. For something more serious it might be a spanking or flogging."

"I thought spanking and flogging were supposed to be fun?"

"They are. But increase the severity and…"

"I get the picture." My lips press together, I don't know that I want to agree with this part.

He sighs, "Nessa; some subs act like brats to provoke their Doms into punishing them because they enjoy it. But I doubt you'll do that. At least, not at first. And the whole thing fits into my duty to keep you safe. I never want you to put yourself in a dangerous situation; this clause will remind you there are penalties for doing that."

Put that way; it doesn't seem too bad. And I can't see me provoking him; I'm someone who obeys rules and doesn't knowingly flout them. And I'm so new to this; I'll be looking for his guidance at all times.

"Okay." My voice is a bit shaky as I agree. "And this bit?"

Now he chuckles, "Yeah, I amended that. The standard contract says the sub will keep herself bare for her Dom, but I like your ginger pubes. I just changed it, so you'll keep yourself tidy."

"What about you? Can I specify how I want you groomed?" It seems a bit one-sided.

"I'm the Dom, babe." He smirks as he reinforces his role then he grows serious again, "This contract just sets out expectations on both our parts. The things that people who go into a vanilla relationship don't talk about. It's not legally binding, and you can walk away at any time. But once you sign it, I'll take it as your agreement that your body will be mine. Mine to do with what I want, mine to pleasure or punish as I see fit."

Those words make me squirm. I've already seen just how much pleasure he can give me when I let him take charge. I'll ignore the punishment clause for now, I can't see myself doing anything he'd want to chastise me for. "And it's just for the club?" I press for the confirmation, not wanting his control to spread into our working lives.

"Yes. Unless we both want to play elsewhere."

I consider it, remembering the expectations with which I'd entered relationships in the past, and how disappointed I'd been when those hadn't panned out. And the thought that I would be giving myself over into his care makes my clit tingle.

He's quiet, giving me time to process. Then, after a few moments, he speaks again, "If you don't want to agree to this now, that's fine too, Nessa. When we're back from Amahad, we'll go to the club, and you can get a better feel for what's going on and how everything works before jumping in with both two feet."

Suddenly I make a decision, "No, I'm in, Sean. I'll sign the contract now."

His arms come around me, and he pulls me to him, placing a kiss on the top of my head, "Always knew you were a brave woman, Nessa." His lips nuzzle my hair, "And I can't wait to start playing properly with you."

Hell, he's turning me on!

"Right, okay. Now that's sorted." He takes the laptop from me and closes the lid.

I suppose he has to get back to Mollie, but hell, I wish he didn't have to leave me in this state. I'll have to get out my vibrator once he's gone. For an unknown reason, a fantasy comes into my head where he's spanking me for some infraction I'd committed. I squirm.

CHAPTER 24

Sean

S he's been taunting me with her too tight tee since I got here, and those shorts she's wearing show her toned legs go on for miles. And fuck, add to that the subject matter of our conversation and I'm sporting an erection as hard as granite.

It's not difficult to appreciate how aroused Nessa's become. My nostrils flare as I inhale her scent of arousal, and I know if I could touch her, she'd be dripping for me. And that bodes well when I eventually get her into the club. But God knows when that will be, we've got to sort out the Amahadian issues first *and* the situation with Danielle. It's a possibility we'll need to extend the month before we even start.

Casting a glance toward the woman in question I can already read her like a book. The disappointment shining out from her face lets me know she expects me to leave her now and go. But I'm not going to do that. We might have just agreed that our official Dom/sub relationship will be restricted to the club, but that doesn't mean I can't give us both some relief right now.

Standing, I hold out my hand. She takes it and then steps toward the door. I give a little pull, and she falls back into my arms with a little gasp. Unashamedly I pull her in tight, so she's left in little doubt about my desire for her. And in case she is, I rub my throbbing erection against her soft belly.

"I thought we had to wait until we were at the club," her breathy voice tells me she doesn't want to, and neither do I.

"Other places by mutual agreement," I remind her. Her sigh shows me she's not going to argue about that.

Lowering my head, I let my lips continue the conversation, my mouth brushing over hers in a light caress. She opens for me, and as I move my hand to the back of her head, I hold her in place as my tongue dances with hers, keeping it gentle. Breathing in through my nose, her unique perfume only fuels my arousal. She moans into my mouth, and I groan in response. Without breaking away, I put my hands on the bottom of her tee and start easing it up. When it reaches her chin, I have to end the kiss. She makes no objection as I slide it over her head and discard her upper clothing.

Inhaling sharply, my eyes settle on her fire engine red bra, a colour that could have been designed to taunt me. I put both my hands on her scarlet covered orbs, and trace the lace with my fingertips. "Are you wearing a matching set?" Fuck, I hope she is. The colour should clash with her hair and skin, but instead, it enhances it. Even the thought's driving me mad.

"Yes," she pants out.

I don't want to remove her bra, but need to see, to touch her. I pull down the cups, and her breasts spill out over the top, her nipples already erect as though seeking my attention. Not wanting to disappoint I bend slightly and close my lips over one, while toying my fingers on the other. Her breaths are shallow now, a red flush spreading down from her face until it covers her whole body. I love the way she's so responsive to me and how her skin betrays her arousal.

She's finding it hard to keep still, and I've having difficulty keeping myself from grinding against her, knowing if I do I might end this before we get a chance to get down to the real business. *Shit, keep control of yourself, man.* But the very fact I'm here, doing this and not abiding by our agreement to keep it in the dungeon shows my lack of control goes bone deep.

Wanting to see the rest of her underwear I undo the button of her shorts, and then the zip. Loosened they fall away revealing a frilly thong which perfectly matches her bra, the material insufficient to prevent her pubes from poking out. Stepping back I take a second to admire her. She's bloody gorgeous, and I can't wait to get my mouth on her.

Placing my hands on her shoulders, I nudge her gently in the direction of the couch and then apply a little more pressure when the back of her knees touches the seat cushion, so she's forced to sit down. Grabbing hold of the neckband of my shirt I dispense with it quickly and open the top two buttons on my jeans to give my cock some much-needed space. Then I drop to my knees in front of her.

"These expensive?" I tug on the waistband of her thong.

"They weren't cheap," she replies with a little giggle.

"Lift up then." She lifts her bum enabling me to remove the scanty article of clothing that's blocking me from my target. I bring it to my nostrils and inhale deeply, being throwing it aside. Her eyes flare at the sight and then darken as I place a kiss on her mound.

Watching her carefully, I push her back and keep one hand on her stomach as I lower my mouth and circle my tongue around her clit. She jumps as I blow a breath on her sensitive nub, but my hand keeps her still and under my control. Touching my fingers to her slit, I collect the copious moisture there and slide them back, circling her puckered hole. My lips curl into a smile, as I remember the limits and what hadn't been excluded. Gently I press a finger inside, feeling the resistance from that band of muscles.

My eyes, still fixed on hers, take note of every slight movement, and as her muscles begin to tighten in an automatic effort to keep me out, I instruct her, my voice rumbling against that sensitive bundle of nerves, "Bear down, let me in."

She scrunches up her face with concentration as she attempts to obey me, and I have a finger inside. I add another, and slowly start pumping my fingers in and out while sucking and nibbling on her clit.

"Oh!" Her mouth drops open in surprise at the sensation, and again I smile. Sometime, we're going to have some fun with this.

My dual assault combined with her already high level of arousal pushes her quickly to the edge and I decide to let her reach her peak, torturing her isn't my main aim today. "Come for me."

She shatters with a scream, and I continue to drive my fingers into her arse, extending her orgasm and forcing another from her as I bite down on her clit.

"Sean!" She screams out my name and tries to rise from the seat; my arm anchors her down.

This time I take mercy on her, and with a last soft caress lift myself away from her body. Her eyes are closed, her head thrown back, and her chest rises and falls quickly. Her breasts, still overflowing from her bra, look like plump cushions that I long to get my cock between. But that will have to wait for another day.

After a short while, her eyes open and meet mine, and her lips curl. As I rise on my knees, my jeans slip over my hips, and my cock bounces up eagerly, knocking against the hard muscles of my stomach. A drop of pre-cum leaks from the tip. Eyeing it, she licks her lips.

I take it as an invitation, and draw myself onto my feet, feeling the twinge in my leg reminding me kneeling on it so long wasn't perhaps one of my greatest ideas. But the throbbing in my loins overrides the residual pain which recedes to take a back seat for now. Leaning over her, my cock bobs just in front of her mouth.

Again, her tongue flicks out, but she makes no move toward me, and her eyes meet mine, widening in anxiety and it hits me she might never have done this before. Placing my hand behind her head, I draw her toward me. The head of my dick touches her lips, and I smear the pre-cum over them, analysing her every reaction. I don't want to force her to do something she doesn't want or isn't ready for, but my cock's crying out to get inside that damp, warm haven. It might be wishful thinking, but I interpret her hesitation as fear of doing something wrong, rather than distaste. If I'm wrong, I'll pull away.

That's it, her mouth opens, and I push an inch inside. Now her tongue's swirling around, teasing me, and I groan in satisfaction then push inside a little further, pleased to see her pupils dilating again as she starts to comprehend the power she has over me.

"Put your hands around my cock. Control how much you want to take."

She responds to my direction, seeming to relax as I tell her what to do. Knowing I won't now be giving her more than she wants I start to thrust gently, her mouth sucks me in, not too far, but in time she'll be able to take more.

My head goes backwards as the feeling of being inside her in this way is a slice of utter heaven. Her hands start to move up and down my shaft, and then she's massaging my balls, little squeezes only just the right side of pain. I won't be able to last long, and as the tell-tale tingle starts in my spine and my cock begins to swell I warn her, "Pull away now if you don't want me to come in your mouth."

She does, but I don't care. One day, she'll swallow. What we're doing is all new to her, and I don't mind taking things slow as we explore more ground. But I'll be pushing her boundaries eventually. It's my job, as her Dom.

When one door closes, another opens, I mentally remind my painfully steel hard cock, as I take a condom from the pocket of my jeans and smooth it on, noticing she's watching my every move. Using my upper body strength, move her, so she's lying on the couch. It's a tight squeeze, but I manage to come down on top of her, resting on one arm to keep my weight off of her.

Positioning myself at her entrance, I push inside. She's tight, so I thrust gently, gradually gaining more ground until I'm fully seated, then give her a moment to adjust. When her legs come up around me I know she's ready, and again move, quickening my pace and thrusting harder.

I'm already close and know I won't last long, but I refuse to take this just for myself. Noticing the frustration on her face, I move my hand down and begin to strum her clit. Her muscles begin to tighten, her brow furrows and her teeth clench. Her eyes start to roll back in her head, and then almost violent tremors shake her body as she tenses around me and goes over the top. A few more short bursts triggered by the spasm of her vaginal muscles and I'm right there with her.

Careful not to crush her, I rest my forehead against hers, our ragged breathing in unison as we both struggle to recover. I feel her heart beating against my chest and her lungs heaving. Her skin has a faint sheen of sweat covering it making it shine in the overhead light. God this woman will be the death of me. How does she make me come so fucking hard?

Starting to recover I ease myself down beside her, shifting her slightly, so she fits against my side. I hold her tight, close up against me. The contract we so recently put out signatures to seems to mock me. Keep sex to the club? Yeah right. That's just not going to happen. Not when it's this incredible between us.

As Nessa sleepily snuggles beside me, she gives a lovely

little snore which makes me glance down. Her breasts are still bulging; she must be uncomfortable like that. Noticing it's a front fastening bra I undo it and let those large globes drop free. If it wasn't so late, I'm be tempted to get my hands on them again, but we've got a plane to catch in the morning. But fuck me, another round wouldn't go amiss. My hand hovers in mid-air, but I manage to restrain myself.

Who am I kidding? I'll be wanting to have this woman as often as I can. Perhaps every night if she moves in with me. A full-time sub ready and waiting for me at any time I want. Hmm. My cock twitches as though it likes the idea.

Wait a minute! What am I thinking? Nessa and I would never work; that's why we were going to keep this part of our lives separate and compartmentalised. I've got a baby to consider! It wouldn't be fair on her or Mollie to even suggest it. It's going to be hard enough keeping them apart in Amahad.

CHAPTER 25

Vanessa

S ean's worn me out. I'm barely conscious as I feel his strong arms go around me and carry me to bed, and only just register the brief goodbye kiss to my cheek. Then I turn over and drift off into one of the best sleeps I've ever had in my life.

Waking the next morning and remembering the events of the night before, I know I'll be embarrassed later when I see Sean again. Some of the items on the limits list were not things you'd discuss with a work partner. *But he's more than that now. He's my Dom.* Entering my kitchen, I check the bottle of wine in the fridge realising I can only have had two glasses at most, and that wasn't enough to blame signing that darn contract. *Had I really agreed that he could punish me?* Only in the club, I must remember that. Only in Club Tiacapan and it was all for play. Not serious. *But still.* But we hadn't been at the club last night. And I got carried away, *again.*

In the cold light of day, signing a contract to agreeing to give a man control over my body doesn't seem something I'd do at all, but that's exactly what I appear to have done. And neither can I forget what happened after I added my signature. My body is feeling slightly sore, muscles I've not often used making their protest known makes me recall precisely what happened after we'd put away the laptop. Christ, that man can make my body sing! I have to be careful, I could become addicted to his touch. No, I'll have to explain to him, leaving it to the club is by far the best idea. There'll be less danger of me getting too attached to him and less chance of becoming the type of woman who'll want to cling to him. And then I won't have him at all. This is Sean, the original manwhore we're talking about.

The flight we're booked on leaves just after midday, so cutting my thoughts short I get a move on sorting out and packing what I need to take, then get off to the airport to meet the others. It's easy enough to spot Ryan and Nat, like most of Grade A they're tall and stand head and shoulders above the rest of the crowd. Joining them we exchange greetings and pleasantries to while away the time. Discussing the business of our trip is not something we'd do in public. Hunter appears next, but as the minutes tick down to the gate closing I'm anxiously looking around for Sean. It's not like him to be late. As the final call or boarding is announced over the loudspeaker, he's only got a short time left.

Then, at last, he appears, sleeping baby in one arm and all the paraphernalia that comes along with that over one shoulder and carrying a duffle with his clothes on the other. Ryan steps forward to relieve him of some of his burdens, and I take a step back, distancing myself from him and Mollie. *How embarrassing if I have a panic attack here.* I concentrate on taking deep breaths.

There's no time to delay; we need to head to the plane.

When we board, I make sure to take the seat next to Nat, leaving Sean, Hunter and Ryan to sit way back down the aisle.

But that's not the last I hear of my companions during the flight, well, one at least. Travelling with a young baby must be an eye-opener to Sean. She isn't too bad on the way out from London, but as we transfer planes at Dubai Mollie starts to protest, and Ryan laughs at Sean's embarrassment as he tries to keep her quiet and amused. This time, seated close by, I've a good view as Mollie starts exercising her lungs when she drops her dummy for the umpteenth time, and I watch Sean rummage in her bag to find a clean replacement. I recall the number of times I've cursed people with crying babies wondering why they can't keep them quiet. Now I'm experiencing it first-hand I'll have more sympathy in the future. Sean's doing everything he can, but it's obvious nothing's going to pacify his baby. Caught up in the drama I'm commiserating from afar, and for once, the sight and sound of a young child doesn't trigger my normal reaction.

By the time we arrive at the airport in Al Qur'ah we're all exhausted as well as partly deaf, and relieved that Kadar's arranged transport to take us to the palace. And when Cara steps up and takes Mollie from Sean the relief that floods through him is palpable.

Cara grins sympathetically at him, "You look done in!"

"You're not wrong there." Sean stretches his neck and shoulders. Mollie might not weigh much, but he'd been holding her for nigh on ten hours straight now and must be pleased to be relieved of his burden.

Zoe has come out alongside her sister-in-law and is rubbing one hand over her seven-month baby bump while stretching out her other to look at the baby in Cara's arms. "Oh, she's beautiful, Sean. She looks just like you!"

For some reason, this comment and seeing them cooing over the baby gets to me, and a strangled sound escapes involuntarily. Sean glances down, and catches a glimpse of my face which I can feel has paled. Touching his fingers briefly to my shoulder, he whispers, "Why don't you go ahead and get settled in? I'll join you shortly."

My head jerks, he's given me the excuse I need, but I answer with a small shake of my head, I don't want to appear unprofessional.

Zoe's watching me closely. "Are you okay?"

Sean answers for me, "It was a long flight; we're all tired." I give an inward sigh of relief that he hasn't given away my secret.

I feel a nudge in my back; Sean's pushing me away and toward the houses in the compound where we'll be staying. "Go get yourself sorted out; I'll be along shortly."

Giving in I nod, and leave them to it.

Reaching the same small but perfectly adequate house we were assigned last time, I step inside feeling like I'm coming home. Was it really only three days ago, that we left this place? Seems like so much has happened in just a few days. Going upstairs I open my carry-on bag and start taking out my clothes, and then I stop. With the way, we're moving from place to place I can see why Sean doesn't bother to unpack. Perhaps I won't this time either. Replacing my clothes and pulling out my washbag instead,

I go to the bathroom and splash my face. Being around Sean and the baby today woke me up as much as the cold water from the taps has done. While sex with Sean is great, keeping everything to the club and not letting it spill over into our everyday lives is a bit like having my cake and eating it. He's not the man for me, not with the responsibilities he has. At last removed from the company of the baby I allow myself to relax and breathe normally for the first time in hours.

I don't know how long I've been daydreaming, staring at my tired reflection in the mirror, but a banging door brings me to my senses. *Sean's back.* And now it's time to face the music, Sean, Mollie and I are going to be living in close proximity for the foreseeable future, and I can't avoid them forever. I can't stay hidden up here. Taking a few deep breaths to prepare myself, I go downstairs. And find Sean alone.

"Where's Mollie?" I ask, looking around in the unlikely even she might be hiding somewhere.

It's impossible to miss how tired and drained he looks as he replies, "Cara's taken her for the night. She's staying in the palace nursery."

To say I'm relieved I'm not going to be forced into dealing with my issues with her tonight is an understatement; they haven't invented a word to describe how I feel about the reprieve I've been given. I let out a breath I hadn't realised I'd been holding, then, when I look at Sean, I see how selfish I've been thinking only of myself. His complexion is tinged with grey, red around his eyes, "You look exhausted."

He tilts his head to the side, and his eyes, gleaming with intent, fix on mine, "Come here."

Automatically my feet start moving across to him, but I stop before I get too close. His arms reach out, and he pulls me into him. I've got suspicions of what might be on his mind, and I'm not certain it's a good idea to go there. Had last night been a mistake? If we repeat it, it would be. I'm not sure how long I can keep my heart from getting involved if he thinks us making love is going to be a regular thing. I try to stop him, "Sean, I..."

"Just give me this." His lips come down to mine, and he kisses me with the lightest of touches. As my traitorous body starts to respond, he deepens the caress, his tongue demanding entry. My hands go up to tunnel through his hair, pulling his head closer to mine. The touch of his hair feels like silk beneath my fingers, his musky male scent so enticing I breathe deeply through my nose to get the full effect. A tingle runs down my spine, and I feel myself growing wet. *How can I resist him?*

He pulls away, resting his forehead against mine, "Tell me you want this too."

I'm fighting for sanity, forcing myself to remember he comes with strings. Some sense of self-preservation stirs, "Sean, it's a bad idea." If I allow my baser instincts to let him into my bed tonight I know I'll never want to let him go. I don't kid myself that I'm anything more to him than here, and available. I'll be letting myself in for a whole lot of hurt unless we keep sex to a pleasurable activity between us, and limited to the club.

"The way I'm feeling right now, it's a very good one."

I don't know how, but from somewhere I summon up the strength to pull away, "It won't look that way in the morning." It takes everything I am to reject him. "We agreed on our roles last night. I'll be your sub at the club, but nothing more. I'm going to bed now, Sean. Alone." I swallow, my mouth suddenly dry, "Repeating last night would complicate everything. Don't, don't push me Sean. Please?" I know my eyes are leaking as I plead with him to let me go. Another night in his arms won't be enough. I'll want to go back for more the next, and the ones after that. I won't be able to stop.

He lifts his hand to my cheek, gently cupping it, his fingers gently caressing my skin and it's all I can do not to give in to temptation. *If he makes one more move toward me...* But after only a few seconds he nods, and turns away. Dismissed I make my way upstairs to my lonely bed.

I toss and turn, falling into a proper sleep only shortly before dawn. Morning comes far too soon. I wake, disorientated, before remembering where I am. As I go downstairs gurgling sounds greet me, and in the sitting room I find Mollie lying on a play mat kicking out at a baby's play gym. She seems happy and content. I quickly flick my eyes away from her as I make my way into the kitchen where I find Sean making breakfast, and, thank God, he's already got the coffee on the go.

As I walk in, he nods toward the room I've just left, "Cara brought her over earlier. She's a good kid. Happy to amuse herself. When she's not on a plane, that is." He laughs, obviously remembering the torment of the day before.

Moving over to help myself to a drink, I take a moment to examine him, and immediately wish I hadn't. His jeans hang low on his hips, the top button open, and his chest is bare allowing me an uninterrupted sight of the glorious V arrowing down to what I already know is an impressive package hiding underneath. Why does he have to be so devastatingly handsome and so hard to resist? He catches me staring, and smirks, his boyish charm attracting me like a bee to honey. I feel so drawn to him it's hard to keep my distance, but as I'm wondering how to keep away a knock at the door breaks my absorption in the hot man in front of me.

With Sean's eyes on me, I remember to check who's there before turning off the security system and opening it. As I expected, it's Ryan and Nat who come bearing gifts which they pass over to me, nothing special, just a couple of ID tags so we can get into the palace without needing an escort. I lead them into where Sean's dishing up some food on plates.

As Ryan reaches over to snag some bacon, he catches a glimpse of Sean's state of undress, "Oh my God," he exaggerates putting his hand over his eyes, "Put some clothes on man, please. Not all of us like to see your junk hanging out first thing in the morning."

His words make Sean look down at himself, and he throws a towel at Ryan when he confirms he is suitably covered. Nevertheless, he does up the top button. "Nessa, could you grab a tee for me from my room, please?"

Nat swings round from the coffee machine that he'd made a beeline for, "Nessa?"

Sean shrugs, "Van makes her sound like something you cart gear around in; she doesn't like Ness, and Vanessa is too much of a mouthful. Thank you." He adds the last as I hand him his shirt, and leans down to whisper in my ear, "Though a very tasty mouthful."

As usual, I hate my complexion, unable to do anything to stop the flush coming to my cheeks. Ryan gives me a sharp look and then barks a laugh, "Like that is it?"

Shooting my fist out I thump his arm, "No it isn't, like, well, whatever it is you're suggesting." I realise my quick denial has probably only confirmed what he's thinking.

Sean's raises his eyebrows, and I redden even more. Ryan's outright laughing and Nat's sniggering behind his hand. At that moment I'm saved as Mollie starts to cry. No one moves for a second, then Ryan gets up and goes to collect her, bringing her in and jiggling her around until she starts laughing and giggling. Sean heats up a bottle in the microwave and holds it out.

"Want to feed her?"

Ryan glances at me, and goes as if to pass her over. I take a step backwards, not wanting to risk dropping her, I'm starting to shake as it is. With a puzzled shrug, he takes the bottle, perches on a stool and expertly puts the teat to her mouth. She starts to guzzle noisily, and I'm impressed by the way he's handling her.

"You've had some practice at that," Nat observes.

"Two nieces and a nephew," Ryan informs him, "And a worn-out sister who takes advantage whenever I go around."

Sean's giving me a careful look; I nod to show him I'm

fine, and proving it, go and fill a plate with some of the food he's cooked, my hand only slightly trembling. He's dished up bacon, scrambled egg and toast, enough for all of us, so he was obviously expecting the others to turn up. By turning my back on Ryan with Mollie in my arms, I'm able to eat it all.

Another coffee later, we're all done. Sean's disappeared and then returned with a now fresher smelling Mollie, and after having visited the gun safe and taken out the weapons we each prefer, we make our way to the palace. Once again I'm stunned by the wealth blatantly on display, and doubt I'll ever get used to it. Although I've coped quite well this morning or, in other words, have successfully avoided having anything to do with her, I'm pleased when Sean drops Mollie off at the royal nursery. Then, knowing the place the best, he takes the lead as we make our way to the government offices. Once there we're offered seats in Kadar's reception area.

The emir has clearly had an early start to his day, and we aren't shown straight in. The reason for the delay becomes evident as just before our meeting is supposed to start, his office door opens, and out comes several robed men with weather-beaten faces. It only takes me a second to appreciate these must be the famed desert sheikhs that I've heard so much about.

One pauses his steps as he reaches us. "Sean, it's good to see you again. How's the leg?"

"Much better, thank you, Sheikh Rais," Rising to his feet, Sean accompanies his words with a bow of his head, "And how are you and the Haimi?"

"My people and I are well," Rais, a fierce looking man narrows his eyes, "But what I hear about the threats to our country are not so. You've come to help us, I believe?"

"Grade A will do their best," Sean assures him.

"As they always do." Rais claps his hand on Sean's shoulder, almost making him stagger, and then goes off to catch up with the other tribal leaders.

A sound draws my attention, and I turn to see Kadar waiting at his office door. He's looking toward his assistant, "Ma'mum, could you ask Sheikha Cara to join us, please?" Then he turns to us, "Please come in." Standing aside as we enter his office he then waves us to the conference table in front of the windows. "Please, sit. Help yourself to refreshments."

Knowing from my last visit the coffee here is dense and strong I avoid it, but my colleagues busy themselves rattling cups and saucers, and I take a moment to study the emir, now seeing him in a formal setting. He's still only in the first year of his rule. He's a tall man, olive skinned and wearing traditional robes, his headdress secured by a golden agal. His dark eyes seem penetrating, as he waits for people to get settled, landing on each man in turn as though assessing them. Finally, his gaze lands on me, and he offers a small smile which lightens his face, making him instantly more approachable.

At last everyone has sorted themselves and taken their seats when Cara enters the room. Accompanying her is Hunter, guiding her in with his hand on her elbow. Instantly Kadar's eyes darken at the sight. He grunts a greeting, adding, "Hunter, please sit there." He points to a chair at the opposite end of the table from Cara making me wonder what the history is between them.

"Oh, for goodness sake Kadar," Cara raps her brother-in-law on the hand, "Get over yourself, Hunter's my friend. You know that perfectly well."

Hunter's grinning widely as he winks at Cara and shrugs, making his tousled hair flop down over his forehead. He brushes it back.

The door opens, and Nijad comes in and takes his place by the side of his brother. Both sheikhs are strikingly handsome men, but as my eyes flick toward Sean, with his boyish charm and roguish looks, I find myself comparing them to him and finding them wanting. Even Hunter can't hold a candle to him. *And, for a while at least, he's mine.* A shiver of a different sort runs down my spine as I recall just what he's capable of doing to me. Which is not the right frame of mind for a serious meeting.

Kadar acknowledges his brother with a nod, and then, after giving a piercing stare round the table gets down to business. "Thank you for coming here today. I've invited Cara here as she's been looking at the chatter on the web and seeing if there's anything there that can help us. Cara?"

Cara, who I now look at with more interest having a greater understanding of the Dom/sub dynamic now, has definitely grown in her relationship with Nijad. I watch her with interest, Grade A had been providing bodyguards for the sheikhs during the period when she'd first come to Amahad. She'd been a shy retiring woman then, but is so full of confidence and poise today and perfectly at ease being a woman in a roomful of powerful men. Deciding I could learn something from her, I watch as she opens her laptop. "I've been trying to hack into the emails that Amir al-Fahri sends and receives, but he's obviously updated their encryption. All I can tell you is the volume has recently increased, but I can't get into who they're from or to, or the content. So, I'm sorry, but I'm of no immediate help there."

"Cara," I say her name to get her attention, "Is there anything I can help with?"

She knows my area of expertise, and I haven't got the hacking skills she has, "No, I don't think so at the moment, Vanessa. I'll keep working on breaking the encryption, and if I do get in, no doubt the messages will be in code, and that's when you can help."

I nod.

"So," Kadar begins, "We know there's a credible threat against Amahad, notably our tourist venues. But we don't know exactly when or where, just that it will be soon."

Everyone nods or offers another gesture of in agreement at his succinct summary.

"We've tightened up security, and have doubled the checks at the airports," the emir continues.

"We'll post Grade A men at the airport, casino and souk as well. They'll wear local clothing, so they'll fit in," Hunter announces.

"Do you think the harem will be a target?" Nijad consults his wife as he refers to the part of the palace recently converted to be a hen party venue.

"We've only just started taking bookings, and we've not got

anything definite for another month. And as the newest renovation to the palace, we took security seriously. I'm not sure there's much to worry about." Cara's looking thoughtful.

"Wouldn't hurt to put a man there as well."

"Or a woman?" Sean raises his eyebrows at me. He's offering me a role, but is it just because he thinks it's the least likely target?

It brings Hunter's attention to me, "Do you want to take responsibility for the harem?"

Put on the spot, I can't see how I can refuse. I'm an operative, and the most junior and least experienced at the table. "I'm fine with that."

"Zoe would be heartbroken if all her good work was destroyed, so thank you, Vanessa. You'll have palace guards there as well," Kadar reassures me.

"Perhaps they'll offer you a cheap rate for your hen party afterwards," Ryan laughs, and my face goes red. But I can't stop my eyes flicking toward Sean who's grinning at me. I look quickly away.

Kadar's taken the suggestion seriously, "I'm sure we'll be able to do something."

"Thank you, but I'm not getting married!" The words tumble out of my mouth as I squirm in embarrassment, wanting the focus to be taken off me.

"I'll take the casino." Sean butts in, making me thankful to him for turning the subject away from my non-existent wedding. "I know it fairly well, and can work with the security that's already in place." There are a few sniggers as people realise just how he knows it so thoroughly.

And of course, Ryan can't resist, "Hopefully you know

more than the bar where you picked up your conquests, Sean."

Sean throws a balled-up piece of paper at Ryan, "I set up their security, you jerk."

Hunter taps on the table, impatient to get us back to business, "I'll take the airport." He points his finger across the table, "Like Sean and the casino, I already have knowledge of the weak points as I did some work for you there before, Kadar, when we were beefing up all around as the oil workers started to come in."

Ryan and Nat are having a private discussion; then Ryan speaks for them both. "We'll take the souk. Be useful if we have some of your men with us. Our Arabic is pretty good, but our accents would give us away. They'll help us to blend in better and with more manpower we can cover more ground."

"Of course," the emir agrees, "Every man we can spare will be at your disposal."

"The desert sheikhs have offered some of their warriors; I think we should take them up on it," Nijad proposes.

"Good idea, brother. And the soldiers at the garrison in Ẓalmā?"

Nijad wipes his hand over his face, "That's a difficult one, Kadar. The information tells us that the threats are directed at our capital city, Al Qur'ah, but I don't want to put all our eggs in one basket and run the risk that the information is to put us on the wrong track. There's always a chance it's the oil field construction that's the main target. If we pull the army away from the southern desert, it could leave us wide open to attack."

"I'd advise increasing the guards around the oil field in any event. And the patrols along the pipeline."

"That's just what I was thinking, Hunter." Nijad nods at the man who's been working closely with him to ensure the construction of the oil wells goes smoothly.

"From the list of names on the thumb drive, I've tried to work out who could be possibly involved with the threat here. Interpol has supplied me with images where they can, but facial recognition hasn't pulled anything up so far. None of them has entered the country recently." Cara pauses, "It's strange, I don't recognise any of the names. They're not people I've heard of before."

"That's why the information is useful. Normally al-Fahri's lieutenants keep themselves well under the radar. At least we've got something to look out for." Kadar looks pleased, as though this is some progress.

Sean's shaking his head, "Could be helpful," his words are positive, but he looks doubtful, "We'll be dealing with foot soldiers, fanatics who'd give up their lives for the cause. Not sure any of the leaders would appear."

"But they might," Kadar again throws a smile toward Cara, "So if we can get the photos circulated we can make as many people aware as possible."

"I don't want people getting hung up looking for faces which they don't find," Hunter throws in, "They have to be looking for anything suspicious or out of place. Abnormal behaviour, mysterious packages and such."

"Good point," Nijad agrees, "But as long as we make that clear, I still think having the photos might help. Thanks for sorting that." He places his hand on the arm of his wife causing her to turn and smile at him. As he looks back, love and respect shine from his eyes. Love can be found in unexpected places, I think to myself, remembering how she was kidnapped to be his bride.

For the next hour, we sort out details and then when our plans are firmed up, make the decision to get to work. With the imminent threat, no one wants to delay becoming familiar with the place they've taken responsibility for.

Cara offers to show me to the harem, but before we leave the room, Sean pulls her aside, and I overhear he's discussing arrangements for Mollie. Once the sheikha has reassured him his baby will be in good hands in the palace nursery, and that it's no trouble having her there, she takes my arm.

"Come, I'll show you to the harem now. I think you'll be surprised at the alterations, even though you didn't see it before. It was decaying away before Zoe got her hands on it, but the restoration has just about finished now." At last, she pauses for breath, but she's not finished, "We've got a photo shoot lined up with a couple of the major bridal magazines the week after next. We want as much publicity over the world as possible."

"Have you put together what you're offering as a package, yet?" I ask, just to be polite, not seeing how I'd ever be able to partake of anything that's offered it doesn't overly fascinate me. But it seems to be her pet project, so I'll let her talk about it.

She laughs, "Interested, are you? Yes, I can give you a brochure if you want."

"Not for me, personally," I take the opportunity to refute that suggestion and also to show I'm thinking with my professional head, "But it occurred to me if you're sending brochures out into the public domain, it's possible Amir al-Fahri has got hold of one. In which case, I'd like to know as much he does."

"Good idea! We'll stop off at my office and pick one up."

I already knew the palace was huge, but after the brief detour my legs are growing tired by the time we eventually reach large golden doors which were the original entrance to the harem from the palace. As Cara unlocks them, she explains, "We've opened up the external entrance, and any visitors will come in that way. When it's in use, these doors will be locked and barred so no one can enter the palace from here." She indicates a series of metal bars which will come down to prevent the doors from being opened. "For now, we're just relying on the original lock, but once we're up and running, these will be in place."

Reverently I reach out my hand and touch the surface of the doors and throw her a questioning look.

"Yes," she laughs again as she correctly interprets my silent question, "Real gold." As I whistle through my teeth she continues, "Kadar was horrified when Zoe said she was only using gold plated fittings inside, but as she pointed out, we didn't want anyone running off with a solid gold tap."

I can see her point. These doors alone must be worth a king's ransom, but being so large, it's unlikely anyone could make away with them, and certainly not undetected.

You'd need a crane to lift them. The wealth in this palace is simply staggering.

She ushers me through the golden gateway, and I get a first glimpse of what even I have to admit is a magical place. Immediately I'm drawn into the romance of how it would have been in its heydey. There are separate rooms around the outside which Cara tells me used to be the concubine's cubicles, but for modern privacy have now been roofed and given doors. A tiny en-suite is provided inside each one, and larger bathrooms with original Victorian plumbing that Zoe had sourced from somewhere, are available as well. There are twenty rooms in all—this place is vast! In the centre of the area is a pool with a beautiful mosaic.

Cara presses a button, and huge glass windows roll aside to reveal the gardens as well as allowing the hot air to flow in making me appreciate the air conditioning that has been installed in the interior. Moving ahead she leads me outside. I follow behind, my eyes wide open as I try to take in everything there is to see.

"Zoe did a lot of the work herself out here." She points to the low walls surrounding flowerbeds overflowing with beautiful blooms, "You wouldn't think all this was crumbling away, would you? The artisans Zee employed did a great job of using the original stone, or where they were unable to, getting a good match."

It looks magnificent, and the fountain playing in the pond full of colourful fish tops it off.

Cara touches my arm again, "This way," she points back into the interior, and as we enter, closes the glass doors again. I welcome the coolness not, as yet, being used to the harsh climate. She takes me to one side; there's a spectacular bar set up, with tables around, and every alcoholic drink imaginable on the shelves. The whole thing's been constructed with consideration to the Arabic theme. Well, ignoring that this is one of the few places in Amahad where alcoholic drinks will be served.

"Accommodation is available for staff this way," she leads me across to a small, almost hidden door. "They don't need to live in the palace, but we're providing them somewhere to stay if they need it." She leads me up a narrow staircase. "This was where the sultan would sit and pick out his favourite for the night. The cubicles had no roofs back in those days, of course. And this, through here, was the old sultan's suite of rooms. This part of the palace hasn't been occupied for a century or more, so we've extended the staff accommodation out. There are security doors so even they are restricted from entering the palace proper."

Swiftly becoming the professional, I pull my mind away from the romance this place evokes, and examine the security set up instead. It seems more than adequate. Steel doors have been installed complete with alarms. "What about in the case of fire?"

"The doors will open automatically if the fire alarm sounds in this area."

They seem to have thought of everything, but there is something I'll have to discuss with Sean. What if there was an attack on the harem? If they set a fire, could intruders enter the palace via these entrances? Hmm. I make a mental note to ask him later.

"What about catering for your guests?"

"The harem had a kitchen area downstairs, we've modernised it."

"And the staff? Have they been recruited yet?"

"Zee's working on that now. We're having fun trying to decide on the 'eunuchs'. Of course, we can't castrate them, but she's working on a uniform that includes compression pants. Would be a bit of a giveaway to have men walking around with visible hard-ons."

I burst out laughing. "I can think a few men I'd like to volunteer to be castrated." I'm thinking of Simon for a start. Then I still, it's the first time I've ever thought of him in a joking sense. *Could that be an indication that I am moving on?*

She's giggling, "I've met a couple of those too, but," she sighs dramatically, "While it's a lovely thought, I don't think I'd get Kadar to agree." Then she thinks and says, "Though if Hunter was on the list…"

Grinning, I ask, "What is it with you and Hunter?"

She waves her hand in the air, "Oh, we go way back. He's very demonstrative, and Kadar is a stickler for protocol when it involves a man touching a woman. Hunter likes to hug me, and the more Kadar protests…"

"The more he does it," I finish for her, then give her a curious look, "What does your husband think of him?"

"He's not too keen on him cuddling me but knows he's just got to get used to it. And he's been working with him a lot more closely lately, so I think they're becoming good friends. Right, have you seen enough?"

I nod, "But where are the guards I was promised? I'll

want to talk to them," I pause, then add as the thought hits me, "I'll need an interpreter."

"I'll sort that out for you. Come, I'll take you to the guard room, and you can introduce yourself to the men in charge."

My eyes narrow, "Will they be okay with a woman directing them?"

She shrugs, "As long as you know what you're doing then they'll respect you."

As we make our way out of the harem I can only hope that I do.

CHAPTER 26

Sean

Even though it's only just afternoon by the time I reach the casino, it's already buzzing, reminding me again that casinos all over the world are set up to make time meaningless, to keep patrons at the tables as long as possible, giving no indication of whether it's night or day outside. A place like this never sleeps, and staff work around the clock, making themselves inconspicuous as they tidy and clean. It's never quiet, bells ringing and the clink of coins paying out from the slot machines, music playing, the loud sound of voices placing bets and the cries of croupiers encouraging them. It's an exhausting place to be.

I make my way through the massive central area and, by showing my Grade A identification, am allowed through to the security rooms on the mezzanine floor. A wall made of one-way glass lets me look out into the casino and, behind me, a mass of monitors, showing various zoomed in views from the tables below, all being carefully scrutinised by men and women who sit, staring at them intently. I know they'll be watching out for people like Danielle; people who cheat.

Taken into a small office for our hastily arranged meeting, I sit across from the Head of Security and bring him up to date. His face falls as he digests the implications of my news, and I give him a few seconds to process it. His expression darkens as he considers the information, showing me he's taking the threat seriously. My initial impression, that this is a man who gives his all to his job, is confirmed once we get down to discussing the details. His immediate concern is for the safety of his staff and customers; the building comes second.

"I've got three security teams working shifts," he explains.

"I'd like to brief each team as it comes on duty."

"I'll tell the six to two team to stay a bit longer today, so you can bring them up to speed as they hand off to the next."

"That would be helpful, thank you."

He considers for a moment, "I'll give you the grand tour, shall I?"

Immediately I indicate my assent, the sooner I acquaint myself with everything, the better. As he leads me through the areas the customers don't normally see, I'm pleased to find that as well as the interior cameras, the outside of the casino is also able to be monitored. I show him the photos of possible people to look out for while emphasising anyone looking suspicious or out of the ordinary should be viewed as a potential threat.

Checking my watch, I see we've got a couple of hours before the next shift change, so take my leave of the security head and decide to re-familiarise myself with the layout on the floor below.

Walking around the tables, I'm reminded of the night I

met Danielle, and pause at that fateful table. I'd been playing roulette and losing—only the small amount that I could afford to; gambling's not my addiction. But as I'd glanced up, with a frustrated sigh at yet another loss I'd met her eyes, unable to miss the interest that flared there.

As I pushed away from the table, not wanting to be tempted to lose any more and had gathered up my few remaining chips, she put something in my hand. My wallet. Stunned, I'd felt in my pocket, not realising I'd lost it. Having confirmed mine was indeed missing, I asked her, "Where did you find it?"

"Dropped on the floor." Her voice was husky, sexy. "I opened it and saw your ID card, then when I saw you at the table, recognised it was yours.

I might have been dumb, but never for one second had it occurred to me that she'd stolen it herself. Everything about her reeked of money, her clothes, her perfectly styled hair, and even the perfume she wore. I simply thanked her, bought her a drink then, at her invitation, followed her to her room where she had apparently enjoyed her reward.

More than enjoyed it, as the truth's now come out. And she'd pilfered far more than fifty euros that night.

Now, standing, looking at the table my head shakes from side to side. How could I have been so naïve? And then the vision of Danielle morphs into Nessa's face, and the way she reacts to my touch. Fuck, both occasions I've had her now were times to remember, unlike Danielle who I can barely recollect. Visions of Nessa's innocent reaction to being restrained and her untutored attempt to take me into her mouth make my cock so fucking hard it's clear I was a fool to think I'd only want her the once. There's no comparison between the two women. Sure, I was able to perform with Danielle, but it was perfunctory, pleasant enough. But Nessa? Her reactions blew everything else out of the water.

She'd stopped me last night, when I was eager for round three, strangely having to be the one to remind me we'd agreed to limit our sexual interaction to the club. It wouldn't have taken much for either of us to give in, and I suppose she'd been right to call a halt to it, but fuck me; I wanted her again. The experienced subs and women like the Danielle's of this world haven't got much to learn. But a blank canvass? There had been wonder in her wide-open eyes as she'd shattered as if she'd never come so hard in her life. The sense of accomplishment that gave me was what made it outstanding for me too.

But boundaries have been drawn and must be adhered to. We have to work together after all.

My thoughts are interrupted when I feel something rubbing against my leg, and looking down see an enthusiastic black and white springer spaniel. I've worked with both him and his handler before, so as my eyes follow the lead upwards, I'm not surprised to see it's in the hand of a dour looking man in his fifties. My lips curl up as I greet him, "Hi Frank. Good to see you here." As he gives a nod in return and what passes for a smile for him—he gets on better with canines than humans—I sink down on my haunches. "And what about you, Butch fella? Are you a good boy? Yes, you are. You're such a good boy." I ruffle the spaniel's head and am rewarded by an enthusiastic lick on my ear and a glance of warm approval from his handler. From previous conversations with Frank I know at four years old Butch, about halfway through his working career, is an experienced sniffer dog and has often proved himself since passing his obligatory nine-week training with flying colours.

Wiping away dog saliva from the side of my head with the back of my hand, I stand. "You're going to be patrolling here at the casino I take it?"

"Yes, we've already done one sweep, and Butch and I will remain on duty until our shift ends. As it's a twenty-four-hour business, we've another team taking over later. He's found nothing of interest up to now." Frank takes a ball on a rope out of his pocket. "You're a good boy, Butch," he tells his partner and proceeds to play a quick game of tug with the dog. It's how he keeps the dog interested and motivated in his search.

"The rest of your team with you?"

"Gray is at the airport, and Masters is joining Ryan at the souk."

The dogs are great allies in discovering concealed bombs. However, we do need to be careful in this Muslim country where canines can be considered unclean. That's why Butch is wearing a harness clearly saying in both Arabic and English; Working Dog Do Not Touch.

I give Butch another pat, then Frank gives him a command which reminds him he's on duty and waves his hand toward the next area to be searched. The pair go off, the dog's tail wagging nineteen to the dozen and his nose sniffing as he looks for the prize. While Butch is animated and lively, I have no concerns, but if he stops moving, I'll be worried. If he finds something suspicious, he'll sit still and point with his nose and eyes toward where he can sense explosives might be. For obvious reasons, his behaviour is unlike a narcotics dog who would bite, scratch, and worry at where they think drugs are concealed. Which certainly wouldn't be safe in the case of a bomb.

I continue the day briefing the security teams, then hand over to Jamie, one of our backup Grade A protection officers, and eventually make my way back to the house on the compound. Nessa's already back—she'll have handed off to Matt her backup CPO—but her bedroom door is firmly closed, and I can hear no movement behind it. Packaging in the bin suggests she's already eaten, so I heat up a meal for one and relax in the sitting room to eat it, a welcome beer within easy reach. My phone pings. Cara's sent me a picture of Mollie fast asleep in the nursery, and an update that she's had a good day, eaten well, and apparently had a couple of poos and sufficient wet nappies. Personally, I feel that was information I didn't need, but fuck it, I'm new to this parenting lark, and maybe there's some reason for me knowing.

As she's down for the night, there's no point in going to see Mollie now. I promise myself I'll pay her a visit in the morning. Hopefully in time to give her a bottle. Already I'm starting to consider her needs, along with my own.

Leaning my head back on the sofa, I consider how she'll fit into my life and the changes I'll need to make. I never expected to be a single parent, but hell, I'll give it the best shot I can. That kid is not going back to her mother.

"Sean? Didn't you go to bed last night?"

What? Oh fuck, I must have fallen asleep on the couch. Damn it. Sitting up I roll my head, feeling the stiffness in my shoulders. My hands go up to my neck, and I try to rub the pain away. "What time is it?"

"Seven. I'm taking over from Matt at nine. And we've got a catch-up meeting with the others at eight."

"Shit!" I lean forward, putting my elbows on my knees and resting my chin on the back of my hands, "How did it go yesterday, Nessa?"

She comes over and sits on the chair opposite me, "Fine, I think. I wanted to talk to you about a couple of security issues."

"Go on." Tilting my head up, I encourage her. For a few minutes, we discuss her concerns about the access to the harem, and I make some suggestions. All in all, I'm encouraged by her intelligent observations and she's on the right track with her ideas, she just doesn't yet have the confidence to trust her own judgement.

I shower, dress, and am just about ready when Hunter, Ryan and Nat join us. Two coffees later and a bite to eat—just cereal and toast this morning as we've no time for much else—and I start to feel human again.

Like an extension of the conversation I've just had with Nessa, we update each other on the security at our various locations, reporting on any weak points identified, and tossing around ideas of how to strengthen them. Then, in time for the nine o'clock shift change, we go our separate ways, ready to start our day of keeping eyes and ears open and hopefully keeping the tourist hot spots of Amahad safe.

The next couple of days proceed in the same way. When I return from the casino, I spend as much time as I can with Mollie. I've taken to bringing her back to the house in the evenings where she sleeps in a cot that the palace has lent me and that I put in my room. I'm lucky, the symptoms of teething have died down again, and now more comfortable, she's been sleeping the night through. During the day, she seems content enough in the royal nursery, the nanny competent and quite happy to look after an additional child.

Every time I see Mollie I get a pang in my chest as I'm beginning to comprehend at a bone-deep level, she is actually mine. And then I feel the fear, wondering if I'll be able to do right by her. It's a huge responsibility, but one I'll not shy away from. Already I can't imagine her not being in my life, and have started looking forward to seeing her grow.

My only issue is that when I bring the baby to the house, Nessa makes herself scarce, or if she's in the same room, ignores the child kicking about on the floor or lying in my arms. I'm not sure how much Mollie's presence is hurting her, or if she's trying to prevent another episode like the one when I asked her to hold her. I'm sad and angered for her. As I see her struggling it makes me want to put that bastard in the ground. I've suggested she swap accommodation with Ryan or Nat, but for some reason, she prefers to torture herself and stay here.

It's the third morning, and Mollie's woken me early. I've

just fed and changed her when I'm interrupted by a call from Jamie at the casino. Butch has been doing his job and has alerted Frank to a suspicious package. The casino's been evacuated, and bomb disposal experts are on their way in. Though there's not a lot I'll be able to do, I tell him I'm on my way over. The casino's my responsibility after all.

"Nessa?" I call up the stairs, "I've got to run, there's trouble at the casino."

It's only a few seconds before she appears, my shout obviously having roused her, her hair's all over the place, and she looks startled. But as she tears downstairs, I'm pleased how fast she's put on her professional hat. "What is it? What's happened? What do you need me to do?"

"The sniffer dog has found a suspicious package at the casino. Suspected explosives."

"Shit. Do you want me to come with you?"

I'm grabbing my keys and suddenly remember, *fuck!* How could I have forgotten? There is something she can do, but I hesitate to ask her. But there's nothing else for it; I've no time to sort anything else out. "Hate to do this to you, but could you get Mollie over to the nursery? They're expecting her about nine." Which means I'm leaving her watching the baby for nearly three hours. Seeing her face fall I add, "I'm sorry Nessa. If there was anything else…"

"Go, Sean. Go. I'll handle it." Her hands wave as if she's shooing me out of the door.

"She's fed and changed. I've already prepared her bag for the day. The bottles and everything else is in there, spare nappies…"

"Sean, GO!"

With one last look at Nessa, and after leaning down to give a quick kiss to a happy gurgling Mollie I leave my two girls alone.

My job by its very design is fraught with danger. I look death in the face every time I start my working day. But my mortality has never hit me so hard as it hits me as I go out of that door, with the thought, what if it's today my luck runs out? If the terrorist attacks on Amahad have started, will I be returning to them?

Fuck. I haven't given a thought about what would happen to Mollie if I didn't come back.

But I'm out of time, and I can only trust to luck I'll see them again. Running to the next house along I bang on the door, then jump into the SUV provided for my use and have the engine running as Ryan, Nat and Hunter emerge, Jamie having rung them after speaking to me. I gun the engine, and we're out of the palace grounds before we start any conversation.

CHAPTER 27

Vanessa

Sean's left me in charge of the baby. Shit!

What do I do? I glance down at Mollie, lying on the floor, seeming happy enough kicking her feet and giggling when she manages to hit a toy hanging from her play gym. Then I look down at myself, realising I'm still wearing the pyjama set I wore to bed. Well, she's not going anywhere.

Racing back upstairs, I run through the shower clocking up my fastest ever time and throw on some clean clothes for the day. Given the heat here I just put on some Capri trousers, a tank top and, in respect for the country, a loose cotton blouse over the top. Then I'm back down, and thankfully Mollie doesn't even seem to have noticed she was left alone.

Six-thirty am. Over two hours until I can take her to the palace. I sit on the settee; my legs pulled up under me. *Does she need feeding? Changing?* No, Sean said he'd already done that. Then the sobering thought comes to me of where her father's gone and why. God, I hope he's careful today. If there is a bomb I hope he's sensible enough to stay well out of the way of any flying debris. If the terrorists have started their attacks, where's next?

That reminds me, grabbing my phone I send a quick text to Matt telling him I'll be a bit late as I've got to drop

Mollie off at the nursery first. I also add that it might be a good idea to have a look around the harem and check that nothing looks out of place. I wonder whether we should ask for a sniffer dog to check it over and make a mental note to ask Sean once this immediate crisis is over. It's only a moment before I get a text back acknowledging the contents of mine. I then replace my phone in my handbag, so I don't forget to take it out with me.

Mollie gurgles happily on the floor.

Maybe I won't have to do anything?

She's kicking out furiously, and now she's rolled onto her stomach. Wow! I'm sure she hasn't done that before. What a shame Sean missed it!

Now she lifts a wobbly head toward me and is smiling and giggling as though she knows she's achieved something. It's Sean's smile. Every bit of her is Sean.

"Er… Hi…, Mollie? Who's a clever girl?" It seems strange, alien talking to a baby.

"Ga gah!"

What the hell does that mean?

"Ga, ba ba, GAH!" Having pronounced something, her arms pummel the floor, and her feet kick furiously in the air. She starts to let out a keening wail.

Perhaps she can't turn herself back?

My hands are shaking, my body is trembling. *Dare I pick her up?* Remembering what happened last time, I'm terrified. But if I don't hold her at some point, how will I get her to the nursery? Gingerly I get to my knees, and turn her onto her back, and reaching out my fingers, tickle her tummy. It distracts her, but then her hands reach for me, and her face starts to scrunch up. Taking a couple of deep breaths to steady her, and before I can have second thoughts, I pull her into my arms, bringing her close to me, holding her against my body. It's safe, I'm at floor level, if I start to go lightheaded, I can put her down. Holding her seems to have settled her for now. I breathe a sigh of relief.

All at once the perfume of baby hits me, the smell of her shampoo and baby lotion. *This could have been what holding my baby would have been like.*

I smooth my hand over Mollie's back, and as if some innate instinct comes to me, I reach round to check that she's dry and doesn't need changing.

"Ouch!" I extract the handful of hair that she's got in her tiny hand noticing she's got a surprisingly strong grip. "Now we don't pull hair, do we?"

She giggles and goes for my hair again. Flicking it back over my shoulder and, to distract her, I risk standing and start jiggling her in my arms. This she seems to enjoy. I glance at the clock, just over an hour and a half to go now, and I can hand her over to someone who does know what they're doing.

It's at that point I hear a knock on the door. Crossing the room, still bouncing Mollie in my arms, I peer through the peephole. A man in the uniform of the palace guards is waiting behind it. In a flash the thought goes through my head that something's happened at the casino. *That something's happened to Sean.* As fast as I can with a baby in one arm, I disable the security system and open it. As soon as the door's cracked open the palace guard pushes inside, followed by another man. They're both carrying guns and they're pointing them straight at me. He spits something at me in Arabic, I shake my head, showing I don't understand. But whatever he's said isn't something pleasant. My eyes open in shock and fear, this wasn't what I'd expected.

The second man isn't in uniform. Instead he's wearing western clothing, but has the olive toned skin of a native. He puts his gun in the holster and reaches out his hands, "Give me baby."

Mollie? No way.

Stepping back, I place my hand protectively over her head, "No." My gun is in my bag, on the table. But how can I reach it? And while my scores on the range were good, how could I defend myself against two armed men? I'm not going to put Mollie down, not if they want to take her.

"We take baby," the man pronounces.

Violently I shake my head, "The baby is going nowhere."

Who are these men? What do they want with Mollie?

"She come," he says again.

I stare at him in disbelief, the practicalities racing through my mind. "Why? Where do you want to take her?" My voice is shaking, "What are you going to do with her?" Are they here to kidnap her? To hold her for ransom?

"Not your business. Give baby, or we take."

The loud scary voices or perhaps the tension in my body gets to Mollie, and she opens her mouth and lets out a loud scream. The men look at each other and wince. I try to calm her, holding her close and rocking her.

There's a conversation in their language, and then the man who speaks English, and appears to be the leader, makes a decision, "You come. Keep baby quiet."

Well, I've probably no more chance at keeping her quiet than them, but going along has got to be better than them taking her away God knows where on her own, so it only takes a split second for me to decide if they're taking her, they won't be leaving me behind. Remembering the bag Sean left, I dip my head toward it. "Have you got stuff ready for her? You can't just take a baby unprepared."

As the English speaker shakes his head, I suggest, "Let me get her bag, it's got her food and nappies for the day already in it."

He eyes the colourful bag-come-changing mat, apparently unthreatened by its innocuous appearance and gives a sharp nod of permission. "Get bag."

Thanking several deities, I move across to the table where Mollie's bag is conveniently lying underneath. As I pick it up, one handed I surreptitiously slide my handbag into it. They don't seem to notice. Placing it on the table, I start to rummage inside.

"What you do?" The snapped question stills my hand.

"Getting her dummy, her pacifier out. You wanted her to be quiet." Making a meal of finding what I'm looking for, my hand slides my gun from my bag into a side pocket, and I hide it under some baby wipes, regretting I'm not confident enough to use it, doubting my ability to shoot two men without bullets flying at the baby and me. *But if I can take it with me...* Extracting the dummy, I put it in Mollie's mouth. She begins sucking and immediately stops her tears. The man comes over and checks the contents, taking out my handbag and leaving it on the table giving me a look as though he's outwitted me. *Damn, my phone was in there.* Then, giving only a cursory look at the baby items inside, he zips up the bag and puts it over his shoulder.

"Move." His tone shows he's lost patience, and he gestures to the door with his gun. As I cross the room the men flank me, walking so close, I have no chance of escape. *How am I going to get out of this?*

Hoping there'll be someone in the vicinity outside that I can call on for help, I go through the door. Immediately outside the house is a covered military style Jeep. Another wave of the gun and I'm in the back seat, the man in civilian clothes sitting beside me. He pushes my head down and covers Mollie and me with a tarpaulin. The bag's in the foot well below the front seat; there's no way I can reach my gun.

Although the sound's muffled, I hear the man's voice telling me, "Keep quiet. Don't move. Shout I shoot you and baby." He sounds so cold, it's easy to believe him.

The Jeep starts to move off, and then halts, and it seems we must be at the palace gates as there's a brief exchange of words and a snort of laughter, and then the vehicle is moving forward again going over some bumps then picking up speed. I huddle with Mollie, holding the dummy to her mouth to keep her quiet.

I'm not sure how long we've been travelling, I've lost track of time, but at last, we come to a halt. Then, as the canvas is pulled away, I realise our journey hasn't ended.

There's a helicopter waiting, and Mollie and I are pushed inside.

As Sean discovered on the journey from England and I'm finding out today, Mollie doesn't like flying. Even the dummy doesn't keep her quiet. Without earphones, it's loud and noisy, and all I can do is to cover her ears as best I can and pray for the flight to come to an end. When we at last land, for a brief moment, my relief overwhelms the fear of where the hell we've been taken to. Then my curiosity piques when we're waved out, guns threateningly held in the men's hands, and I see squat adobe buildings around us. There are about ten in all and are impossible to age. I'm not allowed to linger long, with one hand on my arm, the non-English speaker drags me toward the nearest building and pushes me inside. With the barrel of the gun against my back, Mollie and I are directed to a room at the rear. The other man throws Mollie's bag down, and then we're left alone.

Immediately I try the door, it's bolted or locked and doesn't budge. Still holding the baby to me, I study my surroundings. There's a pile of dirty blankets on the floor, and one small window high up on the wall that's got iron bars concreted into it. Standing on tiptoe I can just about see out, but my view is of a couple of other similar buildings and then sand. Miles of sand. The sound of an engine starting and rotors whirring tells me the helicopter is flying away.

Why have we been brought here? And who'd dream of bringing a baby somewhere like this? The idea they want to hold her for ransom seems the most likely one, and I thank God I came along with her, else who would be looking after her if she was on her own? The menacing men? It's a chilling thought.

Going over to the pile of blankets, I sit down on them. As I'd seen on my initial inspection, they're not particularly clean, but it's all there is, and we'll just have to make do for however long we're held captive here. At least after her terror of the helicopter journey Mollie must have tired herself out, she's now asleep. Remembering there's a small baby blanket in her bag, I shake it out and lay Mollie on it, flexing my arms as I've been holding her throughout the flight. I stare at her, unable to resist smoothing my hand over her fine hair. *Fuck, Molls, what is going to happen to us?*

I go to examine the window again. Now my hands are free I try the bars, they won't budge. The other houses don't have the same metal fixtures, so why were they put here? To keep someone in, or to keep someone out? Peering out at the buildings I can see they look deserted, and not in as good a state of repair as this one, at least one roof has fallen in. What is this place? It looks like they've brought us to the middle of nowhere. Quickly, I think through any possible options. Can I loosen the bars? Even if I could, the window's so small I'm not sure I'd be able to get myself out, let alone Mollie as well. How long do they plan on keeping us here?

Taking advantage while she sleeps, I explore the square room further, seeking any nook and cranny that might hold something to aid an escape, but there's nothing to be found. There's no light bulb or electricity, in fact, absolutely nothing at all. Returning to the window, I once again pull on the bars, but they're set too tight in the wall to move even a little. I scrabble with my fingers, but I only end up breaking my nails, the bars haven't budged at all.

As the sun rises to its zenith, the heat increases. The thick mudbrick walls keep out the worst of the hot air, but even so, it's still very warm. No longer caring for my modesty, I throw off my shirt so I'm only wearing my tank top, and try to fan myself in the airless room. After a while Mollie wakes, and I give her a bottle, hoping that not keeping it refrigerated won't cause her to get an upset stomach. Since they left us here, I've seen no one. They haven't even come to check on us. *What would have happened if I wasn't here?* Would they have left her to starve?

Checking, I find Mollie needs changing. Rolling out the mat as I've seen Sean do, I take a while finding out which way round it goes, but at last the new nappy is on. "There, Molls," I tell her, "I'm not as useless as I thought." She gurgles at me and giggles. I guess she's giving me marks out of ten.

I play with her, tossing her around, getting her to laugh and chuckle again, trying to be brave, so my fear doesn't affect her. It's not easy, I'm terrified. But determined. No one is going to take her from me. With a start, I recognise the feeling of being like a lioness protecting her cub. No matter that she's not mine, no harm's going to come to her while I'm here to protect her.

I've no watch, no phone. The only indication of time passing is the golden orb moving across the sky until, at last, it starts to sink beneath the horizon. Darkness falls fast here; there's barely any twilight before the room is shrouded in darkness.

Suddenly I hear a scuffling outside, then the sound of a bolt sliding back, and the door opens. The man who seems to be the leader enters carrying a torch. As it shines directly on my face, I put up my hand to cover my eyes.

"I need the bathroom." It's the first thing I say, a sign of my desperation.

The man nods at someone behind him and the second man enters carrying a bucket. When he places it in a corner, it only takes a moment before I comprehend with disgust what it's supposed to be used for. *Yuck!* He also brings a plate which has some bread on it and produces a bottle of water from a pocket. *At least they don't want me to starve or dehydrate.* Though it's hardly adequate fare.

"You stay."

"Look, you can't keep us here. This is no place for a baby." *Or a woman, or anyone,* I add to myself.

"You stay."

"For how long?" I want answers.

He shrugs. His dismissive gesture gives me nothing at all to go on, but before I can press him again, he adds. "Baby go tomorrow."

I pull Mollie closer; she's going nowhere without me.

He sees me trying to protect her, and snorts, presumably to let me know if he wants to take her, I'll be unable to do anything about it. But he doesn't know I've got a gun, and when the right time comes, I won't be afraid to use it.

But first I'll need to find out just how many men are

guarding me. The two here have holsters by their sides, weapons at the ready. That was the first thing I'd checked. Presumably it's just the two of them, the pilot must have flown away when the helicopter left.

After giving me and Mollie one last sneering look, the English speaker waves the other man out, and I'm left alone.

With only the starlight coming into the room, I wait until my eyes become accustomed to the dark once more, and then, with a grimace, use the bucket, sighing with relief when at last my bladder's finally empty. I eat the bread on the plate, sipping the water to help the dry dough go down, trying to conserve as much as possible in case they don't bring any again.

Then, finally, I pull the baby bag within reach and cuddle up with Mollie, grimacing at the hardness of the bare stone floor under the inadequate blankets. I wrap my shirt around the baby as well as her blanket to keep her warm in the cooler night air. When my brain gets tired of looking for explanations, I finally give in and succumb to an exhausted sleep.

CHAPTER 28

Sean

I t's a decoy." Ryan announces, kicking at the offending object, "Someone's toying with us." He kneels down, and ruffles Butch's ears, "You're a good boy, but they fooled you too, lad."

The Amahadian bomb disposal expert, still suited up in all his gear, although he's removed his helmet, nods, "Must have had sufficient traces of explosive for the dog to have sniffed it out, but there's no bomb."

Thank fuck for that. I slap the back of the brave man who'd entered the casino alone, luckily to find there was nothing to disarm.

We're all staring at the innocent box as though we'll see the answers written there.

"Why?" Hunter glares down.

I shake my head, "It could be a message of some sort. A 'look how easily this could have been a real bomb'." But if that's the case, I can't fathom what the point would be.

"It's a decoy," Ryan repeats. He lifts his head and looks around at each of us in turn. "It's brought us all here, away from where we should be."

"But only us. We weren't due to take over from our seconds until nine. Nowhere has been left unprotected." As soon as we'd found nothing amiss here, we'd checked with our counterparts to find everything as it should be at the souk, the harem, and the airport.

Ryan's like a dog with a bone, "Is there somewhere else we should be focusing on? Or was it something to get *us* away from the compound."

It doesn't make sense. Kadar's palace guard is well trained and the compound secure. What would it matter if we weren't there?

"Why?" Hunter repeats. It seems he's a man of few words today.

My phone rings, and I walk away to answer it, briefly taking note how strange the casino looks with lights up high and no punters playing at the tables. "Cooper. Speak to me," I answer in my normal way.

And then, as I listen to Cara, my blood runs cold.

"No, they're not with me."

"Shit!"

"We're on our way back, now. Was there…?"

"Nothing? No note?"

"Her bag and phone are there?"

"Okay. We'll see you shortly."

The tone of my voice and my rushed questions have drawn my colleagues' attention. I gaze at them, having difficulty processing what Cara's just told me. Somehow, I manage to stammer out, "Mollie, *my baby*, and Vanessa have disappeared."

Ryan's staring at me. He doesn't have to say a word. He was right all along.

Hunter's phone rings, "Nijad, talk to me."

"What's the damage?"

"Thank fuck for that."

"Okay, will do."

He ends the call and turns to us. "There was an attempted attack on the oil field earlier this morning. Nijad said it's under control. A dozen men causing a diversion, three suicide bombers who were supposed to get to the rigs but luckily, as we increased security, they were stopped before they could do any damage. A couple of our men were injured, but not fatally, thank God."

"We were supposed to withdraw security at the oil field," Seth states, frowning.

"Instead we strengthened it."

They could be talking in double-dutch for all I can understand right now; there's only one thing worrying me. Seeing me bouncing on my feet in impatience, Hunter takes pity on me, "Come on, let's get back to the compound."

Minutes later we're in the SUV heading back to the palace. I want to go straight to the house to check for clues that might have been left, and anyone else may have missed, but there's a message waiting for us at the gates, we're to go straight to Kadar's office.

Dismissing my protests, Hunter drives past the house and parks close to the entrance to the modern part of the palace housing the government buildings. With a hand on my arm, he encourages me inside, and leads me through to the main offices, Ryan and Nat following hot on our heels.

Not Mollie. Not Nessa. Where have they gone, and why?

Kadar's ready and waiting with Cara at his side, Matt

sitting opposite, and a conference call already in progress with Jon and Ben back at Grade A. Their conversation briefly pauses as we enter.

My hand trembles as I put out a chair and sink into it. Never has anything touched me so closely before. I'd rather go through being shot all over again than have this fear inside me, the dread that something awful has happened. I glance across to Kadar, "Speak to me. Tell me what the fuck is going on?"

"I'm sorry, mate," Matt flicks guilty eyes toward me, "Van texted me, told me she'd be a bit late as she had to drop Mollie off. I didn't think anything of it until an hour had passed. I just thought she'd got held up. Then I tried to call her, but there was no reply. I went to the nursery…"

Cara takes over, "Vanessa didn't turn up with Mollie, so I sent the nanny over to see if she had a problem. When she said neither Vanessa nor the baby was there, I went myself. With my guards." The final three words she directs at Kadar as if to forestall any objection that she might have put herself at risk. "There was no sign of them, Scan. I'm so sorry. As I told you, her handbag, with her phone in it, was on the table. I didn't touch anything, and security is over there now looking for fingerprints." She looks down at her hands, and then up again, "There was no sign of a struggle."

"Could Vanessa have taken Mollie somewhere herself?" Hunter asks.

Would she? But why? And where? She doesn't even like picking her up.

"She's not in the compound, we're pretty certain of that.

Obviously, this place is vast, and search parties are still out. If they do find them we'll know soon enough, but Sean, I'm sorry, but I think it's more likely someone has taken them."

"We've looked at the CCTV footage from the gate," Kadar interrupts his sister-in-law, "A Jeep pulled out around eight o'clock. The man driving was dressed as a palace guard. It wasn't searched; the men on the gate saw no need to. They stopped the driver as normal, had a joke and a laugh about being lucky he was going off shift and then let him through. There wasn't anything about it to raise suspicion. Even though the Jeep had blacked out rear windows, they didn't think anything of it. A lot of them have. But there could have been someone inside they didn't see." He pauses, leans forward and steeples his hands, "We've questioned the guards, they said they didn't recognise the driver, but then there's more than two hundred employed here so that's not unusual in itself."

"But the Jeep wasn't one of ours. I checked the number plates." Cara adds. "They were fake plates, the number wasn't traceable."

"We've got to work on the premise that it's an abduction," Ben's voice booming through the speakers makes me glance up at the screen. I nod, incapable of speaking, worry burning in my chest, making it hard just to breathe.

"And we've got to work out the fuck why." Hearing Jon's familiar voice is calming. I know he'll understand exactly what I'm going through, Mia, his wife, had once been taken too. Luckily that ended well, and we got her back.

And now Kadar leans toward me, his palm covering my shaking hand, "I know how you're feeling, Sean, but we've got to talk this through. I know you'll want to do something, to take some action, but until we figure out why, we've fuck all chance of knowing where, let alone who." And he's another who can sympathise. When Zoe was kidnapped, she barely came out of it alive. I'm only too well aware of the harshness of this country and the extent some of its citizens will go to. My leg throbs as if to remind me.

Again, I give a sharp nod, but now I'm feeling a little more in control. Kadar's right, we have to take the time to think what could be behind this. Why take Nessa and the baby? It doesn't make sense. Sure, it's a kick in the teeth to Grade A, and a personal affront to me, but in the greater scheme of things it means nothing at all. Certainly, al-Fahri would have little to gain from it. If it had been either of the sheikhas, Cara or Zoe, it would have sent a hell of a stronger message.

After peering at me intently, Kadar sits back again. "All the fuss about the threat being here in Al Qur'ah could have been to mislead us. Turn our focus away from their real target. The oil field."

"But it didn't work," Hunter looks up as Kadar's personal assistant comes in with a couple of women who proceed to place an assortment of food and drink on the table. When they leave, he reaches for a bottle of water and opens it, "We increased security. Nijad and I had a discussion yesterday and deployed a second platoon to guard it. There were an extra fifty men there last night."

"At least," Kadar adds, "Sheikhs Rais, Fadi, and Tamir

sent some of their warriors along as soon as they heard there had been threats to Amahad. They're nearest, and wanted to protect their investment."

"So," Ben's voice again, "Let's explore for the moment that the oilfield was the main target, leaving aside that it was successfully foiled."

I'm hearing the conversation around me, but wondering what the fuck any of this has to do with a four-month-old baby. "But where do Mollie and Vanessa come into this? Why take them? Could it be completely unrelated?"

"Look at the timing, Sean," this from Jon, "The attack coincided with their abduction, if we're working on the premise that's what it was. But that might have been a coincidence. Focusing our attention here in Al Qur'ah was what they intended, and to that end, it could have happened anytime over the past few days. But the bomb scare at the casino this morning…"

"Was meant to get me away from the palace," I complete his sentence for him.

Cara's fingers are tapping against her mouth, "I don't think it's anything to do with Vanessa, I think she was just collateral damage. This all started with Mollie, Sean. Think about it. Let's take it from the beginning."

"Danielle arranged for her to be left for me at Grade A," I start going through what everyone already knows.

"And then you set off to find her mother," Ben is too impatient for my fogged mind to wade through the facts.

"And she gave you a thumb drive which held the information about the planned attacks," Jon's speaking for me now too.

Shaking my head to try to clear it, pulling the coffee that someone's just placed in front of me closer, I think, "You're suggesting it's got something to do with Danielle."

"If it wasn't for Danielle, we wouldn't have had the information in the first place."

Narrowing my eyes in thought, I look at Kadar. "And it seems it was fake information. But why involve a baby?"

Cara gives a mirthless laugh, "It's the biggest bargaining chip she had, Sean. Tell me, would you have run to Danielle's rescue had she not dangled Mollie in front of you?"

"Fuck no." I shudder, remembering what I'd thought of her when I'd met her. "She's a cold-hearted bitch."

"And if she'd come to Grade A for our protection, once we'd researched her, we'd probably have decided her safety could best be provided for in prison."

"Could it have been set up when she first met me?"

A brief pause as we all think about it, then Jon gives us his opinion, "I think that's pushing it too far. In my view, what she told you about the baby's conception is probably true, the selfish bitch just wanted a baby and saw you as a convenient sperm donor. She couldn't have known you'd be at that place at that time. Something's happened since, and Mollie just proved convenient bait to dangle in front of you."

"Let's continue going over what we know." Kadar's sitting in his familiar pose, his hands steepled in front of him. "She entices you with the baby, lets you find out you're the father. Entices you to Paris then sneaks you the information which brings you to us. Conveniently she disappears. We act on the information, believing her story that she came across it by accident. But what if she didn't? What if somehow she's part of the plot?"

"But that would mean she's got links to Amir al-Fahri. And that list of names, surely he wouldn't have wanted us to have that?"

Kadar shrugs, "Could be a list of people he no longer trusts, or who are dispensable. From what I know of the man, I wouldn't put it past him."

"She gave up her baby…" I break off, thinking.

"Because she was going to get her back. I don't think she would have gone to such lengths to have a child, only to abandon it. It's her, Sean, I'm certain. She's behind this; she's taken Mollie. It's the only thing that makes any sense."

Slowly my head dips up and down as I consider Cara's allegation. It fits. She's right; she has to be.

Abruptly I stand, pushing my chair away from the table. My hands brush through my hair. Danielle's got Mollie, which is what she wants. But she's got Nessa too, who is of absolutely no use to her at all. Fuck! I don't want my baby in Danielle's hands, but she is her mother, and even if she's used her like some pawn in a game, I doubt she'd do anything to harm her. But the woman with her? That's a whole different story. And the thought of Nessa being in such danger is chilling.

"We've got to find them. And fast."

A knock at the door sounds and Ma'mun enters, he's carrying a note which he hands to Kadar. Kadar reads it and then dismisses him. He glances around, all our eyes are on him. "The Jeep was found abandoned about thirty miles away. It seems they've taken off in a helicopter from that point."

"Any chance of tracing them?"

He's shaking his head, "They were probably flying under the radar."

Hunter leans forward and waves at the paper in Kadar's hands, "Anything else?"

Kadar's scanning it again, "The marks in the sand suggest it's a small helicopter, possibly the R44."

Ben clears his throat, "That would give it a range of about 400 miles in total. Check whether they fuelled at the airport in Al Qur'ah, if not, they haven't much in the way of flying range, and I doubt they'll have been able to leave Amahad."

Nat picks up his phone, gets to his feet and nods at us. "Dave's at the airport; I'll give him a buzz and get him to check it out."

Kadar presses the button on his intercom, "Ma'mun, can you set up a conference call with all the desert sheikhs in half an hour? Thank you." He turns to us, "If they're in Amahad we'll find them."

But can we find them in time? The more I think we're right to think Danielle's returned to take Mollie back, the more concerned I get about Nessa's safety.

"Is there anything that would suggest they were after Vanessa?" At my flinch, Hunter shrugs, "Just exploring every avenue."

It's Ben who jumps to her defence, "I've known Nessa a long time, and unless they wanted a puzzle solver, and I can't for the life of me think why they would, I doubt anyone would want to take her. As a Grade A employee, her background was fully investigated when she started."

I tend to agree. Nessa isn't going to be important to anyone, certainly not as important as she is to me. A wave of nausea hits me at the thought I might never see her again. It dawns on me just how vital she's become to my life. I can't imagine losing her, not before we've had a chance to explore what could be between us. But thinking on that isn't going to get me closer to finding her. Trying to suppress the recognition of my growing feelings for her, I try to treat it like any other case.

Forcing myself to think rationally I join in with the others as we chuck ideas around in case we're missing the blindingly obvious, but nothing floats to the surface. Within the half hour Nat gets a call back that all helicopters in and out of the airport this morning have been accounted for, so unless they've got another fuel dump somewhere, it seems likely the helicopter flew in from elsewhere. Which would suggest Mollie's within two hundred miles of us. But that would still mean we're looking for a needle in a haystack.

Leaving Kadar alone to conference in with the sheikhs, we exit his office. Ryan grasps my shoulder as we walk through the palace, a tactile but silent reassurance of his support. I clench and unclench my fists as I walk, never before in my life having felt as helpless as I do at this moment.

CHAPTER 29

Vanessa

M ollie had stirred three times in the night. I'd fed her and changed her nappy twice. The third time I'd noticed that I'd only one bottle and two clean nappies left for her, and not having a clue what was going to happen in the morning, decided I was going to have to start eking things out. The final time she'd woken, I'd just rocked her back off to sleep. I'm muddling my way through this only able to hope I'm looking after her as best I can while knowing I'm just making it up as I go along. But she's become my responsibility, so can only hope my best is going to be good enough.

One would assume, as they've kidnapped a baby the men would have been prepared to look after her, but something tells me not to be overly optimistic. Hell, I don't even know if the men will turn up today. They said they would, but all's been quiet during the night. Either they're sleeping, or they've left us here alone.

Dawn breaks, and I hear some sort of car's engine, and voices speaking Arabic outside, but no one comes to us. By the time I estimate it's about mid-morning and I've no option but to relent and give Mollie half of her last bottle, the poor mite is screaming and stuffing her hands in her mouth, letting me know she's desperate to be fed. She cries when I take the milk away, but when I replace it with the dummy, it calms her down so hopefully her little tummy is at least no longer completely empty.

After I use up one of the last remaining nappies, I cuddle her close and rock her, hoping she'll go back to sleep. From somewhere I dredge up ancient memories and start singing Twinkle Twinkle Little Star to her, followed, for some reason, by Away in a Manger as no other songs come to mind. She doesn't seem to mind I've anticipated Christmas by a few months, nor that some of the words are replaced by la la la when I've forgotten them. My rusty singing voice helps her to relax, and at least, for now, there's peace.

"Oh Molls," I place a kiss on her forehead, "Your Daddy will be looking for you, you know? He'll come and find you soon." I know I'm making promises I have no way of knowing I'll be able to keep. But hope is the only thing that keeps me going. Hope, and knowing there's no one else to look after her. Whatever happens to me, Mollie has to stay safe.

The sun's past its highest point in the sky before the men eventually return. This time there's three of them. Only one enters, but at least he's carrying a plate of bread as before, along with another bottle of water. Guess I'm on a diet whether I want to or not. The other men hover outside.

"How long are you going to keep us here?" I call out to the man who'd spoken English and who's one of the two waiting by the door.

He lifts his shoulders to his ears and drops them, "You stay."

"The baby needs milk." I tell him as forcefully as I can, "And more nappies." In case he doesn't understand, I wave an empty bottle and the clean nappy toward him. In fact, I'd have thrown one of the soiled ones at him but I didn't want to invoke violence around Mollie.

Now he tilts his head to one side. I can see he understood me, but is at a loss as to how to provide what I've asked for. The men put their heads together and have a discussion that I can't understand. Finally, he looks at me, "We bring."

Well, that's one thing I suppose, though where they'll find what we need in the middle of nowhere I've no idea. *Perhaps we're near some village or town?* The men leave, shutting and bolting the door behind them. I sit and think, if I can get out of here, maybe there's somewhere close by I could walk to.

Three. Is that all of them? I've noticed they don't enter with guns drawn, but have their hands hovering over their holsters. Am I faster than them? If I catch them unprepared, can I get three kill shots off before they're able to respond? As I've never shot at a live target before, I'm not sure I could do it. And if they return fire, they might hit Molly. And what if there's more of them than I've seen? The third man must have arrived in the vehicle I heard, but there could be others who'd accompanied him. The gun will have to be the last resort when I've given up all other hope of rescue.

Time drags. Aware she's far too young, I attempt to teach Mollie to count her fingers and toes, she takes no notice of the numbers, but laughs along as I tickle her. Then her face scrunches and she begins to cry, so hoping

I'm doing the right thing, I feed her the last of the bottle and make use of the final nappy.

That's it. There's no more.

They'd told me Mollie would be taken today, but as the light starts to fade, and I know it will only be minutes before full darkness descends again I realise something must have happened to upset their plans. I'd heard an engine going away from the building some time ago, but nothing else since.

Expecting another long night ahead, worrying that Mollie has nothing to eat and no clean nappies if she soils herself, I'm relieved when the engine noise becomes audible once again. My ears trace the sound which gradually gets louder and then ceases abruptly. Again I hear voices, and as they get closer, I pull Mollie tightly into me. *No one's going to be taking her away from me.*

When the door opens, the man who enters is the one who knows some English. Again, he has two companions who are standing blocking the doorway. My gun's hidden. Close at hand, but the odds are still too great for me to risk going for it.

"Milk," he says, producing a jug with a flourish and setting it by my feet.

Shit, I should have asked him for formula.

He must note the way my face twists. "Goat," he continues, "Baby good."

Well, even if a baby can drink goat's milk, it's probably not going to be very gentle on the stomach of a child who's been fed properly balanced formula to date. And it's not sterile.

"No," I try to explain, "She needs proper baby milk. And I'll need to sterilise her bottles."

He doesn't understand anything but my denial, and points to the jug. "Baby drink milk."

Resolving to leave it until I have no option but to give it to her, I sigh in defeat. Suddenly something else appears on the floor. A pile of rags which I presume are the answer to my other request. They don't even look particularly clean. It's the sight of the meagre provisions and the fact I'm the only person Mollie has to try to keep her well and healthy that makes me want to cry. Not wanting to show any weakness I force myself to get angry.

"Look, how long are you going to keep us here? You said we'd be gone today. This place is no good for a baby."

I don't think he's going to answer, then he gives a shrug, "Mother come for baby, 'innaha ta'akhkharat." I understood the first part which is enough to send a shiver down my spine. At my confusion with his Arabic he scratches his head, and then comes up with the translation, "Mother delayed." Then he leaves, and bolts the door behind him.

Danielle. He must be talking about Danielle. And she's been delayed? Yeah, right. That sounds like what I know of Danielle, dumping her baby on a man who she can have no idea as to whether he'd make a good father or not, and now *delayed* and leaving her to languish, dirty and hungry, in a hovel. I wonder what's delaying her, the need to get her nails touched up? Another bottle of champagne to drink? Does she even know I'm here with Mollie? Or was she perfectly content to leave her with these rough men? If I hadn't decided I'd hated the woman before, this would have settled it. And now she's going to have to prise Mollie from me over my dead body!

I grow cold as I understand that's very likely her intention. She's coming for the baby, not me.

The jug of goat's milk is at room temperature, and has a faint odour which I don't know is right or not. When Mollie wakes and cries for sustenance, I try giving her some bottled water instead, but she's not fooled. She wants more.

I hold out until she's screaming with hunger, and then, with great reluctance, put goat's milk in her un-sterilised bottle instead. As she sucks, her little face scrunches at the unfamiliar taste but the demands of her stomach dictate the show; she relaxes in my arms and proceeds to suckle. When she's had her fill, and I remove the teat from her mouth it seems, at least for now, it's given her some comfort and hasn't immediately made her sick. Lifting her up I put her over my shoulder to burp her, just like I've seen Sean do.

This second night is worse than the first. The darkness is never ending. Mollie's sleeping fitfully, and I'm sure she needs changing, but I'm trying to work out whether nappy rash from a wet nappy is better or worse than using one of the pieces of dirty cloth they've provided. But when morning comes, there's nothing for it but to change her. And oh shit, literally. The goat's milk has come out almost as runny as it went in.

Having to resort to the tools they'd left me, I wipe her up as best I can using water from my scant supply I leave her lying on the floor on my, by now decidedly worse-for-wear, blouse having had to discard her filthy blanket. Today I'm going to have to do something, the poor little mite can't survive like this. Dehydration is dangerous for babies. I might not know a lot about them, but even I know enough to grasp that.

Sliding the gun out of the bag, I slip it into the back of my waistband, then pick up Mollie, pulling her into my arms. After which I sit. And wait.

And then I hear it, the sound of a helicopter approaching.

Friend or foe?

Soon I hear voices outside, men's voices, and I try to distinguish the different tones and count them. There's a woman's too, speaking to someone in English. A voice I recognise. *Danielle has arrived.* I cuddle Mollie closer, vowing I'll breathe my final breath before I allow her undeserving mother to take her.

The door opens, and the woman I last saw in Paris enters, looking equally well turned out, while I'm standing in the middle of the room dishevelled and covered in baby shit. Entering alongside is a man I've not seen before. Of the others, there's no sign. She steps into my bare cell, wrinkling her nose at the smell, then her eyes fall on Mollie, and she reaches out her arms.

Scooting backwards and never taking my eyes off Danielle, I lay Mollie down on the blankets behind me and stand in front of her like a human shield.

"Why are you here?" Well, it's obvious, but I'm trying to find out whether this is a rescue or not, though I very much doubt it is.

"For *my* baby. Give her to me." Danielle sounds almost bored.

"Your baby? The baby that probably needs antibiotics and a doctor's care after being kept in these unsanitary surroundings and given goat's milk to drink? Your baby that doesn't even have clean nappies?"

A fleeting chastened look crosses her face, "I should have been here yesterday, but we had a little trouble getting into the country. But no matter, Mummy's here now." She calls the last in a sing-song voice that makes me want to wretch.

She takes a step forward; I put out my arms to either side to block her.

"Oh, for goodness sake, Nasir, can you move her out of the way?"

As the man beside her makes to move, a hiss comes out of my mouth, "Where are you going to take her?"

"Not that it's any of your business, but home of course. Home with myself and Nasir. He's going to be your Daddy, isn't he, Mummy's little precious?"

Mummy's little precious takes that particular moment to let out a howl of distress. It tugs at my heartstrings, though seems to have the opposite effect on the person who birthed her, and the man who's supposedly going to be taking a paternal interest in her who both give near identical grimaces.

"Give her a pacifier or something," she instructs me.

I don't want to turn my back else they'll see the weapon, "None of her dummies are sterilised," I tell her, but Mollie's inadvertently helping, her screams providing a good distraction. I want to keep her talking, I'm waiting my chance until they relax and take their eyes off me.

Speaking loudly to make myself heard, I ask, "What's all this about, Danielle? Why did you let them bring Mollie to this godforsaken place? And me?"

Airily she waves her hand, it's the same gesture she used in Paris, "You weren't meant to come along, but considering I was unable to get here sooner, it's all to the good. You were able to look after Mollie." If she knew me better, she might not have been so quick to trust her child with me. But then it's not the first time she's trusted this precious little girl to a perfect stranger.

"It was all a ruse, you see." Now she's talking, she doesn't seem to want to stop. "I knew Sean wouldn't go for it if I simply told him what I wanted him to know, so Nasir's father set up the USB drive with information that needed to be decoded. Then all I had to do was leave Mollie with her convenient parent and assure him I was in danger."

I let out a breath, "The information I decoded was false."

She seems surprised, "That you decoded? I thought you were just his lame girlfriend. And a jealous bitch at that." She laughs, "You wanted to scratch out my eyes in Paris."

I couldn't blame her for dismissing me. I hadn't exactly shone in her company. I have another question having latched onto something else she's said, "Who's," I point at her companion, "Nasir's father?"

She gives him a look of complete adoration, "Amir al-Fahri."

And just like that, it all falls into place. "There was never going to be an attack on Al Qur'ah, was there?"

"No," she sneers, "It was the oilfields that were going to take a hit."

Right now, it's not the most important thing on my mind, but professional curiosity makes me ask, "And did they?"

This time a shrug, "Not as much as was planned. Instead of sending the guards to the north, they beefed up security there too. They caught and killed the suicide bombers before they got to their targets." She seems as concerned about the failed attack as she does about her baby. I glance at Nasir wondering whether he will show any greater regret about the loss of life of his comrades.

She notices the direction of my eyes and clears her throat to get my attention back to her. With a disdainful look, she queries, "Is there anything else you want to ask me? As I'm eager to get my gorgeous little pumpkin back and leave." Every frigging time she talks around me to the baby, she uses that stupid voice. I'm watching her carefully, and the man beside her. With a terrorist as a father, there can be no doubt that he's armed. But her? Mmm.

"Oh, for goodness sake Nasir, this woman bores me. She's no use to us. Just shoot the bitch and we'll take the baby."

CHAPTER 30

Sean

Two whole days. That's how long Nessa and Mollie have been missing. And we've still no idea where they could be. For the first forty hours, I had no sleep until I all but passed out from exhaustion, and my colleagues persuaded me to take a break. And even then, I found myself sleeping not in my bed, but in Vanessa's, with one of Mollie's blankets bunched up in my hands. I closed my red, bleary eyes breathing in the combined scent of baby and woman and at last my tired brain shut down.

Only a couple hours later I awake feeling as though I haven't rested at all, and even the short time I'd been asleep fills me with guilt. Where are they? And are they still alive? Rolling onto my back, I stare up at the ceiling. Will I ever find them? Getting air into my lungs is an effort as my gut twists and my stomach rolls. will I ever hold my baby girl again? Or Nessa?

There's been complete silence. We are working on two options, one that Danielle arranged the abduction so she can take her daughter back, and the second that they are being held as hostages. Only the second holds the better chance that both of them are still breathing. But as the hours have passed and we've received no ransom demand, the former begins to seem the more likely. So where does that leave Nessa? Surplus to requirements? That thought sends a cold shiver down my spine.

Sitting up I pull her pillow to me, breathing in deeply. It's still full of a perfume that's all her, and I remember those two nights we spent together, the nights I have every intention of repeating. Why did I tell her I would be happy limiting our liaisons to the dungeon? Who had I been kidding? I want her. My fist smashes against the pillow, why am I realising that only now, when she's lost to me?

There's a strand of auburn hair on the pillowcase, I touch it reverently, remembering the touch of her pubes, so strangely enticing when I usually like my women bare. Nessa was so different from the subs I usually played with. Innocent and pure, just waiting for my corruption. Was I never going to have the chance to touch her again? No, I can't think that way.

But she's still naïve. Despite her training, she's no natural in the field, forgetting to set the alarm system, or going out without her gun. And there's my worry, how she'll be able to look after herself, let alone care for a baby. Her weapon's missing, has she somehow managed to take it with her? No, it's more likely, the abductors found it and took it away. And even if she managed to hold onto it, would, could she bring herself to use it? Or possibly worse, fire it when there's no chance of escape? Fuck, she's no idea how to handle herself in hostage situations, all her knowledge is theoretical.

If we get them back, I'll be talking to Ben. Nessa will be staying safe behind her desk for the rest of her life if I have my way. If she's still alive.

Oh Nessa, oh Mollie. Where are you?

It's coming up for nine, and the next scheduled meeting with Kadar. Maybe overnight there's been some news, I can only hope.

No one looks any more refreshed than I. In Kadar's office, we take our seats, the mood sombre. With every passing hour, hope is rapidly fading.

"The fire at the oil wells has been capped." Kadar starts the meeting by giving us the update.

Although it's only five am in London, Ben and Jon have again joined us via video conferencing. "That's good news, Kadar." But Jon's face betrays while that's great for Amahad, on the more immediate front we've got nothing to be happy about, and he addresses our main problem, "We've gotten no further tracking down Danielle Smith. Any news from your end?"

"I've spoken to Sultan Qudamah, he's got eyes at the airport in Ezirad in case she tries to come in that way, and King Asad is monitoring Alair." At least they've got the neighbouring countries covered.

"She could be coming overland, or might already be here." I nod at Hunter, who grimaces, we'd discussed this yesterday.

"Are we sure she'll be coming for the baby? They might have delivered Mollie to her."

Kadar frowns, "Everyone's on the lookout for anyone taking a baby over the border."

Yes, but as we all know, the borders are almost impossible to control the entire length, particularly the southern desert between Amahad and Ezirad.

Ma'mun swings the door open and enters, I don't bother to look, expecting him to be bringing in yet another round of coffee, necessary now to keep us all awake and our senses sharp, but sit up straight when I hear a different voice and he usher in another person.

Kadar stands to greet the newcomer, swinging around I see Sheikh Rais, the rugged looking sheikh who's unofficial spokesman for the other nine tribal leaders.

"Rais, my friend," Kadar greets him warmly, but his eyes narrow fast, "Have you brought news?"

"I have, Excellency, but I don't know how useful it is." As Kadar points him to a seat, the Sheikh pulls his robes under him as he sits down. He leans forward, putting his elbows on the table. "Sofian contacted me earlier; a man came and visited one of his nomadic tribes to buy goat's milk, yesterday. He was a stranger, Arab, but not Amahadian."

Goat's milk? I don't immediately see what that's got to do with anything. My brow creases as I look at Rais, he sees my unspoken question and answers it.

"It was mentioned that he was buying milk for a baby." Rais nods as he sees we're all catching up with him. "The villages didn't know the man, or where he could have come from. The woman who gave him the milk said she didn't care for him."

Goats milk! "If it's for Mollie, would it be safe for her to drink?" That's my first thought.

He raises his shoulders, "If they've run out of her normal feed. How much did she have with her?"

I'd made up the bottles myself, "Six," I tell him,

"Enough for a day and night." Mollie prefers to drink little and often, but if she was sensible, Nessa could have eked it out a little longer. *But she doesn't know the first thing about looking after a baby.* And those bottles should have been refrigerated. Christ, Mollie, I hope you're alright. I shudder. But surely, anyone who kidnapped a baby should have been prepared to look after it?

Ben butts in, "Where is the village, Rais?"

"Map?" Rais jerks his chin toward Kadar, who summons Ma'mun and tells him what we need. Very shortly he returns with a large-scale map of the southern desert and lays it on the table, efficiently anchoring it down with cups. Leaving our seats, we all crowd around it. He points to an area which has nothing marked on it, and, in the way of someone who knows the desolate region like the back of his hand, circles an area which to the untrained eye, appears to be completely void. "Some of the Alah, Sofian's tribe, have made camp here. That's where the milk was purchased."

"Is it a permanent camp, Rais?" Ryan asks.

Rais waggles his hand, "Semi," he explains, "They're farmers, herders. For now, they are based around an oasis, so they'll stay a while."

"So, anyone in the area would know they were there." Ryan's nodding, thoughtfully.

"Quite possibly, yes, especially if they'd flown over it."

"Have they heard a helicopter?"

"Sorry, that's all the information I've got. There's no phone signal in the desert, and the tribe doesn't have a satellite phone."

"How did they get the message out?"

"Sofian and all the other desert sheikhs sent messengers out to their nomadic tribes. We're doing what you asked, Kadar, covering as much of the desert as we can. One of the Alah rode to the nearest permanent settlement and found someone with a phone."

Kadar taps on the table with his fingers, "It's not much, but as it's the only thing we've got, it's worth following up. Let's think this through. All conjecture, but if they flew over the camp and noted it when they needed supplies they would have gone to the closest place. So," he breaks off, and circles an area around the place that Rais had pointed out, "We send up a helicopter and search in this area."

"They'll hear a helicopter coming, Kadar." It worries me that if they think we're closing in on them, they might not leave anyone alive.

"The tribespeople will help us search on the ground."

"Give us the coordinates and we'll use satellite images," Ben suggests.

Rais quickly rattles the information off.

"Hold on, and we'll get back to you in a few. Christ, I wish Van was here, Nafisa's good, but not…" His voice trails off; it seems he'd been talking to Jon, not us. The view on the video is of an empty room now, both men in London have gone off to see what they can do to help.

It's not long before they're back, then suddenly there's a big screen shot displayed in front of us, "There's one structure that's of interest. Rais, I don't know if you can shed any light on this? There seem to be a few derelict adobe buildings about ten miles north north-west from the nomad's camp. There's no sign of movement, though; I can't tell if there's anyone inside." He rings it on the image with a pointer. "Other than that, I can make nothing else out. There's rocks behind. Do you know the area, Rais, are there caves in those hills?"

Rais is shaking his head, "I'd have to check with Sofian, I don't have much knowledge of that locality." He magics his phone from somewhere out of his robes and shows it to Kadar, "May I?"

"Please."

Rais places a call, and in quick fire Arabic is questioning Sheikh Sofian about the adobe buildings. When he ends the call, he gives us the gist of the other side of the conversation. "It's an ancient settlement, abandoned about five hundred years ago, when the oasis dried up. In its time, it was fairly prestigious hence the permanent structures. While they look ramshackle from the air, it's possible at least one of the buildings is still habitable."

"They're that old?" Nat asks.

"Adobe buildings can last millennia," Rais informs him, "Mud bricks are some one of the most durable building materials you can get. They may have had to remove blown sand from the inside, but otherwise, they could still be used."

"Why don't we check the buildings out anyway? It makes sense that they would have travelled to the nearest camp to get the milk, and if nothing else is showing up on the satellite image, it seems possible that's where they could be."

It's the only thing we have to go on, and I'm anxious to start doing something, anything, rather than just waiting around. Even if it turns out to be a dead end.

"Nafisa's just pulled something up that we missed earlier, there's a Jeep that's about halfway between the nomad camp and the adobe huts. It looks like it was heading toward them." The picture on the screen zooms out, and a pointer appears near what at first seems a very small black dot. When it zooms back in we can all see it's an old Jeep of some sort.

"It must be it. Why else would there be movement in such a desolate area?" My knuckles are white, my hands clenched in frustration from sitting here doing nothing. I can't face many more hours like this.

"We can fly into the nomad's camp, Sean, then go by whatever transport we can scrounge off them from there." I raise my chin to show my appreciation of Rais's suggestion.

Hunter is looking at me, "At this point I'd rather go on a wild goose chase than sit here twiddling my thumbs." It warms me that he's thinking along the same lines, "Sometimes you have to go with a gut feeling and the smallest clue before waiting for everything to drop into place."

The satellite image of the huts disappears to be replaced by the faces of Ben and Jon, "Sean, you go along with Hunter, Nat and Ryan."

"I'll go too," Rais offers, "The desert's my home." Now I lift my chin in his direction; he'll be an extremely useful man to have along.

Kadar wastes no time; he's already on the intercom to

Ma'mum asking for one of the larger choppers to be made ready for us. "Do you want any of my men with you?" he offers, once he's finished with his assistant.

Looking at my colleagues, I shake my head, "We'll need to sneak up on them. We're skilled, Kadar, if we go in numbers, it might be too easy for them to spot us."

"I'll be in contact via satellite phone," Jon's voice captures our attention, "Once you can give me the layout I'll talk you through the best method to extract them." Having been a member of the British army's elite force, the SAS or Special Air Services, and an expert in hostage extraction, Jon's input will be invaluable.

Taking advantage of Kadar's offer we swing by his well-stocked armoury, before making our way to the helipad, collecting a variety of weapons as well as suiting ourselves up in lightweight Kevlar body armour. It will be hot wearing it in these temperatures, but better sweating than taking a bullet to the chest. At last prepared, we go to where the helicopter is waiting for us, the pilot already in his seat. Rais sits up beside him, and for a while, they look at the map and set coordinates for the nomads' camp.

The journey isn't quite as far as the desert city, but will still take an hour and three-quarters to get there. My leg starts to bounce; I'm anxious to get on my way. At last, the rotors start spinning, and we lift into the air.

Conversation is stilted and then fades away altogether, each of us thinking our own thoughts. If we're right, and we *have* to be, we could be going into a fight, and it's possible not all of us will be coming back. None of us can guess what we'll find when we arrive. Or if it is indeed the right place. And, of course, even if I find my girls, there's no guarantee both or either of them will still be alive.

In a sombre mood, I look out of the window. The endless miles of barren desert pass beneath us, broken only by the shadow of the helicopter itself, but the emptiness of the landscape is nothing compared to the hole in my heart. They've got to be safe and still breathing. Both of them.

CHAPTER 31

Vanessa

I'd known as soon as she started being indiscreet that my time was running out, she'd implicated herself too deeply for her to let simply let me go. I'm prepared, understanding it's take action now, or do nothing and let them kill me. Knowing I've nothing to lose, as soon as she starts to voice her instruction to her companion, I jump to one side so that any return fire won't be directed toward the baby, and in one swift move pull out my gun and drop into a firing stance. I shoot Nasir with no regrets; made in his father's mould he's no loss to the world. It's an unfamiliar gun and pulls slightly to the right as I fire, missing his heart, but it's done sufficient damage that he collapses to the floor. I adjust my aim, firing again and this time place an accurate shot to his forehead.

There's a stunned silence. Then Danielle gasps, her eyes narrowed at me in horror then she lets out a scream, but the shots have frightened the baby and have elicited such loud shrieks from her, they drown those of her mother right out. With absolutely no remorse I pistol whip Danielle hard to keep her quiet, feeling no regret when she too falls to the floor. Quickly, I check she's out for the count, but just to be sure, pocket Nasir's weapon and check he's carrying nothing else she could use. Danielle, herself, is unarmed as I'd suspected.

Mollie's cries decrease to pitiful wailing, but I force myself to ignore her, moving cautiously to the door, trying desperately to remember the layout of the building when I'd been brought in. I hear footsteps, and a voice outside shouting. Fuck, I'd forgotten there was probably at least one pilot with the helicopter. There are at least four men, I know of, who I'll need to deal with.

I stay still, glad when Mollie quiets, as I'm hoping if someone comes down the short hallway to investigate the shots, I'll hear them. A moment passes, and but no sounds reach me. Then I hear two voices outside laughing. It suddenly hits me why no one's come at the sound of the gun; they were going to kill *me*. Presumably, the shots fired have been dismissed as being from the execution they were expecting Nasir to carry out.

Inching along carefully, keeping up close to the rough stone wall, I make my way to the front of the building moving slowly and cautiously through the doorway and spinning around with my gun in front of me to check the entry room is clear. Then I cross to the door which is open to the outside. The third of my guards and a man who I assume to be the pilot are smoking cigarettes a few paces away from me, and looking at the helicopter instead of in my direction. For some reason, the thought that they're casually smoking and sharing a joke just after Nasir's apparently murdered me causes my rage to rise. I take aim, shooting the guard first, firing three times until he hits the ground. It would have been better to keep the pilot alive, but he's recovered from the shock fast, and already his hand's gone to a holster. At the second his weapon appears I put two bullets through his head.

Loud shouting now. By my reckoning, there are at least two men left alive. Investigating the shooting a head peers around the corner but disappears before I can take aim. *They know where I am now, and that I've killed their comrades.*

Quickly I check my ammunition; I've got eleven bullets left in my Glock 18, my preferred weapon as it's lighter than the Sig Sauers the men tend to favour. The voices go silent as I slide myself back into the safety of the doorway. As shots fire through both windows, I drop to the floor, hoping not to be hit by any ricochet. There's a man either side of the house. *How the fuck do I get out of this?*

Taking a rock, I throw it through the doorway as hard as I can. It hits the Jeep waiting outside. The sound draws a hail of bullets in that direction. In the confusion, I come out from my hiding place and carefully sidle around keeping my back to the outer wall. At the corner, I turn, aim, and shoot as soon as I'm lined up on my target. I'm faster than he is and I keep firing until he drops to the ground. *That took four bullets. I'm down to seven.*

And there's at least one man left. Carrying on round the oblong house, I throw another rock toward the front then run around the back as quietly as I can, thanking God I've got on my sneakers and that the sounds are absorbed by the soft desert sand. Swinging around the last corner I immediately see a man with his back to the wall, his gun wavering left and right in front of him, his erratic movements showing I'm not up against a trained soldier.

For the final time, I take aim and fire.

As the echoes of the gunshots fade, the only sound breaking the silence of the desert air that of the baby, still crying inside. I wait and watch, listening for the slightest noise that would indicate there were any other men, straining to hear anything over Mollie's cries. But there's nothing. I've left no man alive.

My adrenaline rush fades, and I put my hand on the door to balance myself, vomiting the meagre contents of my stomach onto the sand. I've never shot at a live target before; have never killed anything, let alone a human being. And now I've taken the lives of five. My hands are shaking, my palms sweating, and stars begin to form in front of my eyes. *One of those dead bodies could have been mine.*

Mollie's cries keep coming. *Shit! Danielle!* I shake my head, knowing I've got to pull myself together. I rush back to the room that so recently had been my prison, checking to see Danielle's still out for the count. I then go back to the entryway to see if there's anything I can use, nothing. But what about the Jeep? Yanking the door open I check what's there. *Yes, rope!* Thanking God for small mercies, I grab it and take it with me then make myself search the bodies of my erstwhile guards, uttering another prayer of thanks when I find a knife. I made quick work of trussing up the woman I've grown to hate. I haven't done it a moment too soon. She starts to stir as I'm tying her hands.

I'd hit her hard; I'd had to. I feel no sympathy as she starts to come to with a groan, neither do I care that there's blood in her hair, and some has seeped onto the ground.

She was going to do worse to me; she'd planned to kill me and leave me here. As it was I'd only been seconds away from death.

I see her starting to move, but know she'll be feeling groggy for a while. Returning my gun to my waistband, I pick up Mollie, trying to soothe her as I carry her outside to get an idea of our surroundings. I've not leaving her anywhere near her birth mother any longer than necessary.

Outside it's quiet and still. The helicopter sits, taunting me. A way of escape so close, and yet, impossible for me to use.

Awkwardly I move the baby around in my arms, and kneel down, making myself rummage through the pockets of the closest dead man trying to swallow down the bile that rises in my throat. Already flies are starting to settle on him, and I know it won't be long before he starts to bloat in the heat of the sun.

In his back pocket, I find what I'm looking for, a mobile phone. Pulling it out I find it's an iPhone, but the screen is locked. Luckily, it's a later model. Swallowing down bile, I take hold of the still warm hand and press his finger to the home key, elated when the phone responds. But my joy doesn't last long, no bars show, and presumably, the equivalent of 'no service' in Arabic shows mockingly at the top left-hand corner. Having another thought, I press on the map icon, then swear loudly. Sure, the GPS works sufficiently to show us where we are, we're a blue flashing dot on a pure white screen. There's nothing to say where we are, or in which direction I should make my escape.

Damn! Throwing the useless item away, I rise to my

feet, and go over to the helicopter. *Is there a radio I can use?* Clumsily, with the now calmer bundle in my arms, I climb inside. Yes, there's a radio and a headset lying on the instrument panel. I look at it, realising I haven't a clue how to work it. And if I picked it up and somehow managed to get through, who would I end up talking to? It's highly possible it would be someone who might be very interested to find I'm still alive, and for all the wrong reasons.

It's even hotter in the interior, the sun's beating through the glass windscreen and is not doing either Mollie or me any good. With one last yearning look at the radio, realising I daren't try it, I leave the helicopter. I walk around the buildings, taking note of my surroundings for the first time since I escaped my cell. They're all squat adobe houses made of sun-baked sand; very old and in places the walls are crumbling. *Why was such a village built here? Surely it can't be that far from some sort of civilisation?* And when I asked, the men got milk from somewhere. But where?

There are no roads leading up; a gentle wind is blowing covering any tracks that might have previously been there to show from which direction the Jeep had arrived. This small village seems ancient and long since abandoned except for its current use as a prison. The settlement is surrounded on three sides by desert going on for miles, to the rear of it sheer rocks rise to the sky, the range continuing as far as I can see in either direction. I'm in the middle of nowhere.

There's the Jeep. But where to go? Which direction? The keys are in the ignition, so I turn it on, the engine starts with a satisfying purr. Checking the gauge I see the tank is half full. *What do I do?* If I stay here, is there any hope of rescue? Or is it more likely Nasir will be missed and more men would be sent out to find him? To stay could land me in trouble all over again. But if I set out and drive in the wrong direction, I could get lost in the desert.

Returning to the house where they'd kept me prisoner, I explore the inside. Apart from the entry room and my prison cell, there are just two others, one which the men had obviously used to sleep in, and another with a table and chairs. There's a roughly hewn stone dresser, and there I find two bottles of water and a box that had obviously contained food. But from the empty wrappers strewn across the floor anything edible has already been consumed. I put the water in the Jeep, cursing there's nothing else for me to take.

The sun is coming from a different angle now and, hazarding a guess it's already mid-afternoon. Not too long before night falls. The buzzing of flies now fills the house, making me shudder. If I'm staying here another night, I'll have to move the bodies further away. And to do that, I'd have to put Mollie down, and I'm still holding her tight to me, not wanting to let her go.

Returning to the room I was kept in, I find Danielle now fully conscious, her eyes glaring at me as I enter.

"Untie me, and give me my baby." Her demand is in the tone of someone who, up to now, has always gotten her way.

"No." I stare her down, equally determined. "You were going to kill me."

She shrugs as though it's of no consequence, and then her eyes go to the prone form of her boyfriend, and for a second it's possible to see regret in them, but her expression quickly turns back to one of hate, "You killed Nasir, you're not going to get away with that."

Right now, I couldn't give a damn about that. I'm wondering how I'm going to get away full stop.

She starts to shout.

"You can stop that right now; everyone is dead."

Her eyes open wide, and her mouth works, but in the end, she doesn't speak, but I think I see a new admiration for me, tinged with not a little amount of fear, in her eyes.

"Danielle, this is important. Do you know where we are?"

I don't think she's going to speak, but just when I've about given up, she replies, "The Southern Desert of Amahad."

Well, that's a great help! Knowing that we're somewhere in the middle of hundreds of square miles of sand is not particularly useful.

I crouch down in front of her, "Danielle, this is the situation. There's a little water and only that jug of gone over milk for Mollie." As I speak I glance down at the baby, she's flushed red, and I don't think it's just to do with the heat. Putting my hand to her forehead, I can feel she seems to be burning up, "Mollie isn't well, and needs medical attention." Mollie punctuates my words with pitiful whimpers. "We need to get out of here. There's a Jeep, with half a tank of petrol." I sigh, "So we can just drive, but I need to know which direction to go in."

Danielle's eyes open wide, she'd been so focused on her anger toward me, I don't think she understood the seriousness of our position before. "You stupid bitch, if you hadn't have killed everyone Mollie would be safe by now. Why did you kill the pilot?"

"Because it was him or me." As she goes to speak again, I talk over her, "We're in trouble, Danielle." I consider driving away and leaving her here to die, but know I can't do that. It would be kinder to put a bullet in her head. But I make her aware of my options, "I could leave you here."

Her eyes widen, and the colour leaves her face, "You wouldn't do that," she whispers, trying to read my face.

"No," I reply, simply. Much as I hate her, I can't. I've already killed more than enough today.

While I'm loathe to have her out of my arms for a second, I put Mollie on the blankets, and taking hold of the knife, stand over the woman on the floor. "It's getting late, and we haven't much daylight left. We'll have to leave, now."

Her eyes flick toward the knife in my hands as if she's expecting me to cut her throat.

I pour the remainder of the milk into Mollie's bottle, then regard the woman on the floor again. "I'm going to cut the binding around your feet so that you can walk. I'll take you with me, but if you try to harm me, be aware that I'm well trained in self-defense, and armed, and I *will* take you down and kill you."

She's such a spoilt bitch I've no concerns she'd be a match for me. I wait until I see her nod, then lean forward and cut through the ropes. She stretches as if to remove any cramp there, and I feel not one iota of compassion.

I help her to her feet, then let my hands go immediately, feeling like I'm touching a poisonous snake. She staggers, but I don't offer any further assistance. Taking out my gun I wave her in front of me then pick up Mollie again, balancing her on one arm, together with one of the stained blankets and the filled bottle and we make our way to the Jeep.

Now how am I going to play this? Pausing by the vehicle, I make up my mind. I motion Danielle to stand well away from me then place the blanket on the floor in front of the rear seats and form a secure soft cradle for Mollie and lie her down. Once she's secure, I turn to the woman. "You're going to be driving." I cut through the rope around her hands, and train my gun on her. "And you're going to do everything I say." I motion with the gun, "Get in the driver's seat."

She wants to protest but looks around her. "You knocked me around the head pretty hard. I feel too dizzy."

"Either you drive, or I'll leave you here." I threaten as I wave around us, bringing her attention to the bleakness of this spot, "And you're in no danger of hitting anything here." I'm giving her no choice. The thought of leaving her behind is an attractive one. I had thought of tying her up and driving myself but felt there was too much risk she might get free, or headbutt me or something. No, balancing everything up I think it's safer if she drives. *I'll have to tell Ben there's a gap in his training programmes; he should introduce one called 'How to escape with a baby and a prisoner'!*

With a huff, she gets into the driver's seat. I get into the passenger side, and only then give her the keys. She puts them in the ignition.

"Where to?"

I have no fucking idea. As she turns on the engine, the instrument panel comes to life. And the GPS. I point to it, unwilling to reach over her. "See if you can find a town or something."

She fiddles with it, minimising the map. Eventually, the desert city of Ẓalmā appears, but it's far, far away, and well out of the range of the fuel in the tank. There must be other settlements around. I know there are ten tribes living in the desert, surely if we keep heading in one direction we'll come across one eventually?

Clenching my fingers into fists I know I need to make a decision. "East," I tell her finally, selecting the direction for no particular reason, "Go east." Before she moves off, I warn her, "Keep your eye on the compass and sat nav, and continue going straight. It would be too easy to go around in circles if you lose concentration."

She turns to look at me, and for once, without anger, "We might not get out of this."

Wondering why it's taken her so long to come to the conclusion I'd reached some time ago, I look quickly over my shoulder at Mollie, restless in her makeshift bed in the back and decide to keep my pessimism to myself. "We will," I tell her firmly, "We have to."

CHAPTER 32
Sean

If there was any way the pilot could make the helicopter fly faster I'd be yelling at him to do it right now, but I know he's already pushing the craft to its limits. Both my legs are bouncing, and I can't get comfortable on the seat. Ryan tosses me a sympathetic look but thankfully doesn't offer any platitudes as nothing he could say will help. *Are we too late?* My hands form such tight fists my fingernails dig into my palms, but I welcome the bite of pain. *What if my girls are going through worse?* Mollie's far too young; she hasn't even had a chance at life yet. *Oh God, please don't take her away from me now.* And Nessa? I just want the chance to hold her in my arms again and tell her how I feel.

While such thoughts are racing through my head, the pilot gets a call on his radio. He pipes it into the headphones so we can all hear. It's Ben; the satellite makes a pass every twenty-four hours, and now he's got an updated satellite image, this one showing a Jeep parked behind the adobe building. The buzz of excitement that I feel does nothing at all to put a rein on my impatience. We were right about where the Jeep was headed. *We must be on the right track, who else would be in a dilapidated building in the middle of nowhere?* Despite the fact we can get there no quicker, the news has helped raise our spirits.

At long last, there's a change in altitude, and we start our descent to the temporary settlement which we're headed toward, black tents surrounding a small oasis. As we descend, our unexpected visit brings the tribespeople out to see greet us. Rais gets out first, and in fast Arabic explains why we're here, and sheikh that he is, he calls for the man who alerted Sofian to the stranger's visit, congratulating him on his astuteness in knowing that something was wrong. He, in turn, calls his wife to his side and says she's the one who should be praised, making the connection between the request for milk and a kidnapped baby, and had questioned the stranger to confirm it.

As I go to step forward, exasperated with the delay, Hunter holds me back. I shake my head in irritation, just wanting to get going. But after the greetings, Rais isn't wasting any more time and is now requesting that we borrow transport. At last, we're led to two run-down trucks which look we'll be lucky if they go anywhere at all. But Hunter reassures me the tribespeople will keep them well maintained, getting into difficulties in the desert would be suicide. The trucks might be old, but knowing the tribesmen, they'll be in good running order.

As Rais explains where we're headed, the head of the tribe recognises the buildings he's describing and offers to come with us and show us the quickest way. Sure, we can follow the GPS, but the desert can be treacherous, and he'll know of any quicksand or other perils we'll need to avoid. With thanks, we accept.

Then, at last, we're piling into the trucks and setting off.

At first, we cross the rocky terrain, having to hang on as we bounce across the rough ground. Then, Afeef, our guide, points the way to the edge of some sheer cliffs and suggests we can approach out of sight and be able to get nearer if we hug the rocks at the bottom. After another half an hour he warns us to come to a halt, suggesting if we proceed further, we'll be both audible and visible from the ancient village. From here, he proposes we proceed on foot, estimating we're only half a kilometre away.

Weapons prepared and ready and sobering looks exchanged, we proceed in silence. Afeef leads the way, though Rais has told him we won't expect him to take an active part in the rescue, he's a farmer, not a fighter.

Ignoring the pain in my leg, I manage to keep up with the others as we make our way over the rock-strewn land, but I'm starting to limp badly by the time the adobe buildings come into sight. The first thing I notice is that there's no longer a Jeep parked between the dwellings and the cliffs, the location Ben had identified. Either it's round the other side where we can't see it, or it's no longer there. But what we didn't expect to find here is a helicopter. Now it's even more imperative we approach with extreme caution, knowing they've got the means of a quick getaway if they hear us coming. Or, of course, they might take their other option and stay to fight. We've no idea how many men we're going up against, and the new mode of transport makes me concerned; there may be more than we expected.

Rais taps me on the shoulder and points up above. Vultures are circling. *Oh shit!* Birds of that species are attracted by rotting flesh. Despite the heat of the day, goosebumps cover my skin, and I shiver. Oh God, no. Please let it be an animal rotting in the sun. Fuck, I can't think of the alternative. For a second I stagger, my thoughts hitting me like a physical blow. Trying hard to keep moving, while part of me doesn't want to see what we're going to find, my dire predictions are interrupted by Jon's voice in my earpiece.

"Sean, status update."

Quickly I describe the sight in front of me.

"Okay, it sounds like you're close enough now. Ryan, Nat. Go do your thing," Jon instructs.

Ryan and Nat drop down and begin their leopard style military crawl, hoping to approach the building unnoticed. I stay back with the others, my rifle aimed to give them cover. They move fast, their bellies to the ground, and soon I see them stand, one covering the other as they look into the windows. Within moments they're waving for us to come over, Ryan gesturing showing it's all clear. *All clear?* Wait, have we come to the wrong place? What about the helicopter? There must be someone there. *Unless they're off chasing a woman escaping across the sand.* Then I watch, unbelieving and then with total horror, as Ryan brings his hand across his neck in a cutting motion, a clear signal letting us know there's no one alive.

What?

Still unsure what to expect, my heart is in my mouth as I dread what I might find. *What about Nessa and Mollie?* I run as fast as I can, my leg screaming in agony but forcing myself to ignore it, reaching the house just before my companions. Ryan waves me to a stop.

"There's been a gun fight…"

"Nessa? Mollie?" I gasp. They're all I care about.

"No, no. No sign of them." He reassures me that they're not amongst the dead. "Just men. Five. Four outside the building and one inside. As Ryan waves me closer, I go and take a look for myself.

As he said, there are four dead bodies scattered around the perimeter of the building, all riddled with bullets, the bodies already starting to swell in the desert heat. Brushing past him I go inside, where I find another man, different from the others, dressed in clothing reflecting a more affluent way of life, in a room that looks like a prison cell with bars on the window. The room smells of death and decay, and more, of shit and other unsavoury things. A bucket is in the corner which someone's obviously had to use, and dirty nappies stacked beside it. I recognise Vanessa's blouse on the floor, and beside it, blood.

What's happened here?

Rais comes and notes the bars on the window. Reaching out his hand, he tests them, then traces the concrete with his fingers. "Turds," he exclaims, "Scum of the earth."

I throw him a questioning look.

"Drug runners use places like this. The bars are to stop people coming in. It's becoming a problem. We'll have to keep an eye on this place."

His explanation was a moment's distraction, but the stench in the room is overpowering, not that I need a reminder of our main objective, and I go back outside, preferring the heat to the smell and the realisation of the terrible conditions in which my girls had been kept.

"What's going on? Update me, Sean?"

"Jon, we're here. There are five dead men. Five, Jon. The baby and Nessa were obviously kept here, and the conditions weren't good." By that, he'll know I mean bloody awful. "But there's no sign of either Mollie or her."

"Good girl," he breathes in my ear.

"What?"

"What do the wounds look like? Any idea of the calibre weapon used?"

His no-nonsense tone makes me re-examine the bodies; the clear head shots show me that the weapon used could very well have been the Glock Nessa had chosen from the gun safe. Suddenly I cotton on to what he's thinking. "She took them out?"

"She passed her tests at the range with flying colours. If she waited for the right moment, I wouldn't put it past her."

"But where is she, Jon. There's blood here. She could be injured." Even though I'm trying to keep professional, my voice falters.

Nat steps in front of me, "The Jeep. She took the fucking Jeep!"

"*Walllah! hdha lays khubranaan jayidaan baldrwr.*"

Rais's exclamation makes me swing around, "What do you mean it's not fucking good news? She's escaped!"

For an answer, he sweeps his hands around, indicating the bleak sandy landscape all around us. "If she's gone in the wrong direction she could be driving for days before she comes across anyone."

Fuck it! He's right. A woman, alone in the desert, with a young baby. Suddenly it seems her troubles might only be beginning. We'd seen no sign of a Jeep passing us, so she's not making her way to the only settlement within miles. But how would she even know it was there?

"Jon, can you get a new satellite image?"

But I know it before he tells me, "Not until the satellite passes over again. In about twenty hours' time."

Raising my eyes to the sky I again see the vultures circling above, patiently waiting for us to leave before descending for their meal, and at the same time notice how fast the sun is descending in the sky. It's almost nightfall.

"Rais," my voice is little more than a whisper, "Can we track them?"

Like me, he's looking up, and now he turns and shakes his head sadly, "We can try to find the tracks, but with this wind blowing, they'll soon be covered."

"*Ymknny tattabie lahum.*"

Oh, thank God! Thank fuck the tribesman came with us. "*Hal tastatie?*" Can you? I ask when Afeef tells us he can follow them.

The Amahadian's head nods furiously, "*Walikun lays fi alzzalami, fi alssabah.*"

I take a deep breath, I want to get going, I don't want to waste any time, but deep down I know Afeef is right. However good a tracker he is, he can't follow them in the dark, and we'll just have to wait until the morning.

"What about the helicopter?" I'm grasping at straws.

Rais rests his hand on my shoulder, "Like looking for a

needle in a haystack; we don't know in which direction she went. We can get an idea from here, but there's nothing to say she is heading in a straight line. If the Jeep runs out of petrol, the lights will soon go off. Our helicopter only has enough fuel to get us back to the capital. It can't fly around for hours."

I'm still not giving up, "What about this one? There's another chopper here."

He pats me, then moves away, swinging himself up into the pilot's seat. He looks at something, then speaks to Jon, "Jon, this is an R44. It's got just under half a tank of fuel. What range are we talking about?"

"About two hundred and fifty kilometres if there's less than half a tank. One hundred and fifty miles. Even if the Jeep's done only half that distance, we'd never find her. Unless we know which direction to go."

I bow my head, so close, and yet so far. What if it was her blood on the floor? What if she's bleeding out? What about Mollie? Is she hungry, sick? Slowly I sink to the ground, my legs suddenly unable to hold me up.

"Sean, you okay?" Nat, with his unruly shock of hair, is beside me.

"Sean," Jon's calling my name, but I rip my earpiece out.

Suddenly another body drops down, "She's a brave woman. It looks like she took them all out. By herself. How did she manage that? Fuck, I don't know. But she did. If she's survived so far, she'll keep going another few hours. First light we'll set off, but for now, there's nothing to do but to wait. Look at me, Sean." Ryan waits until I lift my head, unashamed that tears are leaking from my eyes, "She's got your baby, she'll keep her safe."

A bolt of rage goes through me, "You're making assumptions! What if one or more their captors survived? What if they're with them now? What if they had a fight among themselves? Fuck! We don't know anything, do we? Not really. It's all supposition!"

He considers it briefly, "You might be right, but I don't think you are. She's killed a lot of men here, Sean, if she'd left anyone alive, I would have expected to find her body too."

He's right, but we can't know for sure. Not until we catch up with her.

And there's something else that concerns me. "She doesn't know the desert, Ryan. Doesn't know about the snakes, scorpions. She's no idea about jackals or hyenas. She could roll the Jeep on a dune, hit quicksand… anything could happen."

"As long as she stays with the Jeep, we'll find her."

But what if she runs out of fuel and starts walking? Neither she or Mollie would be safe.

I might not be able to do anything about the girls now, but there's one thing I have to do. Pulling myself together as best I can, I place a call to Kadar, updating him and requesting that someone to come and dispose of the bodies, and keep guard on the building. If the helicopter doesn't return and the dead terrorists don't check in, sooner or later, someone will surely come to find them.

CHAPTER 33

Vanessa

A*re we heading in the right direction?* My gun unwaveringly pointed at my driving companion, I'm mentally repeating the question with no way of knowing how to answer it. But staying in that deserted ancient settlement wasn't an option. Someone could have been waiting on Danielle's return, or Amir al-Fahri might have started missing his son. To stay and wait for a rescue was likely to have been more dangerous than heading into the unknown.

"So, you and Sean?" We've been driving for about an hour, and this is the first time Danielle has spoken to me. For my part, I'm not here to make friends.

"There's nothing between Sean and me." Well, a Dom/sub relationship is not something I'm going to explain to her.

"Oh, come off it. You're protecting the baby as though it were your own. Which it isn't, of course."

"*She* isn't." Correcting her automatically, I again have to wonder about her maternal instinct.

She throws me a quick grin, "I think that proves my point. Unless you just like babies."

I could tell her I try to avoid children completely but can see by my recent actions that she probably wouldn't believe me.

I'm sitting at an angle; my back half turned toward the door so I can keep my eyes and gun trained firmly on Danielle. I don't trust her one inch. And I neither do I believe that she's suddenly become friendly. "Just keep driving steadily, Danielle. Don't try anything. I've got no particular love for you and won't hesitate to pull this trigger."

"Aw, shucks. And just when I thought we could be friends. We do have a man in common. He's pretty good in the sack, isn't he?"

I can't deny that, but a shudder runs through me at the thought he's had her too. I decide to turn the tables on her, "Why were you with Nasir al-Fahri?"

I watch as her hands tighten on the steering wheel, her knuckles turning white. The only indication that the death of her boyfriend upset her. I don't think she's going to answer, but then she seems to shake it off, "He was interesting."

That seems a funny way to describe someone. "Go on."

"What's more to say? I like excitement in my life."

My face feels tight. Excitement by way of setting bombs and killing people? Directing suicide bombers? Not trusting what might come out of my mouth at this particular moment, we drive on in silence. The next time I look at the dashboard clock, it's to see another hour has passed, and the fuel level is dropping. Night has come, and we're now driving in the dark. Mollie starts fussing in the back, but she's whimpering, not crying. It's a sound that worries me.

"Pull up for a moment; we should check on Mollie."

With a sigh, Danielle stops the Jeep. My hand steady on the gun, I instruct, "Get out." As she does so, I back out of the passenger side door and move quickly around the Jeep. "I'm not happy giving her more of that milk," Just by looking at her I can see the last lot has again simply run out of her. I'd been hoping that we would have got to civilisation by now. Danielle just stands there.

"Oh, for goodness sake, woman. Get your baby out and see to her."

Tossing me a look, she reaches in and takes Mollie out, handling her awkwardly as if she's not used to doing it. Reaching over I toss some Danielle some rags, "You'll have to use these to clean her up, we should try to make her more comfortable at least."

She doesn't seem to have a clue what to do. "Wipe her as well as you can," I offer.

"The nanny usually deals with that." She picks up a cloth with a look of disgust on her face.

Oh my God, she doesn't even look after her own baby? I'm surprised she didn't pay someone to have her for her.

Sensing my impatience, she does her best, and then, again under my instructions, moves the blanket around so Mollie has something dry to lie on. It's getting colder now, so I tell her to cover her up. Mollie's plaintive and weak cries are concerning me, I'd rather she was letting us have the full brunt of her little lungs. Once we've done what we can to make her comfortable, we resume our places in the Jeep.

As Danielle starts the engine, she turns to me, "Are you sure this is the right direction?"

I'm sure of nothing at all. Just that I want to reach something that passes for civilisation. Scanning the horizon, I hope to see lights or something that would show we're heading the right way. "Just keep driving."

"You sure you want to keep heading east?"

Change and go north or south? We could end up going around in circles, or we could be missing a settlement by just a few miles. "We carry on."

"You're in charge."

She might sound confident, but her fingers are tapping on the wheel, and she's glancing just as anxiously as I am at the amount of fuel we have left.

"This is stupid. We're going to run out of petrol in the middle of nowhere. We should turn back. They'll come searching for Nasir and me soon."

Yes, she's confirmed I was right to get away. And they might come searching for her, but they won't bother rescuing me. It occurs to me she might be naïve, "So Al-Fahri's men will come looking for his son. You think they'll have much fondness for you?"

She shrugs, "I can pay them." Then she thinks for a bit, "Look, Vanessa, why don't we make a deal? We'll go back, and I'll get them to take you with us. Then you walk away."

It's not going to be as simple as that, and I'm not stupid. "Just drive on as you are." I can see the compass heading from here, and so far, she's continued to do as I ask.

Another sixty minutes have gone by, and suddenly there's a difference in the way the Jeep's handling, it feels as though the wind is buffeting us. Then, in the light from the headlamps streaming in front of us, it looks like it's starting to rain. And then I recognise it for what it is. *Sandstorm. Shit, this was never going to be easy, was it?* It's like driving through a thick fog; we can't see a thing. The desert is rocky, and although we've been driving as straight as possible, Danielle's been making small course corrections to avoid the worst of the ground. Now we can see nothing at all; it's too dangerous to carry on.

I tell her to stop. Danielle switches off the ignition but leaves the interior lights on. I don't comment; it's scary enough as it is without being unable to see a hand in front of your face.

The howling wind and the sound of sand particles crashing against the windows and doors is deafening. The Jeep rocks as though it's going to be blown over. Dust is swirling around us, so I reach over to cover Mollie's face with the remains of her blanket, then I hang on to the panic strap with one hand, still clasping my gun in the other, just hoping we're going to be able to stay upright. Danielle's holding tight to the steering wheel, her face white in the reflected lights from the dashboard. Like me, she's scared. Sand piles up outside which has the beneficial effect of stabilising our vehicle, but on the other hand, I begin to have doubts whether we're going to be able to drive away. Or even open the doors to dig ourselves out. Driving away from the only place of safety, the house where they'd imprisoned me, could have been a fatal mistake. With a sick feeling in my stomach I begin to accept none of us will be getting out alive.

Eventually, in reality after only a few minutes but

having felt like a lifetime, the storm moves on. We're both coughing from the dust that's swirling around the Jeep. Once I see the air clearing, I open the windows, and to try to clear the fine particles. I pull the material off of Mollie's face and am concerned as she hardly stirs. *We've got to get somewhere. Anywhere.* Right now, I'd be happy to see a terrorist if it means Mollie will have a chance of life. Even if I don't myself.

Danielle restarts the engine without being told and puts it into gear. The wheels spin. She revs, tries to go backward, and then forward again. I hold my breath, then just as I'm about to suggest we get out and dig, the Jeep jumps forward with a lurch, and we're on the move again, but more slowly as we're now travelling over loose sand.

I've only just had time to savour the relief that we've successfully come through the storm when the engine starts to sputter. The damn gauge is reading just under a quarter of a tank, but it's clearly not accurate. The Jeep comes to a juddering halt. Then the lights go out. All I can see is an ocean of stars above us, and nothing, no lights or anything, whichever way I look. This is it. There's no point in walking, in a few short hours it will be daylight, and in the heat of the sun it would be suicidal. The only shade we'll have is staying with our vehicle. We're stuck. Until someone comes to our rescue. If they ever do.

The thought is a sobering one. If I had a choice, my companion would be the last person I'd want to spend my final hours with. And Mollie desperately needs medical attention. I was right to leave the stone hut, but wrong to insist on the direction of travel.

CHAPTER 34

Sean

I doubt any of us will get much sleep tonight, particularly as a sandstorm blows up. I toss and turn listening to the howling wind whistling round the stone hut, knowing it was likely to obliterate any tracks. Pulling my sleeping bag up over my head trying to keep out the choking dust, all I can think of is Nessa and my baby. If we're right, they're somewhere out there alone. Has the same storm caught up with them? Are they too suffering the worst nature can throw at them in the desert? There's a part of me that hopes they do have guards with them, at least they'd have knowledge of how to survive in such a harsh environment. If not, Nessa will certainly be out of her depth. Fuck, I wouldn't give much for my odds if our positions were reversed.

My leg is throbbing, I overdid it today, and lying on the hard ground doesn't help. But that's not what's keeping me awake. Even when the storm passes and an eerie silence falls, broken only by the coughing of my companions, I think of my girls, out there in the wilderness. If I get them back, no, *when* I get them back, I'm never letting either out of my sight again, or out of my control. The fact I can't protect the females who are important to me is a pain I feel right down in my soul. I'm a Dom, and I've failed them.

As soon as the skies start to lighten Afeef scouts around outside, but he's not optimistic. "*Allaylat almadiat ra'ayt 'annaha aittajahat ghurbaan, walikun min alssaeb altt'akkud min dhlk alan.*" Last night, he tells us, he saw she headed out in a easterly direction, but this morning the tracks aren't clear enough to confirm they continued in that direction. I know he's right, but it does nothing to lessen the burning frustration inside me.

Soon after this disappointing news, a truck arrives carrying barrels of Avgas, aviation fuel to top up the helicopter's tanks. Rais, as do many of the desert sheikhs, has his own helicopter, almost as necessary as a car living in the desolate desert. Once he'd checked the abandoned helicopter was flight worthy and hadn't taken a stray bullet, he'd offered to pilot it for us. Shortly afterwards another helicopter flies in, the one we'd flown into the nomadic settlement. I start to feel some optimism knowing we've two craft that will be able to circle and search, despite not being certain which direction Nessa will have taken.

Studying Afeef, watching the elderly Arab staring out across the sands, I come to a decision. "We head east," I tell my colleagues, firmly.

"But she could have gone in any direction," Hunter protests, he's looking concerned. Like me, he knows time is running out. We have to find her soon. "We should wait for the updated satellite image."

"But that will be hours," I protest. And if they don't have water that could be too long.

Rais is staring at me, his hand brushing his beard, and then stopping to cup his chin. "Sean's right." As I look up in surprise he continues, "She's an analyst, Hunter's been telling me. She'll be thinking logically. And that logic will tell her to avoid going around in circles. A desert Jeep will probably have a compass even if it doesn't have GPS. She's got no desert survival skills, has she?" This question is thrown out to all of us, and we shake our heads, no. Because at the time we didn't think she'd need them. "In that case," he continues, "Her thought would be to get far away from this place in case more men come to find them."

"Could she have simply driven a short distance away? To get behind the rocks?"

Rais indicates the solid cliff wall to the rear of the building. It seems to stretch for miles in either direction. "Personally, I think she'd head out and keep driving. She probably has no idea how vast and remotely populated the desert is."

Particularly if she's headed east. There was nothing on the map for hundreds of miles until she hits the border with Alair, and even after that, there's just more miles of sand.

Shaking his head, Nat checks his ammunition.

"Got something to say?" I ask.

He huffs a breath in, "I don't mind chasing off after her, but fuck knows where she's heading. She might be coming back this way, and we'll miss her again."

Rising up on the toes of my desert boots, I settle back down on my heels again. This hanging around is not doing anything but getting on my nerves. I just want to take some action, but I don't have a clue what's the right thing to do. I hate this lack of control.

Ryan appears, even though it's early he's already wiping sweat from his brow, "Just finished filling up the tanks. We've got some left for refuelling later if necessary."

Afeef has been walking further away from the camp, but he comes slowly back, his hands gesturing he's found nothing of use. *Fuck.*

The satellite phone rings, Ryan goes to answer it. His hand comes out to touch the adobe wall, and he smacks it a couple of times. "That's fucking fantastic news, Jon. Thanks for that. Send the coordinates. Cheers mate."

"What is it?" I'm by his side in seconds.

"Kadar's pulled in a favour and has got info from a French satellite which was crossing the area as dawn broke. They've had people examining it since first light and have found the Jeep. It doesn't appear to be moving, and he's given me the coordinates." He waves at Rais who brings over the map. As Ryan reads out what Jon has sent, Rais marks the spot. Using the spread of his hand he measures the distance. I note it's due east of here. "It's about a hundred and forty miles, just under an hour's flying." And the good news is, that will mean we've got plenty of fuel to get her back out to safety. "Praise Allah!" Rais raises his eyes to the heavens.

The relief I feel almost sends me crashing to my knees.

Without waiting for any instruction, we gather our packs, put guns in holsters and make our way to the two choppers. Rais walks to one, the pilot who brought us here, to the other. Hunter and I choose to go with the desert sheikh while Ryan and Nat go with the pilot who brought us to the desert. Soon rotors are turning, and the helicopters are lifting into the air, their tail rotors spinning as we make a stomach lurching turn and set off on the heading we've been given.

Hang on Nessa! We're on our way.

Nessa must have had a tedious journey, though relatively flat with no large dunes to go over, it would still be difficult driving for someone not accustomed to it. The ground varies from a hard-packed gravel where she could have picked up some speed, to a rocky terrain where she would have needed to take good care. And a large part of it is visibly soft sand which would have caused her real problems. Nessa did well to cover the distance she had mostly in the dark. Full of sympathy, I realise not knowing help was on the way, she must have just kept driving on, hoping to get to civilisation for help. And now she's probably run out of fuel. And will have given up hope. *Hang on, Nessa. We're coming!*

After what seems an inordinate amount of time, but is no more than Rais's original assessment, Ryan points excitedly from one of the rear passenger seats. Up ahead is a Jeep. My jaw locks tight, my muscles are tense as I understand I've no idea what we're going to find. *Is she injured? Is Mollie alright?*

We land a short distance away, the terrain's rocky and the pilots have had to look for suitable ground to set down. Before the rotors stop spinning, I'm out of my seat and on the ground. The other helicopter lands alongside.

Now on foot, me with a decided limp, we draw closer and can see the sound of our engines has attracted attention. Two people step out from where they were sheltering in the small amount of shade provided by the broken down vehicle. One is carrying something, it's Nessa, with Mollie in her arms. The sense of relief all but overwhelms me.

With every second we're getting nearer, but much as I want to run, I know I have to be cautious. Two people is something I didn't expect. Unless it's a guard…

"Fuck! There's another woman with her." Ryan points out. "Who the hell is that?" The woman is slightly behind Nessa and has her head bowed, and from my position, I can't tell who she is.

Covering my eyes against the sun's glare and squinting to bring her into focus, it's then I recognise her, "Danielle! What the fuck is she doing here?"

"Come to get her baby, I expect."

But she's not the one holding Mollie close in her arms.

I start to run; Nessa is coming toward me fast, holding that precious bundle so tightly to her. She near enough for me to see tears making channels through the dust caking her face. Danielle's up close behind her. Suddenly both women stop.

Nessa's eyes are staring, her mouth open wide, and she's mouthing something which looks suspiciously like *oh shit!*

"Don't come any closer," Danielle calls out. "I've got a gun. Throw your weapons on the ground."

"That right, Van?" Hunter calls out.

"Yes." Her face twists and her eyes drop down.

"Where are the people in the other helicopter?" Danielle sounds mistrustful.

Glancing around, I see no sign of the pilot or his passengers. I offer her what I hope is a plausible reply,

"The pilot is waiting with the chopper. He's a civilian pilot, just here to help with the search." I can only hope she believes me as knowing my colleagues they'll have something planned.

"I'll take the baby and be off, then." She grins, and it's easy to see what she's thinking. Offer the pilot enough money, and he'll take her anywhere.

I take a step forward, keeping her attention on me, seeing a movement in the sand off to my right. Ryan has descended from the other helicopter and is crawling slowly across the surface, his camouflage desert clothing helping to hide him from view. Out of the side of my eye, I see him successfully reach some low rocks. Nat's doing the same, but coming up from the opposite side. I've got to keep her talking and her attention on me.

She considers the two aircraft, her brow furrowing. "One of you, shoot out the tail rotor off that helicopter." She points to the one Rais had flown.

Hunter and I exchange glances, if we do that, we won't all be getting out of here. The helicopters are R44s with only room for four people. She's obviously opting to go with what she's probably hoping is a neutral pilot.

"You planning on leaving some of us here, Danielle?"

"I'm sorry, Sean," she sounds anything but, "It's just the way it has to be. I'll be leaving. With my baby."

I hear a gasp from Nessa, and watch as her arms encircle Mollie in a more secure hold. Her eyes are on me, pleading. I take a step forward. "You can't do that." I need to ensure her attention is on me.

"Watch me. And anyway, your woman's dead already

but just doesn't know it." Danielle shrugs nonchalantly.

"What the fuck are you talking about?"

"You know who she killed?" She's glaring at me, fire in her eyes.

Another step toward her. *Just keep her talking and her focus on me.*

"Stay back! Or I'll shoot her. A bullet through the spine."

"Shoot Nessa, and you risk shooting Mollie as well." The likelihood of a bullet going through them both is dubious, but at that close range, possible. Although the sun's blazing down, I shudder.

Behind me, Hunter scuffs his boot against the ground and stamps.

"Keep still!"

"Scorpion." He calls out to explain, perfectly plausibly, particularly as he quickly sidesteps away from where he was standing.

That's enough of a distraction to allow Nat to come up behind her. I just need to buy him a few more seconds. To keep her looking at me I play along, "Who did Nessa kill who's so important?"

"Nasir al-Fahri." She calls out.

Shit! Amir al-Fahri's son. A man so elusive we hadn't recognised him as being one of the bodies left back at the dwelling.

Nat's right at her back. His gun cocks audibly in the still air, and I see Danielle's body go rigid as she feels metal against her ear. He reaches round and takes the Glock, *Nessa's Glock,* from her hand.

Nessa steps away, her breath coming in fast pants as though she's just run a mile. Knowing Nat has the bitch who birthed my child safely contained I close the gap between us, rushing to my woman, putting my arms around both her and my daughter, relishing the feel of them both. And then I notice. Mollie's quiet, too quiet. And still.

"She needs a doctor, fast, Sean." More tears are flowing now, "God, Sean. She needs a doctor!"

Nessa herself looks in a bad way, her eyes are sunken in, obviously dehydrated. I go to take the burden from her, but she's clinging onto Mollie as though she's never going to let her go. As I try again, a small whimper comes from her mouth, and her dull eyes plead with me. Never had I expected her to bond with my child in such a way, especially after everything she'd told me, but now she seems terrified of letting anyone take her, even me, her father.

"Let me have her, Nessa. You're dead on your feet." I keep my voice quiet and low, soothing.

"No." It's a refusal, but also a plea.

"Let's help her to the helicopter, Sean," Rais is speaking quietly for such a big man. "Let her keep hold of the child."

I jerk my chin, not understanding why, but somehow, I know she needs this. With the sheikh on one side and me on the other, we half carry woman and child to the chopper and help her inside. Once there, Nessa's head lolls back. Peering into the blanket I see Mollie; she's barely breathing. She's naked beneath the covering, her body blazing red. *What the hell have they been through?*

Rais waits only for Hunter to join us then lifts off almost before he gets into his seat. As we rise into the air, I see Ryan and Nat have Danielle restrained, and are dragging her toward the other helicopter. I don't give a fuck how they treat her, as far as I'm concerned, if that's the last I ever see of her, the better it will be.

The half hour flight to Ƶalmā seems too long. I sit, my arms round both of my girls, hardly able to believe I've got them back. Mollie worries me, she's so still and quiet. Far too young to have gone through the ordeal she has. Nessa rocks her constantly, and coos to her in the type of voice I never expected to hear. Unresponsive to me, all what remains of her strength is directed toward comforting the baby in her arms.

Rais radios ahead and arranges to land at the helipad at the desert city hospital, one well equipped to deal with the effects from exposure. Medical staff are awaiting our arrival and quickly whisk Nessa and baby away. Nessa's only partly conscious, and still they have to pries Mollie from her arms.

And then I can do nothing but play the waiting game, pacing, unable to relax in the room they've directed me to. My hands alternate between twisting together in anguish then fisting in frustration that there's nothing else I can do but kill time until I hear news.

Rais stays with me during what seems an agonisingly long hour. After a short discussion where I'm able to function rationally, if only for a few minutes, he's on his phone, and, as we'd agreed, informing Kadar of the name of the person who had been killed on Amahadian soil. If the country hadn't already been attracting the attention of al-Fahri, it certainly would be now. The son of the world's most wanted terrorist is dead. Like Rais, I expect there will be fallout from that, and I dread what form that could take.

Finally, the door to the waiting room opens and a doctor appears. He bows his head as he acknowledges the sheikh, and then turns to me.

"Mr Cooper?"

"How are they?" I can't be bothered with introductions.

"The woman you brought in is suffering severe dehydration and exposure but she's now on a saline drip, and the initial tests didn't suggest there are going to be any lasting complications."

Thank goodness for that. "And Mollie, my baby?"

As he starts to explain he hasn't been treating her, another doctor appears. Immediately I take heart that his expression isn't somber.

"Mr Cooper, we were told your baby had been given non- pasteurised milk in an unsterilized bottle." I knew that part, Nessa had been conscious enough to tell them that. "She's got a high level of bacteria in her stomach as a result, and a high temperature. We've given her anti-biotics, and are treating her with intravenous fluids to help with the dehydration. The prognosis is good, and she should make a full recovery."

The relief is so immense, I have to put my hand out to the wall to keep myself upright for a moment. Rais claps me on the shoulder, his hand resting for a moment, giving a squeeze of support. Then he nods to the door, and leaves, his job done for now.

My first visit is to the children's ward to see Mollie for myself. She's hooked up to all sorts of equipment, and looks so tiny and forlorn. I hate to see her this way. How the fuck could her real mother put her through something like that? If I see her again, it will be all I could do not to murder her with my own hands.

I have a short conversation with the nurses, who assure me that Mollie is responding well, and she's sleeping naturally. They tell me some things about her ongoing care which I know they'll have to repeat before she's released, as right now my powers of concentration seem to be nil. All I can focus on is their certainty that there'll be no lasting ill effects.

Once I'm confident Mollie's in safe hands, I make my way to a different ward to see Nessa. Standing at the entrance to her room I examine the woman lying on the hospital bed, her face glowing red with sunburn but strangely still looking wan, her eyelids closed as though she's sleeping. *This woman saved the life of my daughter.* The thought almost causes me to stagger with gratitude, and I don't know how I'll ever be able to thank her enough for that. I don't know the whole story yet, but all the evidence suggests seems she protected her, killed the men who'd taken her, and cared for her to the extent that even in her semi-conscious state she wasn't going to let her go. This woman, who'd told me so emphatically that she 'doesn't do babies'.

As if she senses my presence, she opens her eyes. "Sean," she breathes, her voice still husky and dry.

I'm at her side in seconds. Mindful of the drip still

running into her arm, I pull her to me. I might be a man, but my masculinity doesn't stop tears falling from my eyes as I think how close I came to losing her, to losing them both. Her hands grip my arms with a strength I don't expect, her fingers digging into my skin as if to prove I'm here, and her eyes stare up into my face, drinking me in as though she's afraid I'm a vision and I'll disappear.

I'm not letting you go again. I vow, silently, *I am never going to let you go.*

CHAPTER 35
Vanessa

I don't know how you managed to kill five men, Nessa; that was fucking good going."

I'm sitting up now, drinking a welcome cup of tea. Some time ago the nurse came and removed the drip from my hand. Apart from a throbbing headache and the skin feeling hot and tight over my face, I'm feeling more human now, and well enough to answer Ryan's question.

"I was lucky only Danielle and Nasir came into the room. I was certain she wasn't armed, she just didn't seem the type of person to get her hands dirty herself. I decided to shoot Nasir, and made sure Mollie was out of the line of fire," I impress that on Sean, and wait for his nod showing he believes me. "The men outside just assumed it was me that had been the target." I shudder, knowing just how close my brush with death had been. "When I got outside I took two out immediately, they were standing, smoking, and didn't see me coming. Then it was a bit of a game of cat and mouse with the others." I shrug, "I got lucky."

Sean takes my chin in his hand, "Fuck, Nessa." He's shaking his head in disbelief.

"I took lives, Sean. They're dead because of me." I know I'll have nightmares, will be reliving those bullets smashing into flesh, the blood… Putting my hands on my face, my body shudders again.

Sean covers my hands with his, "And if you hadn't, it would be your body lying rotting under the desert sun."

I nod, he's right, but it doesn't stop tears pricking at my eyes. Before Ryan had joined us, I'd filled Sean in on what had happened from the time he'd left the house in Kadar's compound to the moment they'd saved me. I also let him know in my opinion how unfit Danielle is to be a mother. And now I need to be assured she's safely out of the way.

"What's happened about Danielle?"

"You don't have to worry about her anymore. She's still in Amahad but in prison. Kadar's talking with the FBI and Interpol about her. They're very interested in her relationship with Amir al-Fahri. I can see a lot of interrogation in her future."

Just the name makes me shiver, "And what about al-Fahri? Does he know about Nasir?"

Sean and Ryan exchange glances, but it's Sean who continues to update me, "Not as far as we know. Well, it's not as if we have an address to send a card of condolence." That's true, I suppose, and as Nasir had been the one who would have dispatched me, I shouldn't feel much remorse about it. "He'll know he's missing, but not anything else. Yet."

As my eyes widen at the word Sean ended with, Ryan takes over, "Kadar destroyed the evidence. Al-Farhi will find out his son is dead, but hopefully, we can conceal your part in it."

"How?" I pull myself up straight, wanting to know

everything that's been going on. "Tell me, please, Sean."

"Kadar arranged for the removal of the bodies. His men staged a helicopter crash in the desert; the wreckage burned out. All that was left were charred bodies. That an unknown helicopter crashed and five unidentified men were killed has been reported on news channels."

"Once Amal al-Fahri finds out it was his son, he'll want an investigation, surely? Forensics will show they were shot."

A twisted grin appears on Ryan's face, "The wreckage was found by Sofian's tribe, and you know how primitive the desert people can be. They buried the bodies. Somewhere, in an unmarked grave. Before reporting the 'accident'." His fingers put his description of the crash in quotes. "Everything's been cleaned up; there's nothing to find." Ryan stands and prowls around the room, "Cara's monitoring the dark web, but there's nothing yet about anyone trying to locate Nasir. I think she's working with the American security forces and plotting about leaking news on his whereabouts to try and trap al-Fahri. But it's nothing for you to worry about, there's nothing to link you to his death. Nasir's father will have suspicions, but there's nothing to confirm it. No body, no evidence."

"Supposition is enough for al-Fahri to declare war." My eyes narrow as a thought comes to me, "And Danielle knows. If she gets the message out…"

"Nessa, don't you think we know that? She's being held in solitary with only Kadar's most senior and trusted guards having anything to do with her."

I'm not convinced; it's still a risk. And if the most

wanted terrorist in the world gets to know I'm the one who fired the gun taking out his only son? I don't give a lot for my chances. If there's any way Danielle could make my part in it known, she will do so out of spite; I've no doubt about that.

Leaning over, Sean takes my hand, "You didn't have a personal beef with the man, Nessa. You were doing your job, working as a Grade A operative. If anything, I think his sights will be set on the organisation, not an individual. And as we're on Amahadian soil, I suspect al-Fahri's fury would be directed at this country, and not at any us in any event. He's already got the hots for Kadar, remember? But we're not taking chances, the whole team is still here, and as soon as possible we'll be returning to England." He squeezes my fingers, trapping them in his palm, "We're taking every precaution to ensure Danielle doesn't talk to the wrong person, and unless she does, the only information that al-Fahri will be able to surmise is that it's probable Nasir went down in a helicopter crash. And even that, he won't be able to confirm."

It doesn't help much. It was only months ago that Kadar's most trusted employee turned traitor on him for the promise of sufficient reward, as Sean knows only too well. Danielle has money, and everyone has a price. While she's still alive and breathing, there's a danger my part in Nasir's death will come to light. Frowning, I appreciate that working in the field carries more risk than just being prepared to take a bullet for the person under protection. In defending them it's all too easy to make yourself a target. But I'd been protecting Mollie, and I don't regret a single thing I'd had to do to keep her safe.

"I'd do it all over again, Sean."

Closing his eyes briefly, he opens them again and stares at me intently, "I know you would. And I'll never be able to thank you enough for saving my daughter. Fuck, Nessa, another person might have let them take her. But you put yourself at risk, sticking by her side. Caring for her better than her real mother." As he breaks off his breath hitches, "If they hadn't taken you with her, she might have died through lack of care. Her mother didn't seem to think about her comfort at all."

I contradict him, "In her own way, does. She cares about her as though she's a possession. What she did wrong was having not thought about her well-being. She'd made no preparations for her care. All she wanted was to get her back."

His blue eyes stare into mine, "As I said, she didn't give a fuck about her. You're right; she's nothing more than a toy to her."

Sean's kept me updated with Mollie's progress, but suddenly I want to see her to assure myself she's not suffered permanent damage from my inept attempts to care for her.

"I want to see Mollie." I can't wait to see her any longer. In the two days since we were rescued, Sean's been spending half his time with me, and the other going to the opposite end of the hospital to check on his daughter, but now I need to see her with my own eyes, to know that my efforts to keep her alive had been enough.

Ryan and Sean exchange glances and seem to have a

silent conversation over my head including raised eyebrows then nods. Ryan disappears but returns shortly with a wheelchair.

"Let's break you out of here," he grins.

"I can walk."

Sean waves away my protest, "You're still weak. Wheelchair or nothing."

Narrowing my eyes, I can tell by the way he speaks it's a Dom's instruction, and the sound of it makes my toes curl. There had been moments over the past few days when I never thought I'd see him again, let alone hear his voice. But the impulse to see the baby I've grown so close to drive me to give in without further protest, and soon I'm being wheeled through corridors and up in a lift to the area reserved for children and babies.

Seeing the drip in the little baby's arm is distressing, but she's awake, her eyes scanning the room. When I draw closer to her cot, her arms come up and reach for me, and a smile crosses her face.

A nurse comes up alongside, "Babies are more resilient than we give them credit for," she tells me with an easy smile as she reads the concern in my expression, "You can pick her up, it would do her good to have a cuddle."

I step back, making way for Sean, but he surprises me, "I think it's you she wants, Nessa." He pulls up a chair and waits for me to sit down, then gently lifts her out of her cot and places her in my arms. Immediately she grabs hold of my hair and pulls it. *She's alright. She's going to be okay.* Seeing her smiling face, knowing she's safe, fed, rehydrated and clean now and looking like she'll make a full recovery, I understand how much we bonded during the days we spent together. My heart almost stops as I remember she isn't mine, and I have no sway over her now.

But as her father kneels beside me, putting his arms around us both, I feel a sense of coming home. A home which doesn't belong to me. Holding Mollie, breathing in her scent, tears prick at the corners of my eyes. I signed a contract with Sean, sex as he wanted it, but only in situations which meant neither of us were involved in each other's lives. It was something I thought I'd wanted, but now I know I agreed to it as it was a way to have an exclusive relationship with him. I no longer want restrictions, I want him.

Sean, the manwhore. The man who doesn't do relationships. In any form.

He holds us both, his arms tight around us as if he doesn't want to let either of us go. But it's an illusion.

He's murmuring something, but I can't process the words he's saying. He's repeating them, over and over again and at last, they seep into my befuddled mind. "You're both mine, now. I'm never going to let either of you go. Ever again."

I look up to tell him that I'm an independent woman, that I don't want to be around children, that I've got a career... But the words don't come out of my mouth. Instead, I rest my head on his shoulder staring up at him in disbelief as he continues, his words smashing the walls I'd built around my heart into smithereens, "I reckon Mollie would like a brother or sister eventually, how do you feel about that, Nessa?"

My gut clenches. Me? To have Sean's baby? Balancing Mollie on one arm, I reach out my hand and grab his as though it will give me strength. A baby with a man who won't walk away? Who I can trust? Who's saying he *wants* a child with me? Pulling away from him, I place his baby in his arms.

"Sean, neither of us should make decisions now." Playing down the words he's said cuts me to the quick when he's offering me everything I ever wanted, but I know I have to be the sensible one, "It's a reaction to what we've been through, what you've been through. Your worry about Mollie and me."

He holds his daughter with such gentleness and care, my stomach twists with the thought that could be my child. His face, though, is dark, "Are you saying I don't know my mind? That having you in my life wasn't something I'd been thinking, dreaming, about while going frantic with worry about where you were, how you were? Whether you were still alive?"

I force myself to be strong, to be logical, "That's the point, isn't it? The fact you lost us both. A reaction to your concern. This," I wave my hand around the room of the foreign hospital, signs in Arabic on the walls not letting us forget for one second we're still three thousand and more miles away from home. "I don't want promises made in the heat of the moment, Sean."

His eyebrows crease, "Then I'll just have to show you when we get home, won't I?"

And home is where I'm headed the next morning, much sooner than I expected. When you know an emir things happen quickly. As soon as Mollie's pronounced fit to travel, we're whisked by helicopter to the capital where the plane is waiting to fly us back to England. Ben, himself, meets us at the airport, as though wanting to ensure we're okay with his own eyes, and drives us himself to Sean's home.

The conversation during the journey is more of a debrief with the boss. As we pull up outside Sean's apartment building, Ben clarifies the last bit of information he needs, then gets out of the car and gets Mollie's stuff out of the boot.

Sean turns to me, I refuse to look into his eyes. "Are you coming in?"

It's all I want to do. But I'm still convinced Sean's still not over the shock of his baby going missing, and his invitation has more to do with his feeling of gratitude toward me for keeping her safe, along with his guilt we got taken in the first place. *I need to give him time.* "No now, Sean. Let's put some space between us. Some time to come to terms with what's happened." That's the sensible thing to do, isn't it?

I hear him sigh, "If that's what you want, Nessa. But it won't change anything." He gets out of the car and I feel such loss as he walks away with his baby in his arms that I almost call him back, but I bite my tongue.

One of us has to be rational. Leopards, or manwhores, aren't known for changing their spots. We need to get back to normal, settle into the familiar routine before making decisions that will affect our future.

I know my mind and what I want. Now I'm giving Sean space to discover if he really knows his.

CHAPTER 36

Sean

Why won't she believe me? What can't she see that she's come to mean everything to me?

Entering my lonely flat with my baby, something only a few days ago I'd feared I'd never be doing again, I know I'm a completely different man from the one who set out to find Mollie's mother. Putting the sleeping baby down in the cot that Mum had bought and set up for me, I pull up a chair and sit staring at her, unwilling to leave her alone, even for a second. I've changed since Nessa and Mollie's abduction and rescue, but if I'm truthful the change started much earlier than that, from the time I was kidnapped and shot. Or even a few months before that.

As Mollie snuffles and kicks her blankets off, my introspection continues. I might have the well-earned reputation as a switch, but when I'd been sent into a BDSM club to rout out a wannabe Dom who'd been stalking Jon Tharpe's woman, I'd laid myself open to abuse. The scars on my back will fade, but will never completely disappear, and the damage done to my mind will always remain. The horror of being at someone else's mercy, a man who'd ignored my safeword taking away all my control is hard to shake. I thought I could bounce back, could return to my old anything-goes way, but I haven't, and I won't. I've denied the overriding Dom side of me for too long. I'm not playing at it, this is what I am.

And there's only one woman I want to be my sub. And not just in the club.

Nessa needs someone to watch out and care for her, just as much as Mollie. And I'm going to do everything I can to convince her that I've changed and that change has been coming for a long time. I just hadn't seen it. The events of the past few days have been the catalyst I needed to consolidate the revelations about myself. And now I know she's the *one*. The woman I want to spend my life with. *I've just got to convince her.*

Mollie kicks out again and gurgles, I pull her blanket back up. Then go to the single bed beside the cot in my guest room, unwilling to have her out of my sight. Laying myself down, I close my eyes. *Mollie's home. And now I'll just have to work on Nessa.*

The next morning, I take Mollie to see my Mum, who is delighted to have her back safe and sound. I sketch over what happened, sparing her the more horrific details of what had gone down. When I explain, from now onwards, Mollie is going to be my sole responsibility, that's all she needs to hear. Her pleasure in the reunion makes her more than happy to have her granddaughter in her care for the day, leaving me free to go to work. After the requisite hug to reassure her we really are both back safe and sound, I leave and make my way into the city.

And now here I am, entering Grade A, and it seems hard to imagine the events of the last week have really happened. I wave at Sandra and quickly jump into the lift to evade the nosy receptionist who's left her desk and is heading my way. I hide my grin as the doors slide closed when she's only a few feet distant, not missing the disappointed frown she sends my way. Oh, she probably knows the gist of what's been going on already, but I'm not going to satisfy her curiosity any further. I don't want every Tom, Dick and Harry in the building knowing everything about me.

Making my way to Ben's office I pause to get a coffee, and then arrive on time for our pre-arranged meeting. But he's not alone. I walk in, then pause, seeing I'm faced with a complete stranger.

Ben nods at me, then wastes no time in making introductions, "Sean, this is Jason Deville."

My mouth drops open. I'd come to believe the man was a figment of Ben and Jon's imagination or at the very least a sleeping partner with no interest in the business. In all the years I've been working for Grade A, I've never actually met the other senior partner and my, albeit elusive, third boss.

As he steps forward to shake my hand, he makes a correction, "Devil." He grins as he tosses out the shortened version of his name, "People call me Devil."

The scar that reaches across his face pulling down the corner of one eye and giving his welcoming expression a cruel twist suggests why. The firmness with which he grips my hand, muscles visibly tensing beneath his shirt make me glad that he's on my side.

As last I get over the shock and recover my ability to speak. "It's good to meet you, at last, Devil. I was beginning to think you didn't exist."

He gives a hearty laugh, "I know. And it's best to keep it that way."

Ben's frowning, "Sean, this meeting is on a need to know basis. Devil will be leaving shortly after, and as far as anyone else knows, he was never here. Got it?"

"He'll have to avoid Sandra."

Ben laughs, "You're not wrong there." Then, as quickly as the smile came, it fades away, "I asked you to come in because we've heard something that concerns you directly. Sit."

As Devil and I take the proffered chairs in front of Ben's desk, I push aside my intrigue at the man I've never met before, and look curiously from one to the other instead, wondering which one is going to enlighten me.

It's Devil who clears his throat, "I understand that you have no particular relationship with Danielle Smith, is that correct?"

My voice is strong as I give him the confirmation he's seeking, "You're right. I had a one night stand which resulted in the birth of a child. My daughter. The baby I love. The mother is not someone I'd want in my life."

"And now you haven't got that choice." As I glance quickly up at Devil, my eyes narrowing as I wonder what he's telling me, he continues, "She was killed. Last night, in prison."

"How?" My eyebrows rise at the news.

A shake of his head, his dark mane swinging around him with the gesture, Devil answers my question, "We're not quite sure on that. Another prisoner or perhaps even a guard. There was a fire set, sufficient to cause an evacuation. In the kerfuffle, someone must have knifed her. Shanked, as our American friends would say."

My relief is immense. Nessa no longer has to worry about Danielle exposing her part in Nasir al-Fahri's death. But, taking a moment to think through the implications, the next thing I feel is anger. Danielle potentially had information about the terrorist organisation that she had yet to share. I sum up my frustration in a simple question. "Who the fuck would want to stop her talking to us?"

Devil and Ben exchange glances, and again, it's Devil who leans forward, "She hadn't yet spoken to the FBI or our SIS or anyone else for that matter. With so many people wanting information from her they were still scratching their arses trying to work out who was going to take the lead. Al-Fahri has caused trouble over a good portion of the globe."

"So, she was stopped before she could talk?" That alone makes me think there was potentially important information she could have told us. But on the other hand, it's good news she's no longer able to implicate Nessa in any way. That alone makes me feel a weight's been lifted from my shoulders.

His eyes carefully scanning me, Ben must see some of the stress draining from my face. He nods, once. "Yes, it means Van is safe."

"I know I shouldn't say this, Ben, but that's the thing that matters most to me." I'm still trying to digest the news.

Ben flicks worried eyes at Devil, before commenting, "I think we might have to thank Kadar."

"*Thank* Kadar? Why would he want to stop her talking?"

I can't see what benefit there is for the emir; surely he had more to gain from getting her to speak rather than shutting her up.

A strange, calculating look from Ben, "Sean, this can go no further. Devil and I are pretty certain what happened, but this stays between us, okay?"

I nod, dipping my head up and down slowly.

"Okay, Kadar's a Dom. He's protective toward women."

Devil leans forward and takes over, "There was a risk she'd get a message out to the wrong people, however well she was guarded. Kadar is only too well aware how easily betrayal can be bought. Part of the fighting between the CIA, the SIS and any of the other acronyms involved was where she'd be taken to be interrogated. Once out of Amahad she was out of Kadar's, and our, control."

It falls into place, "Kadar acted so Nessa's part could never be exposed." The emir's last personal assistant had sold Zoe out for money. And that resulted in both of us being kidnapped, and me being shot. Yes, Kadar knows better than most how easily any man can be turned.

With a grin, much like the one a proud father would give his son, Ben agrees, "At the risk of losing information to protect his country, yes."

It was the action of a Dom protecting a sub. But Nessa wasn't his sub. And as emir, Kadar's first duty was to his country. Something about their supposition doesn't sit well with me. I put my head in my hands, rubbing my temples before glancing back up, "Kadar got the information he needed first. And will be keeping that close. Whatever Danielle knew, al-Fahri will think died with her."

Devil laughs, and smacks his hand on the table, "I like him, Ben."

Obviously, I'm thinking along the same lines as they are. "Where does this leave us? What do we do now?"

"Nothing," Ben asserts. "It makes sense Kadar might have used some of his countries extreme interrogation measures to get her to spill her knowledge, but we won't go into that. We'll leave it in the realm of the theoretical for now. We don't know what Kadar found out, or for sure that it was anything. If we need to know, I expect we'll be the first on his list to call."

"We sit tight," Devil confirms. "And wait. But your girl is in the clear."

Again, I nod and then start, "Ben, Devil. Nessa's not my girl." Not yet, anyway. Not until I can convince her.

"Sean, I can read you. She might not have accepted it yet, but you certainly want her to be. You're good together, and it's time for you to settle down. But she's running scared."

Focusing on Ben once more, I remember he knows something of her situation. And fuck it, he's guessed mine. Then a suspicion dawns on me, "You threw us together on purpose, didn't you? Shit, Ben, why the hell did you put her through it? Sending her off with me and a baby? You must have known how that would freak her out."

He looks unrepentant, "She wanted to work in the field. And the opportunity came up." He sighs, "Of course, I didn't know I was sending her into danger at the time. None of us knew who Danielle was, or what she was involved in." He taps his fingers on the table, "Sean, you're a Dom, she's a sub."

"I'm a switch." I say it, even though I know I'm not anymore. I won't be submitting again.

But Ben knows me too well. "No, Sean. You haven't been that for a very long time." He looks sad, "What happened with Hatcher hit you hard. Since then you've been drifting, unable to find yourself."

"So you set me up?"

Now it's his turn to shrug and then throws me a wicked grin, "She couldn't hide her attraction to you, and I always suspected you just needed a push in her direction. It worked, didn't it?"

I can't, don't want to refute that. What's the point in arguing when it's Nessa I want? But it's not a fait accompli as he seems to think. "She's not convinced."

"Well, convince her." It's easy for him to say. He allows a moment's silence while I digest what he's said. And I recognise he's given me an opening. If I'm her Dom, there's something I can do to keep her safe.

"She can't work in the field again," I begin, "She's a danger to herself, and to others. In the office, she's indispensable, she's focused, and her skills are beyond anyone else's. Out on a case, she's all over the place."

"That's not your decision, Sean."

"You've just told me I'm her Dom. In which case, it's my responsibility to watch out for her and keep her safe."

"And you will," Devil puts in. "But first, there's another thing we wanted to talk to you about."

Ben slides a manila folder out of his drawer, and my eyes narrow as I recognise it. It's my medical report. "You went to find the mother of your child. It should have been a straightforward enough case, keeping two of my operatives occupied but without any risk involved." He looks apologetic, "I'm sorry it didn't turn out that way."

"We didn't want to have this conversation with you, Sean. But we can't avoid it. I think even you know that."

Suddenly the crease on my trousers seems fascinating; I pluck an imaginary speck of fluff off the material. I'd hoped this day would never come. But, being a Dom also means understanding yourself, admitting your weaknesses and knowing your flaws. And I know exactly what they are going to say. They intend to pull me from active duty. Permanently.

"Do we need to say the words?"

Glaring at the folder in Ben's hands with an intensity as if I could make it burst into flames, knowing I don't want him to open it and read out what it says there. It's best for me to take the man's way out. Inhaling deeply, I put my back straight and look across at the man who's been my boss, my partner and my friend since I left the SAS. Then, sighing, I force my voice to be strong, "You're asking for my resignation."

"Fuck, no." Both men answer me, equally surprised expressions on their faces.

"I'm not going to be fit enough to resume active duty." At last, I admit that despite everything I've done to prove the doctor's wrong, I'm never going to have full mobility in my leg again.

"We can't have you working as a CPO, Sean."

Much as I want to, and would have done before my self-analysis over the past few days, I can't argue with Ben. My legs used to be my weapons. And who would want to employ a bodyguard who's not fully functional? Who can't run without pain or risking their leg giving way? There are some jobs than even the disability discrimination act has to concede are restricted to the non-disabled.

"That's the other reason I'm here," this from Devil. "I've been working alone, as you know, but now I'd like to set up a team back here at base to support me. Highly secret work, Sean, but I need the best minds. You and Van are just who I'm looking for." He holds up his hand before I can ask the myriad of questions his suggestions bring to mind, "You'll be mainly based here, but on call to provide your expertise anywhere I need you. You'll need to keep up with your physical training, as some of the situations I deal with can be dangerous. You'll be fit enough for what I'll want you to do. So, what do you say?"

As I'd expected them to sack me, the alternative he's suggesting is a lifeline. I may not know what's involved, but the idea intrigues me. And being based here, I can start to build a life around Mollie.

I don't even need to take time to think about it. "I might be getting involved with the very devil," I say with a grin as a glow radiates from inside and the fear I was about to be unemployed recedes, "But yes, I'm in."

Devil reaches over and shakes my hand, "Good to have you onboard, Sean."

"Now," Ben says, his shrewd eyes looking as though he's scheming, "We've just got to convince Van. And I've got some suggestions as to how we go about that."

CHAPTER 37

Vanessa

At least the time difference between Amahad and England let me have a lie in this morning, but for once I don't appreciate it. My mind is too busy buzzing. I'm unable to stop worrying about Danielle opening her mouth and telling all and sundry about me shooting Nasir al-Fahri. Every creak of the house makes me worried someone is already coming after me.

I spend the early morning hours listing the potential weapons I have lying around the house and come up with a pitifully short list. The knives in my butcher's block are about my best option. Great, if the assassin comes in through the back door. And then again, would I actually be able to stick a blade into someone? Shooting a gun had been bad enough. Every time I close my eyes, I see the bodies falling, and know I am responsible for their deaths. Even though the rational side of me says I'd done what I had to, to protect the lives of myself and Mollie, it still sickens me that I'd been left with no other option. Although, my disgust at the action I was forced to take is not sufficient to prefer that it been me,rather than them.

And the other reason for my insomnia is predictably Sean. Had I been right to reject him? Was I right to dismiss him, to doubt the sincerity of his feelings for me?

And Mollie, she might not be mine, but my arms feel so empty today. Had I made the wrong decision last night? Might Sean have come to his senses and realised I was right? Back in England, he'll have no need for me.

When the clock tells me it's time to get going for my meeting with Ben this morning I'm relieved. My house is spotless, getting up at five o'clock with nothing better to do will help with that. The toilet bowl's scrubbed, the bathroom and kitchen are gleaming, and I've even managed to get the dust off my collection of books. But now it's time to face the music.

Has Sean written a report? Will Ben overlook my deficiencies and put it down to it being only my first time working out of the office? Will he be assigning me to another case? *Do I still want to work in the field, exposing myself to danger again?* And if Ben is going to send me out again, will I still be partnered with Sean?

Oh God, I hope so!

Oh, Jesus, I hope not! Not if he's come to understand it was the horror of the past week that's making him act so out of character.

Slamming my front door shut as I leave the house I slap the heel of my hand against my forehead. I don't bloody know what to do or what I want. In my work or personal life. I'm in no more certain frame of mind when I walk along the corridor at the allotted time and knock on Ben's door. I can hear male voices talking inside, and entering I find not only Ben but my other boss, Jon.

"Er, should I come back later?"

Ben dismisses my suggestion, and waves me in, "No, we

both want to talk to you. Come in, sit down, Van."

As he calls me Van it hits me that I've come to prefer the derivation of my name that Sean uses. It's more feminine for a start. Which pulls me up. Why would I want to be considered feminine in a work environment? It shouldn't make any difference, and I've always preferred to be treated like one of the men.

Jon leans forward, "Van, we've got good news."

As he continues to explain, my jaw drops as I hear the welcome, but also disturbing news that Danielle won't ever be able to tell any tales about me. Reassured of my safety, I probably forget to ask the questions I should, but accept their explanation that in the confusion the culprit couldn't be identified.

When they've told me that revelation and allowed me a moment to absorb it, Ben's fingers begin to drum on a sheaf of white paper in front of him, drawing my eyes to him, and when I see his expression my heart sinks. Then he confirms I'm right to have my suspicions, "I asked Sean for a report on your suitability for working as one of our operatives, Van. As I'm sure you'll have expected. It's standard procedure when sending someone out for the first time."

"I cocked up." I decide to come clean.

Looking at me sharply, Ben refutes my self-accusation, "You saved yourself, and the baby. You shot five men. You got yourself out of there. I don't define that as a complete cock-up."

Am I going to get away with it?

"But," as Ben resumes I see he hasn't finished yet, "You did make a number of errors that make us," he gestures between Jon and himself, "Concerned about your suitability to work as a Close Protection Officer."

Here it comes, "You're taking me off CPO work." I decide I'd rather say it myself.

Jon's shaking his head, "No, we're leaving that decision completely to you."

What? Screwing up my eyes, I'm puzzled. What could they mean? They either thought I could do the job or I couldn't. "You're giving me another chance?"

"No." Ben draws my attention back to him, "We're giving you twenty-four hours to come back and tell us your decision as to what you want to do."

As my eyes flit from one to the other, not quite certain what's going on, Jon stands and kicks away his chair and leans against the desk, his back toward his partner. He scrutinises me, and I start to wilt under his examination. When he sees me growing uncomfortable, he takes pity on me, "You've applied for membership at Club Tiacapan," he starts.

My hand covers my face as I smother my gasp. Of all the things I'd thought he might say, I didn't expect him to refer to that.

"You are aware that I co-own the club, along with Sheikh Jasim Kassis and Jason Deville?"

I nod. A discussion about a BDSM club with my two bosses is sending the blood rushing to my cheeks, and I shift in my seat, feeling decidedly awkward.

Jon gives me another intense look, "You'll also be aware that Ben and some your colleagues are also members of the club."

My sense of insecurity makes me spit out, "Are you saying I can't join?"

"Not at all," he snorts as though I've said something amusing, "I just want to make sure you know what you are getting into."

"It's a BDSM club," I shrug, remembering the one I went to with Sean, "I know what to expect."

"Hmm," he looks thoughtful, "I wonder if you've properly thought this through. I'm aware from Sean that you've been to a similar place, though I use the word similar lightly, and may have picked up some things. But Ben and I both play at Tiacapan, and the likelihood is that we'll be there at the same time as you. And if your Dom wants to get you naked—and he'd be a pretty piss-poor Dom if he allowed you to be fully clothed at all times—the chances are that myself, Ben and the rest of your colleagues will see you too. We can't make an exception for you."

I hadn't thought about that part. Taken aback I think fast, "Sean will be my Dom." Well at least, I'm hoping he'll still want to honour the contract we'd drawn up. I don't miss the look that passes between Jon and Ben or the nods they exchange; it looks like I've fallen into some sort of trap.

Then Jon looks back at me sternly, "Only for a month, or that's what it says on your contract."

"You've seen that?"

"I do own the club." *Shit, he must have seen my limits list too. This conversation is way past embarrassing!*

"Sean and I might agree to extend the contract."

"Hmm, but what happens afterwards?" Jon puts a finger to his chin, "As the contract states you and Sean will be keeping your relationship entirely sexual and restricted to the club, it shouldn't make any difference to your working relationship. When your month is up you might be looking for another Dom. Of course, I'm exclusive with Mia, but it's possible Ben might offer to top you, or Ryan or Seth. You've obviously thought about this and compartmentalise your play in that…"

"No!" The denial is drawn out of me in horror at the thought of being with anyone but Sean, even another experienced Dom. It's him I want, and nobody else.

"No?" Ben repeats me, his eyebrows raised.

I look from one to the other in shock, "I only want to play with Sean." Jon nods and one side of his mouth turns up in a small satisfied smile, "I thought it was that way."

I glance down at my hands, knowing I've betrayed myself.

"Van, you do remember I asked you to give me your answer in twenty-four hours, don't you?"

Without looking up, I nod.

"If I was your Dom, I would want to take you to task for the trouble and worry you've caused him."

Glancing up sharply I defend myself, "I didn't ask to be abducted, and I killed our kidnappers and saved Mollie."

"Oh, Vanessa," Jon sighs, "Your catalogue of failures started long before that, didn't they?"

My cheeks grow warm as I realise he's right, and once again I can't meet their eyes.

"As your Dom, Vanessa, I would think your behaviour

warranted a punishment, so you didn't repeat your mistakes in future," Jon pronounces, his voice stern.

Punishment?

"I think we can safely leave the rest to Sean, Jon. But we'll see you at the club tonight. We'll *all* see you at the club."

"And we'll see you here with your answer tomorrow. Go home for the rest of the day, Van. Sean's waiting for you outside."

Dismissed, I automatically rise to my feet and am halfway to the door before my feet stop. *They'll ALL see me in the club tonight? Sean's waiting for me outside?* What the hell is going on? I want to turn to ask them, but I'm not quite sure what to ask, and part of me doesn't want to extend such a disturbing conversation. Instead, I start moving again, leaving the office in a state of bemusement. Part of me is pleased to find Sean's not there, leaning against the wall waiting for me. Huh, they were wrong about that.

But fragments of the strange and totally unexpected discussion with my bosses keep circling my mind. I want to high five myself that they're leaving the decision to me about continuing to work in the field, but why? That's not usual, either I can do the job in their opinion, or I can't. Surely that's up to them, and not me? *But then, it's not exactly normal to have a dialog about BDSM with your bosses, is it?*

As I shake my head to clear it, Sean comes around the corner. The first thing I notice is that he's limping, and the second is despite that, he seems to have a more settled air about him. *He's not trying to hide it anymore.* As he draws closer, he reaches out his hand, and I immediately reciprocate his action and take it. As warm, strong fingers wrap around mine, he stares down at me.

"You're mine, Nessa." His voice is low, authoritative, as though he will brook no contradiction. His tone makes my stomach clench, and an inappropriate tingling for the office environment shoots through me. This is the Dom in front of me, the man who through his control can bring me so much pleasure. This isn't the man I walked out on. The man I can refuse, the Dom I must obey.

"Come." It's another command, and I'm can't do anything but go with him.

CHAPTER 38

Sean

Leaving the meeting with Ben and Jon, I'd felt like a weight had been lifted off my shoulders. I no longer have to pretend anymore, to myself or anyone else. My leg's hurting like a bitch, my attempts to hide my discomfort putting extra pressure on the damaged muscles, and the ability to favour it without having to keep my incapacity concealed gives some semblance of relief. That I've lost the job I've loved for so long isn't as devastating as I'd expected, in fact, it feels liberating, no longer having to put myself in danger and my life on the line for someone I don't know. Now I can concentrate on protecting those I love.

We'd discussed a lot of things during that meeting. Pulling Nessa from the role she'd trained for so long would devastate her, helping her come to her conclusions would be a different matter. As I pass the time hanging around in the open plan office, I frown. What I now need to organise for tonight won't hold much pleasure for either of us, at first, but should help her come to the right decision. And that's the other thing Ben and Jon helped me with, if I'm going to be her Dom, I need to act like one. The only out she'll have with me from now on is if she uses her safeword.

A text comes through. Ben's letting me know she's out of the meeting. Hmm. I pause, getting my head in the right mindset for what's to come so that I can be the man, *the Dom*, she needs me to be.

She's walking down the corridor looking bemused, and not a little shocked. I hide the smile that wants to appear knowing she wouldn't have expected her conversation with the two partners of Grade A to take the turn I know they'd intended it to. Taking advantage of her confusion, I simply take her hand in mine. "Come."

She's quiet in the car, looking out of the window as though to avoid looking at me, and I let her have her space for now. Deep discussions don't go well when I'm trying to negotiate the London traffic, and particularly the hazards of white van drivers. Christ! Do they all go to the same driving school to learn the bad habits the rest of us try to avoid? I swear under my breath as one pulls out straight in front of me without indicating.

We arrive at the flat and I lead her inside. I see her looking around at my very masculine apartment, and I give her a rueful grin. "Not very child oriented, I know," I tell her, "Reckon we should start looking for a more family-oriented home. Somewhere with a garden."

Ignoring the preposition I'd used, she adds her suggestion, "With good schools close by." That's Nessa, ever practical.

"Fuck me!" I laugh, "I never thought I'd be thinking about things like that."

"You didn't, I did," she corrects me.

Again, I laugh, and leaning over, I can't resist placing

my lips over hers and kissing her, "That's why we make a good team."

She shifts awkwardly, sliding away from my touch. When she looks up at me, her eyes are glistening. With hope? Despair? It's difficult to tell. Her conversation with the two other Doms already today has probably already been a lot for her to handle, and now I'm only going to add to it. Eventually, she asks the question, "What team are you talking about, Sean?"

Running my fingers through my hair, I have to make some things clear. "Partners, as in partners for life." I pinch the bridge of my nose, then look straight at her, "I won't be working in the field again."

She takes a step back in amazement. "What?" Now she's reaching out her hand, her fingers hovering in the air inches from my arm, "Sean?"

I smile, my eyes crinkling, "I'm fine with it, Nessa. Truly." I tilt my head back, my neck muscles feeling loser than they have for some time, and know I need to give her more. "My leg will never be strong enough. I've been kidding myself that it would heal completely, but it won't."

Her brow furrows, "But, I thought you were getting there. I thought it was only a matter of time?"

With my fingers, I smooth away the lines on her forehead, "Sometimes you have to admit things just are. I'm mobile enough, but I'll always have a weakness there. Getting shot and having your bone shattered can do that to you. I should be thankful I've still got a leg. And don't worry, I'm not being put out to pasture." Now I tilt her head up to face me, "It means I'll be based here. We can be together. You, me and Mollie. A proper family, a stable home life."

She tries to step away again, but I hold her in place.

"Sean, I... You... Us... There is no us. You're not..."

"Don't tell me what I'm not. Let me tell you what I am. Haven't I made everything plain enough? I told you, Nessa, I'm never letting you out of my sight again. You are *mine*, my partner and my sub. I can live with only topping you in the dungeon, but I'll be the only man in your life. In every part of your life." Closing the distance between us I take her hands in mine, holding them down by her sides. "You're mine, Nessa. Even if you don't understand that yet."

"Sean, I..."

"Shush. I know you think the change in me is a reaction to what happened in Amahad. I assure you it's not, I just needed that spur to make me understand what you mean to me. Being away together let me see the real you, the woman you are out of the office. You had me from that moment you walked into the dungeon dressed as a Domme, I just wasn't admitting it then. You've ruined me for all other women. I don't want a faceless sub. I want you." For a second doubt sweeps through me, how can I convince her everything I told her in Amahad was true? And even if I can, is she on the same page? "If you don't want this, tell me now."

She swallows a couple of times, I can see her throat work, and I'm holding my breath wondering what words are going to come out. Then her hand comes up and softly cups my face. She looks up at me, then away, and then back again. When she, at last, begins to speak it's as if she's baring her very soul.

"From the moment you first stepped into Grade A I wanted you, Sean. Oh, it was just a crush at first, you were unattainable—maybe that was the attraction?— and the most handsome man I'd ever seen. Then you intrigued me when I worked on Mia's case and learned there was another world, another lifestyle that I knew nothing about. You didn't know how much I admired you from afar. When Mollie came to you, I tried to stop feeling the way I did, but watching you with her, seeing that other side of you... You sucked me in and there was no escape. When I let you down..." there's a hitch in her voice, "When Mollie and I were taken when I thought I might never see you again.... Then when you said that in Amahad, I couldn't believe you. It seemed too much; all my dreams come true at once. But if this is real?" She takes a deep breath, and her green eyes delve into mine, "If you're offering me everything, then I want this. I want you."

Leaning down, I rest my forehead against hers, "It's real," I assure her, "You won't regret it, Nessa. I'll make sure you don't regret it every day of our lives together. I love you, Nessa."

"I love you too, oh Sean. God how much I love you."

As she says the words I wanted so much to hear, I rest my forehead down so it touches here, and take a moment to savour the pleasure. But I don't wait long, I can't. I need her like I need air to breathe.

Now we've said the words, I want to show her. Keeping my eyes trained on hers I release one of her hands. A second later I smile as there's a snick and she looks down to see I've fastened both her wrists together in fur lined cuffs. Placing a finger between the material and her wrist and testing it, I question, "Not too tight?"

She shakes her head. Her pulse speeds up, and I inhale the scent of her arousal. A state of calm comes over me as my inner Dom takes over.

"We'll have to get babysitters to play at Club Tiacapan now, but there's plenty we can improvise here I assure you."

A tremor runs through her as she tries to anticipate what I'm going to do.

Standing back, I look her up and down and grin wickedly. "I would tell you to strip, but…" I gesture toward her bound hands and give a wicked laugh. "I think I need to help you." Crouching I remove her sandals, then undo her jeans and pull them down, taking her underwear along with them. Standing once again, I pull a knife from my pocket and flick it open, the snap sounding overly loud. Her eyes widen as she wonders what I'm going to do. After a moment's pause, I ask, "You particularly fond of this shirt?"

She glances down at what I recognise as a fairly standard plain white tee, and shakes her head, then breathes in sharply as I prove how sharp my blade is, going through the material as if through butter. Another evil grin and the straps of her bra are gone, and her breasts fall free.

"The straps actually come off. It's a three-way bra."

I hadn't stopped to ask or notice and what the fuck is that anyway? "I'll buy you another. Hell, I'll buy you a dozen.

The way you shivered as the cold steel touched you." I ease myself in my jeans to show the effect she has on me.

And I can see I have no lesser effect on her. The shudder that went through her when the knife had cut through her clothes very visible. I'd bet good money that if I touched her there, I'd feel moisture between her legs.

Closing my fingers around her face, I gently pull her to me until our mouths touch. At first, the touch is soft, and then more insistent as my tongue probes until she lets me inside, and soon the kiss becomes uncontrolled, a physical reaffirmation of what we've admitted we mean to each other. I feel myself swelling almost painfully at the contrast of her soft naked body pulled hard against my fully clothed frame.

When we pull apart it's to get air into our heaving lungs, and I stare at her intently, making her a promise that I hope to repeat every day for the rest of our lives, "Now I'm going to make love to you as your man."

Picking her up in my arms I carry her through to my bedroom and almost reverently lay her on my bed. Then, with quick, economical movements I divest myself of my clothes and once naked, I come down over her, straddling her and taking her cuffed hands in one of my own.

She's looking down as though to feast her eyes on my erection, but there'll be time for that later.

"Nessa," I chide, "I want your eyes for this." To keep her captive, I reach to the headboard and pull down a chain and hook her cuffs to it. I hadn't been kidding that there are things to play with in my flat.

Her attention caught, her green orbs shine into mine.

"I meant what I said in Amahad. Every fucking word of it." My voice catches as I try to get her to believe what I'm saying, "We're a family already, but I want a baby with you, Nessa. I want to be with you every step of the way." She stills, so I clarify further, "When you're ready, I want to take you bare."

"Sean, I'm not on the pill…"

"I'm happy to use a condom until the time's right. And it doesn't matter if it's today, tomorrow or next year. But one day, Nessa, I want my baby growing here." I put my hand on her stomach and glancing down know I'd be the proudest man in the world to see my child making her swell.

"I want you to have my baby, Nessa." I can't put it plainer than that.

To give her time to come to terms with my demand, I reach over to the bedside cabinet and extract a condom, leaving it handy to use later. Checking with her, she gives me a little nod, showing she appreciates that it will be her decision. But it's important that she understands everything I want to offer her. Before tonight. Before it could all go so horribly wrong. It's my job to make sure it doesn't.

But now, this is our time. I huff a breath over her chest, just the touch of warm moist air causes her nipples to harden, taunting me so I can't resist having a taste. My tongue swirls and a sharp nip of my teeth encourages them to peak even more. Little gasps and pants are coming from her mouth; my steel-hard cock pushes against her and pre-cum leaks out. *Fuck, this woman turns me on like no one ever before.*

Desperate to taste her I move down her body, my tongue tracing her skin, my eyes feasting on the flush my touch brings forth in its wake. My fingers mapping out her freckles as I go, knowing I've got a lifetime to memorise each and every one. Hearing a little rattle of the handcuffs as she pulls against them, and a softly urged plea shows how I'm taunting her, ramping up her arousal which I'm sure will at least be matching mine.

Taking my time, I inch down toward my goal. Fuck, she's dripping for me, so wet my fingers slide easily inside her. Now impatient and unable to wait a moment more I lower my head, lapping and savouring her particular essence. It's been too long since I was able to indulge. She babbles something incomprehensible as I groan against her slit and the sound goes straight to my cock. My senses are full of her, my eyes feasting on those short curly red pubes, her scent pervading the air I'm breathing in, the softness of her skin under my hands. There's never been anyone like her, and I know it won't be difficult to keep my promise, I won't need to sample another woman, ever again.

My body craves to join us in the only way a man and woman can. Replacing my fingers inside her I curl them round, a gentle assault inside her as my lips close around her throbbing clit. I hum softly, the vibration causing her muscles to go rigid. She's shaking and trembling, and so very close. I could pull away and tease her; I could make this last. But I don't want to. My cock is pulsing and twitching; my balls are aching with need. I close my teeth, gently nipping, then suck and swirl my tongue around applying gentle pressure.

"Oh God, God, Sean!"

She's so close. With my free hand, I try to hold her still. She's thrashing on the bed, the violent jingling of the chain attached to the headboard telling me she's desperately chasing her release.

"Oh. Oh. OH!"

With a scream, she comes, her body bucking up off the bed. I keep on the pressure, not letting her come down.

"Sean. SEAN!"

As she screams my name and comes a second time, her body jerking and shuddering as little after tremors go through her I gentle my touch, pulling away before she becomes too sensitive.

Now it's my turn. Quickly putting on the condom I ease myself home. She's so wet I fill her completely in one thrust. She feels so good as her muscles clamp down around me, and I can't hold back. I nearly lost her; I'm never going to lose her again. The thought of how close I'd come to never having the opportunity to be inside her again incites me, and I can't hold back. Watching her face, I hammer into her. She's with me all the way, little sounds of encouragement escaping her lips. Her body is responding to mine as though it's been made for me. A fleeting kiss to her lips, then I place my mouth on those luscious breasts, teasing her erect nipples all over again. She's rising to meet me as I continue to drive into her setting a punishing pace but she's more than accepting of my furious onslaught.

And then she's there again, her pussy fastening down onto my cock. My balls begin to swell, an almost unbearable pressure and the tingling in my spine starts a reaction that at this point I'm unable to stop. With one final lunge, I feel sperm propelled through my length and reaching its sweet destination. With a few concluding stabs, I empty myself completely.

Utterly drained I collapse over her, taking my weight on my arms either side of her head. Her eyes are dazed, her pupils dilated. We pant in unison as our tortured lungs try to take in a breath.

As her hair starts to tickle my nostrils I lift my head with a grin, "Nessa, you were made for me. You know that?" Reaching up, I release her from the handcuffs and massage her wrists and arms.

Her lips turn up in a lazy smile, "Seems that way," she purrs, "And you were made for me."

Lowering my lips I take hers in a gentle kiss, and as she responds can feel the truth of the words we'd spoken previously, the physical representation of the love that's between us. After allowing myself to enjoy our closeness, I eventually push away and roll over onto my back.

Pulling herself up, she leans over me, her hand tracing my skin. I let her explore, relishing the light touch on my shoulder, my chest. Her touch is calming. Opening my eyes they lock on hers. She's frowning slightly.

"What's up?"

"Ben and Jon left the decision to me, Sean. About working as a CPO or not."

"I know."

"Oh?" Her brow creases into that delightful V again, and she scrunches up her nose, "They discussed it with you?" Then her face drops, "I suppose they were talking about that report you put in about me."

"It was my job, Nessa. I'd have had to have done the same for anyone new that I was partnered with."

"I know that, but mightn't you have been biased as you had feelings for me?" When I don't answer, she continues, "What you said, about us being a family, having a baby. You don't want me to go on active duty, do you?"

No, I don't, but she's got to come to the right decision for the right reasons. Otherwise, she might end up resenting me. Resenting us. "It's up to you, Nessa. Whatever you decide it's got to be your choice."

Lying on her back, she throws an arm up over her face, "I don't know what to do, Sean."

I grasp her hand, "We're going to help you decide."

CHAPTER 39

Vanessa

They're going to help me decide? I couldn't understand what he meant, but Sean wouldn't enlighten me further, and I didn't feel any easier when he told me he was taking me to Club Tiacapan tonight, reminding me that Ben and Jon had said they'd be seeing me there. There's something they've got planned, and I've no bloody idea what it could be. But beneath my concern there's an underlying current of excitement, Sean's my Dom, and he'll be taking me to the most prestigious BDSM club in London. Just the thought of being in his safe, but very sexy hands is enough to keep me in a smouldering state of arousal despite the three orgasms he'd just given me.

There's a delivery late afternoon, and Sean hands me a package with a smirk on his adorable face. Taking it with some suspicion, I open it carefully to find somehow he's had fetwear delivered. It's a two-piece set in white satin and lace, a cropped top which will only just contain my breasts and a very, very short skirt. As I shake it out trying to see if it's bigger than I first thought, a third item falls out. A tiny and very inadequate thong. Holding the skirt up to me, I can see I won't be leaving much at all to the imagination.

"Sean, if I wear this, everyone will be able to see

everything. And I don't *shave*." I punctuate my words with a nervous shake of my head.

The bastard laughs, "You're as beautiful there as everywhere, and as your Dom, I want to show my sub off.

"Shit, Sean. I can't go anywhere like this."

His fingertips touch my chin, "Try, for me. Once you're in the club I don't think you'll feel uncomfortable; you'll be wearing more than some people. Remember Paris?"

I do, and I remember how embarrassed I'd felt. "Sean, I..."

"For me, sweetheart? Wear it for me?"

"This isn't exactly breaking me in gently, Sean."

His lips curl up, "Just try. If you want to come home, if it's too much for you. We can leave at any time."

Biting my lip, I think, "I don't want to disappoint you."

"I've no expectations of you, of our relationship. We're feeling our way here. I don't have our life mapped out to a pre-set plan. If you don't like the club, there's plenty we can do here."

"What about Mollie?" I'm grasping at straws.

"Don't prevaricate; Mum's happy to keep her until tomorrow. We need this time, Nessa, as a couple. We can start being a family tomorrow."

No argument can deter him, so a few hours later, dressed in a totally inadequate outfit covered up by a long coat I walk into the place I've been intrigued by since I first heard of its existence. Nothing could have prepared me for it, certainly not the club in Paris. Oh, as soon as I walked in I saw the similarities, the nakedness, the way people were dressed. But here scene areas are set up around the sides of the massive room instead of equipment littered over the floor. It smells of sex and arousal , but everywhere is gleaming and clean. And, unlike Paris, there's no full-on intercourse conducted in clear view.

Leaving my coat in the opulent locker room that's kitted out in the way that reminds me of the normal sky-high membership fees that I would have had to have coughed up had I not been employed by the owners, I go out to the anteroom to see Sean dressed as I've never seen him before. His long legs clothed in tight form fitting leather which hugs his delicious, tight backside. He's got a leather waistcoat hanging open revealing his bare chest underneath, and he's standing tall and upright. He looks every inch a Dom.

Making my way toward him, I see a couple of women walk through the door, and I swear their mouths are watering from the once over they're giving him. Quickening my pace, I take the last couple of steps and stand in front of him, my head slightly bowed, my eyes lowered to the ground sending a message that this man is all mine.

Placing his fingers under my chin, he raises my head, and smiles into eyes, "God, I love you, Nessa." As he takes in my appearance, he smooths his hands down my bare arms, his touch giving me much needed support and encouragement, "You're so brave." Taking my lips in a brief punishing kiss, when he pulls away he nods, "I've reserved a private room. Come."

Tension leaves me on a wave at my relief I won't be on public display. Excited now, wondering what he's got planned and how he's going to initiate me into his world, I take the hand he offers me and follow him through the grand open play area.

My eyes flick in all directions as I try to take in the sights in front of me. There's a bar along one side of the room, and my gaze lands on a couple of familiar faces. It's Jon and Mia. As they see me, I feel brave enough to give a little wave and get one in return from my boss's wife. As I watch Jon lovingly kisses her, and then stands and nods our way.

A little tug on my hand gets me moving again. With wide open eyes, I pass a couple of scene areas, currently unused but being set up for heaven knows what activities. Sounds fill the air creating a background of thumping music punctuated with laughter, screams, moans and sighs. Eventually, we reach a corridor guarded by a man wearing an orange vest, the letters DM on his chest.

Sean's greets him with a one-armed man hug and a chin jerk. "All setup?"

"Room One. As you requested."

"Thanks, mate."

Set up for what?

It's the first door along. Sean opens it, and with his hand on the small of my back, encourages me inside.

The room's larger than I expected. Red velvet trimmed tapestries cover the walls, each depicting various scenes of dominance and submission. My eyes are drawn to one, where a Dom stands over his naked and kneeling sub, his hand in her hair; the pose so loving it chokes me up. Turning around, another comes into view. This is showing a male sub on a St Andrews cross being caressed by his Domme. Everything in this room plays to the senses.

Muted music is playing, and scented candles fill the air with a background of musk. The bed I expected to find is pushed back against the wall, a four-poster affair with strange looking rings attached to the supports, and more red velvet draping it. Black satin sheets are invitingly folded back. There's a couch against one wall, a gold and red chaise longue, and along the other, looking strangely out of place, five chairs and a carved wooden chest. But taking pride of place in the centre of the room is something I've avoided looking at until now. It's an odd contraption. The top part is made of padded leather and shaped as though to support a torso and pointing down, front to back. The legs and supports form a V shape with the point toward the rear and protruding from the front, two smaller pads sticking out at an angle.

My eyes widen as I get a mental image of a body lying prone on the top, knees resting on the legs of the V. A person lying on that would be at the mercy of their Dom. A shiver goes through me as I realise it must have been set up for me.

Sean's giving me time to process, to take in my surroundings. Not once has he taken his hand away from my back, the warmth of his touch imbibing me with his strength. He must have felt me tense, as he answers my unspoken question.

"A spanking bench."

"You're going to spank me?" God, I wish this thong wasn't so small. Remembering how I'd reacted when he'd spanked me before is making me so wet the tiny scrap of material isn't going to hold it in.

"Come over here, Nessa." His voice, so serious, makes me glance up quickly, but I follow him to the chaise longue. "Sit." When I've obeyed him, he seats himself, angling his body slightly, so he's facing me. He takes both my hands in his.

"We need to have a discussion." His intense expression and his words worry me. "Nothing will happen here tonight without your agreement and consent. You understand that, don't you?"

I nod, understanding that's what the club's all about. "I've got safewords."

His chin jerks up and down, "Good. And you can use them at any time." Drawing back his shoulders, he pulls himself straight, "I need this, Nessa. "I've never been so scared in my life as when you disappeared. I never want you to put yourself in such a dangerous situation again."

"Are we having a discussion about my job?" My brow creases.

"We're talking about your recklessness."

I don't see I did anything particularly wrong. "There wasn't anything else I could do. I couldn't let them take the baby, your baby." I know I'm whining, but I don't want to do this here, or now.

"You shouldn't have been out in the field. You weren't prepared."

He's starting to annoy me, "I thought, in the end, I'd handled myself pretty well when it mattered. I tried, Sean." I tried my best. It was my first time working outside the office after all. Surely, he should allow me some leeway for that.

"Sweetheart, you made mistake after mistake. But I'm not going to catalogue them now. Time for that when the others get here."

"Others?" I query in a shrill voice, my whole body tensing.

He ignores my question and continues, "I'm your Dom, yet you caused me to worry. You're still causing me worry as you're continuing to deny what's right in front of your eyes. I want to make you understand that your safety is of paramount importance to me. I can't have you putting yourself at risk, time after time, or disregard the effect that would have on me. I love you."

Those last three words cause my face to soften, "Sean, I'm sorry for worrying you. But I didn't mean to."

He nods, but there's more to come, "Nessa, tonight may be uncomfortable for you, too much for you. If so, you've got a safeword. But this has been designed to make you comprehend both your weaknesses and your strengths, and what you mean to me. To everyone."

"Everyone?"

That plurality again. What the fuck is going on? Just as I'm about to ask him to explain, there's a knock at the door, and it opens. My mouth drops open as it looks like the whole of Grade A is marching in. Ben, Jon, Ryan, Nat and Hunter step inside. All dressed as Doms and all with identical grave expressions on their faces.

Shit! I'm in trouble here. Rapidly turning back to Sean, I begin to ask him, my voice shaking, "Sean?"

CHAPTER 40

Vanessa

H i guys," Sean warmly greets his colleagues and mine. "Thanks for coming." His tone is serious, though his eyes glow as he turns his attention back to me, "Nessa, we've exchanged our declarations of love for each other." He pauses for a moment, reaching out his hand and lovingly smoothing it down my cheek. "I've invited our friends here to witness our commitment to each other." His hand cups my chin, turning up my face so we look into each other's eyes. "Nessa, tonight I'd like you to publicly accept me as your Dom. Your sole Master. Not for a period of a contract, but forever. To make a lifetime commitment to each other." Again, he breaks off, studying my face before continuing, "Do you understand what I'm asking you?"

My unease of the last few minutes drifts away. Despite being so new to the lifestyle, I know this is something big. A shiver of pleasure runs down my spine at the thought this man intends to claim me. Slowly I nod.

"Say the words, Nessa." A gentle reminder of the need for clear communication.

"Yes." As he waits, I remember what he's expecting. "Sir," I add in a hesitant voice. While I'm proud he's saying the words in front of our friends and colleagues, their presence in some way unnerves me. I swallow a couple of times.

"Master," he corrects me, his voice commanding, but also soothing. "From here on in, you call me Master. Now, kneel." As he gives his instruction, his voice is controlled, but has slight tremor in it, letting me know how earnestly he is taking this, and that he's not unaffected by the situation.

As gracefully as I can, not really knowing the right way to do this, I kneel before him, and he places his hand on the top of my head. Suddenly something appears in his other hand, a flash of silver.

"Nessa, I have invited my fellow Doms here to witness us making these vows to each other. As I commit to you, I wish you to give yourself over into my care. To allow me to love you and to guide you in the lifestyle. It is my utmost wish that you wear my collar as a sign that you accept me as your Dominant. And by wearing it, agree to be my submissive?"

My voice catches as I try to get out the words, not completely sure what I'm supposed to say to something that sounds as binding as any wedding vows that I have ever heard. Swallowing again, moistening my mouth sufficiently to get out something that sounds an appropriate response, "Yes, Master. I'll wear your collar with pride, and as a sign you are my Dom, and I'm your submissive." My heart is nearly bursting out of my chest at the idea of the relationship we're cementing here.

For a second he holds something within sight of my eyes, a gorgeous white gold chain which flashes in the light. Something I could wear every day without drawing attention to what it means to people who wouldn't understand. After a brief glimpse, his hands move and I feel cold metal placed around my throat and hear a snick as a clasp is fastened. It a loose, not uncomfortable fit, and I can't resist fingering it, a glowing feeling as I know this is as significant, if not more so, than a wedding ring on my finger.

He traces it, as though admiring the sight of his mark of ownership around my neck, and then instructs, "Rise, my beautiful sub." Then he holds out his hand.

As I interlock my fingers with his and get to my feet, clapping begins. Ryan and Nat holler and hoot, and then our little audience steps forward to congratulate us.

Sean allows the aftermath of our ceremony to continue for a short while, and then he puts up his hand, and at his signal, quiet descends. He puts his finger under my chin and raises my face, so once again, I'm forced to look into his. "Nessa, my darling sub. Before we can proceed with our life together, there is one thing that I need to ask you to do for me." He brushes his hair back over his head, and little creases appear on his forehead as though he's in pain. It makes me pull back a little, and his hand drops away from my face.

"Sean," I start, and then cast a worried look around at the other men standing in a semi-circle around us, but find no comfort there. They're all wearing expressions as serious as his. "Sean, what exactly do you want me to do?"

His eyes stare into mine, "Do you trust me?"

My shoulders rise to my ears before I lower them again,

then give a little dip of my head. I'm really not sure what all this means, but one thing I'm certain of, Sean would never hurt me, "I trust you." My voice comes out as a whisper.

"Do you trust I have your best interest at heart?"

"Yes," I reply, even breathier.

He takes my hand and gives a reassuring squeeze, "Remember the punishment clause in the contract?"

And here it comes. The thing he alluded to earlier today. I swallow a couple of times and manage to get out a response that's just about audible, "Yes. But I haven't done anything wrong."

Sean sighs, and once more his hand cups my cheeky, "Darling, sweetheart. The problem lies in exactly that. That you don't understand what you did wrong. That you don't recognize your own worth." As I begin to protest, his fingers cover my mouth, "Allow us to show you what you mean to us. Keeping you safe is the most important thing to me, and helping you to understand your weaknesses and strengths is what we intend to do."

I don't want to disappoint him, but I feel on edge. "Sean, I," I look around the room. All five men are gazing at me earnestly. A shiver runs through me as I wonder exactly what they've got planned. "Sean, I don't think I can do this."

"You can, sweetheart, you can. And you have your safeword. You can stop this at any time."

Stop what? Despite his tactile comfort, I start to shake as my colleagues take the chairs that I'd noticed earlier. They look like they're going to watch. *But what?*

Again, he's gone serious, "Each of us has something we wish to say to you. To impress on you. We're asking you to submit, to each and every one of us. To understand the worry and concern you've caused to us, to understand how your actions put you, and others into danger. This is your comprehension of events, and the way the actions you took appear to us. You have agreed to be my sub, to enter the lifestyle. The lifestyle that allows us to communicate in different ways than those in the vanilla world."

"You're going to punish me." For what, I don't know. But that's his clear intention, why he mentioned that clause. I start to stand, wanting only to get out of here. This is too much. This is not how I thought tonight would go. Ben had mentioned punishment, and I hadn't taken it seriously, or if I did, I thought it would be just Sean, and that it would be a bit of a laugh. I open my mouth…

"Vanessa," unusually Ben gives me my full name as he interrupts, having seen my intention, and the way I start inching towards the door, "Don't safeword out immediately. Listen to what we have to say." He pauses, and nods at the men sitting in line, "We have expectations of our colleagues when we are working. It's essential, our lives depend on it. The most important of which is that no one lets their partner or colleagues down."

"You're saying I let everyone down?"

"Didn't you?"

I open my mouth to protest, but because it's Ben who's speaking, *my boss*, suddenly I'm not so sure. Yeah, I made mistakes, but we're all here, we're all alive. No one was injured. That's the main thing, isn't it? But if I'd done a good job, why would they all be here? *It's a kink club.*

Ben's watching me carefully, "As an employee of Grade A, normally I'd have explained your transgressions, reprimanded you, decided the consequences and put them in place. You would have agreed or disagreed with my ruling and would have been left satisfied or dissatisfied as a result. But you have been collared by your Dom, and have joined a BDSM club which affords us a different opportunity."

"And I'm a woman." I spit out.

"No," he refutes it adamantly, "You are a sub. If you'd been a man we would have done it the same way."

"You're a sub," Jon repeats, "And you wish to please, not disappoint your Dom."

I cast a look toward Sean, seeing he's looking worried as though he's unsure what I'm going to do. But the very last thing I want to do is to disappoint him. He cares for me, there's no doubt about that. I breathe in, "You really want me to do this, whatever this is?"

His hands come around my face, and his eyes stare down into mine, "I'd like you to try."

"I don't know what I'm agreeing to." It must be the fear of the unknown that's bringing tears to my eyes, either that or the realisation that these men, all wearing grave expressions, seem to feel I've disappointed them. These men who aren't just people I work with, they're men I like, respect and trust to have my back. Suddenly I know whatever they're asking of me, I'll do it, from just the desire to get back into their good books again.

Sean stands and positions me, so we're both sideways on

to our audience. "Remember you can safeword out. But what we want, what we, as Doms, need you to do, is to get onto the spanking bench and take one strike from each of us by the implement of our choice. Each of us will explain the way in which you let us down. You'll apologise, and we'll move on." He waits for my tentative nod. Seven spanks that doesn't sound so bad. "Saying we'll move on means this will be forgotten. Forgiven. Nothing about this night will ever be mentioned again. You can make your decision and give it to Ben and Jon tomorrow, and whatever you decide, we will all accept it. The decision remains yours, and you'll have our support in whatever way you wish to go."

I'm starting to understand what he's proposing. One spank from each man and they'll absolve me totally? That seems rather strange, totally different to anything I could have dreamed of, but fair. Again, I nod, this time a little more firmly. They are recognizing decisions about my future are mine, and mine alone. I can do this and the end result will be better than I could have hoped.

"What's your safeword?"

"Red or yellow." I read in the Club Tiacapan rules that they use the traffic light system, red for stop, or yellow to take it a bit slower.

"There'll be no slowing down, Nessa. Red is the only word you can say. To stop everything entirely."

"And then the decision reverts to us." Ben's voice makes me look at him. "Or rather to me. I will decide where you go from here. That's the alternative you can take."

A touch on my arm draws my attention back to Sean,

"Whatever you decide it doesn't affect our relationship, Nessa. I meant everything I said earlier today. But if you go ahead with this, it wipes the slate clean, and I'll never reproach you again for this infraction."

Understanding he means what he says, I bob my head again, an affirmation of my permission.

"We need the words, Nessa," he reminds me, "Will you submit to us?"

"Yes, okay." There's a quiver in my voice as I hope I know what I'm agreeing to.

"Right." Sean draws himself to his full height, and his hand drops away. His voice deepens, "We will begin." He takes a breath as he gets fully into Dom mode, the sound making me glance at him. *He doesn't really want to do this.* The reluctance in his expression makes me want to give him strength.

"I'm ready," I say firmly.

He nods, and a fleeting smile crosses his face, before disappearing once again. "Go to that chest over there and open it. There's a bag of rice on top, bring it here."

Rice? What the hell is that for? Are they expecting me to cook for them? But I do as he says, finding the item and handing it to him.

He shakes his head, "No, you hold it." He rolls his head back, and then his stern eyes find mine, and I'm surprised to see moisture in them. "You went out, unarmed in a foreign country. Not once, but twice Nessa. I know you're not used to carrying a weapon, but you had one assigned to you and you left it behind. In a country where you know I'd been shot and kidnapped, and where you also know we were expecting terrorists to appear at any time. You left yourself, and me, your partner, exposed. And," his voice falters, "You exposed yourself to danger. You could have been killed."

The words, the catch in his voice. The thought of how I had worried him. I can't dispute any of that. It's fact.

"Take a handful of rice and put it on the floor." Bemused I do as he says. "While you follow my instructions, I want you to think about how you put yourself in danger. Then you'll thank me, and apologise to me."

I eye the rice on the ground and don't understand what he wants me to do.

"Now, while we sort ourselves out, kneel. On the rice."

I shrug, not understanding why, but it seems simple enough. So rather inelegantly I do as he's told me. Ouch! Christ! Immediately I understand the point of this exercise. Hard bits of rice bite into my knees like slithers of glass, it's biting into me and I realise it's hurting me, like the worries I'd caused had wounded him.

As I quickly look up, I find Sean's watching me, and there's sympathy on his face, but when he speaks he uses that dark voice again, "Stay there, while we prepare ourselves. If you can't take it, you know what you have to say. But your safeword will stop everything." His voice shakes, he doesn't like seeing me in pain, though he knows this will make me think. If only that I'm never going to do anything that will deserve this again.

Gritting my teeth, I try to breathe through the pain, shifting myself slightly from one knee to the other and then immediately back again. Whoever thought this up was a sadist. *Yeah, they probably all are.* I can't help glaring at the men who are taking turns delving into the chest and pulling out various items. And then my glare drops from my face, and my eyes widen as I see what they're taking out. A crop, a cane. A paddle. Shit! I thought they'd be using their bare hands. This is going to be harder than I thought.

As the grains of rice bite into my skin, I pull back my shoulders. *You can take this. Don't show them you're weak.*

They're talking and showing each other the implements they've chosen, seeming to take no notice of me suffering on the floor. Except for Sean, who hasn't once taken his eyes off me, he's watching my every reaction, his breathing shallow as though to mimic mine.

My face is flushed, and I'm sweating. Surely they'll let me up soon? There's no clock, but time seems to slow down before eventually Sean comes over and stands in front of me. "You may stand."

Hastily I do so, brushing away annoying bits of rice that stubbornly stick to the indentations formed in my skin. When I'm grain free, I look at him. He's waiting for something.

"Thank me, and apologise," he prompts.

Oh, yes. Gritting my teeth, feeling like I'd rather hit him, I give him the words he's after. "Thank you, Sean. And I'm sorry I was so careless." Then I see the look of pride on his face, and I repeat it again, this time with more contrition, "I'm sorry. I was careless."

If I'd had my gun to hand, maybe I could have prevented the men taking Mollie, and I. But it was in my bag and across the other side of the room when I'd opened the door.

His arms come around me and his chin rests on the top of my head, "Good girl, but remember it's Master when we're here. And you'll address everyone else as Master and then their name." He nuzzles my hair, then stands back holding me at arms' length, "Ready to continue?"

Doubting anything can be worse than kneeling on rice while casting suspicious glances at the items my colleagues are holding, I nod, then remember he needs the words, "Yes, Sean… Master."

Gently he prods me until I move toward the bench. With a hand at my back, he pushes me forward until I'm lying on it, my knees on the supports, my head pushed down low and my butt in the air. He pushes up my skirt exposing my almost bare backside covered inadequately in that barely-there thong. My face reddens in embarrassment as I turn my head to one side.

"Master Ryan?"

Opening my eyes I see Ryan's holding a paddle; it looks like a table tennis bat from here.

"Van, when Nat and I came to the house you opened the door without checking who we were, and flung the door wide open so we could just walk inside. You didn't use the security system. It was turned off when we arrived. You and your partner could have been murdered in your beds. The system's there to keep you alive. Yet you never remembered to use it. We could have been anyone. You put both yourself and Sean at risk. And anyone else you could have been working with." Ryan's voice is full of emotion, he really means what he says.

"Try not to tense." Sean's soft voice makes me realise my body had gone taut. I relax my muscles and then, wham! Christ, that hurt!

"Nessa?" Again, Sean prompts, his tone commanding, but tinged with concern.

"Oh. I'm sorry. Thank you, Master Ryan, I should have made sure it was you before letting you in." I hadn't understood how much importance they set on it. I'd been expecting them to arrive, but now he's pointed it out, they could have been anyone.

And had been, when Mollie was taken. Could I have prevented that by being more cautious? *I should have left on the security and not opened the door until I'd been certain who the men were.*

Nat's got a flogger. I've heard good things about how sensual a flogging can be, so this time I don't need Sean's instructions to relax. Though I don't get a good view, it seems small and innocent, with thin strands of leather.

Nat clears his throat, his voice chokes with emotion, "Out in the desert, you'd put your gun in your waistband when you saw the helicopters arrive to rescue you. You relaxed and allowed Danielle to get behind you making it easy for her to take your weapon. I was the one who disarmed Danielle. I put myself at risk to rescue you. Not that I wouldn't do the same thing again, but I wouldn't have needed to had you remained in control of the situation. Fuck, Van, I put myself in danger often enough without having to do so in situations where it could have been avoided. I might not have been able to save you, you could have been killed. If you'd been a better operative, you'd have kept your eye on the ball and your gun in your hand."

Of course, it had all come out in the debriefing, I'd had to answer how Danielle had managed to turn the tables on me. And I'd been wrong about the flogger too, each strand of leather bites where it hits, the pain and humiliation making tears leak from my eyes.

"Thank you, Master Nat. I'm sorry you were put in danger." A sob escapes, as I recognise he'd had to put his life on the line for me. *And he's right, I could so easily have been killed and others injured as well.*

"Van, you're taking this well. Are you okay to continue?" Jon asks, his tone heavy with concern as he steps toward me carrying a cane.

"Yes," I confirm on another sob.

"I don't think you know what you mean to us, Van, to all of us. When you were taken, and I had to direct operations from London, it was killing me not to know whether you were alive or dead. You're one of our best employees, Van, you've been with us a long time. With your disregard for your safety, you caused us all hurt and worry."

He doesn't make me wait long before I feel the cane come down across me just when my thighs join my bum, smarting and stinging as it lands, a localised pain rather than the paddle which covered a larger area.

Right now, I'm not sure what is worse, the physical hurt from the blows or the mental one, knowing how much these men care about me and how much I'd let them down. "Thank you, Master Jon," I remember to say, "And I'm sorry for worrying you."

A movement catches out of the corner of my eye, wiping my tears away I see Ben. He's not carrying anything, but his hands are going to his belt. Very, very slowly he unbuckles it and slides it through the belt loops. He doubles it and cracks it in the air, the sound making me jump. I swallow, *oh God, that's going to hurt!*

"Vanessa, I've got nothing to add to what Jon has said, but let me tell you I was just as concerned as him. You scared the shit out of both of us."

He flicks the belt. It lands across both cheeks, and a yip escapes from my mouth. But still, I remember. "Thank you, Master Ben. And I'm so so sorry." Tears are flowing freely now, but not from the pain, from the anguish I caused to these men.

Apart from Sean, there's only one person left, Hunter. Vaguely I wonder why he was left to last. As he comes toward me, like Ben he's not holding anything in his hands. He must see the question in my eyes, as he huffs a laugh, "I'm going to use the tools God gave me, pet." Having seen the size of his instruments of choice and his muscular arms, I doubt it will be any the less painful.

"Van, Nessa," he corrects himself, borrowing Sean's pet name for me. "My beef with you isn't that you let me down any more or differently than the others, but that you're letting yourself down. You're the best fucking analyst I know. By denying your strengths, trying to do something you're not geared up to do, well that's preventing me getting the support I need when I'm out doing my job. That you can't see the gift you've been given and that you're intent on being something you're not, that's what makes me angry."

The palm of his hand slaps down hard, and I jump. My breath hitches as I try to get out the words through my sobs, "Thank you, Master Hunter. And I'm very sorry."

As if a flood has been released tears start falling down my face, and now I'm crying in earnest. Sean gathers me up into his arms and carries me over to the bed. I hear the door opening and then closing. The others have left.

CHAPTER 41

Sean

I hold her close, hugging her to me, telling her over and over again how beautifully she submitted to us, how brave she is and how strong. I know it doesn't matter much the actual words I'm using, it's the sound of my voice she needs to hear, to know she has the approval of her Dom. I love her so much, more than I ever imagined I'd love any woman.

The ordeal she's just been through hurting me almost as much as it did her. When Jon and Ben first suggested it, I railed against the idea, never having enacted the punishment clause before, except when a sub acted out on purpose, and the ensuing flogging or spanking had just been for fun. I haven't cared enough to punish a sub. But care for Nessa I do, and keeping her safe is my role as her Dom. There's no doubt she had to come the right decision herself, imposing my view on her would not be a good start to our life together.

I care. So fucking much. My recent past might have shaped me, but that I've changed out of all recognition is mostly down to the woman in my arms. Her love and support consolidating everything that I've become until at last, I know who and what I am. A look in the mirror no longer shows me a man who is lost, a man who lives only in the moment, looking only for play with no responsibilities.

Instead, my reflection is that of a Dom, and a father. A man who wants only to care for the woman and child in his life. That I've found myself is a revelation.

No, I didn't want to punish Nessa tonight, and for a moment didn't know if I had the strength to go through with it, too frightened I might scare her off from the start. But this way allows the slate to be wiped clean and negates any embarrassment when meeting her colleagues again.

As I smooth my hand over the hair of the woman lying in my arms I'm pleased with the outcome, her reaction was even more than I expected. She'll be giving Ben the right answer in the morning; I'm certain of that. And Hunter, fuck, he knew the right thing to say. Rather than concentrating on her failures he'd told her what she did well, and which of her services Grade A can't do without.

Her sobs are starting to slow, her tears drying up. Placing my hand under her chin, I turn her to face me. As she tries to pull away, I tighten my grip, needing to see what's hidden in her eyes.

"It's over. Finished. We move on from here."

A look of hope flickers on her face, "Do we? Can we?" Her gaze drops down, "I didn't know how badly I'd cocked up…"

"No need to think about it again, Nessa. Don't beat yourself up. This," I wave my hand around the room, "This was the end of everything. You're the only person who'll ever bring it up again."

She shudders, "I've got to see Ben tomorrow." Her hand goes up to her face, and she worries a nail, "I'm going to tell him that I'll go back to my old job."

I'd hoped that was what she was going to say, but hearing her state it, I let out a sigh of relief. And I've also got Ben's permission to tell her what she doesn't yet know, "No, you won't." As she goes to interrupt me, I explain, "We've both got new roles. We're going to be working with Devil."

"Devil?"

"Jason Deville. I had a meeting with him today."

"You've met him?" She sits up straighter in my arms, "He actually exists?"

I laugh, her reaction was a mirror of the one I'd had, "Yes, he does exist. And he wants us to form a new team to support him back here. We'll have some travelling to do, but will mainly be based in London. Perfect for our family."

"Doing what?" Her eyes narrow.

I shrug, "I'm not sure, but it sounds intriguing. It will play to your skills, and what's left of mine."

That seems to have cheered her up, one side of her mouth turns up, and then the other, then I see a full smile.

"They'll forgive me?"

"Already have. Now turn over for me, let me see the damage."

She turns over, and I wince slightly, to be honest, my colleagues went easy on her, but there are a couple of welts which appear to be red and might bruise. Since her entire butt is glowing red, it's hard to tell. I find myself longing to give her a sensual flogging to see her colour up under my own hand but now is not the time. As I smooth my palms across her tender skin, she starts to moan. And when I reach my hand between her legs she's wet. Good, she's not reacting badly to what she's just been through and is now responding to me.

"Stay here a moment." Leaving her, I go to the adjacent bathroom, gather up the supplies I'd left earlier and return almost before she's processed that I'd gone. I apply a cooling lotion to her burning butt. "You're a wonderful pink," I tell her, "You might have a bruise or two tomorrow, but it shouldn't be much." And if she does, I hope Ben will be able to hide his grin when she sits down.

As my hands circle, she murmurs something incomprehensible as I continue to caress her. The sight and feel of her lovely skin and the little sounds of pleasure she's making make my cock as hard as steel. I turn her, seeing her wince slightly as she rolls on her tender skin. She's staring up at me, biting her lip and looking completely and utterly adorable.

Smirking, I slip off my vest, and her eyes become glued to my hands as she watches me undo my leathers and then slip them off. Taking out my cock I prime it, tugging it with one hand. Whether she does it consciously or not, her legs fall open, inviting me in.

"Touch yourself," I instruct, fair's fair as she's watching me.

Her hand slips between her legs, her face flushes all over again and her eyes open wide as though surprised to find herself so wet. Then they close.

"Look at me." I continue to stroke myself from root to tip. As she obeys, her tongue comes out, and she licks her lips. Fuck, what this woman does to me.

"I…" She lifts her fingers away.

"Don't be embarrassed Nessa, never be embarrassed with me. Do what you do when you're alone."

Her hand moves back, her fingers move and start rubbing, a little sigh comes as she finds out how sensitive she already is. Faster movements now and her muscles start to twitch. She's getting close, I can tell, as her face scrunches up in concentration.

"That's it, circle those fingers around, now pinch your clit." She's still wearing her thong, but it might as well not be there at all, I can see everything she's got.

"Feel your tits, squeeze them, tweak your nipples."

Her breaths are coming in little pants now.

"Sean, I…"

"Stop!" I growl. Again, she complies, but the frustration on her face almost makes me laugh. Throwing myself down on top of her, my arms keeping my weight from crushing her I gaze straight into her eyes, "First rule of a Dom. Your orgasms belong to me. And don't forget who I am in the club."

"You're not going to let me come?"

"Not until I'm inside you."

"Make it soon," her tongue licks her lips again, "Master."

Oh fuck, she pleases me so much. How can I resist? Even though she's technically topping from the bottom at this precise moment. I start to reach for the condom I'd left within reach. Her hand comes to rest on mine, staying it.

"Take me bare, Sean."

It's against the rules of the club, but fuck it. No one will know. Smoothing my hand across her brow, I gaze at her intently.

"I want this, but you need to be sure."

Her teeth worry her lip, but she's nodding. "I'd love to have your baby, Sean. A brother or sister for Mollie."

She doesn't need to offer twice. Like a homing missile my cock goes straight to her entrance, and I thrust my way home. Home. That's what this woman is to me. That's what she'll be for the rest of my life.

Having seated myself fully, I pull out, only to slide back in, a movement I repeat over and over again making sure to hit that special spot inside her with every pass. The pace of this joining so slow, so controlled. Keeping both of us in a heightened sense of arousal, extending both our pleasure as long as we can stand it.

She's close again, her muscles starting to twitch, her pussy tightening around me.

Leaning down I fasten my lips to hers, my tongue mimicking the movements of my cock. Her mouth sucks me in, unconsciously replicating what her cunt is doing to my prick. My balls feel heavy; I start swelling inside her, an unstoppable burst of cum preparing to launch inside her.

Inside her.

"Come with me," I rasp.

Her muscles clench around me sending any remaining control I might have out of the window. As I groan through my release, she screams as she takes all I have to give her.

Rolling over I hold her tight, knowing, accepting and hoping this could be the start of a new life. And very definitely the start of our new life, together.

A flash of white gold reminds me she's wearing my collar. And soon, very soon, she'll be wearing my ring.

CHAPTER 42

Vanessa

Waking the next morning in Sean's large bed with his warm body spooned behind me is pure luxury. Lazily I stretch to ease the soreness in my overused muscles having had a second and third time with Sean when we'd returned from the club. Having to answer an urgent call of nature I leave him still sleeping, gentle but far from annoying snores coming from his amazing mouth —well, amazing as he'd proved over and over again just how talented he is with it. Sliding out from under the covers as quietly as I can so I don't disturb him, I go to the bathroom.

Noticing the mirror, I contort myself to see whether there were any lasting reminders of the night before on my poor backside, pleased that there was nothing I can see. Rubbing my hand over my bum I feel a slight tenderness left behind, but nothing that's too uncomfortable. Turning round to face my reflexion I rest my hands on the sink and lean forward, taking the opportunity to examine my collar in the bright light. It shimmers and shines, and I place my finger to the metal, feeling a burst of pride at the mark of ownership Sean placed around my neck, knowing I belong to him like no woman ever has before. And being aware that he is mine, as much as I am his.

The events of the evening before should have made me embarrassed this morning, fearful of returning to Grade A and meeting my colleagues who'd seen me so exposed. But somehow, instead, I felt I'd been cleansed, forgiven. And the message delivered hadn't been that I was a failure, or only in that I'd failed to recognise my real strengths.

I'd wanted to train as a bodyguard so that I'd be the one in control, the only way I'd seen at the time of taking charge and never letting someone have such power over my body again, or the power to ruin my life. And though my skills saved me, the thought of holding a gun and needing to point it in anger chills me. All along I wanted someone who'd stand up for me, to protect me. Last night, albeit in a rather bizarre and unique way, gave me the clarity to admit that. And without leaving a residual feeling that I was disappointing anyone, including myself.

The door opens behind me, and still watching the mirror I see my lips turn up in a smile as I'm encircled in warm, strong arms. Leaning back I feel, and watch as Sean nuzzles me and whispers into my ear, "Good morning, sweetheart."

Swinging around I put my hands on his chest, "I love you, Sean."

"Love you too." His intense eyes stare into mine, then he brushes his mouth across my lips, the gentlest of touches. "What time are you seeing Ben?"

"Twelve."

A dip of his head, "Then we've got time to go and collect Mollie first."

The pleasure that goes through me is indescribable and I start grinning, "I can't wait to see her again."

As he smooths his hand down the side of my face, he tilts his head to one side, "She doesn't bring back bad memories for you?"

It's not hard to give him the honest answer, "No. She's chased them away. Oh, it will always be there in the background, Sean, I'll never completely forget. Or stop mourning. But it won't destroy me. And being around Molls? I honestly can't think of living without her." I giggle, "If you hadn't have asked me to be with you, I might have tried to steal her from you."

He smiles, and then grows serious. His hand wanders down and caresses my stomach. "I want you pregnant, Nessa. Just as soon as we can."

My stomach churns with excitement at his words and a delightful shiver runs down my spine. My hands tighten against his bare chest as though I never want to let him go. A fluttering in my stomach tells me I wouldn't be averse to continue working on his plan now.

He smirks, well aware of the visceral reaction his words have had on me. But it seems he's got other plans as he reaches around and gives a slight tap to my bum. "Now, get ready and dressed. I want to get our daughter."

Our daughter. For a moment, I forget to breathe.

"Oh, and after your meeting, we'll go to your house and get your things. You're moving in with me until we can find somewhere to raise our family."

He's full of instructions today. *Don't I get a say?* But he's offering me everything I ever wanted, so who am I to complain? But I'm not letting him get away with it entirely. "You going Dom on me?"

Now I get a proper smack. "You love it," he smirks.

And I can't argue with that.

An hour later and we're at his mum's house, and Mollie is in my arms. It feels so right to hold her, as though it was meant to be. Fleetingly, memories of our hardship in that adobe hut go through my mind, we formed a bond there which will last forever. I might not be her birth mother, but now I'm the only mother she's ever going to know. And as she chuckles up at me, I can't help but grin back, even when her fingers get tangled in my hair.

Sean's watching me with Mollie, the gentling of his features betraying what the scene makes him feel. In the kitchen, his mum is making tea, pouring boiling water over tea bags in the cups. Sean approaches her, and tries to make conversation, "How's the work going, Mum?"

He gets a slap on the wrist with a tea towel for his attempt to drive the conversation into mundane matters. "It's going, son." She takes the tea bags out of the cups and disposes of them, then nods toward me so carefully holding the precious bundle in my arms. "Now tell me if you're going to make an honest woman of Nessa here. Give Mollie a mother?"

Wait. *What?* He claimed me in the club, but we haven't discussed what she's suggesting. She's putting him on the spot. I shift awkwardly, but I needn't have worried.

With his eyes firmly on me, he answers her, "As soon as I can."

I gasp, for some reason I hadn't expected that. My eyes widen as I look at him, but both son and mother are ignoring me.

"Good," Anna nods, "I'm looking forward to helping plan the wedding." Then she laughs and covers her mouth with her hand and turns to me, "If my future daughter-in-law is alright with that."

Coming up behind me, Sean draws both myself and Molls back into his arms, "She's already got the venue for the hen party sorted."

I swing around to see him looking at me with a wicked twinkle in his eyes, and then turn back as his mum gasps, "That was quick!"

"I haven't said yes!" I think it's time I contributed something.

Pressing his lips against mine, he then pulls away, "Well?"

"Oh, son of mine, I want to see you do this properly."

Sean's eyes go to his mother who's standing with her hands on her hips, her head tilted to one side as if she's waiting. He sighs heavily, and then sinks down to one knee in front of me.

"Wait!" I call out. As he looks at me warily, I wave my hand at the cupboards, "You wouldn't have any rice, would you, Anna?"

He barks a laugh, and pulls me down beside him. "And there was I thinking you weren't going to be a brat." He smooths his hand over my hair, "Now, you going to marry me, or what?"

"Well as proposal that's a bit lacking, Sean." His mum's laughing, and I'm blushing red hoping she's no idea what implication the rice had.

And then the seriousness of his question hits me, and I

have eyes only for him. And my answer comes out in a rush as though I can no longer hold it back. "Yes, a thousand times, yes!"

"Well, I suppose that will have to do." Anna's grinning. Then she frowns, "But Sean, rice is nasty stuff. You really don't want to kneel on that. A spanking's much kinder."

I'm not quite certain whether it's myself or my new fiancé who's more shocked at that. It renders us speechless and soon we make our excuses and leave. Once Mollie's strapped into her car seat, I'm the first to address it.

"Sean… your mum. Your dad… Er?"

He turns and looks at me with a complete look of shock on his face, "Nessa, I never, ever, want to even think about it."

We stare blankly at each other for a few seconds, and then I can't hold back my laughter. Soon he's chuckling too, and then neither of us can stop, Bent almost double with the effort to try to stop myself giggling, I have to wipe tears from my eyes thinking what Sean's parents might have got up to. I'm not surprised he doesn't want to know. Eew.

When we get to Grade A, Sean lets me enter through the glass doors first, his hand solicitously at the small of my back, in his other he carries the baby seat with Mollie inside. Once inside, I glance over to nod at Sandra, and out of the corner of my eye see Sean placing Mollie's chair on the ground. Next I find myself being pulled back into Sean's arms. Fastening his lips to mine he bends me back over his arm as though we were performing some dance routine. Automatically my hands come up to hold onto him, first to help me balance, and second, well, I'm not going to waste any opportunity to hang onto my man.

After thoroughly ravishing my mouth he lets me up, lifts his chin toward the reception desk where Sandra's standing with her mouth hanging open, picks up Mollie then takes my hand and leads me to the lift.

Once inside I swing around and hiss, "What the hell was all that about?"

"Now we've announced it to the whole company," he smirks, "Saves us time."

I put my fist to his arm, "Maybe I wanted to keep it quiet for a while."

He doesn't look in the slightest bit remorseful, but redeems himself when he says, "I love you, Nessa, and I'm proud you're mine. I want everyone to know what a lucky bastard I am."

How can I stay angry with him after that?

On the third floor I have to walk through the open plan office, and of course, Ryan and Nat are there working. Feeling my face glowing I greet them in my usual way, and any worries I might have had about seeing my work colleagues after they've seen me naked disappear when they acknowledge my presence as if nothing untoward had ever happened. Relieved no one's making any reference to the night before, nor have the slightest sign of a smirk on their faces, I leave Mollie with Sean, and at precisely twelve o'clock I enter Ben's office.

He stands to greet me, "Good afternoon, Van."

I complete the pleasantries and then take the seat he offers to me.

He smiles across the desk, "You've come to a decision?"

"You know I have. I'll stay here and do what I do best."

"I'm glad."

I stare at him, "You set us up, didn't you Ben? Right from the start."

He shrugs, but doesn't look repentant. "Should have realized you'd work it out."

"You never wanted me to be a CPO, did you?" Now he doesn't speak, but simply returns my gaze. And it all drops into place. "You gave me something to focus on, didn't you? To help me get over…" I break off, remembering the day I came to him almost exactly two years ago. But as quickly as the memories threaten to overwhelm me, the thought of Mollie waiting for me outside chases them away.

He sighs, "I didn't know how it would pan out, Van, but I suspected you weren't suited. But your training was an investment, it wasn't wasted, Knowing the detail of what the CPOs go through at the coal face, your experience of working the job on the ground will prove helpful. You'll have far better insight now."

I nod. He's right. I'll have a new appreciation of the importance of getting the right information to the CPOs at the right time.

"Has Sean updated you about working with him as part of Devil's team?"

"Yes, but I'm not sure what that will entail."

He shrugs, "Problem solving, sorting through information, tying things together. Exactly what you do best. Devil will be back next week and will brief you properly. And you may work outside the office too, so your license will come in useful, even though you wouldn't officially be a CPO. And, of course, you know how to shoot if you're ever put in that position again."

This talk about the new job is intriguing, even though it seems Ben has no more idea about it than Sean or I. I begin to get excited about meeting Devil.

Ben looks like he can see the wheels turning in my head, "You'll have to curb your curiosity for another few days. Take the week off. I'm sure you and Sean have things to work out between you." Leaning back in his chair, he clasps his hands behind his neck and chuckles, "I couldn't predict a happy ending, Van, but you always had the hots for him."

My face reddens as it sinks in that I hadn't hidden my attraction for Sean as well as I'd thought.

"You always sat opposite him at meetings, arriving early so you'd get that seat. The looks you were giving him."

I breathe in sharply, "But what about the baby? When Mollie arrived…"

"You had to face up to your fears, Van. You'd either sink or swim. And I'm pleased to say it all worked out. Sean needed to find himself, and you helped him do that."

I toss him a glare, "You're a born meddler, aren't you, Ben?"

Now he laughs, "I think you ought to thank me."

I stare at him, and slowly my lips start to turn up. The bastard might be right, but I'm not going to come out and admit it.

He knows, and snorts. "Now get out of my office, Van. I

don't want to see either of you until next week." He waves his hand, showing me I'm dismissed.

I leave bemused and shaking my head. Outside Sean's waiting for me, and now we're heading off to get my stuff so I can move in with him. I have to pinch myself to make sure the last couple of weeks haven't all been a dream as I take Mollie back into my arms. I seem to have got the man, and ended up with the baby.

And next week? Well, then we'll both be starting new jobs. Working with the Devil.

OTHER WORKS BY MANDA MELLETT

Blood Brothers

- *Stolen Lives* (#1 – Nijad & Cara)
- *Close Protection* (#2 – Jon & Mia)
- *Second Chances* (#3 – Kadar & Zoe)

Coming soon:

- *Dark Horses* (#5 – Jasim & Janna) – summer 2017

SATAN'S DEVILS MC

- *Turning Wheels* (Blood Brothers #3.5, Satan's Devils #1 – Wraith & Sophie)

Coming in 2017:

- *Drummer's Beat* (# 2 – Drummer & Sam) – spring
- *Slick Running* (# 3 – Slick & Ella) – summer

Sign up for my newsletter to hear about new releases:
http://eepurl.com/b1PXO5

Drummer's BEAT

SATAN'S DEVILS #2

Drummer

As President of the Satan's Devils MC I can have every and any woman I choose, and do. That's how I got my name. But I'm happy with the variety, I know I'd never find a woman my equal to be my ol' lady.

Then I meet her, on the road to my compound, standing beside a goddamn Vincent Black Shadow, one of the most iconic bikes of all time. But when she tells me she's Viper's daughter, I know she has to be lying. There's no way he's fathered a child, not one of her age, it's just not possible. I can't deny an attraction to her, but she's the one woman I'm unable to have, I can't go against my brother.

Sam

Trouble, I've found, comes in many forms. Trouble in the shape of the surly president of this MC who just wants me gone. Trouble in that my father denies our relationship, and the trouble that's followed me the fifteen hundred miles I've ridden to come to find him. And when my past catches up with me, I need the protection of the MC to keep me safe.

SATAN'S DEVILS #2: Drummer's BEAT

Brothers protecting their own

ACKNOWLEDGEMENTS

I'd like to thank all my readers for thinking so highly of the books in the Blood Brothers Series. I love this men and their women, and how their lives are entwined, and it's fantastic to discover that you like them too. So know you have my appreciation, the fact that you buy and read my books, gives me the encouragement I need to continue.

Special thanks must go to my beta readers, the wonderful Alex and Pauline who beta read for me, and of course, Steve, who helped pick up inconsistencies.

Thanks Lia, Freeyourwords, for another amazing cover and for squeezing the formatting into your tight timetable.

This is the first time I've worked with editor Elizabeth Wright, and won't be the last. I've enjoyed working with you, and your suggestions and word changes were really useful.

I can't thank my husband enough for his ongoing support and encouragement, and my wonderful son must get a mention, even if it's only because of how often he tells me he's proud of his mum.

If you enjoyed *Identity Crisis*, please leave a review. Writers write in a vacuum, locked away in our lonely towers. We love to know what you think of our efforts and appreciate all feedback we receive.

ABOUT THE AUTHOR

After commuting for too many years to London working in various senior management roles, Manda Mellett left the rat race and now fulfils her dream and writes full time. She draws on her background in psychology, the experience of working in different disciplines and personal life experiences in her books.

Manda lives in the beautiful countryside of North Essex with her husband and two slightly nutty Irish Setters. Walking her dogs gives her the thinking time to come up with plots for her novels, and she often dictates ideas onto her phone on the move, while looking over her shoulder hoping no one is around to listen to her. Manda's other main hobby is reading, and she devours as many books as she can.

Her biggest fan is her gay son (every mother should have one!). Her favourite pastime when he is home is the late night chatting sessions they enjoy, where no topic is taboo, and usually accompanied by a bottle of wine or two.

Email: manda@mandamellett.com

Website: www.mandamellett.com

Connect with me on Facebook:

https://www.facebook.com/mandamellett

Sign up for my newsletter to hear about new releases in the Blood Brothers and Satan's Devils series: http://eepurl.com/b1PXO5

Photo by Carmel Jane Photography